BELOW

ALSO BY ALEXANDRIA WARWICK

The Four Winds Series

The North Wind
The West Wind
The South Wind
The East Wind

The North Series

Below
Night
Hunt

Standalones

The Demon Race

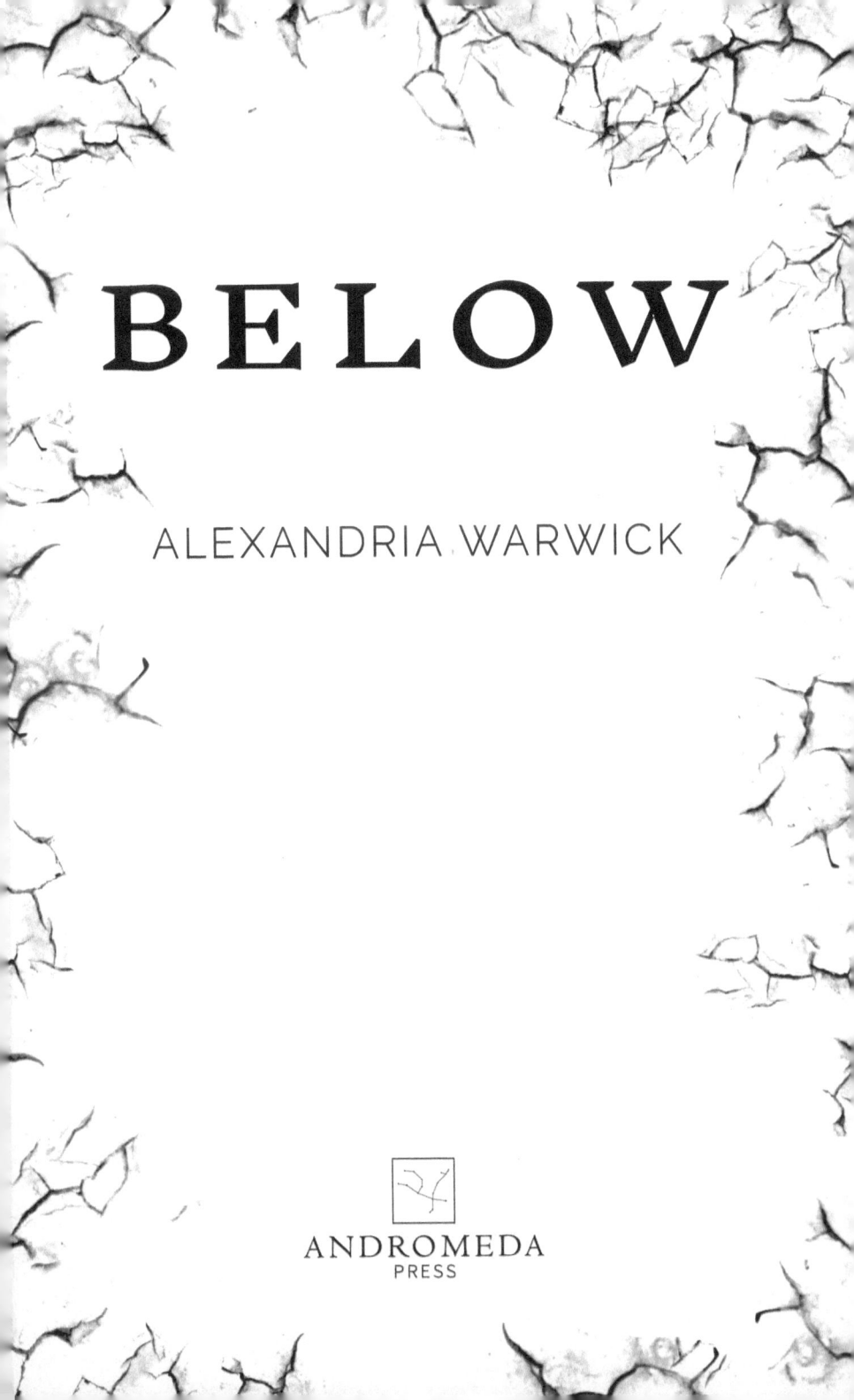

BELOW

ALEXANDRIA WARWICK

ANDROMEDA
PRESS

Published by Andromeda Press, LLC

Cover illustration by Faryn Hughes
Map art © Alexandria Warwick

ISBN 978-1-7330334-0-4
First Edition

For Leah,
because Apaay crossed the tundra to find her sister,
and I would, too

The North

Iniga Fores

Nalwa

Tor
The Western Sea

Northern

Lun

Talguk

Western Territory

River Mitka

Unana

Central

The Atakana

Kesikan
Pass

The Dea

Southern

The
Banished
Lands

Auk

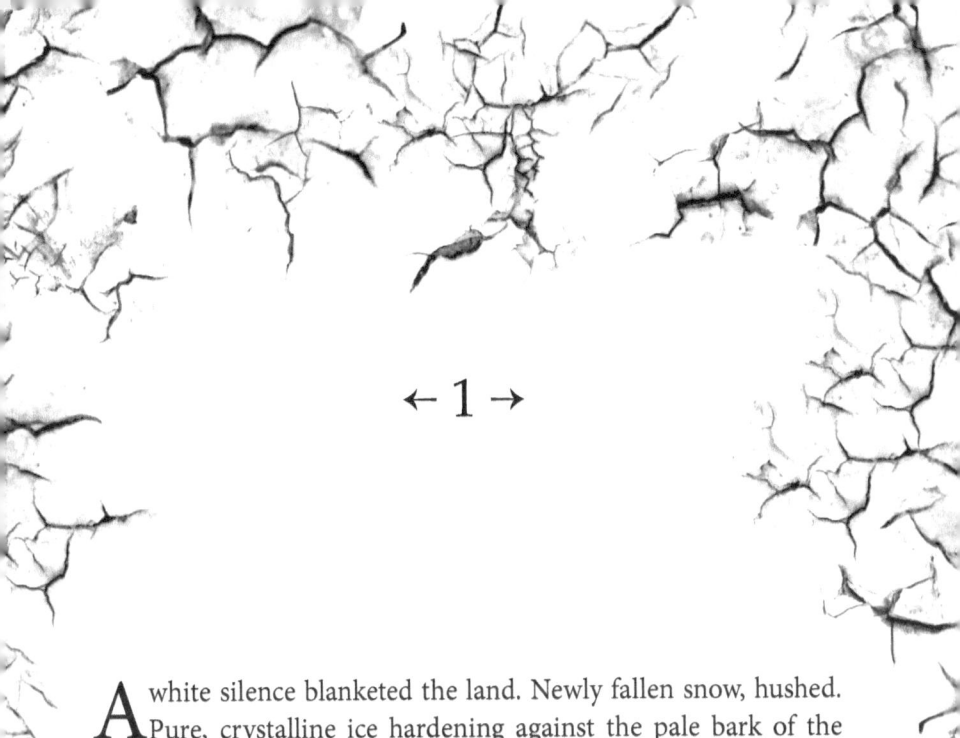

← 1 →

A white silence blanketed the land. Newly fallen snow, hushed. Pure, crystalline ice hardening against the pale bark of the trees. The chilled air that swelled with the slow, sleeping breaths of a world that had yet to wake.

And a girl cloaked in heavy furs, waiting.

Apaay studied the breathing hole in the ice. Her joints ached with cold and the hours she'd crouched, alone save her dog, Nakaluq, who lay quietly curled by her side. It was the third time this week she had come to the frozen plain that was Naga, the Eastern Sea, and she vowed it to be the last. Above, the sky was a spill of black ink. The long night was only in its first month, which left five months of darkness to endure. The moon, a shard of pale light, cast a watery sheen upon the ground. It was not enough.

Keeping her attention on the breathing hole, Apaay slowly removed the harpoon slung across the bulk of her fur parka. She supposed there were worse things in life than lack of sunlight. Here on the frozen sea, she knew true peace. The sea was sleeping beneath the ice. And the seals were, too.

Her gaze slid to Nakaluq's still form. Unsurprisingly, he was sleeping as well. She nudged his flank with one of her sealskin boots. "Wake up." A white cloud streamed from her lips.

His eyebrows twitched, and he curled his body tighter, bushy tail draped across his nose. A clear dismissal that he should not be disturbed.

Apaay rolled her eyes, for this was his absolute favorite game: Feed me, and I will awaken. "You're supposed to be my lookout. You know, to alert me when danger is near?"

One of his large, triangular ears flicked west, toward the direction of her village. No sound, no danger. He grumbled, burrowing further into his warmth. The wind had begun to pick up, and it was cutting.

"I guess you don't want your treat, then," she crooned.

Immediately, Nakaluq sprang to his feet, prancing around as if to say, *Look at me, I'm awake!*

Apaay snorted at the ridiculous display before wrapping an arm around his neck, pulling him close, and pressing a brief kiss to his snout. His pelt was a perfect reflection of the tundra—white flecked with gray. Snow on stone. "Sit still. You're making me tired."

Nakaluq side-eyed her.

"Don't look at me that way." The look that implied maybe she wouldn't be so tired if she were dreaming with Mama, Papa, and Eska in their ice house, warm and safe in slumber.

Dreaming. What a lovely notion.

It was simple, really. They needed to eat. They needed clothes, tools, oil for their lamps. Over the last few years, the seal population had dwindled, and she wondered if someone had disrespected the old rules. The Sea Mother did not take insults lightly. Without her favor, the marine life would travel elsewhere for the remainder of the season, proving for a difficult hunt. Decades had passed since anyone had sighted the Sea Mother beyond her watery silence. The sea grew restless.

Apaay did as much as she could, but often it was not enough. Her earlier attempts at harpooning a seal had ended in failure. The first time, she had struck too soon. The second, too late. *Like this,* Eska would say. *Try again.* And Apaay loved Eska. She did. But she could love her sister with the whole of her heart while also wishing things did not come so easy for her.

When she thought deeper on the issue, it was actually quite ironic. Her parents would be displeased to know she was out here alone, and yet who would come, if not her?

As if sensing her sadness, Nakaluq sidled closer.

"You know how Papa is," she told her friend. "How can he expect to hunt with a broken leg? Or Mama, already busy with sewing and cooking and cleaning?"

A heavy paw settled on top of Apaay's hand, the rough pads scraping against her mittens. She squeezed it. "Or Eska, too busy drooling over Lusa?" Her sister scowled whenever Apaay teased her about it, though admittedly she *did* drool over the girl. A lot.

Leaning close, Apaay whispered to Nakaluq, "Though not as much as you."

The dog huffed as if offended.

Her smile fell as she again examined the breathing hole, huddling only a few feet beyond its slick edge. Black water struck the hard, icy rim. She did not have to worry. Even when her breathing shallowed out, she did not have to worry. This time of year, the ice was frozen four feet solid. There would be no cracks.

Still, she shuffled back to put another foot of distance between herself and the ledge. Her fingers tightened on the harpoon, the head a glint of carved ivory, the line curling along the ground. Drifting snowflakes clung to the ruff of wolverine fur encircling her hood.

Movement in the water.

Apaay held herself absolutely still. She was night, and snow, and hard, glinting ice.

The seal's slick head breached the dark liquid, whiskers twitching, its skin a mottled blue-gray. Its pupils were wet and black, no white to see.

It hadn't yet spotted her. As he'd been trained to do, Nakaluq remained motionless beside her, little more than a boulder among the ice as she lifted her harpoon in an unhurried motion so the animal wouldn't startle. It would only take a few breaths before submerging again.

Her harpoon came down.

The seal vanished in a splash of water.

Apaay swore and lurched to her feet. Two hours of waiting and what did she have to show for it? Nothing. Her stomach hollowed out from the sense of failure, the anxiety of her family's diminishing food stores, which would not last another week.

She waited another thirty minutes despite the unlikelihood of the seal returning. It would instead travel to another breathing hole, one without a sharp stick aimed at its head. The nearest one lay a half mile north and wasn't frequented as often as this one. It would be so nice to return home and slip beneath her furs. Rest, refuel, maybe even dream.

But they needed to eat.

Apaay whistled for Nakaluq as she approached the sled parked some yards away. Grabbing the harness, she looped it around his body and front legs so it hit him high on the chest. He was of stocky build, with powerful haunches built for endurance and a dense double coat.

"My sweet, sweet boy," she murmured, rubbing behind his ears. He nuzzled his nose against her chest like he used to do as a pup. The memory softened her hunting frustrations, and she buried her face in his neck before mounting the sled.

Two short whistles sent him north, the sled's walrus-bone runners cutting lines through the thin layer of powder dusting the frozen sea. The runners' smoothness pleased her, as they had only been recently completed after she had run the last sled, quite literally, into the ground. An accident, she'd claimed, but Papa had been furious nonetheless. Never one to waste anything, she had recycled the old material to build a swifter, lighter sled body, large enough to lash multiple seals to its base.

Above, the stars were hard pinpricks of light. The wind was a brutal, shredding force, stinging her cheeks and eyes, scouring her rough, chapped lips. There was nothing that was not hardened or chiseled in the North. It was a land of contrasts, white and black and gray, uncolored, inhospitable to all except those who had been born here. This was why Apaay admired the land. And this was also why she feared it.

With the temperature far below freezing, the second breathing hole had already iced over when she arrived. Using the tip of her harpoon, Apaay chipped away the thin film, the splintering sound causing her to flinch. She had just settled down to wait when a whistle carried high upon the wind. Three short bursts, followed by a longer note—the signal for friend.

"Apaay!"

Uh-pai.

Two figures approached, their silhouettes bulked in thick layers. Nakaluq perked up, and his tail, curled over his back in alertness, began to wag back and forth.

Apaay waved to Eska and her good friend Chena. "Over here!"

They joined her at the breathing hole, her younger sister ruffling Nakaluq's fur in greeting. "You know most people are asleep right now," Eska said with amusement. "Right?"

Apaay's mouth widened, more smirk than smile. The world was cold, but in her heart, she felt warm. "You know I'm not most people."

"Trust me, I'm aware."

Her attention slid to Chena, who was unusually silent, her small mouth grim. Silver limned the soft line of her friend's jaw.

Apaay said to her sister, "You speak as if that's a bad thing."

"Not everyone is so sure of themselves."

A snort sprang free at how untrue that statement was. What was more, that Eska would think such a thing. Apaay was stumbling along in life, chasing at the heels of those ahead. She shrugged. "Maybe. But let's talk about what's *really* important: my new joke."

"Let's hear it."

"What did the shark say to the whale?"

Eska made a show of thinking deep thoughts, even though she probably already knew the answer. It was a game they sometimes played. Who could think of the most cringeworthy joke? "I give up."

"What are you blubbering about!" She snorted out a laugh. "Get it? Blubbering? Because—because the whale has blubber—"

Eska sighed, her face softening with affection. "That was terrible, you know."

Apaay had always thought her sister beautiful, even as a child, and for the longest time, Apaay hadn't the words to describe why that beauty was admired. People would mention how bright her eyes were, how smooth and round her cheeks were, how precious was her dimpled chin, her mouth like a rosy bud.

But now she understood what had eluded her for years. In a land that knew no warmth, Eska exuded what people craved: light, and a feeling of comfort, and peace.

"Anyway," Apaay said, lifting her eyebrows, "you're one to talk. Why are you out now, except to annoy me? You should be in bed."

"Oh." Her sister ran a mitten over Nakaluq's back and sent Chena an unreadable look. "No reason." She glanced at the sled, its empty base. "Any luck?"

Apaay offered a brief, closemouthed smile, trying to ignore the sudden tension she felt at so few words. "Not yet." Her sister didn't know how truly dire their situation was, and she would like to keep it that way.

"If you need a break soon, let me know."

And risk Eska taking the kill? "I'm fine, but thank you." She turned to Chena. A definite paleness washed out the warm undertones of her skin. It was concerning, but not uncommon. It was easy to catch a cold at this time of year. "How is Muktuk doing?" Apaay asked, speaking of Chena's brother. "Has he learned the name of his new baby yet?" She tucked her braid back inside her hood.

"Not yet. My father is supposed to arrive sometime this week."

Apaay nodded and returned to studying the breathing hole. Chena's father had traveled to one of the neighboring villages, where his mother—Chena's grandmother—currently lived. She and the elders would assemble to discuss the baby's name-soul. This was the Analak way.

Someday when she was old enough, Apaay hoped for the opportunity to choose a baby's name-soul, too. Names did not simply continue individual lives. They continued the life of the community. When the village celebrated a birth, they celebrated both a new person and the return of the namesake, or the deceased person from whom the name-soul was taken. These names, these kinship ties, were the threads that bound their community together.

After a few minutes, Eska said, with an absurd amount of nonchalance, "Pana was asking for you last night."

She very nearly gagged. "Ugh. Spare me."

"Apaay!"

"What? The man is softer than whale intestines. And anyway"—she slid her harpoon free as the water rippled, lowering her voice—"he doesn't actually like me. He just wants to . . . you know."

Chena murmured, "You won't even give him a chance?"

Apaay shot her friend a cutting look. The only reason she'd spent time with him was because he sometimes gave her the smaller of the seals if he killed two. But they didn't need to know that. She had no patience for softness like Pana. It was a hard, jagged world out there. The North would carve you up, spit you out if you let it. There was no place for vulnerability on the ice. "Not all of us have someone like Silla in our lives. And can you both please lower your voices? You'll scare the seals away."

At the young man's name, a flush deepened the bronze of Chena's cheeks. "Right. Silla." Strained laughter bubbled up, and she clamped her lips together.

Apaay looked at her friend. *Really* looked at her. She was about to ask what was wrong when Eska stated loudly, "It's probably for the best. No doubt you'd chew Pana up if given the chance."

It was not untrue. "Yes, he'd sob into his bear skins and then where would we be? Now hush. A seal's coming."

"Apaay—"

The ripple flattened into calmness, and Apaay waited, hoping a seal would breach its warm, liquid safety for the chance to take a breath of air, but their voices must have chased it back into the water's deep. Apaay sat back on her heels, glaring at her sister.

At least Eska had the grace to look apologetic. "Sorry."

Apaay took a breath to quell her frustration. Since the animal would probably not return, she'd have to come back tomorrow. Tonight, she would go home empty-handed. Again.

Eska reached for the harpoon. "I can get a seal for you. I know of another place—"

"I can manage on my own," Apaay said, snatching it away. "I'll come back tomorrow."

"But the breathing hole isn't far."

"I said I'll come back tomorrow."

Something about Eska shrank, became small. "I'm just trying to help."

Apaay hated herself for saying it, because it had been an accident, and Eska was kind, and her sister, whom she loved more than anything, but she said, "You've helped enough, don't you think?"

Chena glanced between them, clearly uncomfortable. "Apaay—"

"What?" If she had come all this way, done all this work, it was not so Eska could take the kill from her. Call it selfishness, but for once, just *once*, Apaay wanted to prove she was as equally capable a hunter as Eska. The seal would be hers. Hers to kill, hers to claim. "Every day that passes is a day closer to starvation. So I'm sorry if I want to make sure we have something to eat next week. If it had been quiet as I had asked, maybe our problem would be solved." It was hurtful, what she said. Disappointment in her performance made her cruel when she should be kind. "But I guess we'll never know."

Eska's eyes swam with unshed tears. Salt water lapped against the ice, gently. "I'm going to go home, then," she whispered.

Apaay nodded, looking to the tops of her boots. "I think that would be best."

"I am sorry," she whispered. "I didn't know about— I didn't know." With one last look to Chena, she left. Darkness soon swallowed her.

A few minutes passed before Chena spoke. Her face was grave. "That was a bit harsh, don't you think? She's only fourteen."

"I know that, but everything comes so *easy* to her." The last word she choked off. Apaay blinked rapidly against the sting in her eyes. Truly, it wasn't Eska's fault. All Apaay asked for was a chance. "Every time I fail to bring in a seal, or forget to replenish the oil stores, or ruin some other task, it's another mark against me. You know I want to lead the hunt this summer."

The men had long ago told her no, and yet she was a burr they could not remove, clinging to their clothes, blowing back in with the force of a blizzard whenever one of the younger men puffed out his chest, claiming this was not her place.

Apaay knew why they told her no. She was too flighty, some claimed. Too lost, others said. A leader commanded respect, exuded confidence, and built trust, acting as a beacon in the dark. Why would they ever choose someone like her, unreliable and drifting, to lead? To which Apaay would counter, how could she prove herself if not given the chance?

"You are under a lot of pressure," Chena agreed. "It would make anyone's patience short."

But. She heard a *but* in there.

Apaay rubbed a palm over her face, dislodging the ice that had condensed around her nose and mouth and eyes. Guilt swam through her. "I'll apologize." Chena was right. She had acted unnecessarily harsh toward Eska out of her own insecurity.

With the hunt a failure, they decided to return home. Nakaluq hauled the sled while she and Chena traveled on foot until they reached the shore. A cairn, as tall and wide as a man, the stones in browns and grays and stacked atop one another, signified the break between sea and unsea, as well as marked the direction to their community.

Snow crunched and caved beneath their boots. This was a still, silent land. Its hush sank deep into the earth, rooting down with those of the bracken and the trees. Their village was located two miles southwest. Boreal forest, thick and lush and evergreen, lay to the south. Open tundra lay to the north.

Chena, normally doing everything she could to fill the silence, was unusually quiet. A slight furrowing of her brow had Apaay resting a palm on her friend's arm. "Is everything all right? You don't look well."

Chena shook her head, gaze elsewhere.

Apaay pulled her friend to a stop and turned the shorter girl to face her. "There is something wrong." The realization was bright.

"Apaay—"

"*Tell me.*"

Chena's glare cut through the gloom. Apaay noticed her fingers digging into her friend's shoulders, and she loosened her grip. "Sorry." There was something between them she couldn't see, filling up the space, pressing out her certainty and ease. The regret she felt for snapping at Eska didn't help.

A shuddering sigh slipped through the chill air. Chena rubbed her mittens over her face, cheeks red and chapped from the wind. "It's about Silla. We slept together last month."

"So?"

"As in we *slept* together."

Oh. *Oh.*

"Was it— I mean—"

Chena cupped her elbows in her palms. "He was good to me." Her throat worked, as if she wished to hide these words by swallowing them down. "But I realized afterward I wasn't wearing my pregnancy charm."

Apaay's mouth parted in understanding as her stomach dropped. And dropped. She glanced at Chena's belly, its softness shielded behind layers of fur. Life swelled beneath it and would one day open its eyes to the world.

Clearing her throat, she looked away, unsure of what to say.

"Eska told me to come to you," Chena whispered. "I need help. I don't know what to do." The words wavered, a touch desperate. "We're not even married. I'm not sure if he'll be able to support me and the child. I mean, he's a capable hunter, a hard worker, and while he's excited to be a father, I can't— I mean—" Her eyes glittered, so dark, so very wide. "I'm not ready for this."

Apaay pulled her friend along, wanting to keep their blood flowing. Chena, pregnant. She could hardly wrap her mind around it.

They walked for perhaps half a mile in silence before Apaay asked, "Have you told your mother?"

"No. I'm afraid to."

The hill they climbed steepened, but once they reached the top, they'd be able to see their village. Apaay glanced over her shoulder to check on Nakaluq and was not surprised to find him only a few feet behind, the sled's runners having carved deep tracks into the snow.

Apaay said, through shallow huffs, "I think you should tell her."

"What if she hates me?"

"She won't hate you. She *loves* you. You're her daughter."

"Yes, and now a pregnant one."

Reaching down, Apaay squeezed Chena's hand. So delicate, so small. "I know it doesn't feel like a joyous occasion, but it will. You're going to be a mother." Not even the worthiest of hunters could overshadow the act of raising and caring for another. "You also have me. If there's anything you need, I will do whatever I can to help."

Chena nodded, the lines bracketing her mouth easing into smoothness. A moment later, her nose crinkled in distaste. She lifted it to the wind. "Do you smell that?"

The scent hit as they crested the hill: sharp and acrid, unclean. Nestled in between clumps of frozen trees, sixty ice houses lay like small mounds of snow upon the ground. Except they were not greeted by glittering white domes. Gray streaks sullied the ice—a spattering of filth. The world rained ash as smoke hissed from down below, pouring into the sky like blood from an open wound.

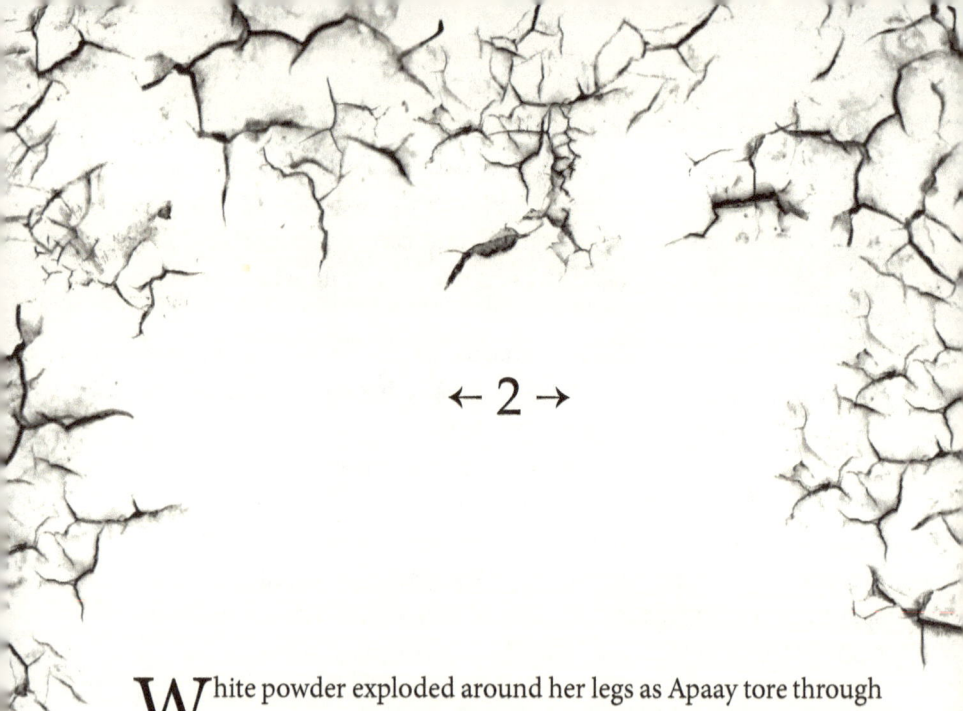

← 2 →

White powder exploded around her legs as Apaay tore through the snow, momentum pulling her down the steep slope, her arms wheeling in circles to help keep her balance. Dense smoke scratched at her eyes, and it might already be too late. The fire had been cast, both signal and protection, and a ring of nausea encircled her throat, because she had not seen it, but more importantly, she had not been here. She had been on the ice, where no one would come looking for her. Where it was safe.

Her heart pulverized her rib cage with each forceful blow. Chena followed close behind, her breathing equally harsh as she called for her parents, and for Silla. Apaay cursed her bulky clothing, the weight of layers able to protect her from the most brutal element but not from something giving chase. A veil of security had been ripped from her, and she could only think, *Mama, Papa, Eska*. What had become of her family?

They reached the initial ring of ice houses, the largest ones serving as meeting spaces. A second, smaller ring housed single families. "Eska!" she screamed. Such silence. A film of ice hardened in her chest, for Papa would not have been able to run far with his injury.

"Do you see them?" Chena asked.

"No." She didn't see anyone.

Within the second ring lay a massive firepit, the flames having been reduced to embers. With so little wood this far north, the fire was only lit in emergencies, to warn neighboring communities of what had come to pass and to not draw near no matter the circumstances. There was nothing and no one around, and the shadows were like long fingers grasping at her legs. The snow had been trampled into frozen soil, scuffed by boots and paws. Even the dogs had fled.

Something shifted in her peripheral vision, and she turned. A young girl, face caked with soot, huddled in the entrance of her home, tears cutting through the grime. Apaay crouched before her. "Kaya, where is everyone?" She didn't ask what had happened, because she already knew. Ignition of the fire represented only one thing. The child was too young to understand.

She touched the girl's shoulders, her sweet, chubby cheeks. Kaya was real. This was not a dream. "Where are your parents?"

The girl shook her head. Fear swallowed her eyes.

"Kaya, *please*. Please—"

One small hand lifted, pointing through the trees.

Apaay ran.

Chena had disappeared to search for her relatives. A young couple clutched each other close, half hidden behind a polar bear pelt they had skinned and stretched out to dry. Before she could utter a word, the woman pointed behind her as if she knew, as if they all knew.

Please, please, please. The cold locked tight in her throat. The small pack she carried, along with her harpoon, weighed upon her shoulders, so she ripped them off and tossed them aside, broke free of the roiling smoke, flying down the winding, snow-carved trail that led to another cairn atop the hill beyond the tree line. She had but one image in her mind. Dark eyes clouded by hurt, an upwelling of tears. Her sister's form as she retreated back home like a kicked dog.

The entire community—close to three hundred individuals as well as half as many dogs—encircled the monument of stacked stones. Fear leaked into the space, the stench of sweat strong. The mass of bodies teemed, never silent, never still. Apaay flinched at a child's bloodcurdling shriek, the hushed whispers slithering along the ground like tendrils of smoke, too afraid to let the noise die, lest the quiet lure back the demon.

Two elders—one man and one woman—attempted to calm the restlessness. The village looked to the elders for guidance in times of hardship and turmoil and need, and people clung to that shred of sanity and control, clung to it desperately, fully awake in the nightmare. They did not step with certainty. They did not put their backs to the trees where the darkness churned.

Apaay shoved through the clustered bodies with all the grace of a newborn calf, not the slightest bit apologetic when she knocked over her neighbor. Ignoring the woman's outrage, she tore apart the huddle until she found her family huddled near the cairn's western face.

Two people, that was all. There was an absence she could not ignore.

Her knees gave out, hitting the packed snow. Not Eska. Not her sister. "Where is she?" Apaay hardly noticed how loud she spoke. How it sounded so like the wind screaming across the snowy plains.

Mama flung out her arms, and Apaay slipped into them as she sobbed, "My little naaja. He took her. He took her from us."

Apaay's body twitched in barely contained horror. She looked to Papa seated beside her, his splinted leg stretched out before him. "How long ago?"

His eyes closed in a moment of relief at her presence, or perhaps denial at what was happening. "A few hours," Papa ground out, fierce despite being unable to stand. "Where were you?" His voice boomed, carrying over the rush of conversation surrounding them. "Because you certainly weren't at home like you were supposed to be. We have these rules for a reason. What if he had taken you, too? We would have never known. And your sister—" A muscle pulsated in his jaw. "You're supposed to watch out for her. You're supposed to *protect* her." A crack in the air that was his voice breaking beneath emotion.

Tilting up her chin, Apaay stared into Papa's tumultuous expression, helpless against the thought that it was her fault, all of it, because she had wanted Eska to leave. If she had only returned after the first breathing hole. If she had only not left at all. "I'm sorry. I'm *sorry*." She tried to piece herself into something that resembled order. "Naattaluk, please."

A gentle touch on Apaay's shoulder brought her attention to an old woman whose chapped skin sank into deep folds. Apaay stumbled forward and fell into the scent of salt and pine, biting the inside of her cheek to hold back the flood. No crying. Absolutely no crying. She must remain strong.

Blowing out a breath, she pulled away. This was the last surviving member of Papa's family. An ear infection had taken her grandmother's hearing when Papa was but a child.

Her grandmother signed, *I saw her run toward Lusa's house.*

Apaay had to take her mittens off to reply. *Was anyone with her?* It was a horrible thought, one that made her feel even more disgusted with herself, but if Eska hadn't been alone, it was possible the other person had been taken instead.

Not that I saw, but my eyes are not what they used to be.

There was only one way to know for certain if Eska had escaped unscathed. "Stay here," she told her family. "I'll be back."

Starting back down the hill, Apaay dashed toward a massive conifer shading a clump of ice houses on the community's western edge, her boots cutting into the soaked, sooty ground. The tree was quiet elegance draped in white. Once she reached its base, she dropped to her knees and shoved her arm through the hole carved out among the ice-bitten wood, grasping for the soft warmth of rabbit fur, a scrap she and Eska would hide away in the event of danger or separation to inform the other they were safe.

But the hole was empty. No fur, just ice.

Apaay pressed a shaking hand to her forehead, feeling lightheaded and faint. She fought the rising panic, stamped it into submission. It was all right. Everything was going to be all right. Perhaps Eska had forgotten to replace the rabbit fur amid the confusion.

She stood and curved her tongue against the back of her teeth. Her whistle soared high upon the frigid air. The village looked so pitiful. It hurt to look at. Fear was thick in the night.

"Where are you?" she murmured, stamping her feet to keep warm.

A small bundle cut through the smoke and snow. Nakaluq stopped near her feet, and Apaay hurriedly removed him from the sled harness, kneeling so they were at eye level. "Do this for me," she said, "and you'll have treats for an entire month. Deal?"

The blue of his gaze swept the area, never lingering on any one place for long. Eventually, his tail wagged tentatively.

He followed her back to their ice house, ever the obedient companion. The Analak, at least those of the coastal regions, used dogs to pull sleds between communities, as well as for hunting and rescue missions. Nakaluq was young, only a few years old, but he was smart. He slept in their furs for extra warmth and knew her sister's scent well.

Apaay grabbed a blanket they had used the night before, an old one cut from caribou skins, and held it in front of Nakaluq's muzzle. A few hours—that's how long Papa claimed it had been since anyone had seen Eska. She would have believed hope to be lost except for one small detail.

Mama's claim that Eska had been taken wasn't quite accurate. It was not how things worked with the demon who stalked the night. He did not snatch people from their homes. He only took what he needed. Which meant she could still be alive.

"Find her, boy. Find her for me."

Apaay relaxed her hands from their suffocating grip on the fur and watched Nakaluq separate Eska's scent from the others as he circled their home. He moved in the direction of the cairn, except instead of ascending the hill, he veered right toward where the land descended into shallow rolling hills, away from the sea.

The snow, gouged deep from where people had fled during the chaos, eventually smoothed save a single set of footprints that zigzagged over the plain, leading to a depression in between two hills. Nakaluq nudged something half buried in the snow.

She stumbled. Her vision swam, broken by bursting black dots. *No.*

Numbly, Apaay sank to her knees. The ground was cold. Her heart was a piece of ice, chipped and cracked from various blows.

Her chest ached as she reached forward, having never experienced this type of fear before. Like she would soon cease to breathe.

The object, drenched and chilly through her mittens, was still. Hands shaking, she dusted the powder from her sister's boot.

It was not attached to a body.

She sagged, her lungs deflating in one long rush. Eska was not here, lying in the snow, dead. She must have lost her boot when she'd fled.

Nakaluq sniffed the abandoned boot, then looked at her, head cocked. Apaay's stomach twisted, because she knew that look. A hunt that led to a cold trail. A bitter end.

This could not be the end.

Her knees groaned as she leaned forward, touching her forehead to his. "Do you remember," she murmured, "the blizzard last year? The one that overtook our hunting party?"

His ears perked at the seriousness of her voice, worn down like water on stone.

"The other dogs weren't able to go on." One by one, they had fallen to exhaustion and hunger and cold. "But not you, Nakaluq. You went on." And saved the men who would have been lost forever to the tundra.

"I'm asking you to try again. One last time." She squeezed her eyes shut and whispered, "My sweet, sweet boy. I believe in you."

Hesitantly, his tail waved back and forth. Always a good sign. He once again sniffed the boot Apaay offered him, and together, they trekked south, winding through the forest of evergreen conifers, frost coating their needles in glittering white.

The darkness was thicker here, and the clacking branches lifted the hair along her body. She didn't think the demon would linger if he had captured his prize, but she couldn't be certain. He could be crouched behind one of the trunks. Or hiding among the branches.

When Nakaluq shot forward, barking furiously, she knew. How could she not? Apaay's instincts, when it came to family, were strong. With hope swelling in her heart, she charged after Nakaluq. He was a bright light cutting through the darkness, and he would lead her to Eska.

Somehow, her sister had managed to wedge herself into a hollowed-out cavity in the trunk. Her hood had fallen back, revealing a long ebony braid snaking over one shoulder. Severe shudders wracked her body.

Relief turned Apaay's legs to water. They buckled before she could reach her destination. On hands and knees, she crawled. "Naajatikaaq." *Granddaughter.* Gently, Apaay tried to draw her younger sister into her warmth. Eska resisted, tucking her face further into the tree's hollow.

"You don't have to be afraid. I'm here. I'm always here." But it was a lie, wasn't it? She had told Eska to leave. Had sent her sister out alone. It was as Papa had said. She was supposed to have protected her, and she had failed.

Nakaluq whined, nudging his nose in the crook of Eska's arm. She stiffened, then slowly sank her hand into Nakaluq's coat and gripped tight. One leg at a time, Eska stirred, as if she were slowly being thawed out. She uncurled, though kept her head ducked, lost in its own shadow. It was so murky in these woods.

"Naajatikaaq." She whispered the endearment. "Come on. Everyone is waiting for us."

Afterward, Apaay would wonder if it had been a cruel dream. For when Eska lifted her head, Apaay had expected to gaze into eyes choked with tears, eyes the color of ripe earth like her own. Except there were no eyes, and there was no nose, and there was no mouth—no lips or teeth. For where her sister's face should have been lay nothing more than a stretch of empty skin.

Faceless.

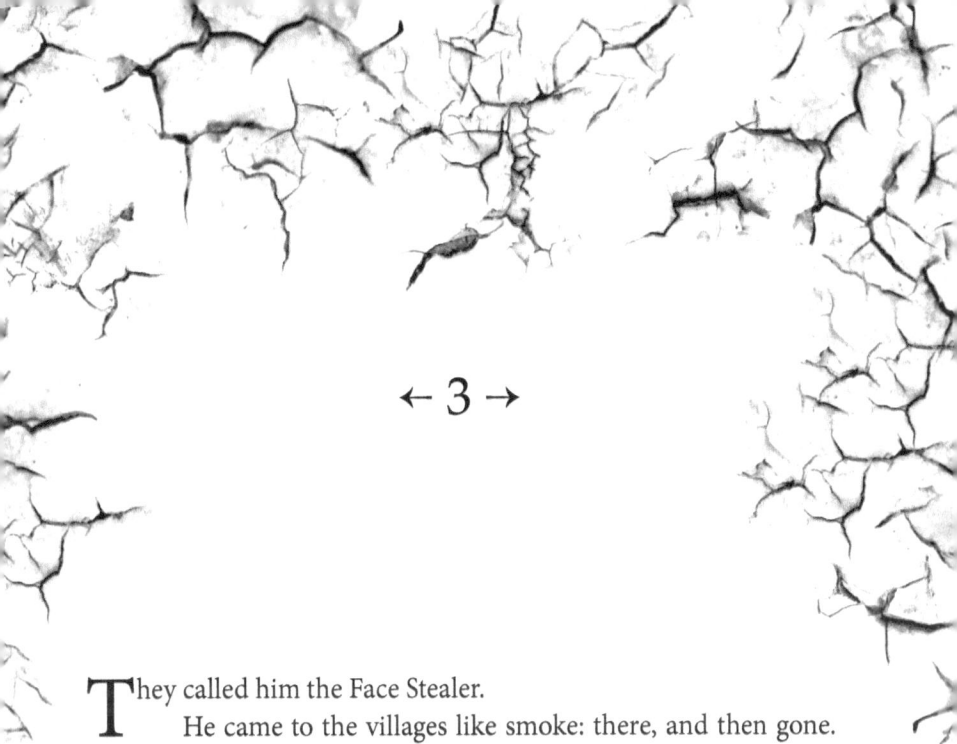

They called him the Face Stealer.

He came to the villages like smoke: there, and then gone. Vanishing into the night.

The Face Stealer was a skin-changer, a demon, a thief. Hoarding people's faces in the in-between where he lived, a place between waking and dreaming, living and dying, here and there, then and now. The in-between, they said, lay deep in the North, lost to the frozen tundra. Once he returned to his lair, or wherever it was he dwelled, that was it. You never saw those faces again.

Despite the Face Stealer's reputation, no one knew what he looked like. You could only see him from the corner of your eye. If you attempted to look at him directly, he remained elusive. They said he was a child. They said he was a man. They said his hair was a deep, fiery red; or pale, pale yellow; or white as snow; or mossy green. They said he was eight feet tall, but in the shadows, he grew to ten, possibly twelve, feet. They said he had fur, not skin, and four legs, not two, and sometimes he grew a tail, but then other times he didn't.

They said many things.

Four hours had passed since Eska's discovery, and the world was a much darker place than it had been. After sending for help earlier, Apaay had carried Eska through the belching smoke toward home, where she and her parents now gathered. They'd settled atop the shelf of ice where they slept, its solidity draped in thick pelts. Eska, blankets heaped atop her form, lay on her side, her back to them. All was quiet. All was still.

Apaay swiped a hand over her face. The shaking of Eska's shoulders had finally ceased, but the sight of her sister's soundless crying—tears locked in a body with no eyes—was an image that would never leave her. Only two small slits carved into her light brown skin remained of her nose, allowing her the air to breathe.

Apaay didn't know how exactly it worked, but those whose faces were stolen did not die. Last year, a young man had lost his face. He was still alive, yet utterly without life. This went for all of the victims. It was as if the act of removing their identity sent them to a waiting place until their self was returned, if ever. Instead, the victims were left with their thoughts. They could touch, but not see. They could smell, but not taste. It was a hollow existence, and many knew not how to cope. Unfortunately, it was not unheard of for a victim to wander out into the cold and freeze to death.

It was this thought above all others that sent her heart into a tumble. Apaay said, "I'm going after him." Since the Face Stealer had not taken her sister's ears, she spoke in hushed tones.

Mama straightened, a blanket wrapped around her shoulders. They had shed their parkas and left them to dry in the tunnel leading outside. Inside the curved dome, the temperature was comfortably warm. "Tell me you don't mean that, naaja."

Apaay very nearly smiled. Her grandmother—Mama's mother—had passed away before she'd been born. Mama had given her mother's name-soul to her firstborn, and thus called Apaay naaja, or *mother*. In turn, Apaay called Mama naajaluk, or *daughter*. She called Eska naajatikaaq, *granddaughter*, just as Eska called her naajatik, *grandmother*. As well, Apaay referred to Papa as naattaluk, or *son*.

"Naajaluk, you know I never say anything I don't mean."

Mama looked to Papa for support. He had yet to contribute to the conversation. *You're supposed to protect her.* Apaay couldn't bear to look at him, instead focusing her attention on the flat, crescent-shaped lamp burning with a small amount of oil they had rendered from seal blubber. The curved walls ignited with warm golden light.

When it became apparent he wouldn't respond, Mama turned back to Apaay. Here was the woman who had given birth to her, and Apaay imagined she was no less fierce than she had been eighteen years ago. "You don't know where he dwells. You don't know anything about him." A pause. "It's not safe to cross over among the territories."

This was true. It wasn't as simple as traveling to his home, knocking on his door, asking him to please return what was not his, perhaps spitting on his boots in the process. The North was an indomitable fortress of fortified white walls. No one knew what treasures it concealed behind its mountains, beneath its rivers and frozen streams. Already, winter began to tighten its grip.

As for the territories, there had been unrest for as long as she'd been alive. But Apaay wouldn't let that stop her. She loved Eska more than she feared this demon. "I know he took Eska's face. That's enough for me."

"And if he takes your face, too?" Reaching out, she clutched her daughter's hand. Apaay felt the calluses from where she held the sewing needle. "Then you'll never get home."

A flurry of wings fluttered in her stomach. "I'm not going to let that happen."

"But—"

"Who is the best hunter in the village?"

Mama looked confused for a moment. "Your father is."

It wasn't the answer she had wanted, even though it was true. She brushed off the twinge of hurt. "Who is the second-best hunter?"

"Muktuk."

All right, so she was not the most effective hunter. But she tried. Even if nothing came of it, she tried.

Pressing her lips together, she tried for a different approach. "Who is the best tracker in the village?"

"Silla is," Mama answered. "Everyone knows this."

Stunned, Apaay could only stare at her. Would it have killed her to pretend, even for a moment, that she believed in her daughter?

Which made Apaay wonder. *Did* Mama believe in her? The possibility that she did not made her feel small. "You don't think I can do it."

"Is that what you think?" Papa murmured. A touch of coldness threaded through his voice. "What reason would we have to send you out into certain death? Because that's what you're doing if you leave. Look at me when I'm speaking to you."

She lifted her chin, cheeks dark with shame. As always, Papa had a way of commanding attention. The lamplight drew out the red undertones of his skin, a color that reminded Apaay of deep autumn, whereas her skin more closely resembled the golden stalks of summer rushes. A ripple of darkness glided over Papa's shoulders, spreading out to cover his knees. Apaay had always loved his hair, the streaks of gray having recently grown in. Small feathers or bits of bone hung from the ends of a few thin braids—goals he had accomplished, significant events in his life. She could not speak for the whole of her people, but for the Analak situated along the eastern coast, hair was deeply personal—a part of their identity. It was never shorn.

"It's a selfish decision," he said. "The only person you're helping is that demon."

"What am I supposed to do?" Apaay snapped. "Watch Eska waste away? He'll come back, and then whose face will he take? Whose life will he ruin next?"

Mama said, "I want you here, where you're safe."

"No one is safe. Don't you see?" She flung out her arms in frustration. "It won't stop. Eventually, he'll return." As he did every few months. The last attack had left an entire family faceless. The youngest had killed herself. The father had followed not long after.

"I'll make a search party." Papa's gruff voice. "I'll gather a few men, and *I* will go after the demon. You and your mother will stay here—"

I. Not *we*.

"You're joking, right?" She stabbed her finger toward his splint. "Your leg is *broken*."

"It's been feeling better lately."

"Naattaluk." The fire in Apaay's voice petered out. She didn't know what hurt more: the lies, or how he did such a poor job of them. "I know you don't think so, but I'm strong. I'm smart."

"I didn't say that."

"So then why? If this were Silla, you wouldn't tell him no. You'd encourage it. But he's not the only one who knows the land. I have good instincts. I'm just as capable of fending for—"

"Because you're our daughter!" he roared, red in the face. His rough breaths filled the enclosed space. "You're our daughter, and right now, you're the only one we have left."

There was only emotion. Bright, painful emotion. Eska was *right there*, wide awake. One daughter left? She should slap Papa for saying something so hurtful.

"Is this how we deserve to live?" Her voice rose, cracked. She lowered it again. "In fear of a demon?" She would not accept it. Apaay had turned this notion over and over, wanting to perceive things differently, but there was no gray she could see. The Face Stealer had hurt her family, so he must pay.

"You don't have to do this," Mama managed in an unsteady tone. "We'll find another way."

How? she wanted to ask. *Tell me how and I will do it.*

Something was swelling inside her, battering its fists against her body, demanding to be released. Truth was a searing white light, illuminating the dark place where Apaay had suppressed her yearning for so many years. For the first time, she saw it clearly.

Eska needed this, but Apaay needed it more. She needed it much, much more. Because beneath the searing white light, Apaay knew that had the situation been switched—had the Face Stealer stolen *her* face, plunged *her* into a lonely dark world—no one would come for her. No one would scale mountains or cross the inhospitable tundra to find her again.

She tried not to feel sorry for herself. The truth did not have to hurt if she didn't want it to. It was nothing she did not already know. But deep down, it ate at her. And the only thing keeping her together was this: If she succeeded at this task, maybe people would look at her differently. Maybe they would see her as someone worthy.

And maybe she would see herself as worthy, too.

Mama's grief leaked into the open. "If you go after him, you'll die."

Apaay wanted to reach out, stroke a finger down her mother's fraught nerves. She couldn't blame Mama. One daughter was already gone, but to potentially lose the second as well? Of course she would want Apaay to stay. "If I don't," she said, "Eska is as good as dead."

Papa wasn't able to completely hide his flinch. "You're not leaving," he said in a tone that was as flat as it was cold. It sounded like he had withdrawn into himself. "If I have to tie you up, then so be it. But at least I'll know you're safe."

Apaay glanced at Eska again. Her little sister, barely fourteen, banished to darkness. No one would help her. Fear had wrapped her family in its smothering embrace, and there was no air for them to breathe. This was a road with no beginning and no end, and Apaay could not walk it any longer. Someone had to forge a new path. Something had to change.

Dropping her eyes, Apaay nodded. "All right, Papa." Already, the beginnings of a plan began to form. Whether they approved of her decision or not, she was leaving. They would not notice her absence until she was far from home. "I won't leave. I promise." Apaay had to bite the inside of her cheek to stop herself from spilling the truth. In her heart, she knew this was the right thing to do. "But I'd like to speak to Eska alone."

After Mama and Papa left, Apaay shifted closer to her sister, but did not reach for her. It felt as if a gulf lay between them, and there was no ice on which to cross. The light had dimmed. Soon the flame would extinguish, allowing darkness to swoop in.

Apaay murmured, "I know you're not asleep. You always were the eavesdropper, after all."

Eska breathed deeply and evenly, unresponsive. The silence crackled. Apaay pressed her lips together and fought the rise of tears. Enough of the cowardice. Enough of the games. She couldn't avoid this any longer.

"I'm sorry, naajatikaaq. I am so, so sorry." There, in the heart of their light-drenched home, Apaay felt the first stirrings of deep, abysmal fear. Fear that Eska would not forgive her. Fear that this might be the last time they would see each other. Fear that what Apaay had done would rot the leaves and roots of this beautiful flower that was their relationship. Above everything else, it was the last thing Apaay feared most: that they would not be able to start anew. "I know Mama and Papa don't think I can do it, but I'm going to get your face back, and when I do, I'm going to kill the Face Stealer." The words were thick, yet steely with the determination that had always lain within her. "And then he'll never be able to hurt anyone else again."

A soft touch against Eska's cheek. Apaay said, as gently as she could, "I will carry your heart in my heart." Because that's all she could offer, and now it was time to leave.

After kissing her sister on the back of her head, Apaay gathered her pack and was beginning to crawl through the tunnel leading outside when a hand wrapped around her ankle, the grip fierce. She turned as Eska threw her arms around her neck, clinging hard. Her little sister shook in silent grief, and Apaay's stomach twisted with such helplessness that she vowed to make the Face Stealer pay. Whatever it took, however it took, she would do it. He would regret ever hurting her family.

Drawing back, Eska interlaced her fingers—the sign for togetherness—before lifting her clasped hands to her chest.

I will carry your heart in my heart.

Apaay caught Eska's left hand. Pressed their palms together, two halves never to be parted, even in distance, even in death. Her heart swelled, the touch seeping into her skin.

As will I.

← →

Apaay did not say goodbye. It was easier this way. Mama and Papa would not understand her reasons for leaving, and she didn't expect them to. After all, Mama was an only child. Papa, too. They had raised their daughters to love each other and fight, always, to keep the other safe. But they did not know what it was to have half of yourself ripped away. And so they did not know that Apaay carried the guilt and the agony and the shame with her as she strode quickly north, finally breaching the village's outer ring. Frozen seal and whale meat, along with a few tools, filled the pack weighing down her shoulder, a spear slung across her back. She climbed the first hill and had nearly topped the second when a sharp bark sounded.

Apaay slowed to a halt, turned.

Nakaluq was sprinting after her.

The sight nearly brought her to her knees. She should have known she could not slip silently into the night. Apaay could no more separate herself from Nakaluq than she could from her shadow. There was no such thing as him and her, apart. There was only them, together.

He stopped right in front of her so there was no space between them. He looked at her, and his eyes glowed with love. She looked at him, and was home.

Thinking they were going on an adventure, he yipped and bounded in circles around her, snow flying around his legs. *Play with me*, he said, and her heart tugged in longing.

Reaching over, she snagged him around the scruff of his neck. "Sit."

He sat.

Apaay did not look at him as she whispered, "Stay."

As much as she loved Nakaluq, she would not risk endangering him out on the tundra. He was a good boy who would not disobey her orders. This she knew.

His whines ratcheted higher, then dissolved into barking as Apaay topped the hill and descended out of sight.

She promised herself she would not look back.

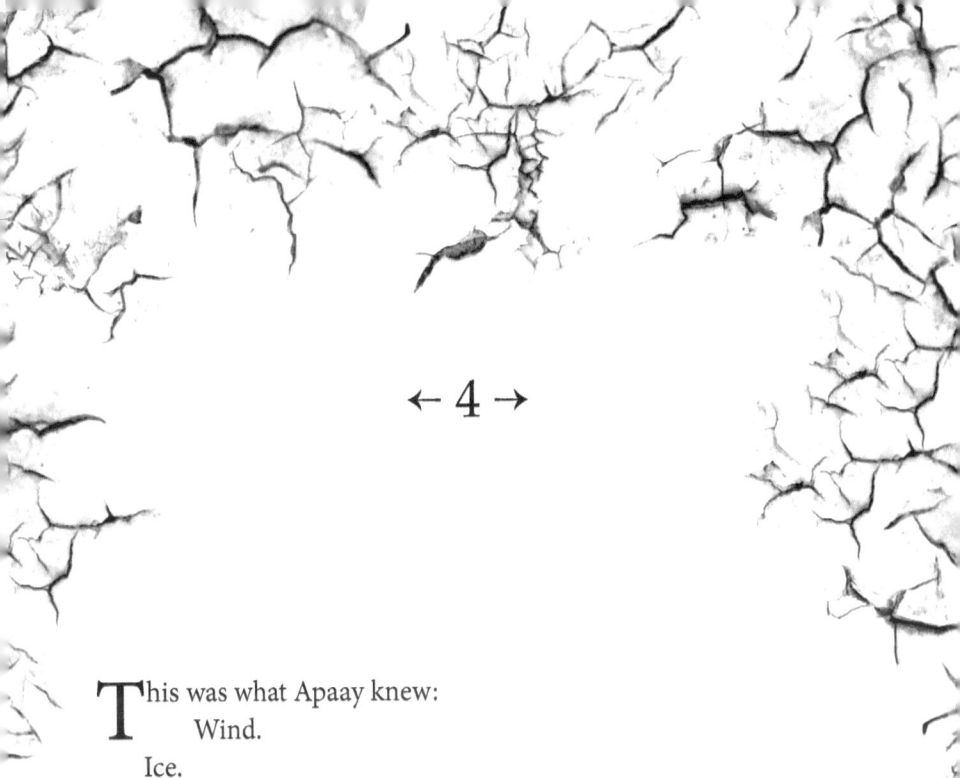

← 4 →

This was what Apaay knew:
Wind.
Ice.
White nothingness.

The days unspooled, no beginning and no end. A ceiling of curved slate broken by constellations was her only guide as the first week came and went, and the second, and the third. Time passed in subtle shades of darkness.

Lifting her legs up high, she brought them down to punch through the thin crust. The cold was a ferocious beast, sliding through the small openings in her furs to rake its claws over any exposed flesh. Apaay ducked her head, concentrating only on the next step, never mind that she had long ago lost count. The North would never be soft or soothing. It was a land carved by wind. If it knew anything less than cruelty, it could not endure. The swiftest, the fittest, the bravest, the most feared. Only those who demonstrated such traits survived, which was why the Analak had endured, and continued to endure, the brutality, the lack of warmth and green. Others were weak, but her people were strong.

She wished things had turned out differently. There was not an emotion she did not feel. The shred of bitter regret, that razor's edge of anger, self-loathing, guilt. Apaay knew she did not have the right to complain. It was Eska who could not laugh or cry or look into the eyes of her family. Eska, who knew only darkness. Losing her sister to the Face Stealer was an agony she could not articulate. It drove her legs forward, through snow and wind and ice. If she failed this mission, there would never again be laughter in their home, or life, because Apaay could not bear to live in a world that Eska was not a part of.

The wind blew from the east, carrying hints of an approaching storm. She trekked across open tundra: a vast sweep of white, the occasional stone or lichen patch. The sea had long since disappeared. To the west lay the Atakana, the single great mountain range of the North, cleaving through the Central and Western Territories. Gray mist cloaked its jagged peaks.

There were five designated territories in the North, and Apaay's people were the only ones not bound to their borders. The Unua, a group of skin-changing races that lay scattered in various nations, had long ago designated which land belonged to whom. Polar bear Unua to the south. Caribou Unua to the north. Seal Unua to the east. Wolf Unua to the west. And owl Unua to the land's center. They kept within their borders, kept within their walls.

It was a shame, really. Apaay did not see the land as something to divide and distribute. She saw it as something whole.

And so it went. Another hour passed, then two. Apaay scanned the land constantly, searching for movement against the snow, which glowed silver in the pale light of the moon. The Face Stealer regularly stalked these lands, but she was not worried about succumbing to the same fate as Eska. Whenever he paid someone's village a visit, he didn't linger. He would take his prize and return to where he dwelled: north. Far, far away from here.

So far, she hadn't experienced anything unusual. It was more of a feeling. A subtle shift to her senses. Frowning, she slowed and glanced over her shoulder. The surrounding dim cast the world in violets and blues and grays. Her awareness of the environment expanded, bumps rolling over her body as blood pumped furiously at her temples. She strained her ears in the lull between gusts—there.

Someone was following her.

Snow crunched and cracked underfoot. Whoever followed her was perhaps a quarter mile behind, their tread light and agile, so unlike her own, burdened by layers of cloth, the weight of food and weapons on her back. She didn't want them to know she was aware of their presence. It was one of the first rules she'd learned as a hunter, and one of the few she hadn't forgotten.

The snow liquified into slush as she descended into a broad valley, and the top layer could no longer hold her weight. Apaay broke through, sinking in up to her knees.

Unslinging her spear from across her back, she used its tip to cut a path through the white mass. Here was exhaustion, and here was pain. It was only the third week, the third week out of many. A small voice slithered through her mind, taunting and breaking down those walls she'd built.

How weak she was, how alone.

How her plan was full of holes, and this failure would prove what everyone already knew: Apaay did not have what it took to see a job through.

"Don't do it," she muttered. "Don't listen to them." She would not go down that path. She refused. "They don't know what they're talking about."

After reaching a rock-strewn area, Apaay ducked behind a boulder, back pressed against its curve, the spear gripped in her hands. The storm must have been traveling more quickly than she first thought, as snow began to fall fast and hard. Whoever followed her was close, but it didn't sound at all like boots.

A head poked out from behind the rock, and there he was. Apaay looked at him in shock. "Nakaluq." The word was soft and pained.

His joy unfurled, and Apaay marveled at how it never failed to catch her unaware—that simple happiness of being with one you loved.

Nakaluq planted his paws on her shoulders and bathed her face in warm, wet kisses. He whined and nuzzled her neck before switching back to kisses, his backside wiggling back and forth as he tried to climb into her lap, all eighty pounds of bulked muscle mass.

Her chin wobbled as she tucked her face into his fur, murmuring, "My sweet, sweet boy. Why didn't you stay home? Why would you come?" So brave, so resourceful. He could not know what awaited them out here.

Pulling away, Nakaluq yipped and bounded off. He lowered his front legs in the signal for play, shot upward, and promptly fell through a mound of snow. Apaay snorted when, a moment later, his dusted head popped up like a flower in spring, tongue lolling happily.

She could not quite help herself. After weeks in isolation, here was family, here was love. Shedding her supplies, Apaay crowed and hurtled toward him. He dashed away, a streak of silver, daring her to give chase.

Heavy, breathless laughter ensued as Apaay attempted to tackle him, an impossible task in the soft, new-fallen snow. Nakaluq raced around and around, tireless, his lighter weight enabling him to prance across the surface while she sank up to her hips, stuck. When Apaay snatched at him, he slipped away. She called him back, and he came.

"All right!" Apaay said, giggling as he rolled onto his back beside her. "You win. You're too fast for me."

Nakaluq licked her cheek before sitting half on her chest. His panting breath burst forth in white clouds.

Apaay allowed herself to rest for a few minutes before struggling to her feet and brushing the slush from her legs. She checked his pads. His gait was healthy to all appearances, save his left hind leg. He must have sprained something on the journey. Under any other circumstances, she would make camp, for the storm's brute force would soon be upon them. But she was afraid of losing more time. Eska needed her.

Hunched against the force of wind, Apaay forged ahead, using her body to shield Nakaluq from the worst of it. The sliver of moon, a delicately carved shard that balanced on the tip of one of the mountain peaks, appeared to wobble as the wind gusted harder, doing all it could to blow the light off its precarious throne. This was a merciless land. People who were not born from its unyielding womb tended to forget. Oh, but not her. Every time the wind smacked her in the face, it was reminding her to wake up, don't forget, don't ever forget what I can do.

"Nakaluq." She reached down, reassured when his snout touched her palm. "Keep up." The snow was coming down thicker, pouring onto them. She didn't want to lose him.

In her lifetime, Apaay had only ever seen three foreigners: men from Across the Sea who knew not how to survive the tundra, who came from a place untouched by cold. They had worn strange clothing, their furs not white or gray or brown, but black or sometimes red. Their skin had been oddly pale, like the moon, their hair in shades of gold. She almost hadn't believed it.

Two years had since passed, but she still remembered crouching next to Papa, studying them from afar as they felled the trees and raised them into dead wooden walls.

"Naattaluk, who are those men?"

"I don't know," he muttered, gaze narrowed.

It was clear they did not belong.

The men spent hours constructing a dwelling of severe angles, the wood rigid and utterly inflexible. It was not enough. The cruel, bone-dry wind would slip through the cracks. Frost would invade and splinter the wood. The square structure would do little to retain body heat, warmth. These were things her people had known for a long time.

That night, a blizzard had blown in. It was sudden. Apaay remembered because it was the day Eska had begun her monthly bleeding, taking those first uncertain steps toward womanhood. It was the harshest storm to have hit in years.

The next morning, Papa and a few hunters left the village to investigate and returned shortly afterward, their faces grave. The men, he'd said, had frozen to death.

The storm had lifted shortly thereafter.

These harsh winds rivaled those of that storm. Drawing her hood tighter around her head, Apaay pushed through the white wall. She could no longer feel her face. The next gust rammed her to the side, and she tumbled into a heap. Immediately, Nakaluq was there, whining at her to rise, keep moving, don't stop.

A few attempts of unattractive flopping later, she managed to right herself. Eska, no doubt, would have laughed. *Like a seal on land,* she'd say. Probably wrestling would ensue. Apaay never missed an opportunity to remind Eska she could happily sit on her sister's head all day if it meant she got to eat the seal's eye for dinner that night.

Tugging on her mitten, Nakaluq led her back to the path, acting as her eyes when the snow blinded her. She huffed and puffed like an old woman. How long had she been out in the elements, pushing forward, not even stopping to rest? It must have been hours. Her joints throbbed with cold, and her muscles grew stiff with fatigue.

Glancing behind her, Apaay scanned the area for a place to make camp for the night, then stopped. Her slow, drowsy pulse began to beat with increasing urgency. "Nakaluq?"

He had disappeared.

Apaay's mind blanked. She walked back the way she'd come, calling Nakaluq's name, snow deadening the sound. The path she'd created was slowly filling in, and any indication of the direction they'd traveled had vanished.

The snow was now as high as her hips. Fumbling to remove a mitten from her shaking hands, she shoved two fingers into her mouth. The whistle carried far and wide, as pure as a gull's cry. Apaay lifted her legs to shake free the soft ice encasing her.

From her right, a high, muffled whine.

Apaay charged blindly forward, the air ringing with the sound of her voice—bitten by cold, shredded by fear. Her spear banged against the back of her thighs as she slogged uphill. "Nakaluq!" The storm was too strong. Sweat soaked through the layers of cloth, chilling her skin. The cold burned.

Apaay slowed. White swirled around her. The condensation around her nostrils had frozen, and there was, quite literally, nothing to see. White, shades of gray. An absence of life.

Except for a shadow on the fringe of her vision, slinking through.

It was not Nakaluq. Her dog did not slink. His shoulders weren't as bulky, his chest as deep. He was small, whereas this shadow . . . this shadow was so very large.

Hands shaking, she reached behind and fumbled for her spear. Pins and needles bit at her fingers, tunneling through her wrists and palms. The shadow slipped closer, circling and circling, not at all concerned with the storm, considering she was a meal standing still. It was huge and long of leg, with an elegant head and a full, bushy tail.

She could count on one hand the number of times a wolf had attacked her people. Wolves were sacred to the Analak. They represented the heart of what it meant to be free.

"Come on," she spat, baring her teeth. "Show yourself!"

It stopped beyond throwing distance of her spear, though in this weather she wouldn't risk losing her only weapon. The wolf watched her, as if waiting for her to die all on her own.

Well, it was going to have a long wait, Apaay thought darkly, because she hadn't traveled this far to die willingly.

Lifting the spear higher, Apaay wedged her body through the hard ice. She was nearly close enough to drive it through the wolf's throat when she faltered. Blinked in confusion. Not a shadow. Not even a living thing, but rather stacks of smooth, flat stones.

It wasn't a wolf. It was a cairn *shaped* like a wolf.

Apaay leaned against the stone structure, trying to tuck herself into the smallest ball possible in order to conserve warmth. Her teeth were chattering so hard she feared she might chip a tooth. Had it been a cairn all along? She swore the wolf had moved.

Apaay pounded her fist against the rock. She couldn't help it. She did not have supplies to build a fire—no oil or wood—and her seal meat was running dangerously low. But more importantly, she did not have Nakaluq.

With their separation, it was impossible to know whether he was alive. It was likely the storm had taken him. And if it had, if he was buried beneath the ice, she would never find his body.

Another shudder tore through her.

She could not turn back. She would perish long before she ever reached home. And Eska was counting on her, which meant she must move forward.

It was as if all the wolves of the North howled their rage at her, this girl who would not succumb, who would go on, even blind. It only pushed Apaay harder. The Face Stealer had stolen from Eska not just a face, but a life. One she would find and return. It did not belong to him. It never had.

She traveled in a straight line as best as she could, moving in the direction she believed was north. The wolf-shaped cairn fell behind, and then, as if chased away by Apaay's curses, the snow lifted its heavy burden, trickling off into a mild flurry.

She stood in a pristine land: untouched white hills, the horizon colored by a faint violet hue. The strangest sight, however, was the smattering of evergreen conifers. They did not grow this far north. Nothing did.

Nostrils flaring, she inhaled.

The air was different.

She didn't know how to explain it. It wasn't a smell she was used to, or even a smell she'd encountered before. It was sharp like frigid water, with an underlying harshness that reminded her of smoke. It smelled ridiculously like a memory, but no memory she recalled.

Apaay strode forward a few steps before coming to a halt. The land swayed. The snow rippled. The hills shifted and reshaped themselves: higher, lower, flatter, broader. Apaay rubbed her eyes to clear them. When she looked again, the land had stilled.

It must be the exhaustion. Apaay slept very little, for that was time she could not get back. Every minute was precious. Since she didn't know how long Eska would last in her condition, she couldn't afford to sleep. Exhaustion, fatigue—yes, that explained the strange shifting sensation.

With a wary glance behind, Apaay continued walking. Eventually, a pile of boulders appeared on her right, one smoothed to resemble a swelling wave. After another twenty minutes, she topped a hill strewn with pebbles. And looked again at a boulder shaped like a wave.

How was this possible? Twenty minutes ago, she'd walked past this same spot. The boulders were arranged in the same formation. There, near her feet, lay the sudden dip in the ground where she'd tripped. Except she had walked in a straight line. She'd made sure of it. Maybe she wasn't the most experienced tracker, but Apaay had a strong sense of direction. There was no possibility of walking in a circle and returning to this place.

"This is all in your head," Apaay murmured to herself, even as a feeling prickled at the base of her spine. She whirled around, spear in hand.

The area was deserted.

Apaay knew how the snow and ice could disorient. White and gray, shades of it. Yet she'd lived her entire life cradled between the mountains and the sea. The only reason she'd be disoriented would be because—

Because this was not her land.

The Face Stealer lived in a realm not of her world. A disorienting, in-between place, easy for someone to lose their way. A place into which she must have crossed over in the storm. The only question was this: Had she found it all on her own, or had he let her in?

Apaay let loose an unsettled breath when something shifted in her peripheral vision. The world went white as pain exploded through her skull, and she fell into dark eternity.

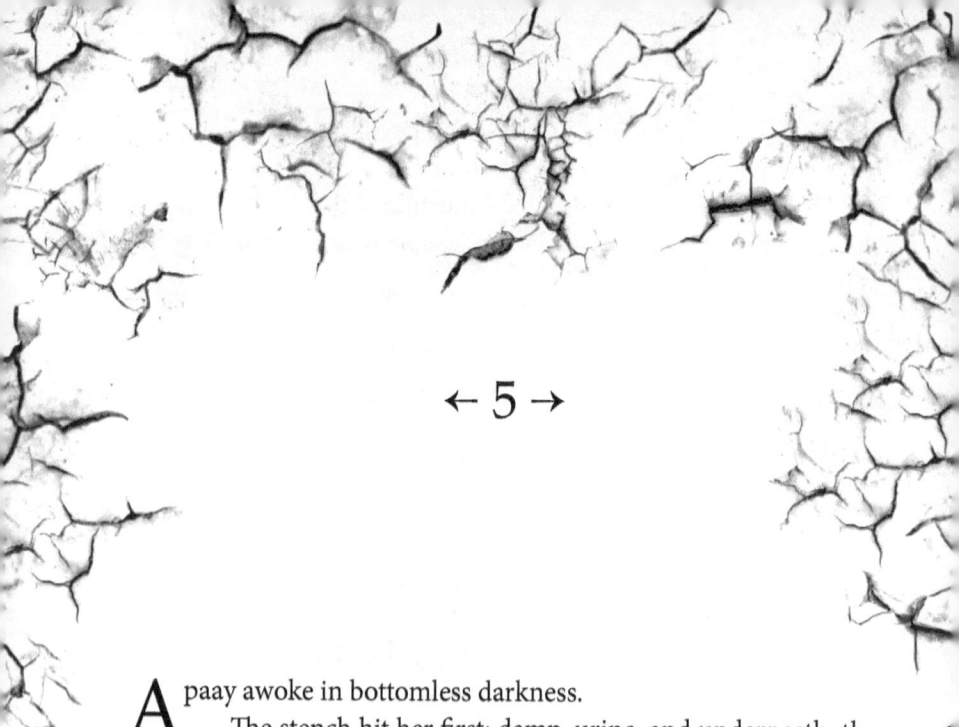

← 5 →

Apaay awoke in bottomless darkness.

The stench hit her first: damp, urine, and underneath, the sharp scent of blood. It was faint, as if time had done its work to dull it. She didn't want to think about where it had come from or from whom. The air was close and stale, biting with cold, but not the cold found aboveground, the type that made her feel free. This was a cold that dwelled below.

A few minutes passed in silence. Apaay lay sprawled on her side, chilled stone digging into her hip. The darkness didn't lift. It curled around her, ran its dark hands down her spine, so lovingly, and yet the slightest movement sent spasms tearing through her shoulders, the muscles locked and wooden, and she nearly bit through her lip in holding back a scream. Her hands had been tied behind her back. Judging from the stiffness, they had been bound for some time, but for how long? Hours? Days? She didn't remember how she got here. This place—where was this place? She smelled spores festering nearby, stagnant water. Like the slowly decaying earth, which always reminded her of death.

The darkness gripped her. A choked gasp burst free as her head swam. An overwhelming fear that sprung from someone else's life experience, now her burden to bear. Sometimes she dreamed, a hazy recollection, the images fleeting. Her grandmother—Mama's mother, whose name-soul she had taken—as a young girl, running and jumping and sliding across the ice. The cracks had been too faint to see.

Run, her mind screamed. *Get away.* But she couldn't move, and she couldn't see. The black cloaked her eyes and made her blind.

Teeth gritted, Apaay braced herself and rolled onto her knees. White heat flared in her shoulder joints, then dulled. She strained her ears. "Hello?" The word ricocheted in the enclosed space, returning softer than before. Wherever she was, the walls were most likely made of stone.

The silence coaxed out her uncertainties and laid them bare, prodded at her fears so they awakened from their slumber, gnashed their vicious teeth. Her thoughts unspooled.

Papa, Mama, Eska. How were they holding up in her absence? Had they sent someone after her, someone to bring her home? They must have known what she'd done as soon as they discovered her pack gone, Eska alone. Maybe now they understood what was truly at stake here. There could not be togetherness when her sister huddled apart. Somehow, she would find a way to bring Eska home. Until Apaay returned, she wished them strength, for they would need it, and each other. Someone in the community would help them hunt or share their food. It was the Analak way.

As for Nakaluq—the storm had taken him. She was sure of it. There was no way he had survived.

Apaay exhaled shakily. In the end, she had not been able to save him. Nakaluq had died alone. Without a proper burial. Without recognition. Without a friend to ease his passing. Without anything.

Apaay had but one small relief: He had not been taken, like her, shoved in this pen to rot. He had died free.

Apaay was about to push to her feet when the floor trembled with faint vibrations.

Someone was coming.

Immediately, she lay back down and closed her eyes. The vibrations lengthened and separated themselves into a steady rhythm. Heavy boots scuffed against the floor lazily. She stored the distinct sound of the tread away for later, along with what direction the footsteps came from. It was likely the only way out.

Red light seared behind her eyelids. A rusted squeal followed, sinking its claws into her mind. Someone halted in front of her, the stench of rotting fish strong, and she was pulled from her shadowy existence by the presence of heat and light.

"Get up."

Apaay managed to open her eyes without being blinded. Firelight emanated from a torch the man held, its golden hue spilling onto the stones constructing the floor and ceiling and walls. The cell was small enough that she could stretch out her arms—if they weren't bound, that is—and touch the walls with her fingertips. Rectangular stones had been stacked on top of one another. Like an ice house, yet without the dome. This ceiling was strangely flat.

Apparently, she didn't move fast enough for his liking, because the man reached down and hauled her to her feet. Apaay cried out in pain.

Shadows cratered the man's face and wavered along his upper torso. He wore what looked to be rags or strips of cloth, gray and algae-green, though she had never seen such clothing before. His boots were strange and black and narrow, not at all fitting to walk atop the snow. "Who are you?" she demanded.

"Silence."

A sack descended over her head, guttering her vision.

When the man yanked her from the cramped room, she could do little but stumble behind him as he tugged her down what sounded like a long passageway, as it took longer for the sound of their footsteps to bounce off the walls and return. Apaay's breath slapped against the thick hide, hot and sticky. She'd never experienced this sensation before. Like there was not enough air or room to breathe.

A moment later, her foot plunged through space where she expected solid ground to be. Apaay didn't have time to scream before the force of hitting the floor punched into her sore shoulder and rippled throughout her body. Her groan filled the bag. "What was that?"

In answer, the man yanked her upright and shoved her forward.

She tried to keep track of which direction they went, but it was impossible. They made so many turns and backtracks she was certain the man was intentionally trying to confuse her. At least there was no wind down here. The air, which was still far below freezing, warmed by slow degrees as they climbed a set of stairs. Over time, the echo of their footsteps lingered, smudged, and was nearly lost as they stepped into what sounded like a spacious area. The twinge in Apaay's chest lessened with each step, for the air was freer here.

"Where are we going?" She needed to know. She *hated* not knowing. The hand on her arm had slackened, but their pace didn't.

"Quiet."

"Not until you tell me—"

"If you value your life," he said, jerking her closer so he could hiss into her ear, "then I suggest you shut your mouth."

A hot ball of rage seethed in her gut, beating back the chill. She clung to it, this fury, because it was the only thing she could control, and if she didn't embrace it, the fear would tear apart all sense of reason. First, they took her hands. Now they wanted to take her voice, too?

"There you are," said a peevish voice. A girl, she believed.

They stopped.

The voice had come from straight ahead, bouncing against the wall behind them, the memory of it lingering after the echo had died. It sounded incredibly young, and yet Apaay unconsciously straightened, blinking behind the sack that kept the girl's face from her. Wondering, too, when she would wake from this nightmare.

"Next time I suggest you try moving a little faster, yes?"

Her nostrils flared as the man's grip tightened on her arm. A sick rush of panic rooted deep down. Apaay was expected. Whoever waited knew of her capture, the cell, the helplessness of her tied hands. How could someone do this to another person? Unless— was *this* the Face Stealer? Her entire life she had believed the demon to be male, but then again, no one had ever seen the demon's face.

"Remove the sack."

Apaay blinked hard against the influx of blue light. She stood in a fortress carved of ice. The circular chamber, as wide across as her entire *village*, soared toward a domed ceiling of impossible heights. Icicles as thick as her head clung to its curved apex, their sharp points glinting with beads of water, the dome's outer band punched through with oval windows where the moonlight draped through high above. The walls were white frost, and so thin they were nearly translucent. Thousands of minute bubbles remained trapped within.

Five arrow-shaped archways cut into the walls leading to yet more passages, with men standing guard on either side. Five mirrors dominated the space between. They were easily the height of two grown men, the breadth of seven. Four of them reflected the blue-and-white surfaces of the ice. The fifth was a void, absorbing the light rather than reflecting it.

Her attention flicked to the floors above—four in total. Small, crescent-shaped oil lamps had been tucked into the cavities of the great hall, casting soft light. It was both beautiful and cold, a pretty piece of jewelry she could look at but not touch.

"Bring the prisoner closer. I want to see her."

In her shocked state, Apaay did not resist as the guard hauled her to the heart of the chamber. Five raised walkways of cut stone led from the passages to converge in the room's center, like a star, while a narrower path ringed the room. A body of frozen water spanned the entirety of the floor. Polished, like bone, but so delicate. Underneath its frozen layer, dark water churned.

Lifting her chin, she took in the first of two people who graced the massive chairs situated side by side atop the dais.

No older than twelve or thirteen, the young girl was nearly swallowed by the stone monstrosity. Fine-boned and dainty, with skin a shade warmer than Apaay's, she considered Apaay with the sleek focus of one who has cornered a hare and now contemplates what to do with it. Her eyes were arresting and quite round. Still black though, like the strands coiled atop her head like a beautiful dark flower. Her clothes were streamlined and elegant, with unusual, shiny fabric cut close to her body in a single-piece bodysuit and what appeared to be netting draped around her thin shoulders.

For the second time in however many minutes, Apaay was again presented with the most absurd choice of clothing she had ever seen. She didn't know how one stayed warm in those clothes.

The girl's face pulled into a distasteful expression. It suited her. "She smells of dead animal."

Apaay bristled and would have returned the insult, but her attention slid to the person sitting in the adjacent seat, and she very nearly forgot to breathe.

The man sat in a graceful sprawl that Apaay suspected was in some way deliberate, a single finger tapping against the armrest, leisurely. Apaay was not sure she could look away even if she tried. The eyes like slices of shadow atop his broad cheekbones, a mouth wide and unexpectedly soft, the nose straight and flaring at the tip, the perfect smoothness of his complexion. The long elegance of his form was showcased in the extension of one leg, the other bent at the knee. The tapping paused for a brief moment, the cavernous silence descending, before it resumed, even more slowly than before.

A wrinkle marred his brow as his nostrils flared.

Beneath the concealing fur of her hood, Apaay took the time to study him as she had studied the girl, the cell, that guard, this chamber—information that would give her some piece of the greater whole of the situation. His hair, braided at the temples, flowed freely down his chest, as if woven from midnight's very threads. A parka, trousers, and sealskin boots all fit him with impeccable precision.

It was disquieting how contrasted they were—a child and a man in his prime. She could feel the push and pull between them, an unspoken battle of wills. They were like two currents colliding, causing a most dangerous drag out to sea. If this girl was the wind—a shriek of sudden, violent intensity—this man was a mountain: quiet in his observations, waiting and enduring, more powerful because of it.

The girl huffed out an impatient breath. "I want to see the prisoner's face."

Apaay stiffened, and a moment later her heavy, fur-lined hood fell away.

The constant tension that had followed Apaay from the cell shifted with startling speed. Her gaze cut to the man's, and when their eyes locked, something in his face sharpened. His eyes were green— No, they were blue— No, they were deep, unending violet fading into black.

His eyes could change colors.

The girl tilted her head in a thoughtful manner, as if perusing a patch of berries and deciding which one to pluck first. "She's rather scrawny. Wouldn't you agree, Numiak?"

He didn't immediately respond. His gaze lingered on her face. "Indeed." The deep, resonant voice slid through her blood.

Apaay shivered.

"Pretty hair though," the girl said grudgingly.

That probing gaze was like fingers scraping through Apaay's scalp, touching the strands and braids that fell to her waist. She didn't have the choice of drawing her hood back up, as they had bound her hands so tightly her arms had long ago turned numb.

"Who are you?" The words came low. "Why am I here?"

The girl's eyebrows shot upward. "Is that any way to speak to a superior?"

Her arrogance was downright insulting. "I don't serve you, and neither do my people." Generally, it was frowned upon—and wrong—to generalize or speak for the whole of the group, but this time she made an exception. The Analak, scattered in communities along the coast and farther inland, had never served under any ruler or form of government. That was left to the Unua.

"And who are your people?" the girl asked.

People of the snow and ice.

People of the battered sea.

Apaay said, gripping her anger so tightly that fear would not leak through, "The Analak."

High laughter struck the ice, ringing in coarse condescension. Apaay flinched, her heart giving a sharp heave at how violent was the sound. She hadn't a clue as to who this girl was. Fear came in not knowing. "I'm already bored, so let's make this quick. Tell me why you're here."

Scowling, Apaay jerked against the guard's hold. "Is this a joke? *You* captured *me*."

"I'm not the one who trespassed on my land, child."

Apaay choked on her words. Spit them out. "Perhaps you should take a good look in the mirror. Or am I mistaken in thinking you're not old enough to begin your monthly bleeding?"

The girl's expression blazed, and the man next to her looked thoroughly entertained by their verbal sparring. Mouth twitching, he leaned over and rested his fingertips on the girl's arm, as if anticipating the likelihood that she would barge down the steps with every intention of bashing Apaay's head into the ground. "Calm yourself, Yuki. I mean, look at her."

The words dug into Apaay, right beneath her breastbone. Yes, look at her. Look at the tattered girl, so small in this open room. If they wanted to underestimate her, then so be it. It was nothing she hadn't been subject to before.

The girl—Yuki—swung her legs back and forth over the edge of the seat, as she was not tall enough for her feet to reach the ground. "My patience is running thin, so I'd advise you to answer my question."

Apaay rolled her shoulders for some relief and glanced around the room to give herself time to think. It was as if the sea had swelled into towers and columns and walls and had frozen there, waiting for spring's warmth to thaw it. "I was searching for someone."

"Who?"

Taking a breath, Apaay let it leak through her nose silently. What were the odds of Eska's face being here? And what were the odds of escaping if it wasn't? She had no idea where she was. Her family didn't, either. A low hum of warning gave her reason to speak slowly and with great care. "My sister." It was not entirely true, but Apaay didn't want to give away too much information before she knew where she stood in this situation.

"Your sister. How interesting." Yuki's hands, covered in thin ebony gloves, came to rest in her lap. "Why would your sister be this far north? No one lives here except me."

"She ran away. She thought—" She thought *what*? "She wanted to see if the rumors were true." Her voice trailed off in a whisper.

"What rumors?"

"About the in-between."

"I see." Her voice was throaty. She stared at Apaay for an uncomfortably long moment before sighing and turning away, brushing a wisp of hair from her face. "I swear, is there not a single decent liar here? Honestly. Searching for your sister." She snorted.

Apaay set her jaw, eyeing the guard to her immediate left in case he punished her for the lie, but he stood obediently a few yards away. "So maybe my sister didn't run away."

"There now, was that so hard? Tell me why you're *really* here."

Apaay girded her stomach as if preparing her body to sustain an extended breath underwater. There were only five exits, and she didn't know whether they led away from this place or deeper into its heart. "I'm looking for the Face Stealer."

The glimmer of surprise was quickly masked, savage delight taking its place. "Don't tell me. He took your face and gave you that hideous one in return." She smiled as if this was nothing more than banter between friends.

Apaay met the girl's wicked gaze stonily. "He stole my sister's face. I have every intention of seeing it returned to me." She must not show weakness, no matter how her heart cried.

"How tragic. You thought you would find the Face Stealer all on your own? He is a demon, after all." Her eyes danced in twisted amusement.

How was it possible that only last month she had been hunting out on the ice? How small her worries had been. "If the Face Stealer isn't here—"

"Oh, I never said he wasn't here. If you wanted to speak with him, all you had to do was ask."

As if it were truly that simple. "Where is he?"

The girl looked at the man, so insouciant on his throne, so still. Then he rose and stepped down from the dais.

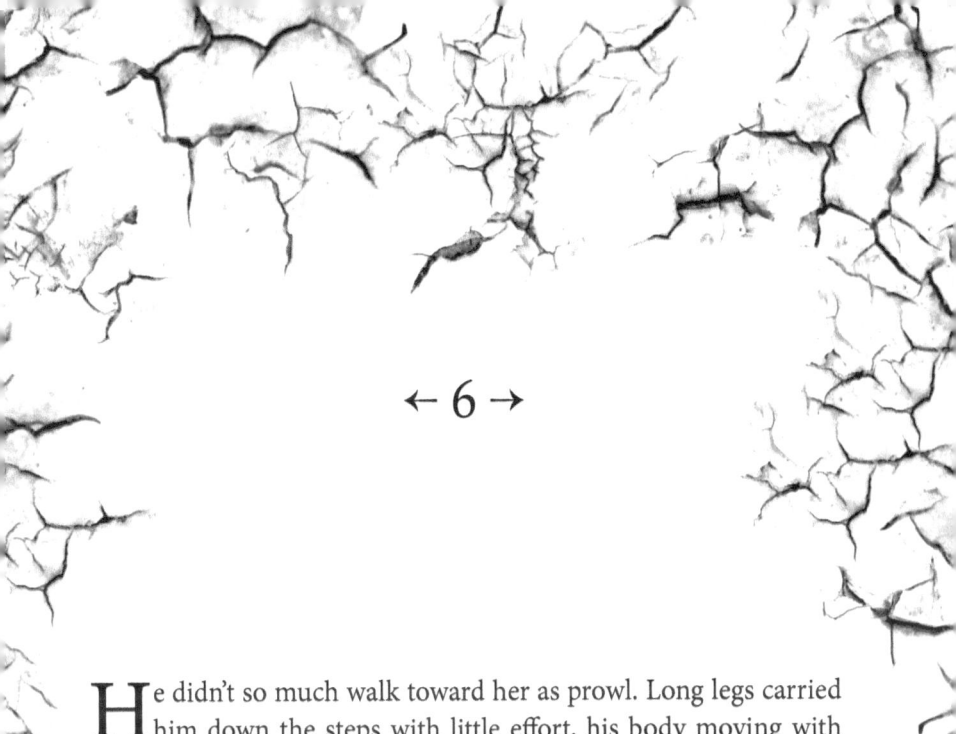

← 6 →

He didn't so much walk toward her as prowl. Long legs carried him down the steps with little effort, his body moving with impossibly fluid grace. Every step was intentional and precise—heel, toe, soundless. There was not an ounce of uncertainty or embarrassment about him, which was more than she could say for herself. This man was the very definition of sleek, polished power. And he knew it.

He stopped only a few feet away. In a voice of pure midnight rippling along her skin, he said, "Hello."

That voice—that was a dangerous voice indeed.

Apaay dropped her eyes and fought to settle the nausea currently sloshing through her stomach. Standing within arm's reach of him in the cavern, she felt the edges of his power feathering against her body. Bravado failed her. Why should he not snatch her face, too? She would not be able to stop it. "You're the Face Stealer?"

He arched one eyebrow. "Were you expecting someone else?"

An animal. A twisted malformation of grotesqueness. Instead, here was perfection—cold, untouchable beauty. But this was not a man. This was a demon. This was her enemy.

The Face Stealer circled her shivering form, hands clasped behind his back. Apaay lifted her chin. "I've come for my sister's face," she said when he stopped in front of her, having finished his perusal. Her tongue felt swollen to twice its normal size.

"I see." He rubbed a palm along his jaw. "Which one was she? I tend to forget what they look like. There are so many, you see."

"I very much doubt that," Apaay murmured. Behind him, the young girl watched their exchange keenly. "She's fourteen years old. Thin eyebrows. A scar on her left temple. One of her top teeth is chipped." When he didn't respond, she continued. "She has a small mouth, but her lips are full. Stubborn chin." And now she could go no further, for the emotion threatened to choke her. "Does that sound familiar at all?" she asked through gritted teeth.

The Face Stealer studied her, one hand on his chin. The ease of his posture reminded her of the wide, slow band of a river, right before the rapids came. "Now that you mention it, the face you described does sound like one I have in my collection."

Just how many identities, Apaay wondered, had he snatched? How many years' worth of faces did he have in his possession? She could not pin his age. He was both young and old and unknowable.

Once again, the demon circled her, keeping his distance, though it still felt too close. She took a step back, toward the plane of thin ice. Fear could weaken, or it could make one feel powerful and alive. Eska—she was here for Eska. She grabbed hold of that thought and made it searingly bright in her mind.

"Well?" she snapped when another minute had passed. Water from the icicles above dripped onto her shoulders.

The skin around his eyes crinkled in what may have been amusement. "If you insist." He presented her his back. "Tell me, does it look like this one?"

He turned, and Apaay screamed and stumbled back. His face was not his face. The bone structure, the iris color, the mouth—it had changed into this monstrous clashing of femininity and masculinity, loveliness and brawn. This face was not Eska's, and it was not anyone's she knew, but it had been ripped from a girl all the same. Somewhere out there was someone's daughter left to a world without color and taste.

His words slid from the girl's pretty mouth, deep and melodic. "Is this what you were looking for?"

Beneath her furs, Apaay's chest heaved. "No," she said, unable to prevent her voice from trembling. "It's not."

He shrugged. "Well, then." His features melted back into his own, his irises returning to their grays and blues and browns. "I can't say for sure I've seen it. Then again, I do tend to misplace things."

He was lying. He had to be. Someone who watched and waited and listened would not overlook, would not forget.

Ignoring the warning hum in her blood, she took a step closer, her hands still bound. The intensity of his focus was near unbearable, but she refused to break eye contact. "I'm not leaving until I get what I came for."

"Then I imagine you'll have a long wait," he said, settling back in his high-backed chair.

"You should know Numiak enjoys playing games," said the girl with much fondness. "He's a twisted little thing."

Numiak. There was a boy in her village named Numiak. *Wolf wanderer* in her mother tongue. His sister's face had been snatched the month before. It was nothing short of tragic irony that the demon shared his name. He had killed the girl, having doomed her to isolation. He had killed the father, having driven him to grief.

"What do you do with the faces?" She had to know. "Why do you need them? Why her?" Had Eska been the target all along, or did he simply show up and rip the face from the nearest person in reach?

Before he could respond—not that he *would* respond—the girl answered for him. "If you have questions or concerns, direct them to me."

Apaay glanced between them in confusion. The demon, having returned to his languid pose, propped an elbow on the armrest, completely unaffected by the girl's interruption.

Who, exactly, was in charge here?

"All right," Apaay said, and focused her attention on his companion.

"That's better." Yuki looked pleased. "All right, we're done here." She made a shooing motion.

A hand clamped down on Apaay's arm, shooting a fresh wave of pain through her body. The guard jerked her backward. "Wait." If they dragged her away, back to that cell of stone, she might never find Eska's face. Something inside her was thrashing to break free, and it was barreling toward shore with untapped ferocity, this vow that would not stop until it broke upon the rocks. "Whatever I have to do, I'll do it!" Pieces of ice crumbled from the ceiling, shattering on the ground near her feet as her scream struck the stalactites above.

The girl lifted her chin with a smile, and Apaay wondered if she had played into her hand. "I've changed my mind." The guard stopped, and Yuki leaned forward eagerly, as if having thought of something clever—or cruel. "Untie her bonds."

The man did as she asked. The pain that followed was nothing Apaay had ever experienced. It was excruciating. Her muscles, having been locked in the same position for hours upon hours, seized, and Apaay bit the inside of her cheek hard enough to draw blood as the inflamed tendons flared with acute agony. Circulation cutoff had been nearly complete. Now the blood surged, through veins and arteries, a furious rush of heat. She screamed as she burned.

Eventually, the fire extinguished. Collapsed on the stone floor, Apaay pressed her cheek against its icy relief.

"So dramatic," the girl drawled. "Get up. You're embarrassing yourself."

Apaay wasn't able to push to her feet, so the guard hauled her upright by her hood. She could not catch her breath, shaky and unbalanced from the lack of empathy in this room.

"Tell me, child. What is your opinion of games?"

Apaay swallowed down her gorge, her gaze flicking between the two occupied chairs. It felt like a trap. "I don't have an opinion."

"Come now. You must. Do you enjoy them? Loathe them?" She flashed a mouthful of tiny, pointed teeth. "Tell me."

The question felt too fragile. Her answer, so heavy in her mouth, would be the stone that cracked the ice.

Growing up, Apaay had played many games: leg wrestle, back push, high kick. These helped her people build agility, endurance, and strength. But as Apaay had entered womanhood, the games had turned toward numbers. How long would she have to wait before she could harpoon a seal, if she harpooned one at all? How many char could she spear in the month of many fish, or caribou? How much seal fat did she need to render so her family would have fuel for their lamp? How quickly could she stitch skins together for a new parka before the long night came?

The games Apaay had played were not games at all. Eat, or be eaten. Survive, or perish.

"I suppose," Apaay said cautiously, "they aren't all that bad."

Crowing a laugh, the girl clapped her hands together. "Numiak, did you hear? She likes games."

"So I heard," he murmured, searching Apaay's expression as if it mattered to him in some way. She did not give any indication it bothered her, though she felt lightheaded from how her heart tried to flee her chest. The less the demon could read her, the better. If she did not showcase weakness, he could not exploit it.

The whiteness of Yuki's smile about burned Apaay's vision. "It's been a long time since I've played a game." She tittered a laugh. "Why, I'd say it's been close to a hundred years."

A hundred years?

But the girl could be no older than twelve, thirteen at the oldest. Or at least she *looked* twelve. And yet the mind, the radiating power, the belief that she had every right to rule—those traits belonged to someone much older.

Gesturing around the room, Yuki said to Apaay, "How do you like my home?"

This did not feel like a question as much as a riddle born of words and wit. She shifted her stance to relieve the ache worming up her right leg, which she had lain on in the cell.

"It's beautiful." And empty. And cruel.

"Yes," Yuki answered, eyes agleam. "It is. When I came to this land, I had it built to my specifications. It's a labyrinth, you see. Someplace you can easily get lost in, so don't try to run. You want to play a game? Then the game is this. Your sister's face is hidden somewhere in the labyrinth. If you want it back, then you must find it without losing your life first."

She didn't know what that meant. Lose her life, as in there would be things in the labyrinth trying to kill her?

The Face Stealer shifted, his expression giving nothing away. Candlelight wreathed his face in shadows so they played upon its hollows. "Yuki. How positively savage of you." His voice was so mild Apaay expected him to pick at his nails.

She preened under the compliment, and Apaay had the sense he didn't offer them freely or often. "A reminder of who makes the rules around here." She offered him a small smile that didn't reach her eyes.

As if remembering Apaay's presence, Yuki turned back to her and said, "It's not often I offer such an opportunity. Say thank you."

Yes, perhaps she *should* thank her. Thank you, she would say, for knocking me unconscious. Thank you for binding my hands, stripping me of all dignity.

Apaay bit back a sneer, silent.

Yuki stood then, slowly. The young girl fell away. In her place stood someone who had never known disrespect or disappointment.

"Since you're new here, I understand you're unfamiliar with the way things work, so let me make clear the consequences of disobeying my orders."

As she drew a hand horizontally across the air, a portion of one of the walls cracked and crumbled, revealing a still, dark form within. "This is what becomes of those who disrespect me, so choose your words, and your actions, wisely."

The form was a man, and he was frozen solid inside the wall.

Apaay cringed and looked away. Her people believed every living and nonliving thing possessed a spirit: bird and tree, rock and sea. But some had the ability to connect with certain material, as Yuki had done with the iced wall. Such people were said to possess a similar spirit within themselves, and that the pull of like affinities— water to water, man to man—allowed the ability to manifest. A girl in her community whose name-soul came from her father's most loyal dog had understood the song of wolves.

Not all who wielded power, however, used it responsibly. Power was temptation. Power was the question: To hurt or heal?

Apaay forced her attention back to the prisoner. The ice had stretched the skin tight over his face, which was partially blackened in places and flaking off. His hands were lifted in front of him as if to block himself from harm. And his eyes: wide open, staring at nothing.

She wondered if he was somehow still alive.

"Take it," Yuki ordered, a harsh ring of sound on stone.

Apaay did not see the demon move. A blur of skin, and then an opaque veil stole her vision, followed by a ripping sensation along her jaw, similar to the tearing of a seam. Heat and ice clashed. Apaay opened her mouth to scream and found a lack of feeling, blindness, like a star winking out.

Her mind splintered with the realization that she was without a face. Like Eska. Like thousands more. She was confined to a void, and there was nothing beyond it save two voices and the temperature dropping by gradual increments. It was suffocation. It was suffering. Mounting pressure crawled up her neck and face, yet there was no place for release, no eyes with which to cry, or mouth to scream.

What have I done? She hadn't said goodbye to Mama or Papa. She'd *left.* Without a word. Without a destination in mind save the in-between.

"This one, I can tell, will be hard to break, but I will delight in doing so."

"Why break her now?" The demon's voice. "You haven't even played with her yet."

It would have been better, Apaay thought, to die out in the storm with Nakaluq. At least they would have been together.

"Good point."

Blue light rolled over the darkness, and the crackling in her ears was no longer blood, but choked gasps and hyperventilation, bile pooling in her mouth.

"Still no apology?" the girl asked sweetly.

Apaay's stomach heaved, and sweat poured down her body in sheets. The Face Stealer had returned to his seat, the slight uplifting of his mouth vaguely pleased. "I apologize." She swallowed the bile down. No matter how she shook, she wouldn't let herself collapse. At least not in their presence.

"You didn't even let me finish explaining the rules." Yuki plopped back down in her chair with an impressive pout, crossing her arms over her narrow chest. "And the rules are my favorite part." She flicked a hand in irritation at the inconvenience. "I'm giving you one chance to find what it is you desire. Twelve hours, nothing more. Succeed, and you can have your sister's face and your freedom. Fail—"

Apaay's head snapped up. She did not dare look at the wall and the man trapped there, bound to eternal winter.

"And not only will you rot here, but Numiak will go to your village and steal another face."

Her attention snagged on the Face Stealer. The truth was etched in every exquisite line of his expression, provocative in its dark cruelty. It was not the end. It was the beginning of a tragic path of yet more destruction. Who would come next? Papa? Young Kaya with her fierce nature?

He would take until there was nothing left.

Tears rose, stinging, but she quickly shoved them down. *The night is long, but the sun will soon greet you.* The proverb was a small comfort. She couldn't give up. She couldn't lose control. If she hoped to escape this place, it was what had to be done. "How do I know you're telling the truth? That Eska's face is even here?"

In an instant, the demon's face transformed. Her sister stared back at her. The features she knew so well, attached to a body that was not her own. Indecision rooted Apaay. She hadn't a weapon. Had nothing but her guilt and regret, and they would not protect her should she charge up the stairs and rip the face from him. In the end, she stayed put. Any sudden movements, and Yuki would no doubt delight in turning her into a block of ice.

The Face Stealer said, to the sound of Yuki's cackling laugh, "Does this satisfy you?"

Apaay turned away, unsure of whether to break down or howl her fury. Her stomach was a fiery, churning pit. "Yes," she ground out, staring at the tops of her boots. "I'm satisfied."

The small reminder of what she had lost was enough to drive a blade through her chest, a fresh wound to remind her now, and every time she forgot, of what was important and why she had bulled through snow and wind and ice. The reason that had driven her here.

There was nothing Apaay would not do for her family.

"One more thing." Yuki stood, her feet silent as she descended the stairs and waved Apaay over to one of the mirrors. The plain metal frame was cold and severe, much like this girl. "I'm doing you a favor, you see, letting you search for your sister's face. But as with anything in life, it does not come free." She lifted a short, slender finger as her attention snapped to the demon. Something wild stirred in the abyss of her pupilless eyes. It only settled when she refocused on Apaay. "Somewhere inside the mirror is a face I'm looking for as well. You can have your sister's face, but only if you find the one I want, too. I imagine they're housed together. There's a sea you'll need to cross to get there."

Apaay blinked at her, thoroughly confused. "Can't you cross the sea yourself?" After all, Yuki mentioned she'd had the labyrinth built to her specifications. If that were so, she should be able to navigate it.

"If I could, do you think I would be asking someone as weak and pitiful as you to complete this task?" she snapped, voice shrill. Ice splintered somewhere in the cavernous space. "Now go, before I change my mind."

In the mirror's reflection, Apaay met the Face Stealer's gaze. Any earlier emotion had been replaced by a cold exterior. Shuttered, unfathomable, telling her nothing of who he was or how he perceived any of this.

It was the last thing she saw before stepping through.

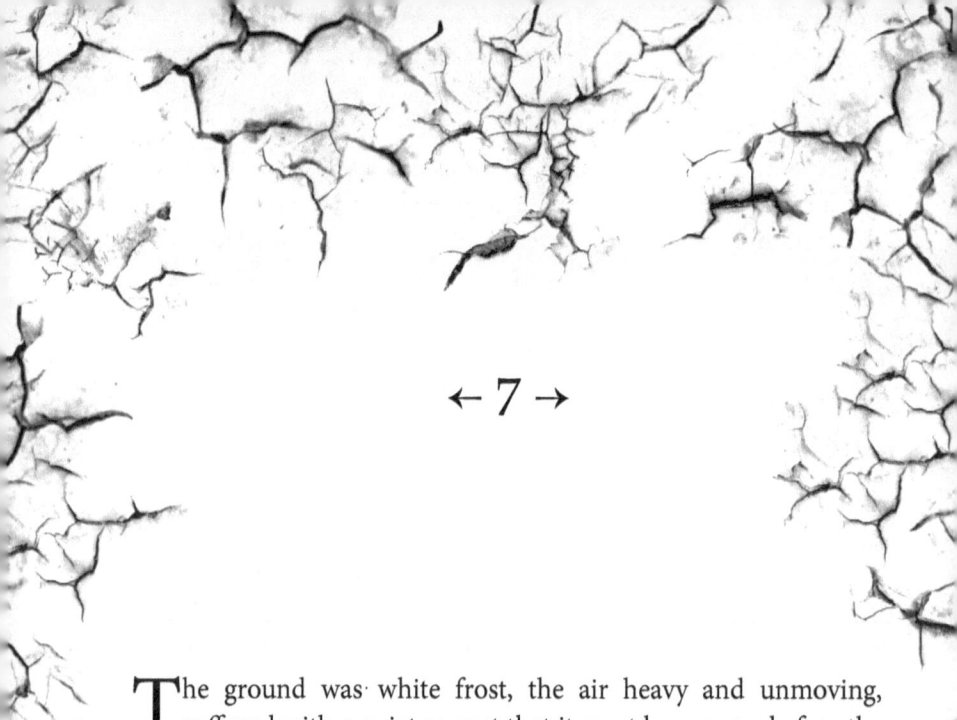

The ground was white frost, the air heavy and unmoving, suffused with a quiet so vast that it must have come before the birds and the grasses and the trees, before light and darkness, before cold, before being. The seed from which the world had been born.

The hair along Apaay's body stirred. Unnatural, this quiet. It was as the silence had been in that stone cell she had awoken in. Even the stillest nights on the tundra did not hold such hollowness. There was the wind, and the salt-drenched willow, and the rooting insects, and a current welling up from deep within the earth.

This was absence.

The mirror had deposited her at the base of a rot-bitten pine, its dark green boughs shading her from an absent sun. The trunk was so wide it would have taken five people to surround it with their arms outstretched. Thinner saplings poked through the blanketed ground, with their bodies of brown scrawn and limp green hats. Tatters of yellow clouds skated overhead, screening the glittering domed ceiling. An outside world contained within.

Keeping her back to the tree, Apaay scanned her surroundings with caution. This place felt wrong. Like a disease. She didn't see any large body of water nearby. It was a wide, sloping ground of shallow hills. An awareness of another's presence touched along her spine, but the area was deserted. Abandoned, more likely. The feeling lingered.

A few paces away, one of the trees caught her eye. Stepping closer, Apaay crouched down and ran one mitten along the bark. There was no roughness. It was silky, smooth, unnatural. As she pressed harder, the trunk began to cave, as if it lacked solidity.

Rearing back, she shot her fist forward. It punctured straight through the trunk, a hollow, flimsy thing. Apaay watched in fascination as the entire structure crumpled.

Once, a man from her community had traveled to Across the Sea and returned with a scroll made of a thin, brittle material that was not quite fabric, its surface stained with ink. Apaay had marveled at the graceful, swooping lines. Had wondered what they meant. The Analak language was oral, their culture passed down through verbal history, song, dance. But somewhere east of Naga, others used what he had called paper to record their histories.

These trees were made of paper.

This was the in-between. Figments of imagination. Objects of nightmares and dreams. How could this be real if she only knew of these things in her head?

Was it all in her head?

"No," she muttered, choosing a random direction uphill to travel in. She pulled her hood up to warm her ears, long strands of charred brown hair tangling in the wolverine fur. Quickly, she set to plaiting a braid before tucking it beneath her hood. Maybe if she said *no* enough she would start to believe it.

Apaay carved a path through the land of paper trees, muttering under her breath of all the ways in which she would delight in ruining the young girl, anything from throwing her off a mountain to something more drastic. Light powder dusted her outerwear in fine bits of fluff that left behind a gray residue, and her body gradually warmed beneath the furs. All the while, she hurried. And sought the sea.

Yuki's inability to cross the water must mean something. Weakness. A lack of control. Wherever Eska's face was hidden, others must be as well. Men, women, children. Identities without a home. Including, Apaay thought, a face Yuki sought. One the demon had taken.

Interesting.

Apaay slowed, gauging her direction. She brushed aside the condensation that had gathered around her nose. Whether she was traveling north or south or east or west, she didn't know. Her chest ached. A lonely, wandering heart.

"You would have known," she said, a single sound in silence. "You would have known where to go."

The space beside her was vacant. The place where Nakaluq would have been, tangling around her legs because all he wanted was to be close to her. He had known what she needed before Apaay recognized she'd needed it. A brief rest, a smile, a reminder: She was not alone and never would be.

Which way? she would have said to him, to which he would have replied with *the look.* Something between resignation and exasperation at his silly human, whose pathetic sense of smell was always a source of great amusement to him.

Her friend, whom she had left to die on the tundra.

"And me," said a small voice. "You left me, too."

Apaay's heart beat still. "Eska?"

In her peripheral vision, something darted through the trees and vanished.

She whirled around. Nothing was there. A branch snapped behind her. Again, swift darkness disappearing before she could pin it down. Human? Animal?

Demon?

"You must hate me, don't you?" came the disembodied voice.

"That's not true," she whispered. The world was bleeding color, hot and painfully bright. "I love you."

"Then why did you want me to leave," Eska asked, "when all I wanted was to stay?"

Guilt swelled in her throat with surprising force. *Because my insecurities made me selfish. Because I'm not like you.* "Don't go."

"I'm already gone." The voice faded as a shadow peeled itself away from the trees and slipped into deeper obscurity.

"Eska!" she cried. "Wait for me, Eska!" Stumbling forward, Apaay chased the silhouetted figure through the woods, not realizing the trees grew more wilted as she ran, stripped and punctured with holes. Not realizing there were no footprints on the ground to follow. Just a voice, movement, tumultuous emotion squeezing her windpipe.

Space pressed outward and upward as the ground rose. A powerful roar reached her ears, borne on a swift wind, and she would have known the sound from anywhere, lulling her village in the summer days.

The sea.

The air burned with the smell of salt. Waves frothed white foam upon the gray-green surface, lapping at the hard rim of ice wrapped around the rocky shore. The sea's thrumming pulse was an ancient push and pull that had come long before Apaay and her people.

On the opposite shore, a large rectangular mirror had been propped against a sentinel tree, snow piled at its base. The figure disappeared through its reflective surface.

Desperation sent her downhill to the stony, ice-crusted shore. This must have been the place Yuki had mentioned, the body of water she needed to cross. The sea crooned, threading its voice around her will with a soft, pleasant sensation. *Trust me*, it murmured. But her heart screamed, *Lies.*

Apaay observed the churning water warily. A faint stench wafted to her nose. Rot. The decomposition of animal flesh. The air was abnormally warm, clinging to her too-tight skin.

Glancing around, she grabbed a nearby piece of driftwood and dipped the tip into the water.

The branch burst into flames.

Apaay screamed and fell back, dropping the stick into the sea, where it was devoured. A red welt rose on her cheek from where the water had singed her. Small pebbles gouged her palms through her mittens. Who controlled what occurred once she stepped through the mirror? Yuki? She could imagine that smirk on the little girl's mouth, the Face Stealer lounging beside her, reveling in their power at knowing how impossible Apaay's task was. Find a face that was hidden. Find it or someone else in her village would suffer.

Success was not, and never had been, a sure, solid thing. It was a trail of fragments that had grown denser over the years as her past failures grew taller, darker, wider, cloaking her in their massive shadows. The fear in the back of her mind made her wonder, *What was the point?* What was the point when she already knew how it would end?

She wanted to give in to that doubt. It was practically a habit. Yet things were different now. There was no room for failure. This was not a matter of pride, but life. Her sister was suffering. Because of *her*. She vowed to make things right.

Her focus returned to the task at hand—crossing the body of water. Fear bubbled in her gut, but she could not think of that now. The resources available were scarce. Plenty of snow—heaps of it— and ice. Pieces of driftwood scattered along the shore. The snow and ice would melt, obviously. The wood would burn unless she had a covering to protect it.

Apaay circled the shore to search for material she could potentially use to help her reach the mirror. Steam hissed as it uncoiled against the colder air, and her proximity to the boiling water brought a warm flush to her face.

She had been walking for perhaps thirty minutes when something materialized in the distance, large and dark and unmoving, sprawled across the pebbled ground. Slowing her approach, she faltered in surprise. A seal corpse. An adult male, by the looks of it, probably weighing close to four hundred pounds.

Apaay allowed herself a grim smile. She knew how she would reach the other side.

Kayak construction did not begin with the hands, but with the mind. The driftwood frame and waterproof casing, a vessel that would lead her across the searing fury of the water. A tedious process, but necessary. The Analak's livelihood depended on it.

Her first task involved removing the outer layer of sealskin. Using a sharp rock, she sliced a line down the center of the mammal's mottled gray belly. A putrid stench belched from the layers of rotting blubber that burst open, making her gag.

With a choked heave, she turned away, eyes watering. The seal had most likely been dead a few days.

As Apaay was pressed for time and lacking tools, she had to make shortcuts. Back home, the elders would moan in horror at the notion, but she hadn't a choice. Slicing the inner layer of blubber away from the outer skin was about speed, not precision. And she only had a single seal to work with as opposed to three or four, which forced her to reduce the size of the kayak. It was not ideal. There was a fine art to it all, and she didn't know what effect the altered measurements would have on the finished product, if it would even be able to support her weight. As such, her hands lacked their usual steadiness. It was the best she could do under the circumstances.

With the skin fully separated, Apaay laid it flat across the ground. The blubber she chucked into the sea, where it quickly sank. Next, she rolled two medium-sized stones closer to shore, arranging them a few feet apart. They would serve to prop up the kayak.

As she hastened to gather driftwood, dragging some of the longer, salt-bitten pieces to her workstation, Apaay could not help but think of home. Time was fleeting, and this memory was especially old, having gathered dust in the corner.

It was summer. The sea pounded against the shore, where she, Papa, and Eska crouched in a circle around a small fire, Mama discussing with the elders how many caribou needed to be killed this season to provide clothes for the most recent newborns. Heat from the smoke seeped into the long strips of driftwood Papa held above the flame until the grain grew flexible. Brine bit at their skin.

Papa, his face freshly shaven, bent the wooden strips into half circles and let them set. Apaay, only seven at the time, grabbed a piece from the driftwood pile, wanting to bend one, too. Eska snatched it away with a wicked smile, the one that said, *Look at me. Look how clever I am!* Apaay stuck out her tongue, and so the day went.

The memory eased some of the tension as she started on the frame. Yet there was heaviness, too, for fear of never experiencing that lightness again.

It began as a set of two runners, which ran the length of the kayak. She used one of the seal's bones and a flat rock to punch holes on both ends of the driftwood pieces. Without any caribou sinew to lash the runners' ends together, Apaay was forced to make do with strips of sealskin.

It was a long, arduous process. She did not have her village. She did not have community—people helping people, sharing laughs. She fumbled with one of the knots, growing frustrated with her inability to remember the pattern. Her head was too full of that slip of dusk in the woods, which may or may not have been her sister. The figure entering the mirror. Eska's voice. She took a deep breath to settle her nerves. Then she untied the knot and started again.

After lashing the short beams perpendicular between the runners, Apaay flipped the frame upside down and attached the ribs, which gave the kayak its curved shape, the wood made malleable from the steaming water. As pain wormed its way into her shoulders and settled into a dull ache, the shadows on the ground grew hazy in the fading light. A reminder that she hadn't much time left.

The frame was complete. She was nearly there.

Apaay stared at the sealskin with reluctance. Sewing. She could think of about a thousand other more enjoyable activities. This had always been Eska's specialty. *Complaining* about sewing, on the other hand—Apaay had been quite good at that, much to her sister's annoyance.

"No, you're doing it wrong," Eska would huff, snatching the material from Apaay's hands as they worked side by side in their cozy home.

Scowling, Apaay watched the small, perfect seams form beneath Eska's nimble fingers. The thread never pierced the outer layer of skin, leading to completely waterproof kayaks and boots. "I was doing fine on my own."

"Oh? Then why do your seams look like the work of a five-year-old, naajatik?"

Apaay never had an answer. No need to argue with the truth.

Dragging the skin over to the half-finished kayak, she laid it across the frame and tacked it temporarily at either end. Then she flipped the vessel right side up, stabbing shards of bone through the outer casing to hold the edges together along the flattened top, since she did not have any thread.

She was not aiming for perfection. A well-made kayak took hundreds of hours and was a community effort, with the men constructing the frame, the women sewing the skins. She was only one girl. Two hands, two legs, a finite amount of energy that was already beginning to sputter. She did not have time to create small, perfect seams. She needed to cross the half mile to the opposite shore, and quickly.

As Apaay studied the kayak, her unease overshadowed the satisfaction of completing such a task. Either it would lead her to safety or send her into a fiery death. Her heart tapped its uncertainty against her breastbone, so light, so breathlessly fast. She couldn't dwell on it. It was done. Now she had to move forward. The Face Stealer would rip another face from someone in her village soon.

Carefully, she pushed the sleek vessel into the boiling water, the liquid hissing and spitting as the foreign object touched its surface. Despite the trembling in her core, fear of the depths beneath, Apaay slid through the hole in the top, gripping a paddle she'd constructed from driftwood and two flattened stones, which were secured on either end. *For Eska,* she thought. Then she began to row.

Waves thrashed on either side of her small vessel as Apaay fought to keep the boat steady, the tide quickly sucking her out into open water. Sweat sluiced down her face. Heat seared through her trousers. She kept her attention ahead, on that distant, distant shore where the mirror gleamed in the low light, a low current whispering in Apaay's ears.

One stroke in the boiling water. Another.

Again.

And again.

Progress was torturously slow. Apaay was no stranger to physical labor, but not in intense heat. The steaming air was so thick it was like blood clotting in her mouth. Flecks of water spattered against her clothes, the occasional drop hitting her neck or cheek, and soon her skin itched and flaked from the heat. It was almost worse than the cramps seizing her legs from squishing them into such a tight space. She bore the pain silently and rowed. It would be over soon, hopefully.

The churning water licked at the outer covering, chewing it away. Her heart leapt, and she paddled faster. If she did not think of how thin the waterproof casing was, if she kept paddling, if she—

Apaay gasped at a sudden burning sensation and shoved to her feet.

The kayak dipped to the left, and Apaay saw her death clearly: searing water licking at her face with its fiery tongues, blisters rising and bursting clear liquid. She lurched to the right to balance the kayak out. A high peal of laughter struck like the squeal of an animal death, tapering off into giggles.

The realization that Yuki was watching made her feel as if she stood on the edge of a crumbling precipice. She wondered if Yuki had lied about being unable to cross the sea, because there was no better incentive to attempt the perilous crossing than the promise of her sister's face on the other side. Maybe that had been the girl's intention. Driven by some twisted form of amusement, to lure the prisoner into boiling flame. Give her hope, then snatch it.

Water now rushed over her boots, trickling through a small hole that must have formed in the body of the kayak. Her center of gravity shifted with the increasingly unstable vessel. The shore was still feet away when the casing disintegrated and the frame dropped through.

Apaay plummeted toward the boiling water as she jumped forward, catching one hand on the rim of ice. Her screams shattered the sky.

She was burning—burning in the deepest, fiery pits of hell. The heat was picking and peeling and shredding and scouring. Layer upon layer of skin shriveled and fell away. She was a raw, lit nerve.

Adrenaline surged through her limbs. A kick, a heave, and Apaay was over the edge. She dove into a snow drift, rolled around and around and sobbed at the sensation of knives gouging into her flesh. Grabbing fistfuls of snow, she rubbed it onto her face and shoulders and chest, but it did nothing to extinguish the fire. She sank further into the cold, packing it onto her body, and let it soothe the wretched tightening, the small white blisters that had begun to ooze.

Eventually, she shuddered and lay still. Her skin prickled with lingering heat. Upon removing her mittens, Apaay cried out in despair. Her poor hands. They were badly burned, having been fully immersed in the water. The slightest touch to the raw, inflamed blisters had her whimpering.

Gingerly, she slipped her mittens back on. Pushed to her feet. Later she would see to treating the wounds. Here was the mirror, beautifully ornate, wolves etched into the silver frame, an entire pack of them. Apaay flinched. The burned face staring back at her was a gruesome sight, but she did not look away. Things could always be worse. She could be dead.

The surface parted beneath her hand, heavy and cool. Her reflection shifted, ripples flaring out from the point of contact. The labyrinth awaited her. And beyond this surface, Eska. Another task, another trial she must overcome. But would this take her closer to her goal, or farther away?

In the end, Apaay didn't have a choice. One leg, one arm, and then she was gone. The only way out was through.

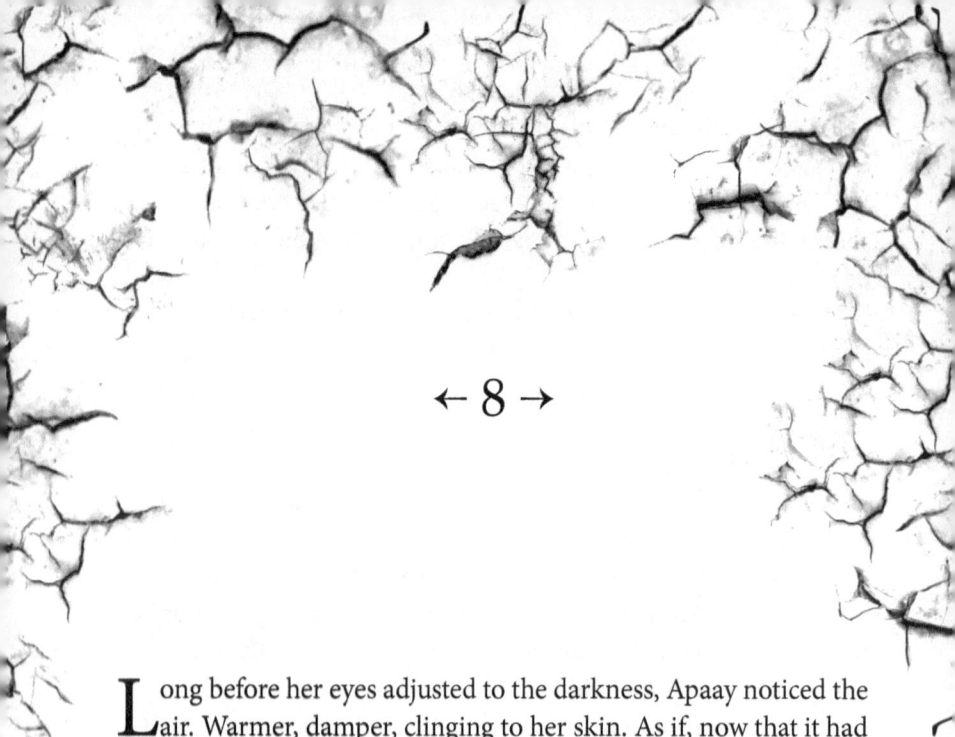

← 8 →

Long before her eyes adjusted to the darkness, Apaay noticed the air. Warmer, damper, clinging to her skin. As if, now that it had found her, it would never let her go.

Apaay pushed her drenched hood back from her face, body racked with shudders. She stood in a long stone corridor cloaked in gray light. It felt abandoned. She knew without looking that the figure, or whatever it had been, wasn't here. The air was close and stale and tasted of chilled, frozen earth. It had been locked away for a long time.

With the warmer air, Apaay could remove her mittens without the risk of frostbite. Trembling fingers brushed against the walls and came away wet. A tremor rolled through her that had nothing to do with cold. Apaay glanced over her shoulder. The mirror had vanished. It seemed that by stepping through, she let go of any possibility of returning to the place she had been.

Deep breath, Apaay.

Shadows streaked the long stretch of gloom. After a few timid steps, she reached a cell on her right. An iron door, the bars bitingly cold. Her blistered palms sizzled against the metal in relief. There was not much inside the cramped area save a single overturned pail and a pile of wilting yellow grass in the corner. No way out of here, either.

She moved on, reaching out her foot to test the ground before resting her full weight on it. If the mirrors could transport her to other places, why not the floors, the ceilings, the walls?

Clamping down on the fluttering fear, Apaay shifted forward. The scrape of her boots lifted the hair on her nape. She'd been so certain Eska would be here. Which was silly, now that she thought about it. She'd heard her sister's voice, had seen a figure moving. It meant nothing. In her desperation, Apaay had forgotten that she sought a face, not a body. A part of someone, not the whole. It felt wrong to reduce someone she loved down to mere facial features. A person was not their face. A person was their heart. And Eska's heart was back home, along with Apaay's.

She needed to resume her search for the faces, then. Eska's, and the one Yuki sought. The stolen identities must be deeply hidden, concealed in a place far from light. And this was a very dark place, indeed.

Apaay ran her hands along the walls, seeking a texture that did not belong. Even though Eska's face was no longer attached to a body, she assumed skin would still feel like skin. There were deep grooves between the stacked stones, more roughness. Nothing soft or elastic. Apaay tried the floor next, her movements stilted as she crouched in the dark on her knees, leaving no corner overlooked.

A stone connected with her boot, breaking the silence with a sharp clatter.

From out of the darkness, a hollow voice: "Back so soon?" The words dragged with sadness.

Apaay froze.

The voice did not speak again.

She rose to her feet, gripping the bars of a cell to ground herself. All the cells were located on her right, with a stretch of wall to her left.

"Who are you?" she asked.

A low, rough sound. A laugh or a sob, she wasn't sure. Apaay braced herself should something emerge from the shadows. She didn't know this place. She didn't know what she had walked into, what awaited her.

"You're not the Face Stealer," said the voice. Gravelly, strained.

And maybe a little bit broken.

"No," she whispered after a moment. "I'm not."

If she strained her ears, Apaay could hear shifting beyond, the quick, shallow breaths of someone trying to calm themselves. She took two steps closer. "Please. Who are you?" She wondered if *this* was the figment she had seen, this man. It sounded like he was crying.

Apaay, unable to see in the dim, did not need eyes to know of this man's agony. It weighed upon her shoulders and dragged at her knees. What had the demon done to this man to reduce him to such emptiness, a shell? Without realizing it, she had let go of the door and now walked toward the soft, shamed sounds.

His cell was the last one, squished into the corner. A place so far removed from everything no one would remember him.

Unsure of what to do, Apaay knelt in front of his cell. The stench of refuse—a combination of feces, sweat, and urine—plowed into her with all the force of a breaking wave. Ack. She switched to breathing through her mouth.

A figure huddled against the back wall, as stooped as an old man. She could not make out his shape, whether he was large or small or thin or broad. The shadows seemed to swallow him, almost as if they were one and the same.

"My name is Apaay." She could barely squeeze the words past the tightness in her throat. This poor man, doomed to spend his days alone in the dark. No one deserved that fate. "I'm a prisoner here." *Like you.*

His breath caught, and he stilled his shaking. Slowly, he uncurled, movements stiff. "Apaay." The shape of her name in his mouth was soft. He had probably not tasted anything so sweet in a long time.

"What's your name?" she asked.

The man didn't respond. The glow of his eyes winked out—he had closed them.

"I—" Roughness clawed at the word, and it fractured. "I can't remember."

The confession caused all the air in her lungs to vanish. She didn't know what to say. How did someone forget their name, who they were at their very core? She locked her jaw to prevent herself from grinding her teeth together. Look at this filth, this confinement. This man was not an animal to be caged. He was a human being. He deserved space and light and warmth, the touch of a gentle hand, the arms of family.

He deserved to be free.

Gently, she said, "Can you come closer so I can see you? I promise I won't hurt you."

His eyelids snapped open. "That's what he said, before he tricked me and locked me up."

"Who?"

His answer was a growl. "The Face Stealer."

Tightening her grip on the cell bars, she leaned closer and asked, "Why did he lock you up? How did he trick you?" So many questions. *How many?* she wondered. How many lost souls had been cast aside and left to die here? Where were they? And why were they here?

The man stiffened and withdrew into the shadows. She had gone too far.

"I'm sorry," she said. "You don't have to answer that."

The silence felt too heavy.

She was approaching this all wrong. Her desperation made her bold, pushing where she should be coaxing, demanding where she should be soothing. It was not the man's fault. This place had been hewn from fear. It was all around, locking them in. The man, it seemed, had learned to live with it.

Though it made her impatient, Apaay settled in to wait. She slipped her hands back into her mittens, wincing from the scratching sensation against her inflamed skin.

"You said you're a prisoner?" he finally asked.

"Yes."

"Since when?"

There was something distinctly hungry about the question, but then again, this man was probably starved for answers as much as she. "A few days, I think. I can't be sure."

Now that Apaay thought about it, when she'd awoken in the cell, it had not been the first time. The memory blurred, dreamlike. The first time, she had vomited before passing out again. The second time, her bladder had let go. She must have held it in for at least a full day. No wonder she had smelled urine when she woke.

"What about you?" she whispered. "How long have you been down here?"

His answer was so quiet as to be nonexistent. "I've lost track of the time, but it's been . . . many years."

How many? Three, five, fifteen? She couldn't tell this man's age, but from his voice she guessed him to be young, possibly around her age or a few years older, which meant he'd come here as a boy. Time had been stolen from him as it was being stolen from her now. While Yuki and her demon ruled from above, they rotted quietly below.

"Please," she said. "I need your help." The seconds, minutes, hours trickled through the cracks. If he had survived for this long, then someone had to bring him food and water intermittently. And if he had spoken to the person, it might give her a clue as to the inner workings of the labyrinth.

"How did you come to be here?" the man asked.

Apaay dropped her head on an exasperated sigh. The story was long and required energy she had lost somewhere back on the boiling sea. Apaay gave him a shortened version. "The Face Stealer stole my sister's face. Someone attacked me while I was traveling. I woke up here, in a cell."

The prisoner considered this information. "Where is 'here,' exactly?"

"I don't know." The in-between, certainly. But not, she vowed, the place where she would die. "It's a fortress. A labyrinth ruled by a young girl—Yuki—and the Face Stealer."

The man shifted closer, yet was still too far away for Apaay to see him clearly. The darkness seemed to thicken over time.

"If I find my sister's face, the girl says she'll let me go, but I don't have much time—"

"You can't trust her," the man barked, and Apaay jerked at the harsh sound. "You can't trust anyone in this place. It tricks you. Makes you believe fake things are real, and real things are fake." He sucked in a breath. "I'm not even sure you're real."

Apaay did not think it was possible for her heart to break further over this man, but it did. "I'm real. I promise you, I'm real. Here, take my hand."

In the gray haze, the man shook his head vehemently and cowered from her touch.

She pulled her hand back through the bars. Her knees ached from digging into the floor. Her skin itched like mad. It felt as if close to an hour had passed. She did not have time to linger.

"I know this is hard for you," Apaay said, an undercurrent of urgency sharpening her tone, "but do you know where the Face Stealer keeps the faces he steals?"

"The Face Stealer . . . faces . . ." He muttered under his breath and rocked back and forth, arms wrapped tight around him. A sad but necessary illusion of comfort. "You'll never find them. The demon hides things in plain sight, but you'd never know where to look."

"How do you know that? Were you trying to find someone's face, too?"

His voice cracked. "Don't leave me. You're the first person I've talked to in so long."

She had to. She could not stay. He had not been much use, unfortunately. "I'll come back for you." He needed to hear this, even if it wasn't true. Nothing was more important than Eska.

"She said that, too. She never did."

"Who?"

The man shot into a sitting position. "Where did you go?"

Shadows pulsed and stretched out their long fingers, creating an opaque shield separating Apaay and the prisoner. She recoiled from the barrier. "I'm right here."

"Hello?" The word was a raw, shriveled thing. "Don't go. I'm sorry! Please, come back!"

Tears swamped Apaay's vision. She reached through the bars, her fingers so close to touching him. A few inches farther and she'd be able to grasp the tattered blanket he wore around his shoulders. "I'm here. Can't you see me?"

The man was crying again. He covered his face with his hands as the shadows grew, until they masked him completely.

A second later, the darkness blinked out, and she was kneeling in the chamber where the challenge had begun, Yuki and the Face Stealer staring her down.

Apaay ducked her head, flinching at the flare of blue light. It seemed the girl could control the labyrinth at will, changing the surroundings when it suited her.

"Where were you?" Yuki demanded.

Apaay held her tongue. Her words curled up safely inside her mouth where they would not cause harm. So Yuki hadn't lied. She really couldn't cross the sea, for whatever reason. Otherwise she wouldn't be asking the question with such desperation, right? Even more curious, she had not been able to track Apaay once she had stepped through the second mirror. This presented an opportunity. Leverage. Knowledge Yuki wanted but didn't have, which Apaay could later use as a bargaining tool. Until then, it was her secret to keep. Something hers and hers alone.

"Nowhere," Apaay said in false puzzlement. "I was walking through the snow the entire time."

"I find that hard to believe." The girl pointed at one of the five mirrors with a pout. "I was being thoroughly entertained watching you roll around like a dog in the snow, and suddenly the mirror went black. Why would it do that?"

"I have no idea—"

"Look at me when I'm speaking to you."

When she lifted her chin, Yuki gasped in delight. "Your face." A tittering laugh. "I'd say it's an improvement, wouldn't you?"

Yes, her face. Her raw, burned face. Skin peeled from her cheeks like scales and scabbed across her nose and chin, the furious red rash disappearing below her neck. She was fully aware of how revolting she must look.

Apaay looked straight at the girl, with her untouched beauty, and then, deliberately, settled her attention on the demon beside her. His eyes were lavender in this light, shocking against the blue-black of his hair, the deep brown of his skin. She was not sure what emotion the color represented. She found she didn't especially care.

"Maybe if I hadn't been forced to cross the boiling water," Apaay began.

"What fun would that be?" She tilted her head. "I'm sure those burns will heal. But you understand why I brought you back, right?" Yuki paused and leaned forward in her seat, the motion too eager to be casual. "Well? Where is it? Where's the face I asked for?"

"Eska's?"

"No. The one *I* wanted you to find."

Apaay's hands were empty. She curled her fingers into fists and set them atop her thighs. "I don't have it."

Yuki's bony shoulders, which had crept up to her ears in anticipation, sank slowly down. "I see." The stone chair seemed to crush her small body.

Yuki didn't look at her as she said, "We're finished here."

The girl's disappointment caught Apaay off guard. "But I still had time." She had, right? She swore she had not lost track of time so easily. It had taken, say, four hours to build the kayak? She'd wandered a couple hours beforehand, sure, and then had spoken with the prisoner afterward, but it couldn't have added up to more than nine or ten hours total. She should have had twelve. "You took the chance away from me. That's not fair."

"I took the chance away from you? Child, I *gave* you the chance. It was quite simple. All you had to do was cross the sea. I even *told* you where to go. Tell me, how is that not fair?"

The girl shifted, her breathing growing more agitated, and still she would not look at Apaay, her gaze flitting from corner to corner as if searching for something lost.

Only when the Face Stealer reached out and touched Yuki's arm did the girl noticeably calm. She whispered vehemently, "Let me tell you what's unfair. Waiting for someone like you to stumble upon my home, to give *me* the chance of finding what's mine." She shrugged off the demon's touch and sent him a glare that said so much in so few words. Fury and betrayal and regret and longing. "You've been without your sister's face for, what, a month?" she said, attention returning to Apaay. "I've waited years in vain, hoping this time will be different. But you failed. And now the price will be paid." The girl gestured to her companion. "Numiak."

A subtle stiffness settled into his posture. He didn't move from his spot.

Yuki turned toward him. She hissed, with truly frightening ferocity, *"Go."*

Unfolding his long length from the chair, he strode down the few steps to the walkway. Apaay kept her head bowed, dismay washing through her as he stepped through one of the five mirrors resting against the wall and vanished.

"Child, you'll want to see this."

Chilled, invisible fingers gripped Apaay's chin, scraping against inflamed flesh, and forced her to peer into the closest mirror. Her reflection blurred before sharpening into white mounds, frosted trees, a large circle of ice houses illuminated by the moon's pale glow. She hissed out a breath. Her village—she was looking at her village.

Apaay bit the inside of her cheek to hold back tears as her people screamed and fled from the whirling cloud of midnight that descended and settled into the Face Stealer's powerful form. He was a dark wolf stalking the night. A horror. Eventually, he cornered a young boy against a tree.

Apaay recognized him. Qavak. In the evenings, he would sometimes demonstrate his bird call imitations, much to the delight of his parents. He was only ten years old.

The boy cowered against the pine, so small, and when he looked up through a shield of tears, his pupils grew impossibly wide. Apaay stiffened as the boy's screams broke off.

His mouth was gone. And then his eyes were gone, too.

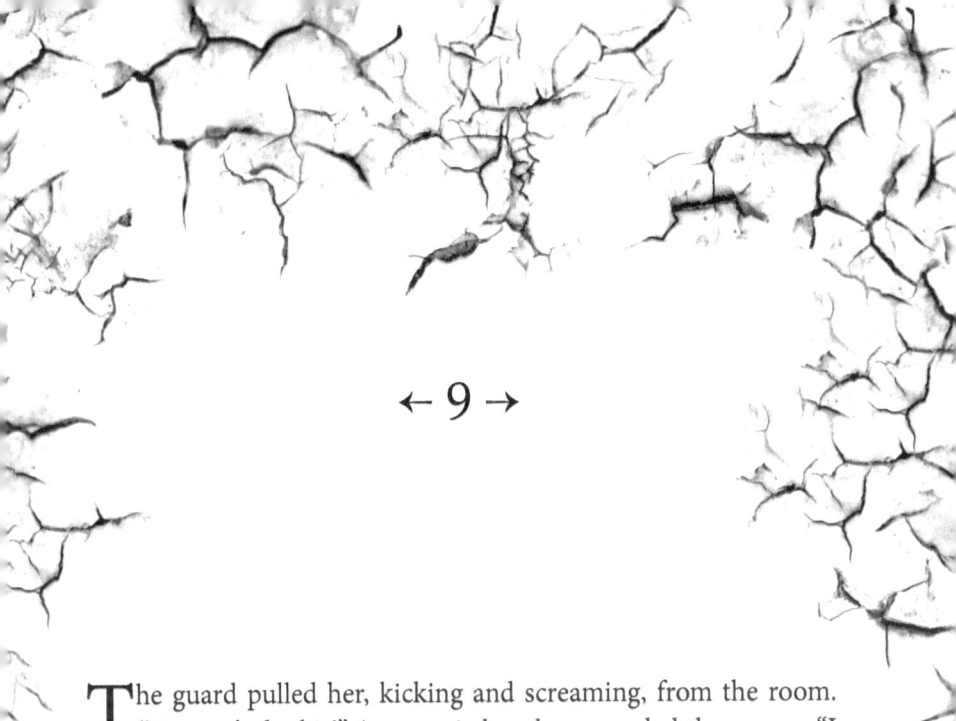

← 9 →

The guard pulled her, kicking and screaming, from the room. *"You can't do this!"* Apaay cried as they rounded the corner. "I still had more time!" She jerked against the man's hold, twisting her body to try and free herself, hissing in pain at the abrasive caribou hairs scratching along her sensitive flesh. His foul odor made her head swim. It wasn't fair. They'd made a deal.

"My game, my rules." Yuki's voice carried, unexpectedly bitter. "Maybe next time you'll prove yourself more useful."

Locking Apaay's arms behind her back, he shoved her down another hallway that led toward her cell. Or what she thought to be her cell. But when the guard yanked Apaay to a halt, she noticed they had taken a different path, one of light, not darkness—there were torches set within the walls.

The door squealed open, welcoming her into its shadowy maw. Apaay held back in confusion. "Isn't this the wrong cell?"

"You've been moved." He pushed her forward and slammed the door in her face.

Well, then.

"I demand to speak to Yuki!" she shouted to his retreating back, shaking the bars of her cage.

The echo faded.

Apaay slumped against the door. That had not gone as planned. The labyrinth was a thick, dark curtain. She had not known what lay behind it. Now she knew how difficult her mission truly was.

On another note, apparently she was supposed to spend the rest of her life wasting away in the dark. Ha! Did they think dropping a mountain across her path would deter her? She'd simply build a bridge.

The air was warm enough that she could safely remove her mittens, and Apaay trailed her fingertips across gritty stone, down the cracks and seams where the rocks locked together in the red-tinged shadows. Her fingertips became her eyes. They told her how high the walls were and how wide. They told her the number of stacked stones, the dimensions of the room, how the floor gradually sloped toward the hallway. There was a stone wall at her back, with iron bars separating the cells on either side of her. Attached to the barred door was a square metal box with a hole wide enough that she could shove her finger through and feel the small pieces of protruding metal. It must be where the guard had inserted his key.

Sneering in disgust, she kicked at a rock on the ground, the clattering bouncing off the ceiling and walls. The last time she'd experienced such helpless fury, Pana had believed it a good idea to kiss her despite her refusal, his breath reeking of fish.

She'd certainly shown him what she thought of that. It had taken four days before he could walk without waddling.

Her people had never been sure, exactly, of where the in-between was located. Between realms? Between consciousness and unconsciousness? Or perhaps it was up to interpretation?

Wherever it was, Apaay had managed to reach it on foot, which meant others could reach it as well. If she could somehow get word to her family . . .

She doused the thought before it took shape. Who would come? Eska, with no eyes? Papa, with his injured leg? Or perhaps Mama, leaving the rest of her family to fend for themselves?

It had never been a choice for Apaay. She loved Eska more than she feared death. Someday she hoped to have someone who would come for her too, should the situation arise. She wanted to be worthy. Her family, as much as she loved them, would do anything for them, was too afraid of the demon's power to venture into the unknown. No one would be coming for her.

Still, a small, foolish part of her hoped.

Apaay paced the length of the cell, hands behind her back. First, she needed the key to the door. The guard, she assumed, would return at some point. Apaay only needed to get close enough to knock him out. A blow to the temple would do it. Once she had the key, she'd have free range of the fortress and could continue her search.

The problems lay with Yuki and the Face Stealer. Whatever her actions, they'd have to be subtle, hidden. They must never know of her whereabouts. They must never learn of her intentions.

She had not learned much of the Face Stealer during their brief interaction. Aside from his horrendous disposition, he was quiet, reserved, an observer rather than a participant. She sensed he was both more than he revealed and less than she perceived. Watching him tear away the face of Qavak, an innocent boy, was one of the most horrifying things she had ever witnessed. The experience of her own face being ripped away had been equally traumatic.

Then there was the girl, barely a child in body, but her mind was a thing to behold, cunning and cruel. The two characteristics did not align, were opposing forces unable to blend seamlessly, for whatever reason. It was both vile and fascinating to watch. Considering how much she already loathed the girl, Apaay wished she weren't so intrigued.

She knew one thing, at least. The girl assumed Apaay would try to flee, not that she had any idea how. She would, in time, but not yet. For now, Yuki did not have to worry. She was here for Eska, to put an end to the Face Stealer. And did they not know? Apaay would do anything for family.

She was about to settle onto the ground when a shape caught her attention in the adjacent cell. A young woman sat in the corner with her knees drawn up against her chest, so quiet that Apaay had not noticed her until now. Light from the torches bathed her form, just bright enough that Apaay could see her without squinting. She did not wear a parka, but rather a long-sleeved top crafted of thinner skins. The girl's pupils were large in her thinning face. Startled, like a cornered animal.

Apaay approached the bars separating their cells in a slow, unthreatening manner and crouched down so they were at eye level. Curling her fingers around the chilled metal, Apaay whispered, "Hello." Soft, like a soothing hand brushed along the brow.

The girl stared. She stared and stared, and she didn't shift, didn't blink. Long, curled locks, like the smoky brown of caribou fur, framed a face that was quite lovely beneath the grime. She appeared to be sleeping with her eyes wide open.

Apaay pressed her cheeks against the bars. "Who are you?"

The girl blinked, focusing briefly on Apaay's mouth. She didn't respond, but neither did she cower away.

Apaay sat back on her heels, mystified. Perhaps this would be a good time for a joke. It might coax the girl out from behind whatever barriers she'd built.

"What do you get when you cross a polar bear with a seal?" The girl was still staring at her mouth when she answered, "A polar bear!" Apaay snorted a laugh, and it was not entirely forced. It reminded her of winter nights beneath the blankets, muffled giggles as she and Eska tried to out-cringe the other. When was the last time she had laughed? It had been too long. "You know, because the polar bear would eat the seal."

Judging by the lack of reaction, the young woman did not think the joke at all funny. She couldn't blame her, really.

With a sigh, Apaay rubbed her hands across her face. It was possible something had happened to the young woman—assault or torture or abuse. And yet the girl saw her. She was staring at her lips as if they were a riddle she was trying to comprehend. .

Threading her arms through the bars so her hands were visible on the other side, Apaay took her time shaping the gestures. Slow, so the young woman, who looked to be a few years older than herself, could see. Three motions: pointing to the girl; hand cupped over her ear; palm flattened against her chest.

Can you understand me?

Apaay would never forget how the girl's face changed. How sweetly it opened, like it had been locked away for so long. The deadness in her gaze thawed into warmth, and suddenly tears slipped down her cheeks and chin in thin streams, cutting pathways through the dirt. Her small mouth quavered.

The young woman lifted her hands from where they had curled around her legs. They trembled as she signed back, *Yes, I can understand you,* and Apaay's heart squeezed.

The girl crawled across her cell. This close, Apaay noticed a thick, knotted scar curved around her skull and behind her ear, a puckered white line that blazed in the low light.

Reaching out, Apaay clasped the girl's hand, prisoner to prisoner. Cold, sharp relief unwound the knots in her back, and her mouth slipped into an easy curve at this simple interaction with someone who understood. For the first time since she'd awoken, bound and alone, she could breathe easily. *What's your name?*

Ila. The girl signed each letter with one hand, a slight alteration to her hand shapes. With communities so isolated in the North, there were bound to be variations in nonverbal communication. Luckily the differences between their dialects did not detract from understanding one another.

My name is Apaay, she responded.

Apaay. Ila blinked rapidly. *Sorry.* She swiped an arm across her cheeks.

Apaay squeezed Ila's hand tighter, letting the action speak.

You're real, yes? Ila asked with a laugh, mouthing the words. *I'm not imagining this?*

She was real. She was here. And for now, she was not going anywhere.

Once the older girl calmed down, she said to Apaay, *Can I tell you something?*

Of course.

Ila said, expression grave, *That was the worst joke I've ever encountered.*

Apaay's mouth stretched so wide her cheeks cracked. *Trust me, I know worse ones.*

When I say the joke was bad, I mean it was bad. She emphasized the last word with more force. *Really bad.*

Then I succeeded. My sole purpose in life, besides escaping this hellhole, is to offer my terrible jokes to all. Even if they're not appreciated.

Shaking her head, Ila smiled. *It's nice to have someone to talk to, at least. I can overlook your bad jokes for that.*

Apaay jerked her chin at a small pile of objects cluttering the far corner of the young woman's cell. *What are those?*

Ila glanced over her shoulder, then ducked her head. She passed Apaay a handful of items through the bars, gaze lowered.

Palms cupped, Apaay lifted the stone carvings in awe. Whale, fox, wolverine. Firelight warmed the sleek edges, the rough points having been smoothed. The darkest had been carved out of rock the color of coal, while the lightest was akin to ivory or bone. *You made these?*

Ila jerked a nod.

Since the older girl seemed embarrassed by the compliments, Apaay returned to studying the carvings. She had never seen such beautiful artwork. Ila had managed to capture the spirit of each animal, cocoon it in stone.

Footsteps in the hall. Ila's face went stricken, and she scurried back to the opposite end of her cell as the guard rounded the corner. He slipped something through Apaay's door without looking at the other girl. Thin, cowered, and nearly invisible in the area farthest from the light, she was easy to overlook.

The guard left as quickly as he had come, leaving Apaay no time to strike. She sighed and went to see what he had brought.

A pail of fresh water.

And seal meat.

Hot saliva pooled in her mouth, and Apaay pounced. She didn't think. Liver, kidney, blubber. The blood was rich and full of life, and it smeared her chin and cheeks. The meat, a deep reddish brown, was soft as it slid down her throat, the scent of iron and salt strong.

But then she paused. The salt of the sea seeped into her pores, and it brought Apaay back to a cold morning when she and her family had gathered around a seal Papa had harpooned, giving thanks to its spirit by allowing it fresh water to drink, before butchering it.

In the memory, it was Eska's birthday, and she was eleven years old.

Hands shaking, Apaay dropped the piece of liver, stumbled to the corner, and retched up everything she had eaten. Her head hung, forehead prickled with sweat.

Ila studied her with concern when she turned and slumped against the back wall, head woozy.

Are you sick? wondered Ila.

Could love be a sickness, or family, or the ache for home? Now that these things were gone, she craved them. Sick at heart. Sick in her soul.

After washing her mouth out with water and cleaning the blood from her face, Apaay offered the pail to Ila, followed by the meat. She did not want to discuss family. She did not want to be reminded of the emptiness in her gut. The *wanting*.

Apaay knew hunger, knew its hollowed face and deadened expression. It was a beast that could not be satiated.

There was only a slight hesitation before the other girl accepted the food, having concluded Apaay would not elaborate.

Unlike Apaay, Ila consumed the meat slowly, one small bite at a time. They shifted so their shoulders touched through the space between the bars, and the small slice of human contact began to unravel the anxious knots snarled in Apaay's chest. No one in this fortress cared whether she lived or died. Not Yuki, not the Face Stealer, not the guards. But she would like to think Ila cared.

After some time had passed, Apaay signed, *Can I ask you something?*

Pushing the tray of food back toward Apaay, the young woman nodded.

Why are you here?

Immediately, Ila recoiled, her gaze shuttering.

Apaay quickly backtracked. *I'm sorry.* After all, she did not know the circumstances that had led Ila here, whether they were traumatic or painful. She knew nothing about this girl, just as Ila knew nothing about her.

So Apaay began with her story.

She told Ila about her community, her family. She explained what the Face Stealer had done and her journey north, the loss of Nakaluq. Then the boiling water, the prisoner who was exactly like them. Occasionally, her hands would falter in searching for the correct term to use, but Ila was there, offering guidance, suggestions.

And then she ran out of words. The past had caught up with the present, and there was little else to say.

Ila's gaze, more open, less afraid, held Apaay's as she signed, *I've been here for a long time.*

The older girl wasn't talking about weeks or months. She saw how Ila interacted with her cell. For her, this was safety and comfort. This was home.

How long?

Ila drummed her fingers against the bar, then said, *I can't remember much of my life before this. I have a few vague—very vague—memories. I remember I had a family, I think. Parents and a sister, but I can't remember what they looked like or what their names were or anything else.* She pulled away and leaned against the back wall. *I'm not even sure if those memories are real.*

You've been trapped here for years?

Yes, though I stopped counting the days long ago.

A queasy sensation slid into her gut. *You've never been out of the labyrinth?*

Ila's expression darkened, strain tightening the skin around her eyes.

No, she replied. *Never.*

In the short time since she'd arrived in the labyrinth, Apaay was already intimately acquainted with the bite of stone against her spine. Already, she came to expect rust-flavored water. Already, darkness and solitude. Apaay had been born free. Ila knew little of it. Here, their two worlds merged, became one of soundless isolation.

I'm sorry, Ila.

She shrugged, her smile small. *I let go of anger a long time ago.*

This was a young woman who could not remember the outside world. Apaay imagined herself in five years, ten, doomed to live her life in dark silence. She vowed to never be subject to that fate. *It's not right.*

The girl's fingers alighted on Apaay's wrist, the touch fleeting. *I'm not completely alone. There's a guard who is nice to me.* The bronze of her cheeks deepened with a slight flush. *He brings me blankets and extra food when he can, and sometimes he will talk to me about the outside world. That's how I learned what those animals looked like,* she said, gesturing to the carvings. *He lets me walk down the corridors so I can stretch my legs.*

He knows how to sign?

Yes. He taught me how.

A small slice of kindness, then. But it was not enough.

Tamping down her mounting anger, Apaay asked, *Why does Yuki keep you here?* What purpose would she have in keeping Ila—sweet, unthreatening Ila—locked away?

From the look she received, Ila had asked herself the same question perhaps hundreds of times. The iron and stone were her companions, and they had no answers to give.

How will you get your sister's face back?

Apaay sank against the bars and pressed against the line of warmth radiating from Ila's side. *I need to figure something out. Yuki won't give me a second chance, and I have no idea how I'll find where the Face Stealer keeps his faces.* She didn't want to dwell on it, the possibility that she had come all this way and was not able to carry out her plan.

What's he like?

Apaay glanced up in surprise. *You haven't met him?*

Fear flashed in the girl's gaze, then was extinguished. *No.* Her lips paused, hands hovering. *He never comes down here.*

Where to start? His arrogance and how he wore it so fittingly? Or those sharp, unsettling eyes, blue and green and gray and gold, which she noticed changed color based on the emotion he was feeling. The cunning of his words, how he stripped her of courage with little effort. Or perhaps his dark beauty, which seemed to have been molded from the night itself.

Apaay smirked. *He has a tiny head.*

Ila clapped her hands over her mouth, giggling through her fingers. So maybe it was an insignificant lie, but at least it lightened the gloom of their circumstances.

How tiny? Ila wondered.

Really tiny. She squeezed her thumb and forefinger together, thoroughly enjoying herself. *Can you imagine how small his brain must be?*

Ila's laughter bounced off the walls and skipped down the passageway. *I wonder if that's the only thing tiny about him.*

Apaay sucked in a shocked breath, appalled and delighted at the turn of events. She looked at Ila, and the space swelled with deep, aching laughs that flooded the cell with a little more light. Her momentary happiness did not belong here. The oppressiveness would soon blanket this fire, and yet she embraced it anyway, the warmth she needed to press on.

Tiny, indeed!

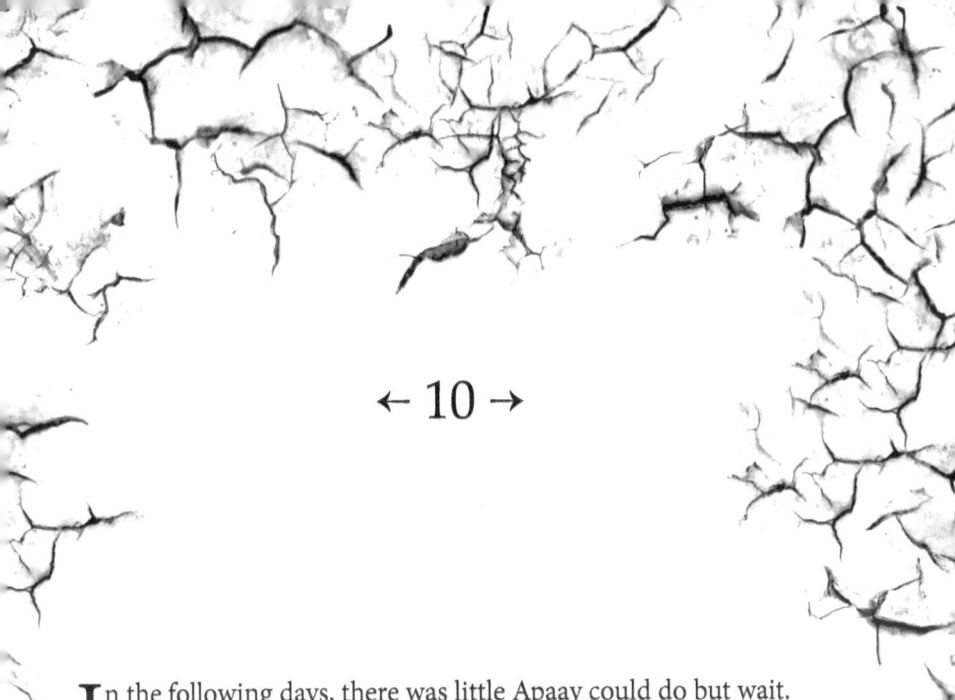

← 10 →

In the following days, there was little Apaay could do but wait.

The beginnings of a plan began to form, shroud-like. How she would take down the guard, and when. What direction she would run. How long before someone found her cell abandoned, the door agape.

Daily, a guard visited them. Once in the morning, or what Apaay believed to be morning, and once in the evening. At first, Apaay couldn't keep track of how many hours passed between rounds. Time was slippery here. She had no sky to bear witness to the cycle of the moon. So she began to tell stories aloud, as some lasted a great many hours. In this way, she discovered that twelve hours passed between rounds. They received food and water every third day, and Apaay scraped tally marks against the wall while Ila chipped away at her current project, a caribou from the looks of it. The guard always came alone.

This was good. Apaay could overtake one man easily enough, so long as she had a weapon. She sharpened one of the larger rocks into a knife. It would suit her needs well.

On the eighth day, she was ready.

As soon as she heard boots scuffing in the hall, Apaay squeezed herself into the corner where the guard usually shoved food through the bars of the door. Close, closer still. Apaay released a slow breath.

The man stepped into view and set his torch into the wall. He began to turn when she lunged, grabbed his sleeve, and yanked him forward so he was pinned against the bars, the rock shard jabbed into his throat. Blood welled at the point of contact, a single crimson tear.

"Give me the key if you want to live," Apaay hissed in the man's ear.

He froze.

Reaching through the bars separating their cells, Ila yanked on Apaay's arm. Apaay brushed her off, but the young woman was insistent, clamping down with surprising strength. Apaay glanced over long enough to see Ila sign, *He's a friend.*

Since she didn't want to release her captive, she spoke aloud so Ila could read her lips. "Ila, this is a guard."

Remember the guard I mentioned before, the one who taught me how to sign? She smiled. *This is him—Irnik.*

For the first time, Apaay peered at the guard's face. He was tall and broad and wearing a keen expression. His hair had been pulled back into a sleek knot, revealing a face as round as the moon.

The hand holding the knife trembled from how viciously she gripped it. She watched, transfixed, as the drop of blood slipped down his neck. His gaze roved over her face, the now-healing burns, if she could call them that. Without salve, they had barely healed and now itched from irritation and infection. If he was appalled, he did not show it.

Ila jerked her arm harder. *Let him go.* Firm.

The knife point pressed deeper into skin, and the guard's eyes narrowed in calculation. He was one of them. The bars separating their forms were a clear divide. The problem was, Apaay had never killed another person before. Didn't think she had it in her to go through with it. The moral implications warred with the need to leave *now*, to find her sister's face *now*, to not pass up this chance. Her eyes stung in frustration, that she still had not driven the knife deeper. She wondered if that made her weak.

Something equally sharp pricked her neck. Apaay stiffened. She hadn't seen him reach for a weapon.

"Step back," he said, voice low and roughened as if from disuse.

Ila signed something to the guard in Apaay's peripheral vision. *Stop this,* maybe. She again tried to force Apaay's hand away from his throat.

Neither moved. They were two walls battering against each other. Was she to die then, after having come all this way? Completing her mission hinged on her survival. And that was more important than killing this man.

If he was Ila's friend, and *if* she could trust him, then he may be of some use. He knew the labyrinth's layout better than she, the places to avoid. If he knew of any weaknesses had by Yuki or the Face Stealer, even better.

Lifting her hand, she released him and stumbled back. Her nose leaked fluid that she wiped away with her sleeve, and Apaay stood there awkwardly, trying not to break down. With a wary look, Irnik approached Ila's cell and began speaking with the girl, who was more animated than Apaay had ever seen her, her hands graceful, swooping birds. It was clear from the ease with which Ila and this man communicated that they cared for each other.

More for Ila's benefit than anything, she said to the guard, "Sorry. For almost killing you, I mean."

"Are you? Sorry, that is?"

Well, when he put it so bluntly.

"No, actually. I'm not." She flashed him her teeth, ignoring the glare Ila sent her. What a relief it was not to pretend. If not for her sister, she would have killed him. She still wanted to. "Or am I wrong in assuming you work for Yuki and the Face Stealer?"

His brows lifted. "Yuki, yes," he said, his words slow and weighted. "Not the Face Stealer. I'm not his to command."

"He doesn't hold power over you?"

"No. He does not even hold power over himself."

Interesting. Even more interesting: She had already reached this conclusion. The thought had materialized after having observed his interactions with Yuki back in the airy chamber. Now that it was confirmed, however, she could figure out how best to proceed. And how best to take advantage of this arrangement.

Ila glanced between her and Irnik in apprehension, tension mounting in the small space. Apaay sent her an easy smile, born of years easing Eska's worries when starvation had lurked beyond the next day, the next week. When Ila turned away, Apaay cut Irnik a look. A simmering warning. *I do not trust you.*

Apaay wandered to the back of her cell, leaving Ila and Irnik to themselves. A part of her wondered what they discussed, if she was a topic of conversation. She leaned against the wall, crossed her arms over her chest, and tried to feign disinterest, never mind that she had given away her intentions to the guard. The longer they spoke, the more agitated she became. She wished he would leave already.

After perhaps ten minutes, Apaay reached through the bars and placed a hand on Ila's shoulder, silently asking permission to speak.

The older girl startled from the contact, as if she had forgotten Apaay was there. Her throat bobbed as she nodded and stepped back.

She had intended to sign for Ila's benefit, but since the girl retreated to give them privacy, Apaay spoke aloud instead. "What do you want with Ila?"

Faint lines creased his brow. The switch to speech had thrown him. "Nothing. We're friends."

"Friends? I find that hard to believe, considering the power imbalance." A prisoner and a guard. A woman trapped and a man free. This guard visited Ila, offered her food, conversation, companionship when the girl had none. The question was, and always would be, *Why?*

"If you hurt her—" Apaay began, lethally soft. In such a short time, the girl had gone from stranger to friend. She was a warm hand in the dark, and her breaths, slow and deep in sleep, calmed the restlessness Apaay experienced when awakening from vicious dreams, her head full of strange, muffled screams she could not ignore.

His expression flashed surprise. "I would never intentionally hurt Ila, that I can promise you. Does one crush a flower in winter? Maybe she's a prisoner now, but it won't always be that way. I want her to be free."

Apaay scrutinized him for a further motive, nothing left untouched, but the young man seemed perfectly content to let her stare at him until her eyes glazed over.

He smelled different. Since she'd been young, Apaay could pick up emotions, fear from others. A gift, her parents were convinced. What she smelled on the man wasn't unease exactly, and it wasn't lies, either. Something in between a truth and a lie. A soft, uncertain shape that had yet to sharpen. She believed him when he claimed he would not hurt Ila. His intentions, at least in that respect, were noble.

"You should leave," she said, hoping he would do so before his hands found their way into his pockets.

He looked over her shoulder to where Ila sat neatly folding her blanket. "Tell Ila I'll be back with more food when I can get away."

"Why are you helping her? What's in it for you?"

He said, with the weariness of someone who had weathered much, "A better world."

He was gone before she had a chance to reply.

Scowling, Apaay stomped over to Ila and dropped to her knees, paying no attention to the rat that scuttled from a hole in the corner. Night had descended once he'd taken the torch with him, and Apaay had not realized how she'd been drawn to the light until it was gone.

I don't like him.

Ila's mouth twitched. She laid the blanket across her lap before giving Apaay her undivided attention. *Why?*

Because he's a guard. And we're prisoners. And if he works for Yuki, then he's as bad as she is. And he doesn't make any sense. Her instincts had saved her many times. She would be a fool to ignore them now.

Maybe you don't trust him because you don't know him. He has been good to me, her friend said, the gestures firm. *You should give him a chance.*

Why should I trust him?

Because he's my friend, and you should trust me.

The comment gave her pause. Trust. She had little of it here, and for good reason. She wondered again why she had been moved to a different cell. She hoped this wasn't another trick.

If he's your friend, why hasn't he tried to help you escape?

I don't know. I've never asked him.

Why?

Ila's chest went still, her breath captured and held as her eyes swept downward. She shrugged. *What if it turns out that I'm not important enough to save?*

Oh, Ila. Her heart went out to her. Truly, it did. *You can't think that's true.* And yet the insecurity touched her as well, because sometimes, in her most vulnerable moments, she continued to hope that someone would come for her, even knowing it was not likely.

Apaay. The older girl looked at her with such compassion that she wanted to collapse in Ila's arms and sob, knowing she was safe from the storm. *I don't know the circumstances that led him to work for Yuki. I'm just thankful he has been kind to me when no one else has.*

Apaay couldn't mask her bewilderment. *That's a bit naive, don't you think? Trusting someone with so much power over you?* She didn't understand how Ila could not see their circumstances clearly.

The young woman stiffened, and Apaay knew she had overstepped. *I didn't mean that.*

I think you did, the older girl said, putting space between them.

All right, so she had meant it. But Apaay wished she had considered the impact before speaking such hurtful things. *Please don't be mad at me.*

Ila sighed. *I'm not mad.*

Yes, you are.

I'm annoyed. She swatted a strand of hair from her face, and Apaay was given a glimpse of a different girl, one with eyes quick to harden. *How can you make assumptions about someone you don't even know? Just because my thoughts or actions don't align with yours doesn't make them less.*

Shame darkened her cheeks as Apaay flinched back. The people in her village did not hesitate to slap judgments on her, to assume the worst based on one mistake, one incident. She was the girl whose word was worthless. She was the girl who tried everything and proved nothing. Of course she would resort to the same judgments.

Tell me about Irnik. How long have you known him for?

Her lips bowed in a tender smile. *All my life. There used to be another guard who would come here* . . . Her hands faltered and fell into her lap.

Jaw clenched, Apaay asked, *Did the guard hurt you?*

Ila shook her head, her gaze shying away. *No, but a few times I think he wanted to. Eventually the guards were switched and I got Irnik. He was stationed here for about a year before being moved to another section of the fortress, but he visits me when he can.*

"Hm." Perhaps the guard was genuine in his intentions after all.

Apaay said, *I'll say he's good for one thing.*

What?

With a devilish smirk, she reached into her pocket and pulled out a key, dangling it from her finger.

Ila's mouth gaped. *How—*

Twirling the key around her index finger, Apaay suppressed the urge to preen at how brilliantly she had slipped her hand into Irnik's pocket when he had been pressed against the door. *I have my ways. Are you coming?* The key slid smoothly into the lock. As soon as the dull *thunk* sounded, Apaay loosed a breath. She had not been entirely sure the plan would work.

The door opened with a rusty groan.

Apaay stepped into the hallway, but Ila still had not moved.

This is our chance, Ila. We might not get another one.

What if we get caught?

The possibility was very real, and uncontrollable tremors seized her heart and limbs at the thought. There would be consequences—severe ones. As swiftly as a braid unraveling, Apaay's bravado folded beneath the harbored terror and confusion and insurmountable pressure to succeed. That sense of something drawing near, yet being unable to glimpse its face, left Apaay with more paranoia. This was a fool's decision. Look at all that had already gone wrong. Nakaluq's death. Her capture. Barely crossing the boiling water alive. She should wait until Yuki called for her. That was smart. That was safe. But it brought her no closer to completing the mission, and she had made a promise to her family.

She could handle the fear, maybe. A little. In time. She could not handle the regret.

Apaay took a moment to gather the scattered remains of her courage. *I'm not going to lie and say we won't, because I don't know what will happen.* Nothing life-threatening, she hoped. *I won't force you to come.* A part of Apaay hoped she would though, that maybe Ila was dying to break free, too.

The beautiful thing about Ila, Apaay thought as the girl set aside her blanket and uncoiled her long, waifish body, was that she did not let her circumstances define her. After pulling on her parka, same as Apaay, the older girl shuffled over the threshold. Huddled together, they ascended the worn stone steps of the stairwell located at the end of the corridor, their bodies flattened against the outer wall and merging with the shadows. It took longer than Apaay expected. Ila was not used to exercise, so they stopped at the first level so she could catch her breath. The second level, when she peeked through the entryway, was little more than faint light and walls coated in hard frost. At the end of the hallway, two guards spoke in hushed tones. Apaay hesitated only a moment before moving on.

Let's try this floor, she said to Ila as they reached the third level, the stairwell bathed in an orange glow. As soon as Apaay poked her head around the corner, she tensed.

She stared into the water. It rushed softly, lapping against the walls, the reflection like an oily sheen. A river spanned the area where a pathway should be, curving around a bend and disappearing into the gloom. Two kayaks and a larger umiak bobbed in the current, adjacent to the entryway.

Apaay stumbled back and would have tumbled down the stairs if Ila hadn't caught her.

We'll go to the next level, Ila reassured her at the sight of Apaay's stricken expression.

Apaay jerked a nod. *Give me a minute.* She sat on one of the steps, Ila settling beside her.

A nervous laugh tumbled from her mouth, and she clamped her lips together. How twisted it was that she willingly subjected herself to a child's torturous games, and yet at the first sign of water, her mind regressed to an incoherent snarl.

It's not all water, Apaay said, rubbing her chilled hands together. *Only black water.* The color she saw in sleep, of night cloaking the world. *I didn't realize there would be a river in this place.* Placing both hands together, fingers outstretched, she motioned the flow of rushing water.

Ila frowned at the gesture. Then her lips parted in realization. She mouthed, *River?*

Apaay nodded.

And it can hurt you?

Only if you don't know how to swim. A soft exhalation slipped out. *I was named after my grandmother—my mother's mother. She died before I was born.*

Confusion clouded Ila's face.

Sometimes during the naming ceremony, certain behaviors or traits can be passed on from the namesake. My mother says my grandmother fell through the ice when she was a girl and was afraid of water until her death. When I was little, I didn't even like getting my head wet. It embarrassed her sometimes, how debilitating the fear could be.

Ila turned back toward the water. She asked, *Will it hurt me if I touch it? The river?* She traced a wavy line over one palm, her own sign for *river*.

Apaay shook her head and watched as Ila crouched by the ledge and dipped her fingers into the slow-moving water, a delighted gasp filling the stairwell. *It tickles.*

Apaay pulled her friend back, Ila's proximity too close for comfort. They both agreed to keep moving.

On the fourth floor, they encountered hundreds of dead, moon-pale trees clustered in a vaulted chamber heaped in pristine snow. The room was shaped like an egg, with the iced walls hugging the snow as if they were the shell encasing the inner yolk. A shimmer of emotion peaked and died, over and over, as Ila's expression splintered and reformed with this newfound glimpse of life. Apaay would have believed herself outside were it not for the walls enclosing them.

Ila pointed across the open space. *The walkway continues on the other side.* She wiped sweat from her brow.

As Ila began to step off the ledge, a whisper crept along the ground, and Apaay grabbed her arm. *Did you hear that?*

Her friend froze. *Hear what?*

I thought— She strained to catch the faint murmuring, but it had disappeared. *You didn't hear that?*

Ila pointed to her ears, as if the answer were obvious.

Perhaps she had imagined it? Or was this a trick of the labyrinth, too?

Apaay glanced over her shoulder to the stairwell. They had wasted too much time standing still. It would be hours before the evening guard discovered their cell empty, but she couldn't ignore the threat of guards wandering the halls.

They did not have time to waste lingering at the trees, touching their smooth trunks, or playing in the snow. Ila seemed to sense this despite her curiosity and focused on trudging through the path Apaay cut for them without falling. Apaay wondered how it felt— living in a world you were not a part of. One day, though. One day they would have time to explore, and Ila would come to know her place.

They were halfway across the open plain when Apaay went still. The voice had returned, and she had not imagined this one. Cloying, manipulative, a sound she would never forget and growing louder by the second. The pale trees and snow illuminated them— no shadows to conceal. Yuki was coming around the corner, and she was almost here.

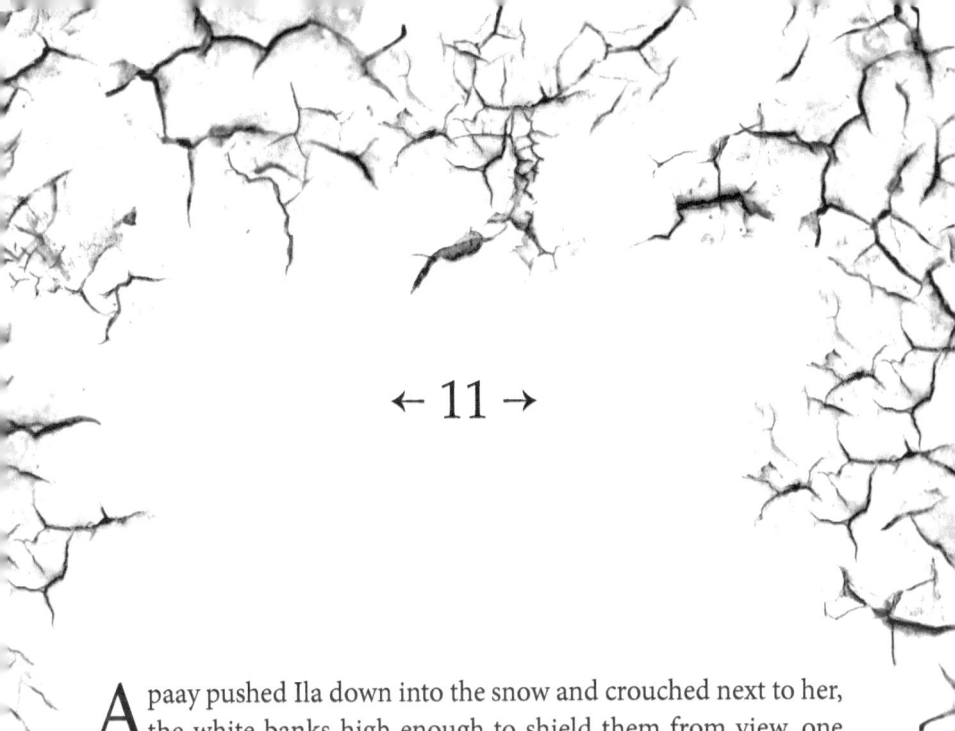

← 11 →

Apaay pushed Ila down into the snow and crouched next to her, the white banks high enough to shield them from view, one mittened hand covering Ila's mouth. A few heart-pounding seconds later, Apaay heard Yuki say, "You're sure the message is legitimate? I don't want to travel all the way to the Southern Territory only to discover it's a trap."

"Yuki, I'm hurt." The Face Stealer's lazy drawl. "Have I ever given you reason to doubt me?" Soft laughter carried down one of the hallways located at either end of the room. Apaay hoped they weren't approaching from the side she and Ila had entered, because then they would see the very obvious path of two people trudging through the snow. "Don't answer that."

"You're despicable."

"I'll admit, I'm curious as to what the council wants to speak with you about." Gradually, the demon's voice sharpened in clarity. "Nanuq, perhaps?"

Apaay mouthed the word. *Nanuq.* Like a half-forgotten memory. Or a dream.

Two sets of footsteps rang in the crystallized silence, then stopped. It sounded as if they had stopped inside one of the entryways to the chamber.

"Where is the path?" Yuki demanded.

"You had it removed, if I recall. You did not want it ruining your view of the trees." He sounded bored.

Apaay did not move, did not breathe. She stared at her hands, ears straining to hear whether they would pass through the room or continue onward. She imagined herself on the frozen sea, poised at one of the breathing holes. She was silence; she was night.

"Do you remember," Yuki suddenly asked, "the summer we first met? You and Kenai were climbing birch trees in the grove, and your brother fell and broke his wrist."

There was a long pause. "I remember."

"I had them planted after the war in his honor, only I wasn't thinking about the climate. So they died." She clucked her tongue, and Apaay wondered if it was more for show, to cover up the true hurt beneath. "Things were good though, weren't they? You, me, Kenai?"

"For a time."

"Do you think it could ever go back to the way things were?"

"No," he replied, a tone of hollow detachment. "It can never go back to that."

There was a silence. Apaay wished she could see their expressions. She wondered if the pain would be as apparent in their eyes as it was in their words. She wondered if they even realized their walls were breaking down.

The feeling was like stumbling upon a washed-up corpse, where Apaay wanted badly to move past it, yet drew near to investigate anyway. It didn't sit well with her, knowing they, too, experienced times of vulnerability.

"I've been thinking lately."

"That's a change."

She spat a curse, to which he laughed and said, "About what?"

"About our arrangement." Yuki cleared her throat as if about to make a grand speech, one she wanted all to hear. "We should rethink it."

Apaay didn't know how it was possible, as she could not see the demon, but she *felt* the Face Stealer's disbelief, as solid as if it had slapped her across the face. Carefully, she pushed back her hood to better hear his response. "That's never going to happen."

"How unfortunate you think so. I, however, think differently."

"Oh?"

"The face, Numiak. I want the face. The girl proved to be completely incompetent, and I'm tired of waiting. It was never yours to take."

"My dear, dear Yuki," the Face Stealer purred, and Apaay stiffened as his voice deepened in that subtle, dangerous way. "I believe you are confused as to how history played itself out."

"Yes. History." The words were faint.

"You take something of mine, and I take something of yours. If you have a problem with the arrangement, then return what belongs to me and I might consider another compromise."

Ila was starting to shiver, so Apaay pressed her body closer for shared warmth. She strained to hear the rest of the conversation.

"Then you remember how much I loved your brother," the girl whispered, "and how much it killed me when he was gone."

"Don't act as if you're the victim. You have only your own selfishness to blame."

"But—"

The Face Stealer's voice harshened, his control beginning to fray, and Apaay swallowed the metallic taste that scorched her mouth at the surge of fear, wondering what would occur should that thread finally snap. "A single life does not equate to an entire nation, and you would be wise to never forget that."

A self-deprecating laugh slipped free. It was the first honest thing she had heard out of Yuki's mouth, and she hated herself for wondering where it stemmed from. "You don't have to worry about that," Yuki said, the words muffled, as if she had turned away from him. "I will never forget."

Once their footsteps died away, Apaay and Ila made quick work of the snow and pulled themselves onto the entryway ledge. Shadows swiftly enclosed them. They left the trees, and the brightness, far behind.

The labyrinth lured them deeper into the unknown, these two young women driven by desperation, and Apaay's breathing grew more erratic as they fled down tunnels or crouched in corners waiting for a guard to pass, searching for a face, a glimpse of skin. On occasion she swore she heard a cry or scream, faint, but the moments were few and far between. It was not Eska's voice and never would be. Another trick of the labyrinth, then.

Her thoughts clashed, adding to the roiling in her gut. This arrangement with the Face Stealer that Yuki spoke of—Apaay could not fathom its parameters, but it seemed to have forced them into this unwilling partnership. She wondered who had stolen from whom first. The Face Stealer had taken the face of someone dear to Yuki, but Yuki had taken something from him as well. She wondered what value these stolen objects held. Sentimental? Monetary? The information might offer a clue to the larger picture. How the Face Stealer and Yuki had come to the labyrinth. Their tangled pasts. The *why* behind the questions she harbored, which grew more numerous by the day.

When they reached a mirror at the end of the hall, Apaay pulled Ila to a halt. The rippling silver surface beckoned them.

I'll go first, said Apaay.

Eyes wide, Ila nodded.

Apaay stepped through into a small, circular room forged completely of ice. Unsurprising. Would a little greenery hurt? Maybe some flowers to spruce up the place?

The room was perhaps three times as wide as her arm span. A single beam of light speared through the gloom, alighting on the five round doors gouged into the walls like overly large bubbles. A boulder took up the center of the room, squat and flattened on top. The floor, which Apaay had first believed to be ice, was in actuality a mirror.

She turned. "Ila—"

The mirror had vanished.

Her mouth dropped. No. *No.* How? Could only one person walk through a mirror at a time?

Her heart beat in her fingertips as the realization of what she had done settled. Without the safety of the cell, Ila had thrown herself into a viperous pit and now dealt with enemies Apaay could not see. Her friend had chosen to come, and Apaay had not stopped her. She should have, though. Ila was too soft for a place like this.

If any guard other than Irnik discovered her, the girl would suffer. She wondered if that was the reason why he had never helped her escape. It was too impossible a task. Apaay needed to find her friend and prevent punishment she did not deserve, but first she had to escape this room.

Crouching down, Apaay leaned close to study the doors. They lacked handles or any structure that would allow her to open them. She skimmed her mitten along the smooth, rounded edge, and at the touch, a whistling sound skittered along her nape—a high whine of ice scraping along the mirror's surface.

The walls were closing in.

Adrenaline surged, lacing her limbs with heat. She charged forward and rammed into one of the doors with her shoulder, the force exploding through her arm, but the door held, as did the second, and the third, and the fifth. She kicked and she punched and she shredded her mittens against the ice, and a broken laugh clawed at her throat. Did she expect to break through solid ice? Maybe next she'd try flying out of here.

Planting her feet, she shoved against the boulder with all her might, thinking there might be a hole to escape through beneath it. Her arms trembled, for the days locked away had begun to leach her strength. The massive rock slid forward, inch by inch, the mirror groaning beneath its shifting weight, but there was no hole, no door, no means of escape. Sweat swelled in her pores and leaked out. There was a good chance that if she was not crushed by the walls, she would drown in her own perspiration, and that would be a sorry way to die.

The walls grew closer. Apaay whirled around and around, as if expecting her surroundings to change, the ice to melt away and free her. She slapped her hands against the wall, braced her legs apart, and *shoved*.

Her boots slid across the floor.

Apaay swore. Her shoulder muscles groaned from the impossibility of trying to stop a wall from slowly, inevitably crushing her. Could she die in here? Probably. One less thing for Yuki to worry about, one less mouth to feed. The Face Stealer would have his faces. Ila would be subject to whatever punishment was given.

The walls shuddered and jerked forward, closing a foot of space in less time than it took Apaay to inhale. She knelt on the ground. Brushed her mittens across the mirror. A small dent about the size of her fist marred the sleek surface, but otherwise, all was smooth. Her hands shook too badly to grip anything, and she curled them into fists, closed her eyes, bowed her head. She needed a moment. Just one moment.

She had forgotten herself. She had forgotten the Analak way. Where was her stillness, her patience? Where was the part of her that sank into cool emptiness and just *breathed*?

She must reduce the situation to its simplest form. A question. What did she know?

Apaay swiped the sweat from her face. Five doors with no handles, unable to escape up or down. It must be a riddle of some sort. These were the resources, and she must decide what to do with them.

Stone, ice, mirror, light.

She could do this. She *would* do this.

It came to her in a moment of clarity. These things were not separate. They were connected. Dependent on the other.

Lunging for the boulder, she wrapped her arms around it, fingers nowhere close to touching, and heaved, back straining, joints creaking. It weighed almost twice as much as she did. There had been a time, not too long ago, when Apaay would have been able to lift it. Now her arms trembled. Her legs burned from lack of use.

She only needed to hoist it a few inches above the dent. Fire seared through her lower back as she lifted the boulder.

And slammed it down.

The mirror buckled at the point of contact and shattered into a thousand fractures of light. Razed angles. Puncturing corners. The floor was a glittering glass sea, a tumble of fragments, heaving upward from the thunderous impact as Apaay snagged a shard so quickly the glass sliced through her mitten. The walls stretched up into the dark. If she lay splayed out on the ground, every hand and foot would be able to touch the hardened ice.

Apaay positioned the mirror shard so the reflected light narrowed into an intense beam, which she directed at the closest door. As warmth hit the ice, it began to melt. A mere trickle at first, but soon a hole began to form, and it grew, grew, *grew* as the walls pushed closer. When enough ice had melted, Apaay rammed her foot into the hole.

"Come *on*," she grunted, clawing at the jagged edges.

On the third kick, the ice snapped. On the fourth, it splintered, spreading like a spider's web, her blows wild and unhinged, her gasps sharp cracks of sound.

The ice shattered. Darkness poured out of the doorway, but Apaay didn't hesitate. She dove through as the walls crunched together, crushing the remainder of the room to glittering dust.

← →

The land was completely hewn of stone. No snow, no ice, no trees, no sea. Soaring pillars of stacked rock jutted randomly from the earth every twenty or thirty feet, their surfaces smoothed by a cold, ageless wind. Against the gray sky, they appeared as rust-red smears—the color of old blood.

Glancing around, Apaay called, "Ila?" The girl would not be able to hear her, but calling out in hopes of a response made Apaay feel less alone. And she was indeed alone.

Pebbles skittered underfoot as she headed toward the largest of the pillars and placed a palm against its surface. It vaguely resembled a cairn, except these stones were not stacked in any particular formation, and they were not strategically placed to identify a pathway or hunting landmark.

After the cramped room she had escaped from, this place was a gasp of air. So much space. As there was no water, the air lacked the dampness she had grown used to. If she somehow managed to climb to the top of one of the pillars, she would be able to survey the land and consider her options.

Apaay had begun to remove her hand from the stone when, beneath her palm, a warm beat pulsed, heart-like.

A hair-raising cry skated across her mind.

It was so faint Apaay believed she had imagined it. Words that, had they been louder, she could have distinguished. But distance ate away at their forms, leaving only a thin, tremulous thread that stretched and frayed, possibly weeping. It was eerily similar to the voices she had heard while wandering the labyrinth with Ila.

She moved to another pillar and pressed her palm to the red stone. The voice was louder, but barely.

Apaay meandered through the stone towers, seeking the thread, backtracking when the connection disintegrated, her feet carrying her to the base of a plateau. She picked up the pace as the connection strengthened, the whisper cutting into two sharp points.

Help me.

Keeping her fingers to the stone, this small point of contact, she leapt over stacked rocks, clambered over a tangle of boulders, and slid down a small mountain of clattering pebbles. If this voice was real, perhaps it would lead to a person, and that person could lead her to the faces, and then she'd kill the Face Stealer and return home and never worry about the demon—

The air rang with sudden silence. She must have missed something. Taken a wrong turn that had broken the thread.

Apaay whirled around, intending to backtrack, and froze. The way was blocked.

By a pair of massive yellow eyes.

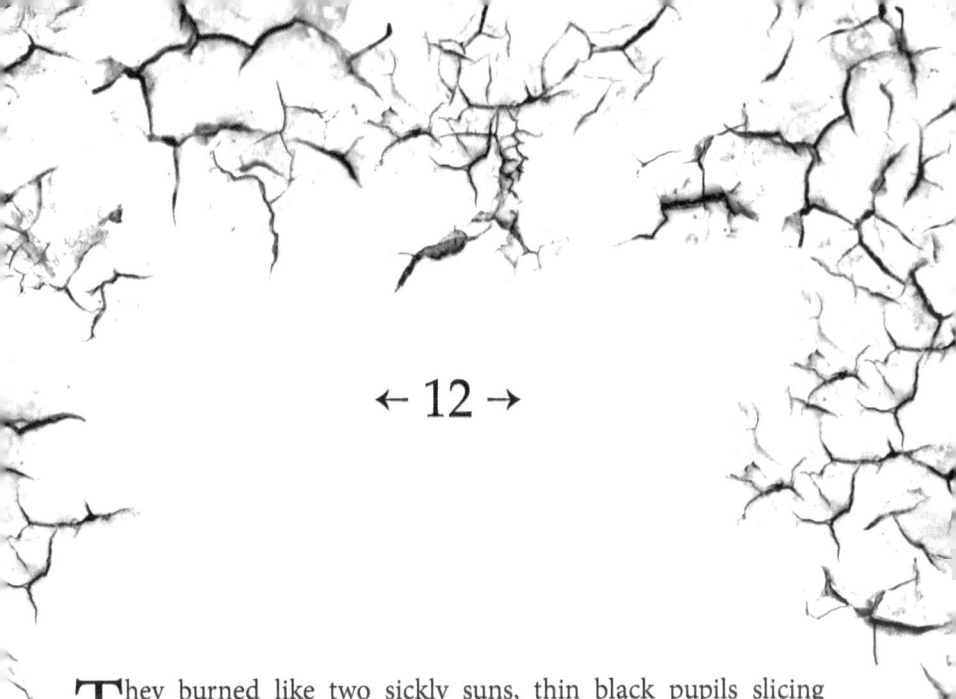

12

They burned like two sickly suns, thin black pupils slicing through. Apaay sucked in a soundless breath, hot saliva flooding her mouth, and she wondered if this was a trick of the mind, too, born of her imagination, born of Yuki's perverse thoughts, born of the rock protruding from the earth. Her vision blurred, then snapped into focus. It was still there—alive, its eyes flickering like dying flames.

Apaay allowed herself the small hope that it hadn't seen her, but of course it had. It was staring at her, eye to eye, nose to nose. A spirit she had only known through song and dance.

Sometimes, her people stumbled across wolf tracks leading to and from the edge of the sea. But these wide, massive prints did not belong to any normal wolf. The Sea Wolf, they said, devoured those foolish enough to wander out after dark. It did not hunt in packs like the wolves she spotted from afar, in togetherness. No, this spirit hunted alone.

Twice the height of an adult man and five times as wide, its bulk towered over her, spindly with muscle, its sloped head tapering to a long snout. The tail curled over its broad back, and dense, matted fur covered its body, white on the underbelly, the remainder black. Like eternity. Like death.

A grotesque snarl ripped from its throat as the spirit gave chase, pounding out a heavy *boom, boom, boom*, nails scrabbling against stone. Its paws were mammoth. Its breath, a hot billow of air.

There was no thought, only limbs moving, a sudden contraction and release of tension. Apaay ran—ran as fast as she could, fighting to keep her balance as the ground rocked beneath her unevenly. She barreled through columns. Leapt over rocks and crevasses fissuring down deep, winding between stacks that were nine, ten, eleven times her height. She needed a plan. She needed shelter. She needed a chance to sit, breathe, *think*.

But there was nowhere to hide. It was all great piles of rock and open sky. Apaay wished for snow and hills, as she knew how to shield herself in the whiteness. Not here in this wide, barren land.

Rock splintered, followed by another vicious growl. A crevasse split the ground in front of her, forcing her into a different direction. Apaay dared a glance over her shoulder to where the Sea Wolf had rammed into one of the pillars, which rocked and tipped onto its side before collapsing in a cloud of debris. She cut right, intending to double back, place herself *behind* the spirit so it wouldn't spot her. She had a few seconds to search for a hiding place.

If these rocks were the earth, then Apaay was the stream cutting through it. What mattered wasn't the direction, but distance. As much as she could manage in the little amount of time she'd been given. By the time her legs gave out, she had covered at least a mile, and could only slump against a rickety column, taking deep, calming breaths. Sweat trickled from her temples, each drop rolling over her flushed skin with agonizing slowness.

There must be another mirror out of this place. Apaay still wasn't sure how they worked, how the mirrors decided where to send her. Nor did she know if it was possible to return to the same place through a different mirror. It might be hours before she found that reflective doorway, time spent draining her energy bit by bit. Apaay didn't think she would survive that long. And if she endured this, imagine what Ila was facing. She accepted that she could do little for her friend at this point except hope and pray she was safe.

A skittering pebble alerted her attention before stone blew over her head in an explosion of grit and dust. Apaay hit the ground. Curling into a protective ball, she covered her head with her arms and braced for impact.

It was a brutal, relentless battering. The crashing was a white wave of sound, drowning out Apaay's screams. Large, heavy masses pounded into her flesh—shoulders, ribs, arms, legs, spine. Something cracked in her ankle. She shrieked as a lick of fire shot up her shin and down her foot, followed by grinding bones.

The last pebbles clattered, then lay still. Silence blanketed the land like the heaviest of cloth, severing all sound save the strangled gasps Apaay fought to muffle behind her shaking hands. Hot tears cut through the dust caking her face. She did not want to go back out there, where terror walked and waited, even knowing she could not stay here, buried beneath the earth. Apaay didn't think she could move even if she wanted to. Her foot was on fire.

Gritting her teeth, she peeked through the rocks currently shielding her, faint light squeezing through the pockets. A growl shuddered in the air nearby. More rocks crashed and caved. Apaay went stiff, and her breathing took on a jagged edge. The dust had yet to settle.

A whiff of the Sea Wolf's rank, musty fur blew on the wind. The air cleared, and she saw its hunched back as it picked through the rubble not ten yards away. As she was downwind of its location, it did not smell her. She was the hare. Prey. No time to wait. She had to move. *Now.*

Keeping her focus on the Sea Wolf, Apaay scooted out from under the rubble, taking care to only shift the rocks when the spirit moved the boulders with its own paws so its clamor covered up the sounds of her escape. She was not quick, but she was quiet. It was one of the things she did best. Biting the inside of her cheek to help manage the pain, she picked her way around the larger rocks. The slightest pressure on her right ankle sent a throb tunneling down into her heel. She had heard the snap of bone.

Then: change, a hard gust shifting upwind. The Sea Wolf swiveled its head around, pinning her. A piercing howl cracked the air.

Apaay wasted no time hurtling across the broken, pitted ground. A breathless sob shredded her throat. The pain was real. The fear was all around.

Apaay couldn't outrun the Sea Wolf. Not with a broken ankle, and not in her weakened, sleep-deprived state. But she was smart. When her back was against a wall and there was nothing to do but fight or give in, she thought of another way. The world shifted and took shape in ways she didn't notice before. A rock was not a rock, a tree not a tree. She saw not what was, but what could be. Resourcefulness, ingenuity—these were her roots.

The crunch of breaking earth chased her with every twist and turn. All the while, she memorized the positioning of the pillars, pieces she would use to strategize. Veering right, Apaay risked a glance back. Debris and dust thickened the air, faint light attempting to squeeze through the particles. The spirit's wrath made it sloppy. It also had a difficult time changing direction quickly. Perhaps she could use that to her advantage.

Within the space of two labored breaths, Apaay had a plan. She cut across a deep ravine, threw herself over the gaping pit, then dropped and rolled as her ruined ankle crunched beneath her weight. But she didn't stop. She *couldn't* stop. This was not about living, not anymore.

This was about surviving.

By now, the adrenaline had dulled the agony in her foot. Apaay backtracked to a particularly dense cluster of red stones, the glowing yellow eyes locked on her small form. A few yards, a few twists more. Earlier, she had passed a blockade of pillars so thick they resembled a wall, sheer-faced and uneven, stretched a quarter mile across. It would serve her purpose well.

The pillars rose from out of the dust. To the right lay a small opening gouged into the rock, the perfect size for a person to slip through.

Ten yards.

She had to do this exactly right.

Nine.

For the Sea Wolf was coming, and it was almost upon her.

Heaving pants exploded past her cracked and bloody lips. The wall was before her. Balancing on the very top of the pillars, smaller rocks tipped from the surge of energy buffeting them. The first one toppled, plunging to the ground and shaking the earth on impact. Apaay wobbled at the shift in her center of gravity but managed to catch her balance. Her lungs were strings of shredded cloth, her feet bruised, her knees rickety knobs, her skin slick and feverish. When Apaay reached the limit of what her body could endure, she proved herself wrong and went far beyond that point.

Four yards remained, then three.

There was no going back after this.

Apaay gasped as the Sea Wolf lunged, its shredding claws lifting from the ground.

The abrupt twist of Apaay's body caused a grinding sensation to pulse through her ankle. She screamed and dove toward the sliver of an opening, a doorway into life.

The Sea Wolf rammed into the pillars with an earth-shuddering explosion. A crack, the sundering of granite. The first stone toppled, and Apaay watched it plummet to the earth. Then came the second, the third. Soon it was all sound and sensation. Massive columns toppled one by one, a torrential downpour that crushed the spirit's body into the ground, a bloody, merciless beating. She felt the tremors in her chest, the rattle in her bones. It was a hail to her survival, and a lament to the spirit's end.

When the thunder and the dust and the shuddering earth lay still, Apaay's gasps were the sole sound in the world. She slumped against one of the few remaining pillars, hardly believing her luck. She was alive. This was real. And to think—

A screech cut into the silence, swift and merciless. Moments later, the rocks melted away and Apaay found herself back in the central chamber, the Face Stealer lounging in his seat, Yuki standing beside hers on the dais. The dozens of crescent-shaped oil lamps splashed shade and light upon the walls.

"So it's true," the young girl murmured, lips pressed into a bloodless line. "The prisoner escaped."

Apaay, in her oxygen-deprived state, had no idea what to say, so she said nothing.

Yuki stomped down the stairs and stopped less than a foot away. Though she was a good six inches shorter than Apaay, it didn't seem to make a difference. Rage made her taller, broader, a flame that burned too hot, too quickly. "How did you do it?" she said. "Did you slip through the bars of your cell? Dig a hole to another part of the fortress?" She smiled giddily, speaking to her as if they were old friends exchanging secrets. "You can tell me."

If Yuki were a bug, Apaay would delight in squashing her. As it was, she stared over the girl's shoulder as if she did not exist.

"Oh, I know! You bribed the guards with your body, didn't you?" Her attention swept from Apaay's sealskin boots to her face. "I'm not surprised. I knew you would flee sooner or later." Reaching up, she adjusted her circlet so the ice refracted the low light. "But to kill one of my own? That was a grave error on your part."

Exhaustion tugged on her consciousness. Her poor, throbbing ankle. Her sad, hollow gut. "I did what I had to do to survive," Apaay said, daring to step closer and crowd Yuki's personal space. "I'm glad the spirit is dead. One less terrible thing you can throw at me."

She responded with a delighted giggle. "Oh, child, you have overstepped. Badly."

Whirling around, she strode back to her throne, perched on the very edge of the seat, and lifted her chin. "Strip," she said simply.

Apaay blinked, not sure she had heard correctly. Her mind was still back in the rock-covered wasteland, running.

"I don't like to be kept waiting," the girl spat. "Now strip."

The blood drained from Apaay's face as comprehension hit, a cold, hard slap. Strip as in remove her clothes?

Without meaning to, she sought the Face Stealer's gaze.

He sat rigidly in his chair—a reaction other than the usual indifference. Today, his eyes were the palest of lavender, the same color they had been when she'd revealed her burns. The color, she realized with confusion, of his shock.

"Did you—" Apaay grasped for words. "Did you just order me to remove my clothes?"

"Still waiting."

Finally, her mind was returning to her. Ah yes, here she was, standing in the fortress, broken ankle, tired soul. No, she had not hit her head. No, she was not dreaming. "Then you're going to have a long wait," Apaay replied. "My clothes stay on."

Before Apaay had time to react, one of the ice pillars melted into a band of water, which slithered along the ground, twined around Apaay's neck, and hefted her ten feet in the air. She scrabbled at the choke hold as the girl said, "Maybe you've forgotten what happens to those who displease me." The back wall slid open, and Apaay was once again staring at the frozen man's peeled skin. Those dead, dead eyes. "Are you truly willing to risk your poor sister's face, your chance at freedom, for your pride?"

The band of water tightened. Apaay wheezed out, so bitter it scorched her tongue, "As if you would give me another chance."

Yuki gave quite an impressive pout. Then again, Apaay would expect nothing less from a girl who looked no older than twelve. "I was considering it." Beside her, the Face Stealer watched the disaster unfold, missing nothing. The tension had bled from his posture, and he was back to lounging.

"Now then." The water lost its shape, and Apaay dropped to the walkway, dampness seeping through the front of her trousers and parka. "You have until the count of five."

Apaay locked her gaze with the demon, sitting so lazily on his throne, unconcerned with everything save his next victim. This was not the same person who had sat straight-backed only moments ago.

"One."

Apaay trembled, half-soaked. He didn't move. Didn't even look at her. She didn't understand why it mattered whether he acknowledged her, but she wanted him to. She was right here. She was a person, and she was afraid.

"Two."

Apaay remembered when Yuki had ordered him to steal the face of another person from her village. There had been the briefest hesitation. In that moment, Apaay had overlooked it. Now she could think of little else.

"Three."

There must be a part of him, however small, that loathed the influence Yuki held over him. Did he not see she was a victim, too? It was the same with every person who had ever claimed a position of power.

"Four."

They set the world on fire and watched it burn.

"Aren't you going to stop this?" Apaay ground out before Yuki could finish the countdown.

The Face Stealer did not look at all surprised that she was speaking to him. If she had suddenly sprouted a third eye, no doubt he would have the same bland expression. "What is there to stop?" His voice was rich and warm, so at odds with the surrounding ice. "I believe the punishment is much deserved, don't you?"

She stared at him, doubt beginning to grasp hold of her. Had she misread his previous hesitation, the tension that had gripped his body only moments before? "How is it deserved? I haven't done any harm."

"You escaped your cell."

"And you're telling me you would not have done the same?"

He did not answer the question, but something passed behind his flat gaze, a subtle emotion he did not desire to think on. "That's the difference between you and me." He dragged a long finger along the arm of the chair lazily, drawing various swirls and shapes. "I would not have wound up in the cell in the first place."

He couldn't know how much the comment stung. As if she hadn't the competence to avoid capture. As if the imprisonment was *her fault*, rather than a desperate attempt to piece her broken family back together, to find love where it had been stolen, and bring it back.

"So you're saying this isn't your own form of imprisonment?" She gestured around the vast glittering hall, wondering if she was overstepping a line. "This girl isn't keeping you here, too?" Irnik had claimed the Face Stealer did not hold power over himself. She was still not entirely sure of his arrangement with Yuki, but after overhearing their conversation only a few hours ago, she assumed the Face Stealer was not here of his own free will.

The Face Stealer's irises were no longer lavender. Now they were a pure, icy green.

"Enough with this," Yuki snapped. Her gaze snagged on Apaay, and that wicked smile softened, something deeper and more honest taking its place. "I suppose this is difficult for you, traveling all this way. I'm guessing you've never been away from home this long before."

Apaay didn't answer, but she didn't need to. It sagged in the droop of her shoulders, the lines of her face.

Yuki nodded, as if Apaay had confirmed this aloud. "I've also been away from home for a long time." Soft. Stilted, as if her mouth struggled to form the words of a language she was foreign to. "The pain of missing it never really goes away."

She had not been prepared for this—this sly sneaking around to the back door, where she was vulnerable and ill-prepared.

The young girl's demeanor relaxed. She spoke to Apaay as if they were friends, and had been for a long time. "I know why you're here, child. Everyone always has something to prove. What were you running from, back at your village? What were you hoping to change?"

Apaay couldn't swallow, couldn't answer, couldn't move. It was all coming back.

"They didn't believe in you, did they?"

They hadn't, and she had wanted them to. She'd wanted them to so badly. She had come for Eska, but she had come for herself, too. The guilt swelled for needing that belief, that trust from those she loved most, to be a reason at all.

"I understand," Yuki said, mouth pinched. "They didn't believe in me, either."

The confession vibrated like the plucking of a gut string. Apaay lifted her head, meeting Yuki's too-bright eyes across the dim, lamp-lit room. For long moments, they stared at each other, sharing in the other's pain. Yuki did not shy away from it. Rather, she embraced it. She accepted her inadequacy. She took the failure and made it her own.

What did that say about Apaay, that such a confession resonated in her very soul?

This was why her parents had not wanted her to go. In the beginning, her determination had buoyed her. Now, with her eyes unclouded, the severity of the situation dragged her down. She deflated at the realization that she would probably never outrun her inadequacies.

"Don't be so hard on yourself," Yuki continued. "I mean, look at you. They had good reason to doubt you, right? What progress have you made except to fail over and over again?" She shook her head in pity. "They were right, you know. You should have listened to them. You're just a sad girl with no hope for redemption."

A trembling spread outward from Apaay's core and rolled down her arms and legs. The truth struck a chord deep within her. She could not escape it. It was a skin she could not shed. A scar that would not fade.

"No one is coming to save you. No one cares." A pause, no doubt for dramatic effect. "I hope you know that."

She had known; she had denied it.

But no more.

Yuki pressed her small hands to her temples in a rare display of exhaustion. "I'm tired of waiting, child. Now, are you going to strip, or am I going to have to come down there and do it for you?"

Had she been wrong? Apaay thought as she pushed back her hood, face blank. Deep down, did she deserve this punishment for not finding Eska's face, for not being enough?

Slow, methodical, and detached, Apaay moved at a glacial pace. Partly because of shock, and partly because no one had ever seen her nakedness save her family. Now she'd bare her body to this girl, this demon. She clung to these last few moments of protection.

A flush warmed her skin as she slipped off her mittens, then reached down and removed her outer boots, hissing out a breath at her swollen ankle, before setting them aside in a neat line. It had taken two caribou—eight legs—to create one pair of boots, as the animals' limbs were so skinny. She remembered sitting next to Mama, chewing the tough skin to stretch it wider and longer. Her soft inner boots followed. Finally, her stockings. Cool air skated along her sweaty feet, chilling them.

Next: her heavy parka. Apaay didn't look as it pooled on the ground, instead focusing her attention straight ahead. If she didn't see the clothes peeled from her sticky body, she could pretend this was not her. This was another girl. The real Apaay was back in her cell. No—the real Apaay was home.

Next: her under layer, which she wore with the fur in contact with her skin so the trapped air warmed between the hairs. The stench of her unwashed body hit, for she had not bathed since she had arrived. As soon as she removed the garment, the cold descended, a relentless pricking sensation.

Next: her trousers, sewn from a caribou Papa had killed, which had fed their community for weeks. When she stood in nothing save her breast band and underwear, Apaay held her chin high as she shed those, too. They could take her freedom, but they could not take her dignity. It was the last wall in a line of fallen defenses, and she did not dare acknowledge the hairline cracks that had recently crept through.

Body bared, Apaay stood tall in the middle of the walkway, ice flanking either side of her. The air was cutting, brutal, but it was nowhere near as painful as Yuki's frigid gaze. The Face Stealer, at least, kept his attention above her shoulders.

"There now," crooned the girl. "That wasn't too bad, was it?" Her eyes were terrifyingly alive. "You are a thin one, aren't you? All skin and bones."

"Maybe," Apaay said, refusing to give them the satisfaction of trying to cover herself, "if I wasn't half starved—" A shudder claimed her as a draft blew in from one of the depthless passageways.

"They're never satisfied, are they?" As if pleased by her own power, Yuki lounged against the back of her chair. "Let's see how well you fare without your precious furs to warm you."

The girl waved her hand at one of the mirrors, the reflection shifting into heaps of slush, a land ravaged by wind and ice.

"Have fun," Yuki said, and a gust snapped Apaay forward and flung her into the snow.

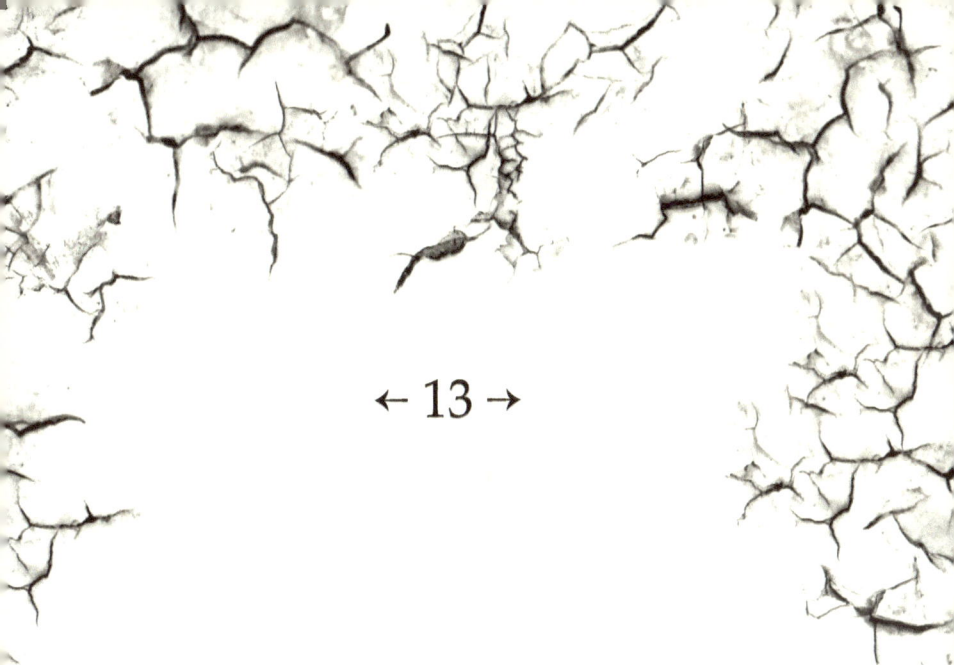

13

A paay sank into a drift so deep the snow closed over her head. She tensed, braced for the smarting of pain, like a plunge into deep water. Her body shuddered and shuddered, and her bones were shuddering, too. The scrape of ice was akin to a thousand stabbing knives.

She needed shelter.

She needed fire.

She needed to *move*.

Pushing into a standing position, Apaay dragged her feet forward. A stumble, a fall. Limping from her useless, broken ankle. Her muscles contracted furiously to pump blood through her shriveled veins and arteries, keep her internal organs alive. Twenty seconds in and her feet were already numb.

The blizzard plunged Apaay into a frozen white nightmare. The snow was so soft she sank in all the way up to her waist and was forced to dig a pathway with her hands, where the slightest curl of her fingers sent shredding agony tearing through her wrists. Stark, unbearable pain. She cupped her palms around her mouth, fingers tinged blue. Her flesh prickled against the heat.

When her legs began to lose feeling, she abandoned the task of warming her hands and switched back to digging through the snow.

Dimly, she recalled how averse she'd been to sewing over the years, unwilling to put in the time and effort toward knitting together furs and skins, a form of protection without which her people would not survive. Apaay could not escape the suffering. There was no part of her that did not burn. She had never felt this cold before. Like it had speared into the very heart of her.

The land may have descended. Apaay couldn't be sure. She did not know how far she had traveled, or if she had only imagined her feet moving. Always, she rubbed her hands up and down her arms, teeth chattering like mad. The whiteout had stolen her sight. Any time she opened her eyes to more than slits, the wind invaded and tears immediately froze against her eyelashes, tugging at the tender folds of her eyelids. She did not see a place to hide or warm herself. Eventually, she stopped looking.

A gust battered her body and sent her face-first into the snow. In seconds, snow heaped onto her naked shoulders, where it sluiced down her spine to the dip above her backside. It piled around her legs, encased her chapped skin, dusted the backs of her knees and arms. It built white walls around her, caging her in.

Drowsiness slipped quietly through her. Awake or asleep, she drifted. Her movements slowed against the twitching of her limbs, which felt heavy and awkward, as if they had been reattached to her body in different places. She blinked woozily, startled by a realization.

Death was not black. It was not red.

Death was the color white.

Tears choked her vision. Apaay wept, and the storm swallowed the sound. She opened her eyes, and darkness leaked in.

Whether it was mindlessness or terror or instinct finally making itself known, she began to dig. Deeper into the snow so it piled around her, fumbling to pat and smooth the sides into a clumsy dome as the knives gouged and twisted. Her breathing grew shallow in the passing minutes, her vision blurry. Sleep and exhaustion touched her with their drowsy hands, beckoning.

With the snow packed in place, Apaay crawled into her cave and collapsed into a ball, knees to chest, her arms, like two frozen twigs, wrapped around them. She no longer had the energy to move. Dazed, she watched the large white flakes pile up against the entrance to her shelter. There was nothing she could do about lying exposed on the snow. Without a barrier between them, it would sap her body heat quickly.

Apaay drifted as her body began to shut down, fingertips blackening as the nerves died. A dark fog rolled across her vision.

Snow dampened the howling of the wind, which sounded as if it had split into two volumes, one high and one low, the tones twining around each other, occasionally snapping in sharp points. Her eyelids fluttered. She remembered she was supposed to do something. Find an object. Return it . . .

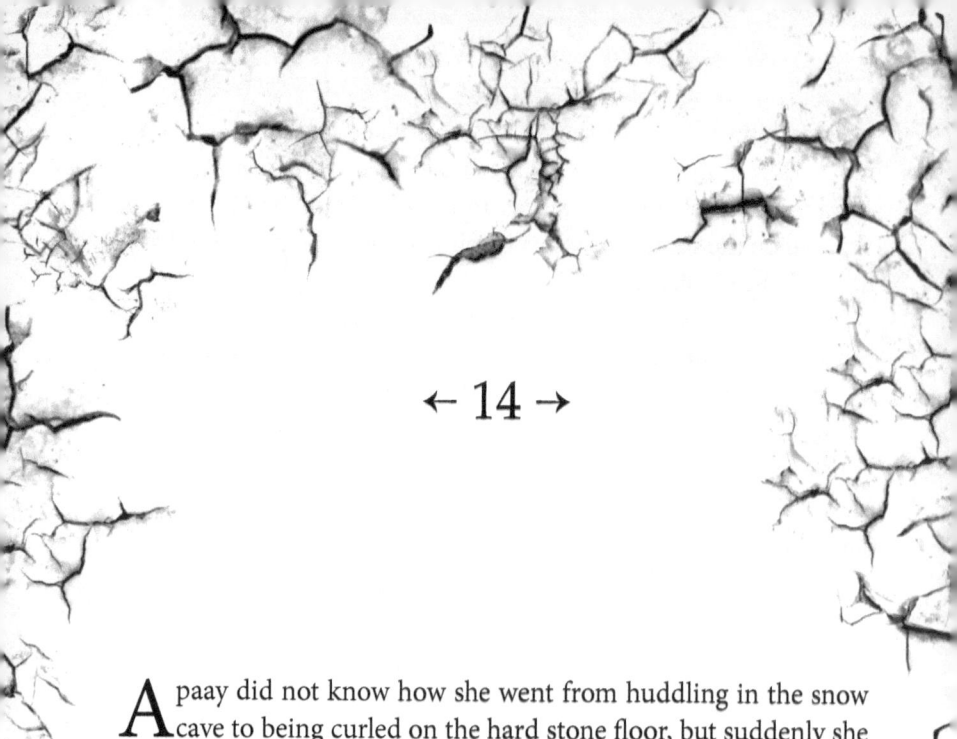

← 14 →

Apaay did not know how she went from huddling in the snow cave to being curled on the hard stone floor, but suddenly she emerged from the dim, into a world that held the shape of dreams: melting colors, soft lines, as if time itself had slowed. Everything held a drowsy feel, but when Apaay squinted, the figures in the foreground sharpened into focus.

Yuki paced the long length of the pathway leading to the dais in the labyrinth's central chamber. Small, iridescent scales winked at her ears and along her neck, catching the lamplight and alighting into muddy gold smears. This was a drenched, colorless world. Each scuff of the girl's feet sent a scraping sensation burrowing into Apaay's eardrums.

There came a deeper murmuring, and the girl whirled around, marched toward her with bared teeth, tearstained cheeks, but when Apaay tried to flinch back, she couldn't. Her legs were deep roots, her arms still branches.

The conversation grew more heated. Yuki's delicate circlet had slid partially off her head, and the ebony strands snagged on the ice.

Something cracked in the air. One of the magnificent columns flanking the dais broke clean in half, a great *boom* reverberating in the chamber as it toppled and plunged through the layer of ice, sinking into the water below. The light guttered. Shadows swooped in and cut into the hollows of the girl's cheeks, the space below her jaw, razing her features into angles. She was a hideous, ugly thing.

And then her face paled. She was staring at something Apaay seemed to be holding in her hand, though Apaay could not see what it was, could not remember ever reaching for it. She knew, however, it was the face Yuki searched for.

Devastation became her eyes, the trembling of her small mouth. Yuki did not reach for what Apaay held, as if knowing she did not deserve it. "What—"

The voice that emerged from Apaay's mouth was foreign. Dark, provocative, wrapped in lush, lush furs. "If you ever want this face returned to you, then spare her life."

Yuki swallowed, still staring. "Do you take that much pleasure in hurting me?"

"It is nothing you haven't done to countless others before."

Another tear trailed down her cheek as she lifted her face. "You don't understand. She destroyed the Sea Wolf. She destroyed what was mine." Her voice was small. Darkness seemed to bleed out from her eyes. "She didn't find the hiding place. Stupid, useless girl."

"I told you your search would be futile. Once again, you refused to listen to me."

"Please, *please*." Stricken. Agonized. "If you just told me where—"

"I gave you my answer a long time ago. It hasn't changed."

Once more, Yuki's focus settled on the face. "You'll never give it back."

"Maybe. But if she dies, I guarantee you'll never see this again for as long as you live. That, my dear Yuki, is a long time, indeed."

Her expression turned suspicious. "Why do you care? She's nothing but a stupid mortal."

For a moment, he said nothing.

Then:

"Does it bring you peace, Yuki, to hurt others when you feel nothing?"

Yuki went rigid as surprise and vulnerability overtook her. "And I suppose you know so much about that? Peace?" She spat the word.

"You bring destruction wherever you go." The muted sounds of this strange dreamworld came roaring into sharpness as she shrieked, "Get her out of my sight!"

Someone lifted her gently. Her vision flickered from dull and muddy to sharp and clear, her heart from the slow, devastating pace of a dying organ to one that was eerily silent.

The arms carrying her were solid, as was the chest her bloodless cheek rested against. Tremors quaked through her body. The arms tightened, one curving around her back, the other supporting her legs beneath her bent knees, their warmth flaring painfully against her frozen flesh. A frail cry slipped out. Blood pulsed thickly through her dead limbs, trying frantically to warm them. Blackened fingers and blackened toes. Apaay turned her head, eyes still closed, and buried her face against the chest. It smelled of wood smoke.

Something nudged at her memory. A bit of dust blown on the wind, slipping through her outstretched fingers when she tried to reach for it. Floating, floating . . .

Gone.

She was laid down on a blessedly warm surface. Heat spread from her shoulders down to the backs of her legs, her oversensitive skin rebelling against the scratch of bristly hairs as a blanket covered her. Apaay's head lolled.

"Drink this," said the voice.

No, she didn't want to drink it, didn't want to drink anything. It was poison. It was—

Dry fingers tilted back her chin. Liquid tipped into her partially open mouth, sliding down her throat, and Apaay coughed and curled onto her side. She shuddered. The liquid burned as it settled in her stomach. For a moment, Apaay swore she saw herself as if from above, so small beneath the furs, lips blue, her braid the same shade as her dead skin.

She tried sitting up.

"Lay back down." A large hand pressed against her shoulder, gently, until her strength gave out and she flopped onto her back. *Like a seal on land,* Eska would say. She was too delirious to care.

Someone gripped her foot in warm hands, agony shooting through her ankle. A sob locked in her throat. She went from feeling nothing to feeling everything as heat spread from her stomach to her limbs, tingles sharpening into relentless points. Hadn't she had enough pain for one lifetime? Two lifetimes? She wanted a world without pain.

Whatever the person near her foot was doing, the pain eventually receded. Her body, too, warmed by slow degrees.

Arms slid under her back, blanket included, and lifted her again. A few minutes later, her eyelids flew open to the sound of a startled cry, though she wasn't yet able to focus.

Clanking keys. The rusted groan of an opening door.

Apaay's head flopped away from the chest, eyes squinting at the figure barreling toward them.

Ila.

A sound akin to a wounded animal shrieked through the room as the girl lunged, clawing in a display of violence Apaay would have never guessed Ila to be capable of. The shock yanked Apaay closer to clarity. She could almost see clearly. Whoever held her swore, fumbling for a hold as Ila attempted to pull her free. She groaned at the jarring motion.

He set her on the ground.

"Happy?" the man snapped.

Ila, half crouched over Apaay, signed something to the intruder, the motions so fast Apaay couldn't keep up.

The man signed right back.

Ila went completely still, her shock apparent. A moment later the door clanged shut, footsteps dying away.

Apaay could no longer hold on to consciousness.

Apaay awoke in the dark, but not alone. Ila, curled around her beneath the blanket, had one arm wrapped around her waist. Heat against her back, breath warm on her neck. For a moment, Apaay allowed herself to sink into the sensation. A memory of another life.

She had forgotten what it felt like to be touched in genuine affection. That hands could soothe instead of harm. It had been this way before. After Mama and Papa had slipped into dreams, Apaay and Eska would sneak outside, giggles muffled behind their mittens, and drag their blankets to the top of the frosted hill where the sky was most open and honest, hiding nothing.

There, they would wait. It never took long.

Black gave way to blue and green streams as the departed souls left one life for another. *Look,* she whispered. *There.* Eska always fell asleep first, leaving Apaay to her thoughts. But in the mornings, they would wake twined together, having pulled toward the other in sleep, safe with the comfort in knowing you were loved.

At the first stirring, Ila sat up and touched Apaay's cheek with smooth, dry fingers, as if assuring herself Apaay was real. *How do you feel?*

How did she feel? Like she had gotten hammered by mounds of rocks and been left to die in a blizzard.

Biting back a groan, Apaay pushed herself into a sitting position. The blanket slipped, revealing her nakedness.

Showing no embarrassment whatsoever, Ila adjusted the blanket so it covered Apaay's breasts, smoothing it into place. For the first time since waking, Apaay realized she and Ila were not separated. They were sitting in the same cell, breathing the same air, no iron bars between.

Ila gripped her arms, waiting until Apaay met her gaze before signing, *What happened to you? You disappeared after stepping through the mirror, and I couldn't find you. I looked everywhere. I thought—* She clapped a hand over her mouth to muffle the sob. *I thought you had died.*

Her heart broke for the girl. *Oh, Ila, don't cry.*

What if I never got to see you again? Her eyes were luminous with tears, her lips trembling as she mouthed the question, hand motions jerky.

You would have, Apaay said, dragging the words up as if from a great depth. *I would have come back.*

I didn't get to say goodbye or tell you how important you are to me.

Apaay wrapped Ila in her embrace. They held each other close, breathing in tandem. She wanted to believe Ila, and a part of her did. The girl's heart was true.

But another part, the part still listening to Yuki's shredding words—*You're just a sad girl with no hope for redemption*—believed she did not deserve it.

Pulling away, Apaay thought back to what had happened. They were bits of time catching the light, then winking out into darkness. She touched her ankle. Smooth, unbroken bone. The deadened skin of her feet had returned to its golden-brown hue, flushed a rosy pink, as had her fingers and palms. Someone had carried her here, given her a blanket, healed her ankle, spoken in deep, alluring tones.

She had an uneasy feeling as to who that person had been.

The memories, as flimsy as they were, weighed so heavily as to imprint themselves in her mind. Heaviest of all was Yuki. That sick, twisted girl wanted to break her. She wanted to break Apaay because in breaking her, there would be no question as to who wielded power. There would be no question as to who was chained and who was free.

Apaay? Ila looked concerned.

It was not easy to begin. There was the room with the shifting walls. There was the Sea Wolf. There was her humiliation at stripping bare, and the blizzard.

She did not speak with conviction. Her words tripped and stumbled over themselves, especially when she mentioned the dreamworld moments, still uncertain as to what exactly had occurred.

Apaay was thankful when she ran out of words. *And you? What happened to you when we were separated?*

I was in the strangest place, Ila began. *There was a large body of water. A lake, maybe?* Palms down, she spread them wide, indicating its size. *Except it wasn't water. It didn't feel like the river we saw. When I reached down to touch it, I felt nothing.*

Apaay, not understanding Ila's situation any more than her friend did, indicated for Ila to continue.

I walked around the lake. The water, or whatever it was, looked like the sky. I didn't know what to do! Ila's hands, slim and graceful, moved swiftly through the dark, parting it effortlessly. *I wasn't sure if I should jump through or find another way around.*

Apaay clamped down on Ila's wrist. *Please tell me you didn't jump.*

All right, I won't tell you.

You jumped? she asked in disbelief.

Well, yes. What else was I supposed to do?

A slow exhalation calmed the sudden spike in emotion. Whatever had happened, it was done. Ila was alive. Safe.

I fell into a deserted hallway, her friend continued. *I was trying to find my way back to the cell when I ran into Irnik.*

Still weakened from her hypothermic ordeal, Apaay lay back down, making sure the blanket covered her. *He didn't turn you in, did he?* She did not feel guilty for asking. She did not know this man or his intentions.

Luckily, Ila didn't take offense. *Silly Apaay,* she must think, *trusting no one.*

If Ila knew how harsh the world could be, she would be mistrustful as well.

No, Ila said, *he didn't. He'd been searching for us after discovering we had escaped.*

You didn't tell him about the key, did you?

A muscle twitched in the older girl's jaw. She said, pleasantly enough, *I didn't have to. He knew you had taken it.*

Her throat bobbed. *Was he angry?*

Leaning forward, Ila adjusted the blanket so it covered Apaay's feet. She seemed tired of the thinly veiled assumptions.

Perhaps Apaay was being unfair. Perhaps it did not matter if Apaay trusted the guard. *Ila* trusted him. Ila, who had protected her when she had been vulnerable, her sweetness both honesty and deception.

He wasn't angry. More worried that something had happened. He took me back to the cell, and then an hour later you arrived, carried by— Her motion faltered. *Was that him? The demon?*

Apaay nodded. She couldn't fathom the reason he had helped her. *Saved* her. She wondered if this would be a debt she owed him, somehow, and promptly pushed it from her mind.

Are you hungry? Ila asked. *Would you like some water?*

Please.

Apaay cupped her palms in the pail of icy water Ila dragged over and drank her fill. Her teeth ached from the cold.

How long was I out for?

Nearly three days, Ila said. She fussed with the blanket again. *Why does Yuki hate you so much?*

Apaay shrugged. Because she spoke her mind? Because her hair was extra dark and luscious? She had done nothing save try to bargain for someone she loved.

That might be the problem, though. In depending on Apaay, Yuki's hands were tied. She would forever search for a face just beyond reach. It must be terribly lonely. Yuki did not seem like someone who had family. What must that do to someone's heart over time? Was it loneliness that made her this way, chipped at her soul? That man, Kenai. The Face Stealer's brother. Dead now.

Together, they leaned against the wall, watching the play of light and shadow on the ground.

What are you going to do now?

She didn't know her next step. A veil had been lifted. She could no longer ignore the dangers lurking near, the ones Apaay had pretended did not exist.

Yuki was immortal. Apaay was not. Her brush with death had made that obvious. A drop in body temperature and she would die. Too much blood loss and she would die. Infection, starvation, dehydration, drowning, decapitation, impalement—the list went on.

Instinct told her to lie low, heal, and accept this cell as enough. She had Ila. She had food and fresh water every three days, and she even had an extra blanket that did not smell of mold. Much.

But that had always been Apaay's problem. It was easy. Doing things because they were easy. Stopping, because it was easy, it was too much trouble, and what was the point?

Her community had been built upon the backs of great leaders. Papa, the strongest hunter. Silla, the most skilled tracker. Chena, the kindest. Eska, the cleverest. Mama, a wonderful mother. And who was she? A subpar hunter, an inadequate tracker, someone who had never finished anything and who probably never would. Was it so wrong though, to feel pride in her individuality?

When Apaay pushed the negative voices away, when she gave herself time to reflect, she could see that illuminated path, all the miles she'd traveled, all the obstacles she'd overcome, however messy. She had worked hard to get this far. She *had* made improvements. Maybe her original plan hadn't worked out, but it was not the end. It was only the end if she accepted a closed door.

Apaay set her shoulders. *I want to speak with Irnik.*

Ila leaned back in surprise. *Why?*

Apaay could no longer continue as she had. Namely, driven by anger and recklessness. These next steps required a more cautious, more deliberate, approach. The steps that would lead her to that shining bright light.

She needed another opportunity to explore the labyrinth.

Can you get in touch with him?

Ila, as if aware her friend had not answered her question, nodded reluctantly but did not press for more information. *He said he would be back tomorrow. You can speak with him then.*

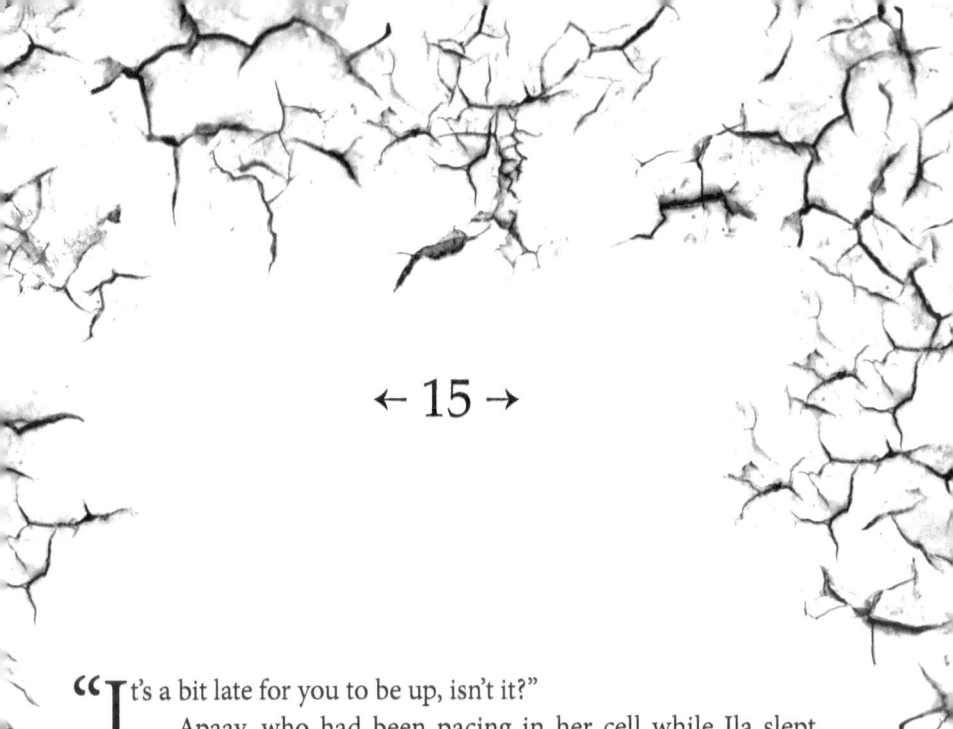

← 15 →

"It's a bit late for you to be up, isn't it?"

Apaay, who had been pacing in her cell while Ila slept, halted as Irnik strode down the length of the hall and stopped in front of the door. Firelight etched an illuminating red line around his strong form, searing against the black. The long shadow of his body eclipsed her.

Her gaze swept from his boots to his face in a quick assessment. She had not seen him since she'd stolen his key, which had been close to two weeks ago. Each day, she had waited. *He will be here,* Ila would say, full of conviction, as Apaay's hope sank lower and lower. Yet he hadn't shown.

"I could say the same thing about you." The skin around her eyes, puffy and tender with exhaustion, cried out for her to rest, and yet she could not sleep. A fiercely clawed animal awaited her in dreams.

With an amused shrug, he said, "I'm a guard. Not sleeping is what we do."

"Is that what you've been doing for the past two weeks? Not sleeping?"

His sharp gaze sought hers at the biting tone, questioning. "No."

"Then what were you doing?" Her face prickled with heat as her temper rose. "Surely you weren't busy every hour for the past twelve days?"

He said slowly, "What is this about, exactly?"

Swallowing hard, Apaay resumed her pacing, needing time to regroup. She wished there was some way to release the nervous energy coiling inside her, but the cell offered little space to run. At least her clothes had been returned to her. The parka weighed heavily against her torso. "You were supposed to stop by. Ila said you would. And I—" She bit off the rest, wondering if she had revealed more than she wanted to.

Each day of his absence, the resentment had gnawed at her, though there was relief, too, at times. Stone by stone, she built up her courage to ask him for help through all the hours of the day. Then, when he didn't show, it crumbled around her as she convinced herself it wouldn't lead to his agreement anyway. Such was the snare Apaay had set for herself. The only way to escape was to chew her own leg off. To ask him, a guard in Yuki's service, for aid.

"Were you waiting for me?" Bewildered. Thoughtful. And something else, something fleeting she missed between one word and the next. "Did you want to talk about something?"

As it was the end of another long day, her courage had long ago fled. Look at her, oily and grimed like vermin. Look at him, tall and proud and without burden. He had no reason to help her. Asking him would only be a waste of breath. "No," she snapped, moving to lean against the side bars. *Coward,* her heart spat. "It's no longer important."

Apaay knew it wasn't his fault. He wasn't a mind reader. But a part of her despised how oblivious he was. He had nothing to worry about save showing up, holding a spear, following orders, wandering down deserted hallways. How easy that life must be. If he had put himself in her position for even five minutes, he would know the waiting and the hoping and the self-loathing was slowly destroying her. Then maybe he would have come sooner.

What she didn't want to consider was the potential of this being untrue, that his life was equally difficult, different shades of the same struggles. If he had family. If his job kept him removed from them, his parents, a partner, possibly children. She had never heard of anyone leaving the labyrinth. It was safer to assume that he couldn't.

Irnik stared at her for a long moment, his face shadowed. "Obviously it was—is. But I didn't know I was needed here. I wasn't able to get away until now."

That word—*needed*. She hated that it was true. "A likely story."

"You're angry with me."

Apaay went still before ordering herself to relax. There was nothing to fear from him as far as she knew. It was nothing more than useless small talk anyway. "How perceptive of you."

His confusion deepened the hollows of his face when he frowned. "Why?"

She huffed a dark laugh and turned away, briefly checking on Ila. The older girl was curled into a ball, fist tucked beneath her cheek, mouth partially open. At some point the blanket had slipped from her shoulders. Apaay tucked it around her body so the cold could not penetrate, but she didn't turn back around. She paused with her hands on Ila's spine, fighting the oily sensation in her gut, the one that had slicked a dirty pathway through her good sense, convincing her over twelve days and twelve nights that the hall remained vacant because Irnik had abandoned them, left them to die in the bitter cold, forgotten.

It was stupid. It was so, so stupid to look for hope in places it didn't belong. She hardly knew the man. But if her family would not help her, why not Irnik? He'd claimed he was, after all, Ila's friend. And a friend of a friend should warrant consideration.

"The fact that you're asking," she said, her back still to him, "tells me more about you than the question itself."

When he did not respond, she turned, but remained in the shadows, for once glad of them. Here, at least, she could watch him unseen.

The guard's face did not disappoint. Strained, closed off. Both frustrated and perplexed, wrapped tightly in what she thought might be guilt. "I only came to check on Ila, and to ask if you needed anything else: food, more blankets."

"We're fine."

"All right, then. I'll leave."

His footsteps were near-silent on the stones, and fading. Apaay rushed to the front of the cell and gripped the bars. What did that say about her, that she wanted him to leave and yet gave chase, and would have kept going were this door not in the way? A look, a laugh, a touch. She did not crave much these days.

"I couldn't sleep," she called.

He stopped at the end of the corridor. She was surprised he did not keep going. "Bad dreams?"

"Something like that." Many nights she dreamed she stood on the edge of her village, an observer unable to approach, and it was slowly killing her.

As silently as he had retreated, he returned to lean against the wall in what she would consider a casual, unthreatening pose. "Have you had many bad dreams since you arrived?"

That, she decided, was far too personal. And none of his business. "As a matter of fact, I have. It's always the same one. I dream this guard comes to my cell and pries into my personal life, and due to rather unfortunate circumstances, the next morning his nose falls off."

The full belly laugh hit her like a spray of cold water. It was the happiest sound she had heard in weeks. It certainly did not belong in a dungeon. The shadows knew, and quickly snuffed it out.

"I guess I had that one coming."

"At least you're not slow."

He rolled his eyes good-naturedly. "What's your name?"

"You mean Ila hasn't told you?" she said, in a way that made clear Apaay knew her friend had.

He shrugged. "I'd like to hear it from you."

Oh, for the love of—

"It's Apaay."

For some reason this seemed to please him more than it should. "It's nice to meet you, Apaay."

"I would say it's nice to meet you, too, but I don't want to get your hopes up."

Using his shoulder to push himself off the wall, he said, "Look, I don't have to be here if you don't want me to be. I can leave. You probably need to sleep anyway."

Apaay touched her forehead to the bars. And slowly the tension in her shoulders drained. "Ila thinks I should give you a chance," she muttered.

The skin tightened around his mouth. "Don't sound so reluctant."

"Can you blame me?" The question was sharp, louder than she intended. She checked to make sure she had not woken Ila, but the older girl's back rose and fell steadily beneath the blanket. She supposed Ila could be feigning sleep. It's certainly what Apaay would have done. "You're lucky Ila likes you."

"Who knows, you might grow to like me, too."

"Don't hold your breath."

At his snort, she said with a frown, "Ila speaks very highly of you. She says she's lucky to have you as a friend."

Irnik slid down the wall and stretched out his trouser-clad legs, crossing them at the ankles. They looked to be sewn of polar bear skins, the soft white pelt coated in grime. "She's a strong woman with an unbreakable spirit. On the contrary, I am lucky to have *her* as a friend."

At least they agreed on one thing.

"She said she's known you for a long time, that she can't remember her life before this." Her anger sparked at the thought and caught fire. "Do you know what happened to her? How she ended up here?"

Long fingers tapped against his knee. "Shouldn't this be something you discuss with Ila?"

Her stomach turned. He was right. It was none of her business. No doubt Ila had asked Irnik this same question. But if she did not ask, she would not know.

"I should." Apaay cleared her throat. "But I thought I'd ask you, too."

He bowed his head in thought. "I can only speak of what I've experienced myself."

Back home, it was the same. People only shared what they had seen or heard directly. If they had not experienced it, they kept their silence, not wanting to spread falsehoods.

Irnik said, "The only thing I know is that Ila had been left to die, and someone brought her here so she could heal. She wasn't that old. Five, maybe? She'd been badly burned. As for her imprisonment—" He shrugged. "Yuki likes things organized, and a cell assured Ila would not be underfoot."

That made sense, she supposed, except . . .

"Has Yuki ever visited Ila?"

The slow shake of his head caused a few strands of hair to tug free of the knot at the base of his skull. "Not that I am aware of."

And yet the girl remained caged, month after month, year after year, until she would eventually pass into eternity.

Yuki did nothing without intention. Every step was planned, cutting into a carefully laid path. Why lock Ila away for all these years? Yuki did not visit her. Did not speak of her. Did not care. And yet she sent food and water. A guard to ensure Ila remained alive, contained. It did not make sense.

Unless Ila was not Yuki's prisoner at all.

Was it possible the Face Stealer held her prisoner instead? And if so, what could he want with her except to eventually add another face to his collection? He may have some use for an older face if he was letting her age. Although it was possible the face would age regardless of whether it was attached to a body or not.

Apaay winced at the gruesome thought, the deadened taste already hot and sticky in her mouth. She would have to consider the notion later, when she was not distracted.

Crossing her arms, she said to the guard, "If you truly are as good a friend as you claim, why haven't you ever helped her escape?"

Somewhere down the hall, one of the lamps doused, leaving the hallway in further obscurity. Irnik did not appear to notice. "You've seen this place. How hard it is to leave." He flung out an arm toward the passage, the stone sooty and burning red from flame. "One wrong step and you're dropped into a nightmare." Drawing in his arm, he frowned. "But that sounds like a load of excuses, doesn't it?"

He chuckled at himself and shook his head, and Apaay convinced herself it was a disappointed sound, self-deprecating, as if knowing he had failed Ila in some vital way. "In your village, do they ever talk about the war?"

Her gaze was keen as she looked at him. Apaay knew little about the conflict, as the Analak had not participated, but from what the elders claimed, it had apparently peaked around the year she'd been born, resulting in bloodshed between the five Unua nations that led to the thick, bold lines of newly marked territories. No longer did the Analak, no longer did the Unua—whether owl or caribou or seal or wolf or bear—inhabit one unified land. The North, once untouched and whole, had broken.

"Not very often," Apaay said. "My people tend to keep to themselves, mostly."

"Understandable. It's a complicated piece of history. It was brutal and bloody, and there's still a lot of unrest, even nearly twenty years later. The times I wanted to help Ila escape, it was too dangerous. We didn't have anywhere to go, as the Unua nations are far more aggressive at guarding their territories than they used to be. I figured it was safest for her to remain here until I could secure safe asylum."

That made sense, she supposed. They would need someplace where Yuki and the Face Stealer would not find them. Yuki seemed like someone who would delight in giving chase.

It was nice to know, at least, that Irnik *had* thought about freeing Ila, even if nothing had ever come to fruition.

"Does that answer your question?" he asked.

She regarded him steadily, not wanting him to know that she believed what he said, even though she knew it was unwise. "For now."

Silence descended, and it was waiting. Waiting for either of them to speak or move or smile or blink. Apaay used the lull to gather her thoughts, however scattered they were, because she could not afford to waste any more time. He was here, and she needed him. Now was the time for action.

"Look, the reason I wanted to speak to you was because I need a favor."

His eyebrows crept upward. "Oh?"

Staring at the ground was cowardly, Apaay decided. She lifted her gaze. "It's about the Face Stealer."

The reaction was immediate: eyes veiled, no longer friendly. A twinge pinched her chest at how quickly the door had slammed shut, blocking her way through. She should have expected this. The demon's name was poison. She wondered if the Face Stealer had destroyed one of Irnik's loved ones.

Apaay shook her head. "Forget it."

"I'm listening."

The man kept surprising her. And it allowed her to view him with a little less suspicion, a little less doubt.

Apaay took the longest, deepest breath of her life. Digging down deep for that bit of courage, punching through the layers of hardened fear, was like taking a plunge into deep water.

The trust between them was tentative at best. If she wanted to take, she must also give. Something personal—a story. Her very personal, very real story.

"The Face Stealer stole my sister's face." At his blank expression, she added, "It's supposedly hidden somewhere in the labyrinth. The girl—Yuki—gave me a chance to search for it, but I ran out of time. As punishment, the Face Stealer—" Her voice cut off. She could not utter what she had witnessed, and even the brief thought brought back a sinking dread.

The lines fanning Irnik's mouth deepened. "What did he do?"

She shook her head. Qavak's life would never be the same. "He hurt a boy from my village. That's all you need to know."

"What exactly are you asking me?"

Now came the difficult part.

"Yuki won't give me another chance in the labyrinth, for whatever reason. But I think—and this may sound odd—" Feeble laughter died in her mouth, caged behind her teeth. She may as well state the world rained fish. "I think the Face Stealer could be of some help." *Deep breath, Apaay.* "That's where you come in."

His curious gaze roved over her face, searching. She was not sure what, exactly, he looked for. "How so?"

She remembered the conversation she'd overheard between the demon and the girl. A gathering. Something stolen. She remembered their pain leaking into the empty space, a history still raw.

"I'm hoping the Face Stealer might be able to sway Yuki. And I'm hoping you might be able to ask him to, uh, speak with me? Without Yuki overhearing, I mean."

Irnik blinked at her in disbelief. "Are you mad?"

"No." Desperate. Though perhaps they were one and the same.

"What makes you think the Face Stealer would ever listen to me?"

She struggled to piece together her reasoning. "Well, you're a guard. And a man. And the other guards would definitely tell Yuki of my plan . . ." She trailed off, aware of the cracks weakening her reasoning. But sometimes you couldn't depend on logic or reason. You had to do what was necessary. You had to do what was right for yourself, for your life. All she wanted was to reunite her family.

She settled onto the ground so they were at the same level. "As much as I wish things were different, right now you're my only option."

"You must be desperate if you're putting your trust in me."

She didn't acknowledge the comment. He was only trying to antagonize her. "Do you think you can sway him?"

"How would I possibly sway him?"

Apaay lifted her hands and dropped them in her lap. "How should I know? Offer him your face. That might put you in his good graces," she muttered darkly.

Irnik crossed his arms over his chest, the caribou hair of his parka rustling. "I'm not giving him my face just so you can talk to him."

"What about your hands? Does he collect those?"

He smirked. "I do believe he's called the Face Stealer, not the Hand Stealer."

Sighing, she pressed her palms against her burning eyes. No matter how sleep tugged at her consciousness, her mind would not quiet. She longed for darkness. She longed for peace, a balm to soothe her overwrought senses. All matters of joking aside, she needed Irnik to speak with the Face Stealer. Not longed. Not wanted. *Needed.*

But, Apaay conceded reluctantly, perhaps she was approaching this wrong. She wanted to demand things of him. She wanted him to feel the bite of stone as his spine hit the wall, darkness pressing in. She wanted him to know how easy it was to slip quietly into shadows, to become the cold and the dark, as she was, fading bit by bit and day by day. Then he would acquiesce. Then he would agree.

It was not right, but did it truly matter, in the end?

Tamping down a surge of irritation, Apaay asked, "How did you come to work for Yuki?"

The tapping of his fingers paused as he went still. "Why do you want to know?"

The harsh tone took her aback. How odd, that his mistrust only made her want to win him over. "I'm curious. It's a simple question."

"No," he said, rubbing a hand over his chin. A faint, prickly shadow edged his jaw. "I don't think curiosity is the reason you're asking. Trust goes two ways." The statement ricocheted off the stone, returning fainter, swallowed by the uncertain quiet. His voice deepened with gritty emotion. "You want me to trust you? Start by telling the truth."

The truth, when this monster of a fortress, and everything in it, were built upon lies?

"Information," Apaay said. "I'm asking to gather information. If I'm going to find my sister's face, I need to know as much as I can about this place and the people in it. If our positions were switched, you would do the same." There now. That wasn't so difficult. "Now, are you going to answer the question or not?"

"Maybe, if you had a little more patience."

Irnik had no idea what he was talking about. She was patient. *Extremely* patient. The most patient person she knew.

Ever the obedient child, Apaay folded her hands in her lap and waited for him to speak, which took longer than she liked, but there was little she could do about it.

"It's a strange story," the guard began.

Nearby, water pattered onto the floor steadily.

Apaay shifted into a more comfortable position, tucking her legs to the side. Her knees pained her if she bent them for too long. "And?"

"I came into her service years ago. I was living in the Eastern Territory at the time."

Where the seal Unua dwelled. Their land bordered the coast, as they needed direct access to the sea, for they were said to be children of the Sea Mother.

A frown tugged at Apaay's mouth. "And you voluntarily wanted to work for Yuki?"

His expression was grim. "I didn't say it was voluntary."

"Then why *are* you here?"

Irnik uncrossed his ankles and said, "Honestly, the less you know, the better. Information is valuable. Being in possession of information only means others can take it from you. It can be dangerous if it ends up in the wrong hands."

"Yuki's and the Face Stealer's, you mean."

A slow nod. "Exactly."

In some ways, Irnik reminded her of a different man, one who was both confident and understanding. One who she had not seen since the month of shedding antlers: Papa.

Apaay slumped closer to the ground. Missing her family was an ache that occasionally flared, never truly leaving her. It was the thought of never. Never hearing their voices, or feeling their touch again. She hoped they were safe.

"Do you have family?" she whispered.

A muscle feathered in his jaw, and he dipped his head so his face was shielded, firelight gleaming against the true-black of his hair. "I did," he said, his response equally soft. "But they're dead now."

"Oh." She pressed her fingertips to her mouth, lips brushing the mitten's warmth. "I'm sorry." She wondered how they had died, but of course she did not want to reopen old wounds, as it was clear the subject pained him. Still, she wondered.

"You couldn't have known. And anyway, it was a long time ago."

But time, she knew, did not heal all wounds.

Irnik rose to his feet, making it clear their conversation had reached its end. But she found she was not ready to let go of his company yet.

Apaay asked, with sudden inspiration, "Do you want to hear a joke?"

He tilted his head, considering the question. "That depends."

"On what?"

"On whether it's funny."

Apaay scoffed. Honestly. "Trust me, it's funny."

"Ila doesn't think so."

Sucking in an outraged gasp, she turned to take in sleeping Ila. Since when had Ila had time to discuss her jokes with Irnik? And the better question: Why was she not raving about them?

With a haughty sniff, she again faced the guard. "Ila has no idea what she's talking about."

A smile broke across his face, and his eyes were lost to folds of skin. Laughter rumbled in his chest, little more than vibrations, and Apaay's lips twitched in response. She could get a bit defensive when it came to her jokes. All in good humor, of course. But seriously. Her jokes were good. Better than good. They were fantastic, and anyone who thought otherwise had a terrible sense of humor.

Irnik waved a hand, telling her to get on with it.

Apaay leaned forward, already anticipating breathless laughter, twinkling eyes, maybe even a wayward snort. "What do you call a snow owl with an attitude?"

"A snow owl with an attitude," he murmured, tapping a finger against his chin in exaggeration. "Snow owl . . . attitude . . ." A minute or two passed as he mulled it over.

Eventually, he shrugged. "I give up."

"Really? It didn't even look like you were trying."

"If I scrunch up my face in concentration, will that convince you?"

"Not really, no. You're sure you give up?"

He tipped back on his heels. "Positive."

Apaay was already snorting at the answer. It was so bad it was good, or so good it was bad. "A scowl!"

Irnik's groan filled the hall. "That was bad." One single, hard laugh. "Very bad."

"You claim it was bad, and yet you laughed," she said, pointing at him. "So the joke's on you."

Palms up, he said, "You're right." With a crooked smile, Irnik stretched the kinks from his legs, which Apaay made a point not to stare at. He half turned, hesitated, then faced her fully. Apaay, who was still sitting on the ground, tilted her head back to see him. "What you asked about the Face Stealer, I need a few days to think it over." His face tightened in seriousness. "But should I ask him, and should he agree, telling terrible jokes will be the least of your problems."

"I'm not afraid of him," Apaay growled, pushing to her feet and shoving her face against the bars. "So if that's what you're worried about, don't be. I can handle one face-stealing demon."

"Maybe not," he said, voice fading as he disappeared down the corridor. "But you should be."

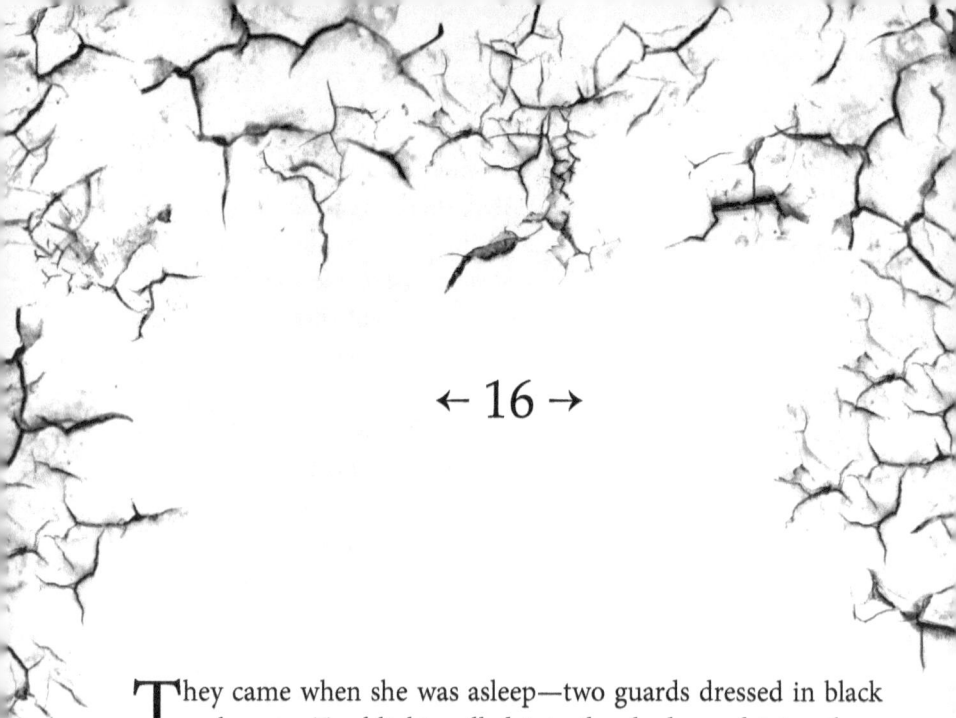

← 16 →

They came when she was asleep—two guards dressed in black and green. Torchlight spilled into the shadows, driving them back into the gaps, where they writhed and lay still. Beside her, Ila stirred, squinting against the brightness. She gasped and sat up, and clamped her hand on Apaay's wrist. Damp skin, trembling. The girl was still half asleep.

Apaay did not recognize the first guard, but she recognized the second. Bile slicked her throat from his stench, fetid like a whale's corpse. They were not here to bring them food, though it had been some time since Apaay and Ila had eaten. Her hollow gut did not lie.

The door screeched open. "The Face Stealer is expecting you."

Barely masking her surprise, Apaay rose to her feet. It had been three days since she'd spoken with Irnik. Apaay had marked the passing time on the walls, shared stories of her childhood with Ila, and tried to remain positive as the bleakness of her situation threatened to intrude. She'd had her doubts that Irnik would pull through. She had not trusted his word because she had not wanted to hope he was anything more than a guard battling boredom, amusing himself with the pitiful prisoners.

Apaay vowed to thank him the next time they spoke.

The guards yanked her out the door and down the hall. They ascended the staircase to the first level before proceeding down a curved hallway, which Apaay assumed wrapped around the central chamber. The next turn led them through a luminous white passage. Everything—floor, ceiling, walls—had been consumed by hard frost.

As their footsteps crunched in the hallway, the walls transformed to thinnest, sheerest ice. Apaay couldn't help but admire its loveliness, how moonlight speared through the oval windows high above and blazed along the fragile surface. It comforted her, to know there could be beauty in ugly things. She focused on that rather than where this walk would lead. On occasion, she passed a mirror and had to convince herself it was her own reflection she saw, not Eska's. Her sister was everywhere and nowhere.

Soon, a breeze skimmed across the fur of her hood, her skin tingling beneath its touch. She leaned toward it, yearning—so much yearning.

This air felt alive.

They reached two massive doors carved of moon-pale wood. One hard push, and they were through.

There was no stone, no suffocation—merely the crunch of packed snow underfoot—and no ceiling save a sky dusted with stars. The night was so dark that it acted as a cloth pulled across her eyes. Apaay sucked in a lungful of air. Dusky light from the low-hanging half-moon pooled across the ground, coloring the snow a pearly gray. A ring of frozen trees, naked limbs laden with white mounds, encircled her, ornately chiseled high-backed benches arranged artfully between them. Beyond, a meandering footpath led to a small frozen pond. Farther onward, a towering white wall encompassed the area. It appeared to be a garden of sorts.

The Face Stealer lounged on one of the benches, watching her. One leg stretched out, head tilted, his casual pose heightened the anxiety snaking through her. What frightened her wasn't his power so much as that he was extremely difficult to read. Rather than a parka, today he wore a snug vest atop lean caribou trousers, which were tucked into calf-high boots of intricate design. Mama owned a pair of similar beauty, which she had acquired from an elder who was recognized for her outstanding and elaborate boot designs. For over sixty years, this woman had chewed and sewed and pieced together furs and skins into reflections of the North so that others might carry that vision with them always. The woman's love for their home was plain.

When he dismissed the guards a moment later, her heart began to pound, and Apaay had half a mind to call them back.

They were alone.

"Have a seat," he said, gesturing toward the space beside him on the bench. She could not read his expression in the dim, but she did notice the three stacked beads attached to the end of a single slender braid. Blue. An unusual color.

Nervous laughter tickled the back of her throat. Did one voluntarily stick their hand into the mouth of a polar bear? "I'll stand, if it's all the same to you."

He lifted his head a fraction, and his eyes, when they caught the moonlight, were reamed silver. Settling into a storm-cloud gray, like the moon in hiding. "A bit mistrustful, are we?"

"You: demon. Me: prisoner." Her voice grated. "What is there to trust?"

He shrugged. "Suit yourself."

Unfolding his long body from the bench, he stood.

Apaay stumbled back a step, unable to catch her breath. Tendrils of night licked along the edges of his leanness. She had never seen that before, that physical manifestation of his power. He'd always seemed less than human, but now he appeared even less so. "What are you doing?"

"I'd rather not shout across the garden." That vulpine smile. "If it's all the same to you."

She measured the space between them. It was hardly shouting distance, as he'd claimed. It was hardly any distance at all.

"Something wrong?"

Her gaze, which had wandered, snapped back to his face. "Nothing." Everything. "I was just wondering if this was real or not." She waved a hand around. "Or if it's all inside my head."

"And what if it was inside your head?"

"I suppose it would be nice to know I could kill you without consequences."

His smile widened, a touch predatory. "Fear not. You are no longer inside the labyrinth."

With a swift nod, she half turned away, using the pretense of admiring the garden to peek at him from beneath her eyelashes. No daggers, from what she could see. At least none that were visible. No spear either. This was good. Apaay would not be able to overpower him—the breadth of his shoulders and chest held much strength—but once she had Eska's face safely in her pocket, she would most likely have to fight him off to escape. It reassured her to know he would not be carrying weapons when the time came.

Casually, he drawled, "Enjoying the view?"

Blood bloomed hotly in her cheeks. It wouldn't surprise her one bit to learn he had eyes in the back of his head. "Don't flatter yourself."

"Is it flattery if it's the truth? Come now. Don't be shy."

When Apaay didn't respond, his gaze dropped to her face, and the smile lost some of its allure. "You look terrible."

Apaay wasn't yet too far gone not to scowl. It was good to know that in addition to his nauseating personality, he had terrible manners as well. She walked a few feet down the path before turning back around, the trees' bare branches arching over her, sharp tines puncturing through the snow like twisted icicles. The extra distance helped clear her head. Even a thousand miles did not seem far enough. "Seeing as I haven't bathed or been properly fed since I arrived here, I'd say I have a reason to." Four weeks she had been here. Two months total of absence from her village if she included the weeks of travel. It wasn't enough time for her family to lose hope. At least, she convinced herself as much. "And anyway, I'm not here to talk about my looks."

Hands behind his back, he began to circle her. "What did you want to discuss? The guard I spoke to was certainly . . . adamant."

Something in his tone put her back up. Three days she had not seen Irnik. She thought he'd been avoiding her. "If you hurt him—"

"And what if I did?" He quirked one elegant eyebrow, mouth sly at his own deviousness, and continued to circle, intruding into her personal space. "Surely you don't care for the poor boy."

She didn't care for him. How could she care for someone she didn't even know? But he had helped her when no one else had, and maybe carrying a spear did not make one as power-hungry as she had suspected. "That," she said, hating the quaver in her voice as he passed near enough for her to feel the caress of his power, "is none of your concern."

His irises sparked gold. She didn't know what he felt, as the rest of his face remained neutral. Challenge? Amusement? If only he was not so impossible to read. "What did you do, throw him in a cell? Were you jealous he had the courage to stand up for what was right?"

The gold flared like two small suns. "Such harsh assumptions." She did not know why he looked so entertained. "You don't need to worry about your precious guard. I did not throw him in a cell. Trustworthy guards are difficult to come by nowadays. And anyway, I do love a good sparring match."

Apaay was about to respond that Irnik was not *her* guard when the Face Stealer said, "So tell me why you wanted to speak with me."

"I'm here to discuss my sister's face."

"Ah, yes. *That*." He sighed as if bored and settled onto one of the benches. "I can't decide if you're stupid or just extremely stubborn."

The barb pricked beneath her breastbone, sharper than she had anticipated. There had been a time when Apaay would have fought for her honor. Even at home, she had resisted others' disappointment and frustration with some success. Not in captivity. Here, she could do little but eat and sleep and think. She started thinking her integrity was too small a thing to matter. Thought there were other, more important, things.

Her shoulders slumped. "Look, all I want is another chance in the labyrinth. Yuki won't listen to me, but she might listen to you."

"You sound certain of this."

"Why shouldn't she listen to you? That's fair."

His smile was more ironic than anything. "My dear girl, nothing in life is ever fair. It's time you got used to it."

Trying to compromise with a demon, while not her best idea, was not the worst, either. Two words: pet whale.

"You're a prisoner, too," Apaay said, going for a different angle. "You work for Yuki." She still didn't know what sway she held over him. "Can't you see why I need this chance?"

His face, carefully blank, gave away nothing, but Apaay recognized the expression. She'd worn it many times. A front to mask her guilt. And her shame.

"You assume much," he murmured.

Apaay bit her lip. "Am I wrong?"

Once more he stood, and Apaay stepped back to give him space. "You are right about one thing and wrong about the other." He wandered to one of the trees, reaching up to pluck a crystal fruit, cupping it in one large palm. She only knew it was fruit because Papa had once traded whale meat for a bowl full of sweet, round foods that burst in her mouth, and they looked eerily similar. "Yes, I work for Yuki. No, I am not a prisoner."

If this was indeed the truth, it was a surface truth at best. Apaay sensed a power imbalance between the two, and yet both possessed something the other desired. The Face Stealer would serve as a powerful ally to the young girl. But maybe his power was greater than Yuki desired, which complicated matters.

"If you're not a prisoner, then what's stopping you from passing along my message?"

"Honestly? Yuki's not interested in your message, nor in giving you a chance after your escape attempt. Be lucky she didn't kill you on the spot."

Apaay didn't understand. What was worse, she wanted the reasoning behind his decisions, because then she would not feel so aimless in attempting to navigate her situation. "Then why did you save me before if you won't help me now?" Apaay had seen death, had felt its skeletal form pull the last breaths from her body. He'd told Yuki to spare her life. Then he had healed her.

His eyes snapped to hers, a swirl of hues, searching. She liked to think a layer separating them peeled away. "How do you know that? You were unconscious."

"I don't know." She really had no idea. The voice speaking to Yuki had come from her mouth, but it had been his. She knew that now. "I overheard your conversation. You could have let me die, but you didn't. Why?"

A faint breeze rattled the stripped branches of the trees. He did not respond for some time, and Apaay wondered if it was purposeful or if he truly did not know the answer to that question.

"I'll admit, I'm intrigued," he said finally. It was spoken with enough arrogance to make her feel smaller than she already did. "I haven't come across a human with such bullheaded tendencies in quite a long time. It's very entertaining." He laughed at this, perhaps remembering her failed first task. "I may think Yuki to be cruel and loathsome, but you have to admit there's a certain artistry to her manipulations."

As far as she was concerned, the Face Stealer was equally cruel and loathsome. "So you *do* dislike Yuki. Is that why you won't give her the face you stole?"

"It's a little more complicated than that. So long as she has what's mine, she'll never get the face back. Yuki knows this. But she's far too smart to give up the only leverage she has over me. So she makes me do her dirty work."

Stealing faces, he meant.

"Don't get me wrong," he said, his mouth a cruel line. "There's something about inciting terror that gets my blood roiling." Deep laughter. "But I'd rather have the choice of when and where I wreak havoc. Yuki, of course, doesn't care. The more faces I steal, the more likely it is that some poor soul will wander into the in-between searching for it, which is exactly what she wants. The thing is, Yuki can't force someone into the in-between. They have to come here of their own free will. It's her hope that one of the prisoners will eventually find where I've hidden the face she seeks." He lifted his head, and his eyes were two slate stars glittering. "But it's a fool's hope at best. No one leaves the in-between. It's a waiting place for Yuki, so it's a waiting place for those who come here."

So that's what Yuki used the Face Stealer for. And that's why Yuki was so furious when Apaay hadn't completed her task. It made her wonder how long this had gone on for. How many people had reached the in-between, only to fail the game Yuki set for them? It sounded like a horrible cycle, to have hope and then find it crushed again and again. Apaay hated herself a little, for finding a piece of Yuki she understood.

"What did she take from you?" Apaay asked.

The demon showed her his back, the thick length of his hair, appearing to fight some internal battle within himself. Deciding, maybe, how to respond. He settled on a resigned, "Something far more important, I assure you."

Which told her exactly nothing, but was unsurprising. The Face Stealer would be nothing without his secrets and walls. "If you want your possession back, why not just kill her?"

He turned around. "How very astute of you." It was spoken in a way that suggested the opposite. Apaay was growing tired of the veiled insults. "I've considered it. However, she's difficult to kill, for reasons beyond your comprehension. Doing so would also ruin any chance I have at seeing my possession returned. I can't obtain it if she's dead. No, I have to acquire it by other means." He studied her as if in a new light.

Apaay returned the stare warily. Everything about this man was sharp and edged. "So will you tell her?"

"Tell her what?"

Oh, he knew exactly how to grind down her patience until it was nothing more than a sorry nub. "The *message*."

He rolled his eyes. "What is it?"

She lifted her chin, a gesture full of bravado she didn't have. If she wanted to survive, he must never smell her fear. "Tell her Apaay demands to speak to her immediately. And if she refuses, tell her I would expect nothing less of a coward."

Low laughter carried across the garden, too intimate for enemies. The shadows seemed to deepen around them. "Bold words for one behind bars." Was that a trace of respect in his gaze? "No doubt you'll regret them."

The Face Stealer tossed up the fruit, caught it one-handed. "You really want me to pass on the message? Fine. But let me tell you something about Yuki." His expression grew serious, and everything inside Apaay went taut at his next words. "She's not one to be crossed. Attempt to play her game, and she will crush you without lifting a finger. There's nothing she enjoys more than exploiting someone's weakness." His mouth softened in thoughtfulness. "I'm not sure whether it's a gift or a curse."

"She's a child."

"If that's what you think," he said, "then you have no hope of leaving this place."

"Maybe if I had a little *help*."

The Face Stealer shook his head, threw the fruit up, caught it smoothly. "You think me passing along a message will help? How naïve of you. You were a fool to come here. You won't leave this place alive."

Apaay flung out her hands. It felt good to express emotion in some way, even if it was not clawing at the demon's face like she wanted, shoving a dagger through his heart like she wanted, watching this place rot and burn like she wanted. "Then let me make this mistake on my own."

A low hum sounded in his throat. "Maybe it doesn't seem obvious to you, but I'm doing you a favor. You stay in your cell, and Yuki forgets about you." A soft tinkle sounded—he had crushed the fruit in his hand. "Unless you'd prefer turning into a block of ice. In which case, be my guest."

It took a moment for Apaay to recover from her surprise. "Don't make this about my safety. This is about you taking the coward's way out."

He picked another fruit from the tree. "You're not doing a very good job at convincing me to speak with Yuki."

"What's the point? You're basically telling me that coming here was a waste of time."

"Not a complete waste. You got to talk to me, didn't you?" The cunning smile made a reappearance.

It was decided, then. He would not help her.

"I feel sorry for you," she whispered.

The night deepened with the tightening along his jaw, a small crack in his façade. "Why?" He threw the fruit up.

"Because you have no idea what it means to love."

His hand faltered, the object slipping past his outstretched fingers to shatter on the ground. He didn't look at her when he spoke. He was staring at the glittering shards. "And you know this because of what? Ten minutes of total conversation?"

"No," she said, voice near a growl. "I know this because of what you *are*."

Apaay would never, for as long as she lived, forget the sight of young Qavak's face twisted in terror as the Face Stealer loomed over him. She would never forget how his eyes, nose, and mouth had vanished within the space of a single breath, and that he had been doomed to darkness, and hadn't a choice.

The Face Stealer finally looked up, and she saw everything in his black gaze. "Maybe you're right," he grated out, ice crunching underfoot. The sharp breaks drove into the stillness. "I don't know what it means to love. I don't know what it means to sacrifice. I could never understand what you have gone through. Of course you know everything about me. I stole your sister's face. Who am I but a heartless demon?"

Apaay struggled to quiet her breathing. Why were his words filled with such pain? "That's right," she said, though now it felt wrong, as if maybe she had, impossibly, hurt him in some way. "You have no idea what it means to lose someone you care about."

No life in his expression. Not even a flicker. "We're done here." Pivoting on his heel, he strode toward a door cut into the side of the fortress. Behind, she heard the guards approach.

Apaay tracked the line of his back as it grew smaller and smaller. He was almost to the door. When he vanished, she would be taken back to her cell, that dank hole where nothing grew and nothing ever would. Fighting tears, she tilted back her head to look at the sky, so much larger on this night. They would take this from her, too, even though she'd just gotten it back.

"Wait." Apaay ran forward a short distance, then slowed when the Face Stealer turned and slid his hands into the pockets of his trousers, his face inhumanly cruel and cold. "I'm—" Sorry? No, she wasn't sorry. He did not deserve an apology, least of all from her.

But she could play the game for a little while longer, at least. "Please. Can you please pass on my message?"

Gaze shuttered, he said, "I'll think about it."

Then he vanished in a pocket of darkness.

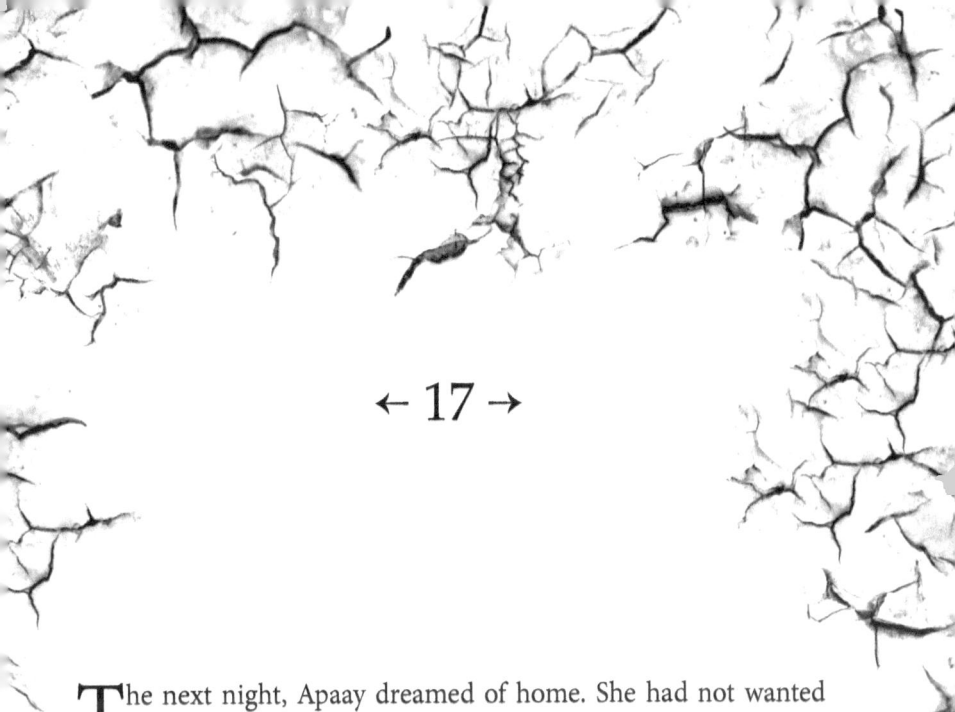

17

The next night, Apaay dreamed of home. She had not wanted to dream, because she had not wanted to hope. In dreams, the world was good and pure, but when she woke, when she threw off that dark, sleeping cloak, the dreamworld fractured and fragmented, and she remembered where she was, and that she was far from home.

In the dream, Apaay passed through the land with silent speed and quiet grace. The sky was beginning to lose its dark luster, signaling the long night was over halfway through. Snow lay thick upon the ground, hills and valleys of hard frost. Apaay moved quickly. She was acutely aware of the vibrations in the earth, whether bear or bird or fox or mole. Her vision was crisp and clear and somehow different, yet the same.

Open plains gave way to frostbitten conifers. Stacked stones arranged in the shape of a sturdy column appeared, this cairn located some five miles from her village. Apaay wanted to quicken her pace, but could do little except growl in frustration. Merely a passenger in this body, she was bound to follow where her feet traveled, no faster or slower.

Soon Apaay stopped at the edge of the tree line atop a rise, her community within shouting distance. People milled about, the ones who hadn't left to hunt for food. It was not many. A polar bear pelt had been stretched out alongside one of the ice houses, the meat no doubt having been consumed. A flash of rage warred with another emotion, though she wasn't sure where it came from, wasn't sure if it even belonged to her. Regret? She wasn't sure why she felt regret when all she truly felt was helplessness and longing.

Why was she standing here, so separate, so still? Stupid, useless legs—move!

A tingle tickled the column of her spine, shooting up to the base of her skull. A rolling fog swept in, and Apaay awoke curled on the ground, one fist cushioning her cheek. Ila was running her fingers through the knots in Apaay's wavy locks, the gentle tugging on her scalp soothing. If she didn't think about this too deeply, she could almost imagine it was Eska's hands touching her with so much love.

Ila pulled on one of the skinny braids mixed in with Apaay's waves, a shard of white bone tied off at the end. *What is this from?*

Apaay reached back and brought it around to look at. She smiled sleepily. *This is from when I made my first kill.*

They had tracked the herd of caribou for nearly two weeks, Apaay barely ten at the time. She still remembered the newness, a feeling like spring. She, so inexperienced, traveling with brawny men, all hunters, instincts sharp, their spears honed.

It had taken months of begging, completing extra chores, not a single fight with her sister, before Papa consented to letting her join the hunt. That morning, Apaay was the first to wake. As she and Papa were leaving, Eska chased after them, tears streaking her face.

Apaay stopped in concern. "What is it?"

"You forgot," Eska whispered, grabbing Apaay's left palm and pressing it to her own.

A small, remorseful smile. So she had.

"I will carry your heart in my heart," Eska said.

Her heart swelled, too big for her chest. "As will I."

Back in the cell, Apaay smiled at the memory. *We must have traveled close to twelve miles that day when we stopped to make camp for the night. That's when I heard rustling nearby.*

Together, she and Papa had slipped through the sleeping woods, an arrow nocked on her bow.

When they rounded a tree, she saw it. A magnificent caribou, its rack of velvet-covered antlers branching out, reaching. It was perhaps in its fifth year, neck bent as it grazed on berries, and the patch of white fur beneath the tail distinguished the sex as male. They never took the females or the young, as the herd needed a viable population to reproduce.

She told Ila this, then added, *My father is the best hunter in our village. I thought he was going to shoot and I would watch, but he said he wanted me to try.*

"Remember," Papa murmured as she lifted the bow. "Make it a clean kill."

Apaay remembered how her pulse had thudded, how she had been afraid of the animal picking up its wild beat. Crouched between two trees, their deep green leaves dappling shade upon the moist earth, she'd drawn back the arrow.

"Naattaluk," she whispered. The bull lifted its head, ears twitching. A snapped twig was all it would take for it to flee.

"You can do it," he said. "I know you can."

On the exhalation, she'd released the arrow. It flew straight and true, embedding itself in the animal's chest.

Apaay had many tokens signifying the accomplishments she'd achieved, but that one, her first one—that was her favorite.

Apaay studied the ceiling and released the tether on her memory. *I didn't want to disappoint him. I'm not great at hunting, to be honest.*

Ila placed a palm over Apaay's hand, and Apaay stilled, unaware that she had tied her poor braids into an anxious snarl. *You do not have to be the best at something to find value in it.*

A halfhearted shrug. Apaay dropped the braids. *That's what I thought, though. If I could do something the way my father wanted, or my mother, then I could earn their respect.*

What does pleasing them have anything to do with respect?

I don't know. She blanked at the question. Truly, she hadn't a clue. *I thought maybe if they were happy, then I'd be happy, too. Everyone would get what they wanted.*

And what is it they wanted?

Someone different.

It hurt, but something was growing in place of that hollow space. The reason why she could never live up to anyone's expectations had unintentionally trapped her in a desperate cycle to please. The things people asked of Apaay were not things she wanted for herself. They were Mama or Papa or Eska or her friend Chena. Other people, other passions, other hearts.

For years, she'd been wearing someone else's boots. Either they were too large to fill, or too cramped for comfort, pinching her toes. Apaay had known this, in some far pocket of her mind. But what was so bad about wearing her own boots? Why didn't she have the confidence to just *be*? Could she not be happy with Apaay, her strengths and her faults, even if others wished better of her?

Everyone brought something into this world. Everyone walked their own path. To seek approval from others, she would search her entire life and never find it.

Ila's sharp features softened, and she smoothed a hand across her friend's brow. *It's not for others to decide who you are. Who do you want to be? That's the important question.*

And one she hadn't an answer to.

Apaay, wanting space from the discussion, sat up, strands slipping through Ila's nimble fingers. *You don't have any tokens in your hair,* she stated, to which Ila shook her head. *Would you like one?*

Ila blinked in understanding. A ring of darkest gray encircled the outer rim of her irises, eventually bleeding into the brown of turned earth. Biting her lip, she nodded, unable to hide the yearning, the desire to be a part of something, because she'd never had the opportunity for more.

Come here.

Ila shifted closer, allowing Apaay to braid a length of her hair, leaving a few inches free at the bottom. As she'd been thinking of this for some time, Apaay already had the tokens set aside: two small stones with holes in their centers. Their friendship was strong like the stone. It would last a long time.

Once Apaay had secured her own token, she lifted Ila's left palm to her own, feeling Eska's presence through the gesture. *Now if we're ever apart,* Apaay said, heat spreading up her neck at how grateful she felt to have met Ila, *we can look at the stone and feel as if we're together.*

The older girl's face crumpled, swiftly and completely. With a broken cry, she threw her arms around Apaay's shoulders and sobbed into the crook of her neck.

They remained there, wrapped up in each other, for a long time. Apaay squeezed her eyes shut, her throat swollen with emotion she was afraid to let show. Once Ila's tears quieted, Apaay leaned back. *Ila?*

Yes?

How— She swallowed, uncertain if this was her place.

Go on, said her friend, her smile perhaps a bit too knowing.

How did you lose your hearing?

Ila's smile broadened, as if she had been waiting for this question as Apaay had, though perhaps for a different reason.

Gestures slow, as if focusing on a memory, Ila said, *I think I used to be able to hear a long time ago, before I came to this place. I can still make out some higher pitches, but over time the sounds have faded.* She added, *Give me your hand.*

The older girl lifted Apaay's hand to the side of her head and the ropy scar curving along her scalp.

You've seen this, right?

Apaay nodded. The tissue was tough beneath her fingertips, yet she touched it gently. In the shifting torchlight, the scar glowed against the deep brown of Ila's hair, freed from its braid, a collection of shining dark threads. At least there was still one beautiful thing in this cell.

I think I hit my head somehow, which caused me to lose my hearing.

But you don't remember how it happened? Or who helped you? A scar this severe indicated the head wound had been traumatic. Had someone not given aid, Ila most likely would not have survived. Someone in the labyrinth had found her, brought her here. Yuki or the Face Stealer or some nameless hero.

Ila shook her head, fiddling with a carved polar bear she had completed last week, its body a pale gray, speckled with white. She set it in between two orcas, their tails lifted clear off the floor. *What about you? How did you learn how to sign?*

Apaay flopped back down on the ground. It seemed she wanted to do little but sleep of late. *My grandmother lost her hearing when she was a child. Bad ear infection.* She pointed to her ear. *She and my father taught me and my sister how to sign when we were young.*

They sat in companionable silence, water dripping from the ceiling. Ila said, *Have you thought of any good jokes lately?*

Apaay snorted, one arm thrown over her forehead. Her hood served as an adequate cushion, the wolverine fur soft and dense. She used one hand to sign, *I thought you said my jokes were terrible,* before removing her arm to see Ila's reply.

They are terrible. But they're less terrible than this cell.

There was one she had been thinking of lately. It wasn't her best, but Apaay thought it at least worthy of a chuckle.

What do you call a walrus in an ice house?

Ila shrugged.

Stuck!

So bad, Ila said as her shoulders shook. *So, so bad.*

The scuff of heavy tread made Apaay sit up, which in turn caused Ila to straighten, their attention locked on the hallway. Ila wrinkled her nose at the fishy smell as their guard appeared and said, "Yuki requests your attendance." His focus flicked between them. "Both of you."

Apaay paused in pulling up her hood. The pounding in her ears intensified as she turned to Ila, doing her best to strap down her fear. Asking for both of them was unprecedented. *Yuki wants to see us,* Apaay said, since the darkness prevented Ila from reading the guard's lips clearly.

Much of the blood drained from Ila's face.

Apaay quickly slid on her mittens, then gripped the older girl's hand once the guard opened their cell door. *Stay close to me.* She did not reassure Ila with falsities. She did not want to lie.

The torches flickered as they passed, shadows gorging on the light. The corridor was long, it always had been, but now it seemed to stretch, an unending continuation of stone. Ila's breathing hitched as the guard led them up the stairs to the third level, where they stopped. The slow-moving river lapped against the walls, the kayaks and umiak bumping together from the current.

Apaay stared at the bobbing vessels as her world narrowed. The ground rushed up. The ceiling pressed down. The enclosed space was shrinking, smaller and smaller.

From this distance, the umiak appeared to be well-made, with rosy, toughened walrus skins stretched over the whalebone frame. It was much longer and wider than the kayak, able to carry multiple people as opposed to only one or two. "We're not taking the umiak, are we?" Her voice was a croak.

"Get in."

"Can't we—"

His shove sent her falling toward the water. Apaay's stomach lurched as she caught herself on the edge of the frame. Spray dampened her face, and she flinched as the umiak heaved upward. Apaay tumbled into the boat on her back, chest rising and falling shallowly, her mind flashing with images from her grandmother's life. A splintering, the sudden plunge into the sea below.

Her fear of dark water robbed her of oxygen. She couldn't do this. She really could not do this. She would die before she ever got off this boat.

Ila hurried to her side. Apaay barely felt her touch. Her vision squeezed and squeezed, denying her the light she so desperately craved. The guard, unconcerned, untied the umiak and pushed off, using an oar to propel them forward.

They glided along the water through the dim. Apaay curled closer to Ila and clutched her friend's leg, sweat prickling her forehead as she fought the urge to vomit. Ila's hands were gentle, they were still, but Apaay was shaking. The current battered against the umiak's casing, nothing more than a thin layer separating her from the water. The frigid temperature seeped through the skins.

Judging from the shape of the ceiling, they curved around the central chamber. As the minutes passed, the darkness began to lift, and a low thrum of voices carried down the passage. When the umiak bumped against a ledge, Apaay practically threw herself out of the vessel, arms and legs splayed out on the wonderfully solid ground. "Sweet rock," she whispered, cheek pressed against its cold surface. "Don't ever leave me."

"Get up," the guard ordered.

Ila tugged on her arm. The guard nudged them through a short hallway, into a place of brilliant white light, and Apaay would have plummeted to her death had Ila not wrenched her back.

They stood on a ledge of slickened ice that ringed a circular pit in a two-hundred-foot drop below—the central chamber transformed. The concave walls curved inward like waves rolling toward shore, making them impossible to climb. The ice was moonbeam white, and glowing.

She and Ila were not alone. Across the way, seven more prisoners shrank away as they emerged from various passages cut into the encompassing wall. Three young men, one young woman, two children, and one elder. She had often wondered about others who were trapped here. The fortress held rooms within rooms, dungeons within dungeons. She hadn't forgotten the young man she'd spoken with before, the one who kept to the shadows.

Ila's waif-thin body was strung like a frightened calf. She gripped Apaay's hand so hard her fingertips bulged.

Voices rumbled through the room, a rush and a roar. Two levels overhead, hundreds of people had gathered, their fur-ringed faces peeking over the crystallized walls, a sea of bronze and brown and gold, though Apaay spotted a few paler complexions in the mix. There was no way all these people lived here. They must have come from outside the in-between. They didn't appear to be Analak, judging from what she observed of their mannerisms, which made her believe they were Unua.

Yuki and the Face Stealer graced their thrones on the lower level directly across the pit. They were near enough for Apaay to read their expressions, but too far to make out the color of their eyes. The ice fortress glittered coldly around them. Sleek, polished, barren. This place, as magnificent as it was, would never be a home. There was too much space with no love to fill it.

The girl perched on the very edge of her seat, back straight, gaze narrowed as it raked over Apaay's form. "You certainly are a bold one," she said, head tilted in consideration. As soon as she opened her mouth, the crowd quieted. "Calling me a coward in your position. Why, I almost left you to rot in that cell."

So the Face Stealer had passed on her message. Good.

"I wanted a chance to defend myself—"

"I'm sorry, but did I give you permission to speak?" The saccharine words drifted from across the pit.

Biting the inside of her cheek, Apaay fell silent. Considering she was, quite literally, standing on the edge of a cliff, it would be wise to hold her tongue for once.

"That's better." Yuki settled back in her seat, the slick, skintight material of her outfit a mottled gray. Strands escaped her upswept bun, as if her hair had been sloppily pulled back, and clung to the sweat glistening along her neck. Apaay could not tear her eyes from the wayward threads. Yuki's appearance was never less than immaculate.

"As I was saying, I almost left you to rot, but I must admit I find you intriguing, to an extent. Numiak mentioned you wanted another chance in the labyrinth. You mortals are so attached to things." Her eyelashes fluttered atop her slitted gaze. "Luckily for you, I'm in a good mood. Go on, ask me why."

Apaay squeezed Ila's hand tighter. "Why?"

Her sweet bell of a laugh struck the ice, so clear, so very young. "It's my birthday, silly."

How old did that make the girl? Twelve? One hundred forty?

"And I can't wait to celebrate with you. Numiak helped organize everything. He invited all the guests—old friends and new friends from the coast." She clapped her hands, and the guards disappeared down the passageways, where the ice closed over the openings, sealing the prisoners inside. "As I'm sure you know by now, I'm very fond of games. And I thought, what better way to celebrate than to play one?"

Please, not the Sea Wolf. She did not think she'd be able to survive a second time.

"It's simple, really. Below, you will find the stage set. One by one, each of you will face a beast. Kill it, and you gain your freedom. Or in your case, child"—she winked at Apaay—"another go in the labyrinth. Fail to kill it, and, well . . ."

Deep inhalation, long exhalation. The taste of metal coated Apaay's tongue.

"You'll die."

The audience tittered.

"Are there any volunteers?"

Apaay looked across the arena at the other prisoners. Tight, terror-stricken eyes, all pupil. Ila wrapped her arms around her middle, and Apaay saw how her teeth chattered. Cold. Fear. She could no longer distinguish the two.

"No one?" Yuki looked around, eyebrows raised. She did not appear upset by the lack of response. On the contrary, she looked quite pleased with herself, if a bit unstable. After all, this was her birthday, her game, and she was master of all the rules.

"Numiak, choose someone to go first."

The Face Stealer's cool gaze slid over the prisoners, one by one. Most flinched from the power of his stare. Otherworldly, with the bitter chill of winter. Apaay's pulse skittered as she watched him deliberate, and her heart skipped a beat when those eyes latched onto her with frightening intensity. The ease with which he considered these men and women and children as little more than animals frightened her.

"I choose her," he said, and pointed a finger.

Right at Ila.

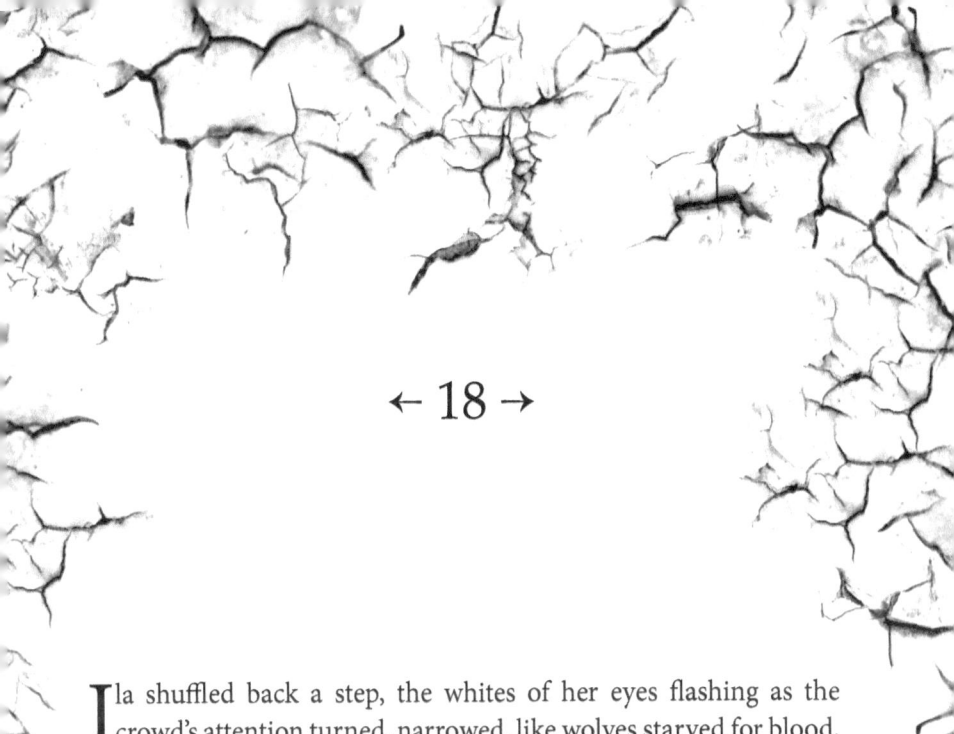

18

Ila shuffled back a step, the whites of her eyes flashing as the crowd's attention turned, narrowed, like wolves starved for blood.

"Wait!" Apaay shoved Ila behind her, as if that would miraculously make her disappear. "I'll go. I'll take her place." She tried to harden the words, but her voice was feeble. "I'm the one you want."

"Too late, child. You had your chance. Now." Yuki dipped her chin, a muscle flexing along the graceful line of her jaw. "The girl."

The floor shuddered, vibrations rolling through the ice so it cracked and groaned. A deep crevasse splintered between where she and Ila stood, and the ice separated, frozen flakes tumbling into a dark abyss, their hands still clasped together, clinging as the distance widened. Ila gasped when their fingers finally pulled apart.

Slabs of ice shot skyward from the ground as Apaay signed, *Stay aware of your surroundings. I'll find a way to get to you. Don't—*

Ila vanished behind a wall.

More groaning of the shifting earth. When it settled, Apaay stood on a column of ice surrounded by a drop on all sides, the platform no wider than an arm span. Across the arena, a guard joined Ila on her own pillar, and it slowly sank, lowering them to the bottom of the pit. The older girl thrashed in the guard's grip, kicking and scratching, even going so far as to bite the arm constricting her throat. A streak of pride shimmered in Apaay's blood. This was when Ila's monsters came out to play.

Each prisoner now stood on an individual column hugging the outer ring of the cavernous pit, like the tips of a many-pointed star. The crowd enclosed the entire arena. Yuki and the Face Stealer were directly ahead, lazy, insolent, thoroughly entertained.

A startling crack struck the air, and someone whistled in approval. When Apaay returned her attention to the arena floor, Ila was on the ground, a hand pressed to her cheek.

Apaay saw red. Her eyes were full of blood—the guard's blood, Yuki's blood, the demon's blood. Too far away, too much distance. She was an island.

She clenched her teeth together so hard a bone popped in her jaw.

"The blindfold, please."

From this distance, it looked like Ila could barely stand. Her knees had buckled from the severity of her trembling, and the guard's hold was likely the only thing keeping her upright. With rising panic, Apaay watched as they tied her hands behind her back. Then a strip of cloth cloaked the girl's eyes.

"Don't do this," Apaay ground out into the silence, a dull throb pounding at her temples. The other prisoners were slack-jawed at the commotion below, immobilized by fear.

The young girl tutted. "Don't worry. She'll still be able to hear."

"She can't hear," Apaay hissed, and itched to wrap her hands around the girl's skinny neck. "She's deaf."

"Really?" The initial confusion gave way to a sharp, ravenous grin. "Then that makes this much more interesting."

Apaay sank to her knees. Her *own* legs wouldn't hold her weight, and she was not even the one in immediate danger. She could do nothing on this column of ice. Only watch, pray no harm would come to her friend. The prisoner on the pillar to her right—the elder—had fainted.

"Release them."

Apaay couldn't breathe, she couldn't *breathe*. A doorway materialized, cut out from the frosted walls.

Three polar bears lumbered from the darkness.

Apaay imagined a small, helpless sound slipping from between Ila's stiff lips. She could probably feel the vibrations from the animals' heavy gaits.

Apaay locked her focus onto Yuki, spitting out, "You're a monster."

The crowd shifted like waves breaking upon the shore, their whispers drifting through the cold. The girl's voice soared, swift as a bird. "You know the law of the land. The strong survive, the weak perish."

The polar bears spread out, pacing back and forth perhaps five yards away from Ila, but drawing no closer. Ice collars encircled their beefy necks. The largest was five times the size of a man, behemoth paws, bulky shoulders, a mouth crowded with daggers. The other two appeared half grown. Blood trailed behind them in thin red streams.

The largest one chuffed air through its lips in a sign of stress. Ila's cheeks glimmered with tears. She had gone from trying to make herself as small as possible to uncurling her body so it stretched tall as a blade of grass. This girl, who would die, and had never learned what it meant to live.

And Apaay decided she didn't need to be a great hunter or a skilled tracker to help her friend. She just needed to be brave.

Crouching down on the pillar, Apaay peered over the edge at the long drop leading to the floor. She shuffled slowly backward on her knees until her legs hung over the side, hands gripping the opposite edge. She was glad to have worn her mittens, as they provided adequate friction against the ice.

Yuki snapped, "What does she think she's doing?"

The Face Stealer replied, "Saving her friend, I believe." A lazy response, and maybe she had spent too long wanting things to change, but she swore she detected a touch of admiration in his voice. Not that it mattered. After all, *he* had determined Ila's ill fate.

"She can't do that. She—"

"Patience." Apaay imagined him resting his fingers against the girl's arm. "Let's watch and see what she does."

Half hanging off the pillar, Apaay slowly slid her hands from the curved edge to the sides and down, her body sinking a little, which enabled her arms to wrap almost fully around the column. From there, it was a slow, sliding descent to the ground.

Someone in the audience laughed, and Yuki's snarl cut through the chatter, rivaling the most vicious of beasts. As soon as Apaay could stand, the bears turned toward her.

Apaay had a single weapon hidden in her furs, a piece of stone she had scraped and sharpened to a lethal point in the hours she lay awake, unable to escape from the nightmares haunting her in sleep. Slowly, so as not to startle the animals, she approached, the stone digging into her palm, every line of her body taut. The bears tracked her movement. Her blood was roaring. It burned through her limbs with the urge to fight, flee.

She was not a violent person, but in that moment, in front of all these people, Apaay made a vow to herself. She would tear into these animals with everything she had. And then, before her time in this frosted hell was over, she would shove a dagger through Yuki's dark heart.

When she reached Ila's side and grabbed her hand, the girl flinched before realizing who it was. Apaay sawed through the rope and, once Ila's hands were free, began to untie the blindfold.

"Remove the blindfold," Yuki cried, "and you both die."

Ila was deaf, she was blind, she was weaponless, yet Apaay did not fear the bears as she feared the people stomping their feet and beating their fists against the rail, crowing for the spill of blood. She could not see herself in any of them. Who was animal? Who was man?

Apaay removed one mitten and signed into Ila's open palm so her friend could feel the shape and placement of her fingers. *We can't remove your blindfold. I'm going to back us up so our backs are to the wall. I'll protect you.*

What's out there?

Danger, blood, pain. An uncertain future.

It's best if you don't know.

The girl tensed, but didn't argue. Keeping one arm around Ila and the other clutching the weapon, she slowly backed them up until Ila's back hit the wall, then stepped in front of her, nerves flighty and on edge. The polar bears paced back and forth, still waiting, still bleeding as they breathed. This was a cage hewn from ice, and there was nowhere to go.

Sharp laughter struck, and Apaay jerked, unable to soothe her jumpiness. The largest bear snorted at the sudden movement. Lowering its head, it rushed toward her.

Apaay did not have time to think. Her head was empty of thoughts. The animal barreled toward her with the force of an avalanche, and it would have crushed her had she not scrambled out of reach. The animal gave chase. Apaay ran in circles around the arena to Yuki's laughter, the mob's jeers, needing time to formulate a plan before her body gave out. A useless wish. The bear cut her off from the inside, and she drove the weapon down, aiming for the animal's gullet. She caught it on the shoulder as it twisted and swiped a massive paw at her legs with an earth-shattering roar. The gash poured blood. The ice streaked red.

Apaay screamed at the shredding of her leg, which buckled and sent her sliding across the floor. Cornered. Prey. In the moment before death, Apaay had never felt so alive. She clawed at the ice and dragged her body toward the wall, used it to brace herself, to stand on her unwounded leg. Sweat dripped into her eyes. She let the stinging whet her mind.

Focus. She was trying to think of how to escape *and* protect Ila *and* maim the animal so they could get away, which resulted in her thoughts bouncing back and forth, leading her nowhere. She decided to first focus on protecting Ila. Escape could come later, after she killed the bear. And she didn't want to kill it, but it looked like she wouldn't have a choice. It was clear only one of them would make it out of this alive, and she intended for it to be her.

Ila cowered on the floor, hands wrapped over her head. Apaay limped backward to draw the bear's attention away from her friend, already breathing hard. Unintentionally, she had shifted nearer to the smaller bears, and distressed wails rolled through the chamber. The larger bear let rip a snarl, planting itself between them. *Stay back,* it said.

They came together again, a clash of skin and fur, woman and beast. The crowd roared and demanded more, the air heady with hostility, and when the polar bear next struck, ramming its shoulder into her body, Apaay flew back and slammed against the wall. Her lungs crumpled and caved, a flower shriveling in the heat. She could not suck in air hard enough, fast enough.

The animal charged.

In her exhausted state, time slowed. Individual voices melted into slush, an underlying buzz. She tracked the bear's gait, waiting until the last possible moment. When a whiff of its breath ghosted across her face, she darted out of reach, ducked under its body, and stabbed the dagger at its throat yet again. But the weapon slammed into the ice collar with a crack, and Apaay hadn't the time to regroup before the bear's jaws descended on her throat. Her spine cracked with how forcefully she leaned back to avoid the strike. She hit the ground and rolled back to her feet, stumbling slightly.

Her gouged leg was a mass of screaming nerves. The weeks in captivity could be seen in the scrawn of her arms, the rounded slope of her back, the shredding of her throat as she gulped down air. Blood splattered the ground. Hers—and the bear's. It all looked the same. There was no difference when it came to life and death, but there was very much a divide between her and the animal she now fought. Animal intelligence, which was nature. Human intelligence, which was complex and layered and strategic. Cause and effect. Right now, it was a hindrance. Her exhausted mind couldn't keep up with her thoughts.

Apaay backed up, keeping the smaller bears in her line of vision. They huddled on the far edge while their larger companion finished her off. As long as the collar was in the way, she'd never be able to kill it. She needed to break it apart.

The animal easily weighed a thousand pounds. The only thing that saved Apaay from death was her speed. She slipped in and out of the bear's reach, hacking at the collar when she could and darting away, circling, waiting for an opening, biding her time. She had given herself over to instinct, yet the sense of wrongness did not abate. The Analak only killed animals for food or clothes or tools—

supplies needed for survival. This was a forced confrontation. A bloody, violent game.

She panted for breath, cold air searing her throat. Then she saw an opening.

The polar bear half turned, as if checking on its smaller companions, and Apaay took her chance. She dove forward, arm muscles coiled as she brought the sharpened point against the ice, driving it through the large crack that had formed. The collar shattered, allowing for the tip to slide through fur and flesh, into the bear's gullet, where the animal thrashed and roared and finally lay still, a mound of white snow atop a pool of warm, trickling blood.

The adrenaline coursing through her soon abated, leaving behind trembling aftershocks. But Apaay couldn't stop. She couldn't sit and she couldn't rest and she couldn't check the gouges in her leg. She had two more bears to kill. Two more lives to end.

She was about to turn her attention to the remaining animals when something caught her eye.

The fallen bear was changing. Limp, fur-covered limbs began to shorten. The body thinned. The snout lost its elongated shape. Apaay backed up, not understanding what was happening aside from the distinct possibility that this was another lie, another trick. The transformation ended with a middle-aged woman, her long gray strands splayed out, soaked in the blood Apaay had spilled.

Utter silence.

Apaay's strangled wheeze was jagged and full of pain. "What?"

Someone coughed from above.

She blinked. This was not a polar bear. This was a woman. And she was dead.

Yuki tsked in pity. "Such a shame. All lives must come to an end, it seems."

The woman did not disappear. "What did you do?" Apaay rasped, glancing up. The girl sipped from a glass before resting it on the arm of her chair. The demon wasn't looking at Apaay. He was looking at the body, his stillness out of place among the shifting people.

"I think the better question, child, is what *you* did." Yuki's perfect eyebrows, like glossy lines of ink, lifted high on her forehead. "You killed her."

"No! I didn't . . . didn't mean to—"

A shriek of laughter sliced through the hall. "Did you not stab her in the throat, or was that my imagination?"

"You *forced* me to." She screamed the words. The woman had been polar bear Unua, the shape-shifting race that dwelled in the Southern Territory. She was far from home.

"I didn't *force* you to do anything. You *chose* to climb down to the arena. You *chose* to fight. That woman," she cried, "died by your hand."

"I didn't know about the collar." That it had trapped the woman in her animal form. "I thought—"

"It's not my fault you broke the collar. If you hadn't done so, we could have bypassed this unnecessary drama, don't you think?"

Apaay whirled around. The smaller bears watched her with wide, unblinking gazes. They, too, bore collars of ice.

Apaay had a sickening feeling she had destroyed something precious.

The girl waved her hand, and the last two collars melted away.

Two boys, having not yet hit puberty, huddled against the back wall. They were naked, shivering, having fallen against each other to cry over the dead woman at her feet. *Mama,* she heard them whisper. *Mother.*

Apaay's trembling mouth parted as the world blurred. She dropped to her knees, head bowed. "I'm so sorry." She was seconds away from being violently ill.

"Well," said Yuki. "I don't have all day. Finish what you started."

Apaay shook her head, a shudder rolling through her. How could she justify murdering innocents? She met Yuki's expectant gaze. "I'm not killing those boys. They're children."

"If you want another chance in the labyrinth, you must kill all of them."

"I won't do it."

"Then you forfeit your chance."

"I—" A small hesitation. Some animal instinct tugged at her. Survive, take, and see another day. But not like this. This was not how she lived. These were children. These were two young boys, ridiculed, tortured, motherless. They were her and she was them, and if their positions had been reversed, she would hope for someone to show her mercy, too.

"I don't care," she muttered. "I want to return to my cell." Where she could retch in peace and dream of simpler times.

Yuki clucked her tongue. "I'm not quite done. You see, I have a special surprise for you."

Apaay fought despair. It would never end. "Why are you like this?" It was so quiet even her whisper carried. "Does it fill the hole in your heart? Does it prove absolutely anything?"

Does it bring you peace, Yuki, to hurt others when you feel nothing?

Carefully, as if aware of the entire audience watching, Yuki patted the sweat from her forehead. She again sipped from her drinking glass. "They don't know it now, but I'm doing them a favor. Someday their mother would have abandoned them. I'm only saving them grief."

"Is that what happened to you? Your mother abandoned you as a child?" She watched the girl's reaction closely.

"I never knew my mother. My father— Well." Sharp teeth flashed. Her fist rested atop her jittering knee. "He made his choice a long time ago. I've come to terms with it."

No, Yuki wasn't even close to closing that wound. And it made Apaay wonder. Did Yuki inflict pain on others because she had so much inside herself that it overflowed? That the only way to reduce the burden was to share it?

"Think what you will of me, child. I'm sure from your perspective it looks like I have it all. But never forget that power is pain. Power is isolation. Power," she murmured, faltering under the word, "is living your life alone."

Apaay looked to the Face Stealer to gauge his reaction. He, too, harbored power. He was alone, as Yuki was. Currently, he was turned away from her. If he felt her gaze on him, he gave no indication.

"Now, your surprise."

The room held its breath. Ila was still curled on the ground blindfolded, though perhaps she had sensed the battle had reached an end, as she was no longer shaking as severely.

In the center of the arena, the ground cracked open to allow a cylinder to rise, bearing a girl burdened by chains. Apaay couldn't see her face.

"Don't be shy," Yuki crooned.

Beside her, the Face Stealer clutched the arms of his chair in a rare show of internal conflict. Though it did not take long before the regret grew clear, he chose to do nothing. He did not try to stop this disgusting display of power, and Apaay wished, foolishly, that he would.

When the bound girl lifted her trembling hands, wrists strangled by thick iron manacles, and lowered her fur-lined hood, Apaay choked out a breath, something between a gasp and a sob. "Chena."

Upon hearing her name, Chena's gaze fell on Apaay, and the girl burst into tears. The chains clanked. Apaay knew how cold the metal must be. "Apaay. Where are we? What's going on?"

She blinked back the sting of tears. It was brutal—helplessness. The ability to speak but no one to listen, to see but be unable to act. How long had it been since she'd last seen her best friend? Two months? Three? Time had unraveled so, so slowly.

"It's— We're—" She swallowed. "It's all right. Everything's going to be all right." She turned toward Yuki, making sure her voice carried. "Release her. She's done nothing wrong."

"On the contrary, the girl trespassed on my territory. I'd say that's reason enough."

"You don't own the land. The North belongs to everyone." She had never understood the reason for territories. The land did not have a master and never would.

The girl ignored her and said to Chena, "Go on, child. Tell your friend why you were trespassing."

Chena looked to Apaay for direction, her face pale, sweaty. Apaay noticed the slight swell of her friend's belly beneath her parka.

"Do as she says," Apaay whispered.

Chena's voice quavered as she spoke. Her gaze, which held Apaay's, said so many things. *I'm sorry. Help me help me help me—*

"Food has become scarcer," she began, wide eyes sliding to linger on the woman's corpse. "Especially seals. I'm not sure why. The village is really struggling."

"My parents? Eska?"

Chena shook her head in worry. "It's not good. Your parents do what they can, but many days they don't eat. As for Eska, it's like she's gone somewhere else. She rarely goes outside anymore. Your parents don't know what else to do for her."

Mama—so warm, like an eternal flickering flame. Papa and his strength. Kindhearted Eska. Struggling. Apaay felt it deep in her soul. She wasn't there for them. She had to get back.

"Why did you leave the village?" She didn't dare mention Chena's condition. She would not put her friend in any more danger.

"I went with a small group of people looking for game. I thought I could help. Then a blizzard hit and we were separated." A sudden flare of agony, dulled. "I think Silla died." Silla, the father of their unborn child. "I got lost and dug myself a snow cave. I must have fallen asleep. When I woke up, I was here."

Which was the worst place she could possibly be. Whirling around, Apaay yelled, "Let her go, you coward." She flung the insult into the open space. Maybe by drawing the girl's attention away from Chena, focusing it solely on her, she would spare her friend in some way.

Slowly, Yuki rose. The crowd parted as she stepped down from the dais and strode to the railing, curling her gloved hands around the frost. This girl had never known what it meant to be inferior. If she had only ever looked down on others, there was no reason to look up. "Coward?" Her voice was faint.

"You heard me, you ungrateful—"

"Stop it."

"Selfish—"

"How *dare*—"

"Sick—"

"—you—"

"Bitch."

The girl's face was positively livid, her cheeks stained red as the crowd tittered under their breath. Behind her, still lounging, the Face Stealer bowed his head, one hand over his mouth as his shoulders shook with laughter.

"Guards," she snapped, but Apaay was ready. She was ready for whatever was to come. As long as Ila and Chena were taken away from this place, she could endure another punishment. She had survived before, and she would survive again and again and again.

"Kindly escort the prisoners back to their cells. The new girl, too." The men did as ordered, dragging Chena and the blindfolded Ila from the arena. "As for you, why, I have a special treat I think you'll enjoy very much." She stretched herself taller, as if to compensate for that brief humiliation, though the motion was stilted. Her chest rose and fell in short, fitful bursts. *"Numiak!"* The shriek rang against the ice.

He didn't move from his position. "Yes?"

"Come here."

"Since you asked so nicely," he purred.

When Yuki spoke, the room was silent out of fear for what was. But when the Face Stealer spoke, everyone was silent out of fear for what could be. The way his voice stroked along the skin. The sense that your face did not belong to you and never would.

He descended the stairs leisurely, hands in his pockets. The crowd gave him a wide berth as he strode up to Yuki's side, towering over her.

"Will you do me the honor of handling her punishment?"

He dipped his chin. "You need not have asked."

"Excellent." That cold, glittering gaze, flat and calm and coolly calculating, had never known warmth and never would. "Let her head be shaved."

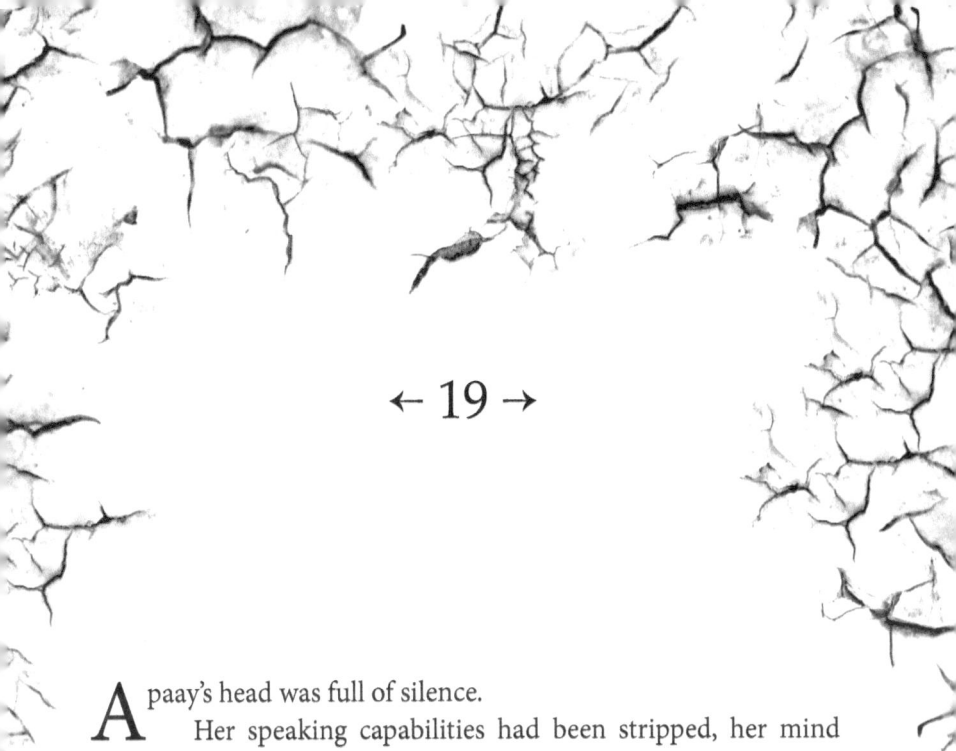

← 19 →

Apaay's head was full of silence.

Her speaking capabilities had been stripped, her mind wiped clean as the Face Stealer suddenly materialized at her side, borne on a phantom wind.

Let her head be shaved.

A fine mist rolled across her vision. She felt faint. Shakily, she reached up and slid her fingers over the long, thick braid hanging over her shoulder, the tips embellished with bones, feathers, stones. Each one, a mark of some accomplishment or defining moment in her life. The bit of vertebra—her first kill. A shark's tooth—her first birthing. The owl's feather for kindness and compassion, which she had displayed after freeing an injured wolf from a snare. And the most recent addition—a stone for the friendship she and Ila shared.

For the Analak of the coastal regions, there was much to be proud of, but hair held the most pride of all. It was a part of Apaay's soul, a brilliant thread that connected her to the very heart of her culture, both history and identity.

Who would she be without it?

The Face Stealer's gaze was hot on her neck. Apaay's head remained bowed, fingers grasping the thick threads, because she could not bear to part from this; she could not bear the thought of losing herself to more confusion, turmoil, fear. Eighteen years had allowed it to grow all the way to her waist.

She glanced at the demon. There was still time to change things. "I—"

"I don't have all day," Yuki snapped.

"Wait." She clutched her braid tighter, so tight her joints creaked. "I want a different punishment. I want something else."

The girl sighed in aggravation, having returned to her chair. She curled against the side and crossed her arms. "It is done."

"Please. *Please.*" Apaay was on her knees, the ground hard beneath her. She would beg if she had to. She would beg for as long as she needed to. "Hair is sacred to me, to my people."

"I know," Yuki replied, mouth sullen. "And I don't care."

"But—"

"Get on with it."

"Tilt back your head," the Face Stealer murmured.

She looked up, and her mouth wobbled. His broad shoulders blocked out many of the stares, all of them hungry save his. The pity in his gaze threatened to gut her. She didn't want it. Curse his pity, and curse this labyrinth, and curse that vile creature of a girl.

"You don't know what you're doing," she whispered to him. "You can stop her. You can stop this."

His throat worked, and he lifted the whale-bone knife in his hand.

The pressure in Apaay's chest tightened as if her insides were shredding open. Mama had always loved her hair. She would brush it in the evenings, the lustrous strands splayed over their bedding furs. In the lamplight, her hair glowed, like light rippling over a true-black sea.

"I need you to let go."

Let go.

He wanted her to let go.

Her voice broke. "I—I can't."

Gently, he unwound her hands from her braid. They fell into her lap.

It was happening. It was really happening.

Apaay tried to suppress the emotion barreling up her throat. Shakily, she lifted her chin. Never in a million years would she have believed things to ever reach this point, but . . . if this was the price for Ila's safety, and Chena's and her unborn child's, then she would pay it. For them.

A single tear slipped down her cheek. The Face Stealer wiped the moisture away with his thumb, and the shock of his touch pinned her, the reaction rippling through her body. His eyes were a color she had never seen before: a shade of green she only saw in the early days of spring.

The cutting began, and soon the weight of her braid vanished. Apaay reached behind, feeling for the place where it had hung, and nearly burst into tears.

It didn't take long. Perhaps thirty minutes for the Face Stealer to shave her hair down to nothing but brown-black fuzz, but when it was over, her head bare for all the world to see, Apaay knew she was not coming back from this.

This was a wound that could not be healed.

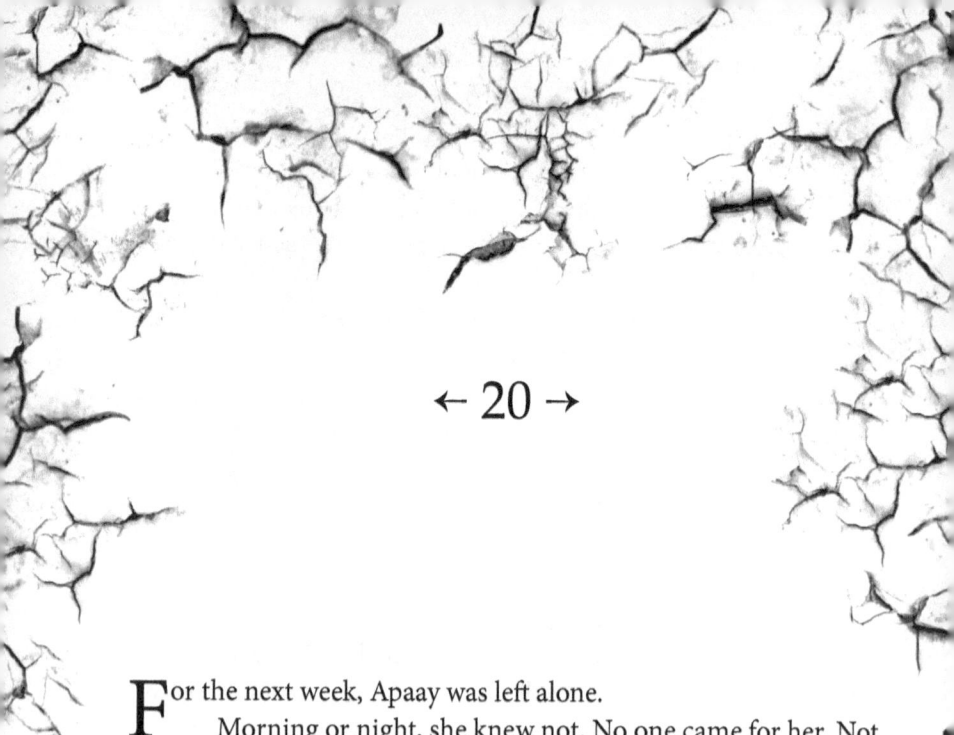

← 20 →

For the next week, Apaay was left alone.

Morning or night, she knew not. No one came for her. Not Irnik, not the Face Stealer, not the guards. She had the stone walls and the pail of half-frozen water and the rats that scurried over her legs while she slept, and she had her peeling skin that itched and flaked off in the coming days, and she had her mutilated leg and aching bones, and she had the darkness and killing cold that haunted her dreams. She spent her days listless, envisioning gray strands soaked in red. The rage that had patiently simmered was strangely absent, as if it had been cut away with her long dark locks.

When Apaay had first returned to her cell, she'd huddled in the corner, facing away from Ila as the girl tugged on her arm, begging her to tell her a joke, the one about the walrus, the one about the whale. Apaay had pulled her hood forward to hide her baldness, a rigid stone hardening in her chest, robbing her of air. She wanted no one to see her shame.

That woman, those poor motherless boys. Apaay shuddered. *Your fault, your fault, your fault.* Behind her eyelids lay a drenched red world, a piece of ice protruding from the woman's torn throat, and the weeping, the *agony—*

Her stomach heaved. This labyrinth was built upon blood and fear, and Apaay had spilled more into the earth so that this nightmare may continue to grow.

Her heart wept for the girl she had been. She had committed murder. She had wasted a life. She had taken away this woman's choice, and the choice of her children, in a rush of power, a single strike to the neck.

And it was a waste. The woman would not bring life with her death. She would not provide food or tools or clothing, the way wildlife did for the Analak. Apaay had drawn a line between them, animal and man, and had decided who should live and who should die, and that she, a girl with a weapon in her hand, would end the life of another.

There was nothing crueler than the voice in her mind taunting what *could have been*. If she had not gotten lost in the blizzard. If she had not crossed the boiling water. If she had not killed the polar bear Unua. If she had not sent Eska away on the ice that one fateful night.

If. The cruelest of words.

Apaay knew one thing, though. As soon as her braid had been severed, something inside her had shifted so severely she did not know if it could be fixed. Maybe Yuki, as much as she wanted to choke on the admission, was right. Maybe she would die here. Maybe she would never be free.

Upon awakening one morning or evening, Apaay uncurled from the stiff position she'd slept in and glanced at Ila, who lay slumped against the wall with her cheek pressed into the bar, one hand a few inches from where Apaay had lain, as if having reached for her in the night. Apaay crawled over and touched the older girl's shoulder.

Ila startled awake.

Apaay met the young woman's gaze and signed, *I'm sorry.*

The girl sat up. *Why?*

Not why Apaay was sorry. Why Apaay had shut her out.

Ila's right hand touched her lips, pressed against her sternum. *Tell me what happened. Did they hurt you?*

In answer, Apaay lowered her hood. Ila gasped, hands flying to her mouth.

Apaay drew her knees inward, close to her chest. Cold air skimmed along her exposed scalp. She had never noticed how heavy hair was, but now that it was gone, it was like a missing limb, so much a part of her, the space where it had hung unusually light. Apaay ran her hand over the short, soft fuzz that remained. Even in the cell, she could not shake the memory of screams, demands, jeers as her braid fell limply to the ground. The wailing of those poor boys after she had slaughtered their mother.

Do you know what this means? Apaay asked. She wondered if Irnik had ever mentioned hair to Ila, who had never been exposed to its importance.

Ila said, so gently, *I don't, but I can see you are in much pain.*

As her eyelids drifted shut, Ila's fingertips traced her cheekbone, the touch featherlight and achingly gentle, as if pressing any harder would cause Apaay to break. Emotion drifted through the cell: her friend's worry, her outrage. That strong, giving spirit.

Tell me what happened. Please.

What was there to tell? The damage was done. *They captured my friend. Put her in chains.* Mouth trembling, she pulled away, woozy and feverish and not at all stable. Her leg throbbed. Everything felt raw. *I killed someone.*

The girl did not respond. Apaay was afraid to look Ila in the eye. *I didn't know she was a woman—polar bear Unua. I was only trying to help.* Acid churned in her gut. *I did it to protect you.*

I know, Ila said, and nudged Apaay's chin so their eyes met. *I know you did.* Her clear, unclouded gaze shone with sincerity. *And I'm so grateful.*

Apaay flinched from the kindness. She was repulsive. She wanted to claw her too-tight skin to shreds and peel it from her bones. She wanted to scour her body in boiling water. She wanted to scrape the sweat and blood and feces from her clothes. She wanted to begin anew.

Ila's expression filled with compassion. *As for your hair, it will grow back—*

Stop. Apaay lifted a hand, tears swiftly rising. *You don't know what you're talking about. This*—she pointed to her scalp, the physical reminder of her loss—*is the ultimate form of shame. I don't know who I am anymore.*

You're right. I don't understand. Ila scooted closer on her knees. *Please, help me understand.*

With her hair, she was Analak. Without it, she was still Analak, but faded. Less. A separation existed between that Apaay and this Apaay, a sharp divide between two parts that were no longer whole. She didn't want to discuss this. Did Ila not see? Her friend was crowding her against the wall when Apaay needed room to breathe.

I don't want to talk about it right now. Apaay started to turn away.

A frustrated sound filled the room, and Ila clamped down on Apaay's shoulder. *Don't shut me out.*

Before Apaay realized her actions, she whirled around and shoved Ila away. The older girl fell onto her backside with a gasp, mouth agape.

Don't touch me. You've spent your entire life alone. How could you possibly know what it feels like to lose your family over and over again because you can't do anything right? How could you possibly know what it means to sacrifice? The motions were hard like stone. They demonstrated outside what Apaay felt like on the inside. *Do me a favor, Ila. Mind your own business.*

The initial shock melted away, and Ila's normally sweet-tempered disposition exploded into something fierce. *What gives you the right to judge me?* Lightning-quick gestures, a blur of motion, which quickly overtook the speed her lips moved. *Do you think because I didn't grow up with a mother or father I don't know what it means to love? Do you think I don't know loss?* The gestures grew larger, more passionate. *Look at me, Apaay.*

Grudgingly, Apaay lifted her chin, heat scalding her face.

Do you think it's easy for me, knowing I once had a family? Do you think I don't wish things were different? Can I not miss my parents or my sister, even though I don't remember them? Ila bared her teeth as tears welled and spilled over. *Maybe I've spent almost my entire life in this cell, but I do know what it feels like to lose family, because you're my family, Apaay. You're my family. I feel you slipping away, and I wish . . . I wish you would trust me enough to talk to me.*

Apaay bowed her head, frustration pulsing at her temples. In the low light, shadows blanketed the floor. She knew of the cracks separating the large stone slabs, could feel the deep grooves when she skimmed her fingers over the flat plane, yet Apaay could not see them. She had never been able to see anything clearly within the cell.

But this hurt was not a matter of light. It was a matter of truth.

She had wanted to blame someone for her misfortune, and instead of recognizing the true culprits—Yuki and the Face Stealer—she had lashed out at Ila instead.

And there was a reason for that. Maybe, Apaay thought with a twinge of guilt, she had said such horrible things because a small part of her resented Ila. The girl did not share in her pain. Her wounds were long-healed scars, not gaping shreds of skin. Sometimes, it frustrated Apaay that Ila did not understand, but perhaps Ila did not need to. She only needed to listen, which her friend had done countless times without judgment or haste. Ila had never asked anything of Apaay. She had given her companionship and laughter and warmth in the cold, and Apaay had stomped on that generosity.

How wrong she had been. Once, there had been a time when Ila *did* have a family. She'd once had a mother who'd birthed her, and a father, and a sister. Woven bits of fabric that had faded with the passage of time.

For her people, nothing was more important than kinship, family. It was the very heart of her culture, surrounded by an even larger network of social relationships. Everything was shared. Stronger together, weaker apart. In the Analak language, the word *family* was synonymous with the word *love.*

Apaay swiped at her damp cheeks. *I'm sorry.*

It's all right.

No, it's not.

Ila was watching her with a strange look in her eye.

Apaay cupped her elbows with her palms. Then she dropped her arms. *What?*

The girl's eyes softened. *Did you know,* Ila said, *that you are beautiful?*

Apaay's shoulders shook with the irony of the situation. Not that she believed Ila to be lying, but beauty, at least in the physical sense, had never mattered to Apaay. Her severe features suited her out on the ice, not warming the bedroll of another.

You're very kind, she replied with a tight smile, her hands moving slower as she thought of how best to phrase her thoughts, *but my face has never been one to draw a man's eye, and it certainly won't now.* She pointed to her scalp.

This seemed to distress Ila, which was the last thing Apaay wanted to do. *You give yourself too little credit,* she said, *but I wasn't talking about your face. I meant here. You are beautiful in here.*

Very gently, Ila pressed her palm against Apaay's heart.

An ache swelled beneath Apaay's breastbone and traveled up to wrap around her throat. Her eyes burned.

You have a strong heart, Apaay, and a kind one. I am lucky to know you.

Who would want me, especially now?

Ila bit her lip and glanced at the passageway, sadness tugging down the corners of her mouth. When she signed, the words came slow. *At least you will be remembered. That is no small thing.*

Apaay straightened at the abrupt shift in mood. Something was different here. A gradual dimming or loss of feeling, like the way her hands felt without mittens in the cold.

Reaching out, she smoothed a strand of hair away from her friend's face. *What do you mean?*

Ila's lashes fluttered low, then lifted, her gray-brown eyes stripped of barriers to reveal something raw and shriveled and festering: a poison, a secret, a fear. *When you're gone from this world, people will remember that you were good and loyal and kind, that you were a sister and a daughter and a friend.* The girl's smile was too sharp, a fracture away from breaking. *When I die, no one will remember me. I will not leave any lasting impact on the world, no legacy. I will be nameless, faceless. I will fade into obscurity.*

That, Apaay said with feeling, *is not true.*

Is it? Ila countered. *Is it really?*

Yes, she wanted to say. *Yes.*

But also—no.

Who was she to dictate how Ila should feel? She, who had family, community. She, who was neither faceless nor nameless, a daughter and a sister and a friend. It was a terrible thought, and Apaay felt sick thinking about it, but how could Ila be forgotten if she had never been known?

Shoving that cruelty aside, Apaay said, *I will remember you. Irnik will remember you. And I won't let you die here.*

Just as I won't let you give up. She touched Apaay's limp hand. *You're too hard on yourself.*

Apaay flinched, remembering all she had done, and that it hadn't been enough. She shifted back. *I need space, Ila. I need to think of what to do next.*

Ila frowned in concern but did not argue, instead moving to the opposite side of the cell and settling against the iron bars. Apaay wrapped herself in one of the musty blankets and turned away, biting her lip until the tears subsided. She could not break. She had to be strong. Weakness did not survive.

The small mountain of animal carvings, their sleek limbs warmed from the glow, cast a shadow over Apaay's form. Reaching out, she grabbed one at random and brought it close to her face, tracing its contours: head, tail, muzzle tilted up in song.

A wolf.

This would help her remember, Apaay decided, tucking the animal against her chest, who she was when she began to forget.

Analak.

Free.

← →

She must have dozed, because a few hours later she awoke to Ila signing with Irnik through the cell door. The guard's face, cast in half shadows, appeared troubled. Ila's gestures were swift with desperation, while the young man's were steady, smoothing away the edges of her temper and concern. She wondered if Ila was telling him what had happened in the arena. Apaay didn't want to think about where they had taken Chena, what she was currently enduring. Sweet, docile Chena. The girl must be out of her mind with fear.

When he looked up, Apaay hunched closer to the ground and shivered. His gaze slid along her shaved head, brow furrowed. Without her hair to offer warmth, she had to rely on her hood, which she quickly pulled up to hide her baldness. Still, he had seen.

The cell door screamed open and slammed shut. Irnik was standing in front of her. His trousers, tucked into his calf-high boots, had been worn soft.

He crouched down so he was eye level with her.

"What?" The word was a void, desolate sound.

"I heard what happened," he murmured, indicating what her hood concealed. "I'm sorry."

Behind him, Ila signed, *I told him you wanted to be left alone, but he wouldn't listen.*

"I don't want your pity." She wanted so many things, she wanted to *change* so many things, and he could give her none of them.

"I'm not here to give you pity."

She sat up and drew the blanket close, gaze narrowed. "Then why are you here?"

Ila watched their exchange in unease. Even if she couldn't hear them, she could read their facial expressions.

"I'm here," he said, "because I need my key back."

Apaay masked her surprise by ducking her head. She hadn't forgotten about the key, but she had hoped Irnik had. Its hard shape dug into her hip bone. "I have no idea what you're talking about," she said, her sorrow momentarily forgotten.

He quirked a brow.

"I lost it," said Apaay.

"You lost it."

"Yes."

"Apaay." The sound of her name in his mouth gave her pause. "The last time you used it, I nearly got caught. If they had discovered it was my key you took, I would have been executed, never mind that I hadn't given it to you. I know you're here for your sister—"

"And that is *exactly* why I need this." Her words thickened with grief, and she fought the rise of tears. "And now one of my friends is a prisoner, too."

Wordlessly, he held out one mittened hand. The man was probably wishing he had not stepped foot inside this cell. "It's for the best."

Mouth grim, she reached into her pocket and passed him the small piece of metal that had been a salvation in more ways than one. Then she turned her back.

"I'm sorry."

"Please," she whispered. "Just leave."

Once his footsteps receded, Ila approached and said, *He wants you to be safe. With Yuki gone—*

Apaay held up a hand, halting her. *What do you mean "With Yuki gone"?*

Irnik said she left and would be back tomorrow.

The girl was gone.

Gone.

The fortress beckoned.

Shrugging off the blanket, Apaay moved to the back-left corner of the cell and counted five stones to the right of the bars, about two feet from the ground. The stone came loose when she jiggled it, allowing her to pull it free from the wall, grit and dust raining down. Inside the hole, her fingers curled around an object.

Tonight, she would find what she had been looking for.

Before Apaay could slip the object into her pocket, Ila grabbed her hand and pried her fingers away.

It was a key, one she had chiseled of stone while Ila slept the week following her first foray into the labyrinth, the idea sparked from Ila's carvings. A key that fit into the iron lock of the cell door. A chance to change things, and a way out.

Please don't tell me you're planning to escape again, Ila said, the press of her mouth severe.

Apaay looked her straight in the eye. *This may be my only chance.*

What if one of the other guards sees you? You'll be punished. Ila gripped her hand. The girl's palm was sweaty.

What would you do, Ila?

I don't know. Her motions burst with frustration. *But you're angry and hurt and it's clouding your judgment.*

Yes, she was angry. Yes, she was hurt and overwhelmed. But there was no other way. Life was full of risks, after all. To open your heart to love, knowing it could lead to pain or death. To choose a less-trodden path.

Apaay did her best to explain. *My sister is counting on me. What if this is my only chance and I miss it because of what* might *happen?* She would hate herself. She would never stop regretting what could have been. *I can't pass up this opportunity.*

She had made this decision long before Ila had known about the key. The very second she had awoken, imprisoned, Apaay had promised herself she would find a way. It was clear now that Yuki would not give her another chance in the labyrinth, at least without forcing Apaay to play one of her twisted games. With Yuki gone, she might stand a chance at unlocking the labyrinth's secrets. The guards she could handle.

Apaay looked at Ila, the older girl's sweet face so full of worry—for *her*. Ila, whom she had known for such a short time. Ila, her dear friend. These gestures and moods had become familiar during their time in each other's company, and they were that much dearer to her.

Ila's look was one of tired resignation. *You're not going to change your mind, are you?*

No.

You're a stubborn girl, Apaay. Very stubborn. But the wry smile softened her disapproval.

Apaay shot her a grin. *You're welcome to come with me.*

She shook her head. *I'll stay here. But be careful, all right?*

I will.

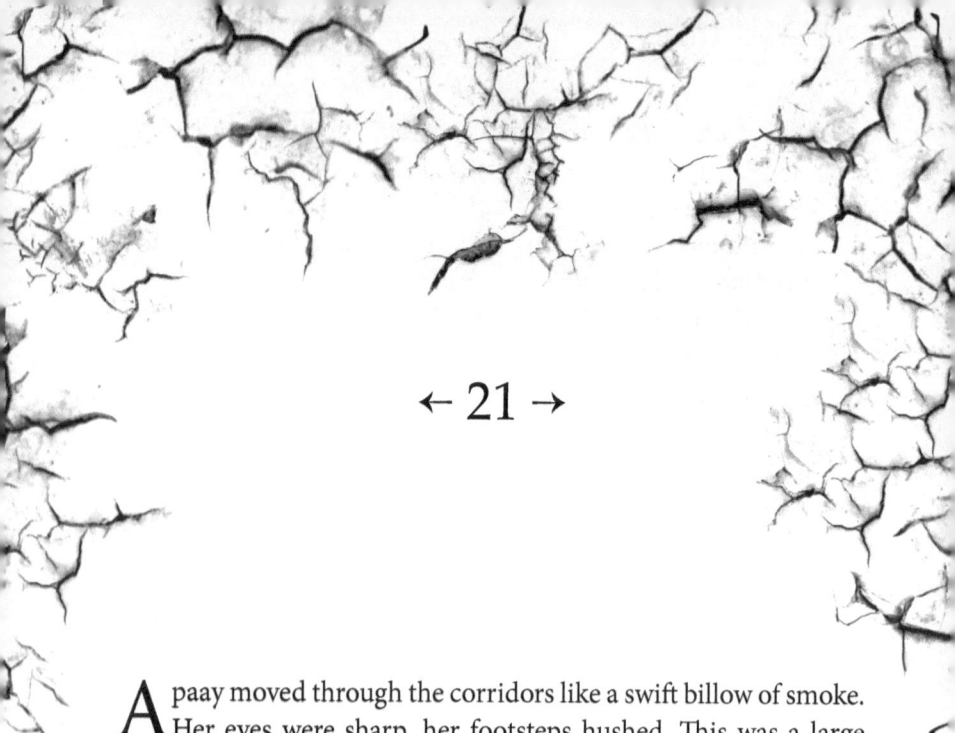

Apaay moved through the corridors like a swift billow of smoke. Her eyes were sharp, her footsteps hushed. This was a large fortress with many halls, many places to hide. The darkness loomed.

The stone wrapped Apaay in deep silence. Every few seconds, a glance over her shoulder. Every minute, a pause for breath. Her awareness tingled, stretching to encompass everything that lay ahead and behind. The space beyond her immediate surroundings locked her muscles in nervous anticipation as she made her way to the central chamber. The sounds she could not hear. The guards she could not see.

When the gleaming ice came into view, her footsteps slowed. The oil lamps had been extinguished. Moonlight speared through the oval windows lining the domed ceiling above, setting the walls—and the five mirrors leaning against them—aglow. Judging by the brilliance, it must be near a full moon.

Apaay hovered inside one of the triangular entryways. The room no longer resembled the arena, that pit of fear. The stands and the people and the corpse and the blood were gone. Everything had been wiped clean.

But the throne still stood, awaiting Yuki's return. With no one to fill the seats, there was an abandoned air to everything.

She hesitated. Normally there were two guards stationed at each entryway, brandishing spears, expressions tight and controlled. Tonight, she had yet to spot a guard, not only in this chamber, but in the entire fortress. Was it possible the guards had accompanied Yuki for added protection?

Apaay allowed herself exactly thirty seconds of uncertainty before she slunk toward the next passage entrance, shrinking away from the patches of light. She removed one of her mittens and slid one damp palm along the wall, fingers trailing through the crevices where the stones had been stacked atop one another.

When the texture of the wall changed, rough to smooth, Apaay flinched back.

It was only one of the mirrors, she realized with a breathy laugh.

But she did not move away. She stared into the sweep of black—the only mirror of the five that did not reflect light—as if pinned by a larger force. Her palm rested against the unembellished frame. The edges pulsed like a darkly beating heart. While the other mirrors acted as doorways to different parts of the labyrinth, somehow Apaay knew the rules did not apply to this one. She did not know what lay beyond its shuddering surface, but it would surely not take her anywhere she wanted to go.

It was an effort to tear her attention away, and Apaay wasted no time slipping down one of the deserted passageways. The first fork she came to, she stopped. The right corridor smelled of clean air. The left reeked of damp suffocation.

Longing propelled her forward, and a feeling like loss, and hope that she would reunite with Eska. What things had she lost in the last few months? How many nights had she lain awake wishing they could be found?

Onward through the chilling quiet she went. The lack of sound was nothing new. Apaay knew how to walk through the world in silence. Hunting had developed that skill. Boots noiseless on the stone, her breath eased through her nose in a slow, steady stream.

Deeper and deeper she went.

The fortress was a maze of halls and dead ends, some circling back to where she'd previously been. Many mirrors lined the walls, though she didn't dare step through any of them for fear of what lay within. Another blizzard. Another room stuffed with carnivorous spirits. Apaay, while not certain of which direction she traveled in, had a tentative idea. She listened carefully for a faint, barely there voice, the one she'd heard in the rock land where she had fallen prey to the Sea Wolf. She had not forgotten that voice. Sometimes she had wondered who it belonged to. A child, a woman, a man?

She thought again. Prisoner, guard, memory, dream?

Wrinkles furrowed her brow. These were the wrong questions. Not *who*, but *what*.

She imagined the questions as water cupped in her palms, lifted, angled against the light so the refractions gleamed. Was it possible the voice had come from one of the stolen faces?

Apaay turned down yet another hall. She was standing at the mouth of the passage when someone whirled her around and slammed her against the wall.

A hand clapped down on her mouth, cutting off any sound she might make. Apaay inhaled through her nose in recognition.

Irnik.

He said lowly, "You're lucky I'm not a different guard, or Yuki would have your head."

Apaay didn't answer—for obvious reasons. Neither did she try to escape. How was it possible that out of all the guards in this place, *he* was the one she ran into?

At least he did not smell of fish.

"I will remove my hand," he said, "if you promise not to run."

Her throat eased its tightening. Perhaps one of the few choices she'd had since she'd been captured, shoved in a cage to die. Yes, she would absolutely take that choice.

She nodded, and his hand lifted.

"What are you doing here?" she asked.

His brows crept upward. "I believe that's the question *I* should be asking *you*. How did you get out of your cell?"

Less than a foot of space separated their bodies, the air between them tinged with cold and secrets and lies.

"I have something to do," she whispered.

"That's not an answer."

It was answer enough for Apaay, and that's all that mattered.

She tried pushing him away, but he didn't budge. "Let me go," she snapped.

Immediately, he stepped back, giving her space. "You won't find the faces. No one has ever been able to find them."

"Is that supposed to sway me? Because it won't work."

He lifted his hands. "I'm trying to save you from disappointment."

"Maybe you haven't looked hard enough."

"Maybe," he murmured, and something in his gaze gave her pause. Eyes that were perfect for the shadows, where no one thought to look.

After listening to see if anyone approached, she asked in curiosity, "Are you looking for a face, too?" It would explain why he had come to work for Yuki, knowing the Face Stealer's cache wasn't far.

"No. I'm just trying to figure out how to build a life I'm proud of. One where I don't have to be alone." The last statement he uttered softly, more secret than declaration. She had never been more aware of their positioning—close enough to share breath, all but invisible in the dark.

"What's it like for you?" she whispered. "To be alone, I mean."

A small, sad smile broke across his face. A story lay there, far beneath the surface. "Hold out your hand."

She did, wondering where this was going.

"See how empty it is?"

"Yes."

"That's what being alone feels like for me."

Apaay struggled for words, because in the past months, she had felt this way, too. A feeling like starvation, the knowledge that your belly would never again be full. She softened toward the guard, imagining Ila experiencing the same sense of loss. She was glad Ila and Irnik had found each other. Companionship was no small thing.

Apaay stepped closer, forcing him back so she could slip away and face him without a wall blocking her escape. "Then you can understand why I need to do this. I don't want my sister to live the rest of her life without ever laughing again, or seeing the sun."

"You'll be caught," he said seriously. "You were lucky the first time. There will be no second time."

"That's a risk I'm willing to take," Apaay said, walking backward down the hall.

He started to follow her.

She faltered. "What are you doing?"

"Coming with you."

"No, you're not."

For some reason, her alarm seemed to amuse him, and he smiled and continued to walk toward her, closer and closer and closer. "Yes, I am."

"I'm going by myself. I don't want you slowing me down."

He snorted as he passed her, melting into the dark while Apaay stared at his retreating back. "I won't slow you down. Besides, I know the labyrinth better than you. It would be wise if you accepted my help."

"How do I know you're not going to turn me in?"

"If I wanted to turn you in, I would have done so already."

With a huff, she followed the guard's lead, albeit reluctantly. Ten minutes passed, possibly more. She had no sense of direction. In hindsight, it was probably a good thing she had run into Irnik, as she would not be able to find her way back to the cell, and to Ila, when the time came to leave.

Then the whispers came.

Hello, my dear
So far, so near
Please help us find
Ourselves, made blind

The singsong voices clanged inside her head, not at all melodic. Shrill with desperation, they clawed at her attention, like sharp nails digging in.

"Do you hear that?" she said, slowing as they rounded a corner.

"Hear what?"

"Voices."

Ahead, Irnik stopped, slowly turned. She couldn't read his expression. "No."

Curling her arms around herself for extra warmth, she leaned against the wall. The clash of pitches, high and low and everything in between, was making her head throb. "This might sound strange, but this isn't the first time I've heard voices."

"What do you mean?"

"I heard them the last time I was in the labyrinth. And sometimes I hear them in my dreams." She glanced at him. "Don't look at me like that."

He shook his head, and she couldn't help but think there was something deeper to his confusion. "If what you claim is true, where do you think they come from?"

"I don't know, but I was thinking. Maybe they're the voices of the people whose faces were stolen." She swallowed, well aware that she was grasping for any sort of connection. "I think they might lead me to where the faces are stored."

Irnik returned to her side, his thoughtful expression overlaid by a thin veneer of curiosity. "And what are the voices telling you?"

"To find them."

Together, they followed the song only Apaay heard, taking the turns where it grew louder, avoiding the paths where it tapered off. They wandered so deeply into the stone she felt buried.

Eventually, they reached a mirror situated in the center of a tidy courtyard dotted with tables and chairs, a glittering ice bridge overlaying a half-frozen stream.

"Wait." Irnik gripped her arm before she could approach. "Let's think about this for a minute."

With a scowl, she faced him. "What is there to think about? I hear them. The faces *want* me to find them."

"You said so yourself you only *think* the voices come from the faces. What if you're wrong? You don't know what lies beyond that mirror."

"I don't have to know. I just have to believe." It fueled her dreams, this tether. Or rather, it had. At some point it had begun to unravel, and was unraveling still. "Haven't you ever believed in something worthwhile, or has this place sucked all the belief out of you?"

"And what's worthwhile?" he grated. "Death?"

"Eska." Her sister would always, always be worthwhile.

"How will you get home? Even if you make it out of here alive, you still have to trek hundreds of miles south. What about supplies? What about the fact that you're thirty pounds underweight? What about food?"

Taken aback, Apaay looked at him for a long moment as realization set in. "You don't think I can do it," she whispered, and was back with her parents on the night she'd left home, sitting in their cozy ice house, their doubts cutting into her as swift as any blade. "You think I'll fail."

Now *he* looked shocked. "What? That's not what I think at all."

With a curse, she pushed him aside and marched toward the mirror. She was a filthy, ragged girl, but there was still fire in her heart. "I'll have you know—" She choked down the quaver. "I'll have you know I am just as capable of finding Eska's face now as I was when I first arrived," she said, infusing her words with false bravado so he would not know how severely his qualms had shaken her, how her own doubts left crumbling decay in their wake.

It always returned to this: inadequacy. This way of thinking was deeply ingrained. Apaay recalled the conversation she and Ila had shared about individuality, self-worth. She wanted to be fully Apaay, unashamed. And the first step was leaving that way of thinking behind.

She topped the delicately arched bridge.

"I didn't mean—"

But she was already stepping through, relieved that Irnik would not be following, as the mirrors only shared their secrets with one.

As soon as she passed into the next room though, the voices quieted. If she strained her ears, she could make out one or two individual pitches, but they were so faint she might have been imagining them. This wasn't supposed to happen. The voices were supposed to lead her to the faces, right? She must have gone the wrong way.

Walls of slickened ice towered on either side of her, framing a narrow path. Shoulders hunched, Apaay walked until she reached a fork: left or right.

A maze. A labyrinth within a labyrinth. How horribly clever.

She went right. The walls and passages were straight with cutting corners, no softness or curves. She wasn't sure how large the maze was, but it must have been massive, as she heard nothing but her own footsteps. An echo of her presence.

When she reached another fork and began to turn right, a crackling groan sounded from behind. The earth trembled. Apaay didn't dare move, straining for a sight or sound, something that did not belong. She braced herself for the possibility of more crushing walls.

From far away, a wolf howled.

Apaay backtracked and picked up her pace, feeling as if something, or someone, was following her. By the time she reached the next fork, she was panting. She went left, all the way down the passage, until she reached a dead end.

There hadn't been a dead end here before. She was sure of it, having kept track of the layout in her mind. Except this ice was a different hue, blue as opposed to white. It did not match the color of the adjacent wall.

Her stomach cinched tighter, a stitch gouging into her side. She couldn't remember where the last turn had been.

Hunching over to relieve the pain, Apaay retraced her steps to the previous divide, intending to take a right instead of the original left, except when she reached that point, the structure had changed. There was no place where the path branched off. The passage continued, on and on, and dread settled heavily in her gut, because that was impossible unless the walls . . .

Unless the walls were moving.

From the corner of her eye, something shifted, and Apaay stumbled back on a sharp inhalation, her back hitting the wall. It was a wolf carved completely of ice.

The creature took two steps toward her. Its fur was white frost. A chiseled snout, the eyes two pits gouged into the ice, the tail tinkling as it lifted in a display of dominance, everything sharp and angular and clinking. Its ears perked forward in demand of her submission.

Apaay's unsteady breath ghosted over her dry, cracked lips. Wolves were not aggressive toward humans. They lived in secret and solitude, rarely seen. Her people held great respect for the wolf, as it was an excellent hunter, full of strength and vivacity, with strong kinship bonds and an untarnished spirit.

But this was not a normal wolf. It was not made of flesh. It was not muscle and blood. It was one of Yuki's toys, and it had come out to play.

Apaay had not yet submitted. She remained pinned against the wall. She should have brought something to defend herself with. A rock. Anything. These thoughts were instinctive, yet wrong, for a deep-seated sense of familiarity held her back. She did not want to hurt this creature.

Its howl was a sound like pure, golden light pouring into the emptiness. Before long, another of its pack joined in song, followed by a second, a third, their individual threads weaving into a complex tapestry.

Apaay was so focused on the howling that she did not notice the wolf shift closer. Lips peeled back, it lunged and snapped its teeth together, an attempt to regain control of a subordinate. Apaay fell to the side, arms shielding her face as ice shards shot from its mouth.

Then it was upon her.

Spurred by instinct, Apaay was already moving, twisting her body in a way that allowed her to reach around and grab its frosted ruff. Using all her strength—which wasn't much these days—she slammed the wolf into the wall. Bits of frozen water broke away in chunks. Its tail. A hind leg. The animal snapped its jaws around her wounded calf muscle, which was still tender from the arena. She screamed, a shrill keening that scraped along the frosted walls, and kicked its muzzle into shards in her haste to flee.

Apaay barreled around a bend, and then another, inking the layout of the maze in her mind despite the knowledge that it could change. She reached dead ends, backtracked, ended up in corridors that had not previously existed. The walls only moved when her back was turned, her attention elsewhere.

She knew she didn't have much time. She needed a plan, a way out. Just as she had escaped the room of doors and the Sea Wolf. Thinking. Searching. Remembering. Digging down deep into her heart. Who was she? Resourceful, adaptable, resilient. The North had taught her the world was always changing. Remain rigid like ice, and you would crack. Allow yourself fluidity, like water, and you could not be broken.

A mournful howl peaked, lifting the hair on her body. The rest of the pack must have discovered their ruined family member.

The walls were impossibly high and thick. She would never be able to break through. She could not see onto the other side. What if the mirror awaited her behind the wall? She would never know.

Apaay remembered, then, the pile of ice from the broken wolf. Sharp, like shattered glass. Sturdy and most likely able to bear her weight.

She turned around and went back.

It was a miracle she stumbled upon the ice pile at all. The wolf pack was gone, likely tracking her scent through the ever-changing labyrinth, and she did not question her luck. Apaay began sorting through the scraps as the howls ripped into snarls. She found four thick shards as long as her forearms and knocked them against each other to chip the ends into spear-like points. Her hands shook so violently that one of the pieces slipped from her grasp and shattered on the ground.

She grabbed another, sharpened its point. After hefting their dead weight in her hands, she decided these were adequate for the job and tied two to the bottom of her boots with strips of sealskin she had saved after building the kayak, the other two gripped in her hands. A growl rumbled on the other side of the wall.

Drawing one arm back, Apaay plunged the pick into the ice.

Ice climbing was a skill she had learned only a few years ago. The picks had been fashioned of bone then, but the concept remained the same. Always have three points of contact on the wall's surface. Alternate hand and foot. Keep your body as close to the cliff face as possible. Lower the heels to lever the picks deeper into the ice.

She fell into a rhythm she had learned long ago. Now it returned to her. Rearing back, Apaay drove her right foot into the ice a step higher, followed by her left hand, followed by her left foot. Her muscles coiled, stretched, allowed her to shift up another few feet. She wobbled, off balance. Her hips were pushed too far back. She tucked them in and quickly found her center. Apaay put trust in her body, in the strength she knew existed somewhere among the pieces of her past. She reached for another hold, digging in. The ice creaked beneath her weight.

Apaay wavered as her pulse surged, then released a breath and rested her forehead against the wall. The sound meant nothing. The ice was solid, without cracks, without flaws. Strong.

Tilting back her head, Apaay dug in one of her hand picks and heaved. Though she could not yet see the top, she told herself it was not far. The next hand or foothold, or the one after that. There was only up. There was only the next step.

A tremor shimmied up her calf. Pain spread and burrowed in, forcing Apaay to shift her weight onto her left leg to ease the cramp. She tried to ignore the pain of her wound, its weakness, blood clotting against the tatters of her trouser leg from where the polar bear had ripped into it. Her upper body, too, had begun to twinge, especially her forearms, the tendons taut at being overworked. Two months of imprisonment had eroded her strength. Water on stone.

Delicate clinking sounded below, cut through by a mournful howl. The wolves had returned.

Her parka was like a dense second skin, trapping the steaming air against her body. Moisture slithered down her back, gathered in the creases of her arms and legs so the damp bristles of her inner layer clung. Her entire body felt heavy and suffused with blood. Each passing moment there was more weight dragging at her limbs, at the picks of ice. It was growing difficult to shove them into the wall, as force of impact had dulled their points. They felt brittle in her hands.

She told herself she would not allow these dark thoughts to take shape, but the strain and stress fed her fears, and she could think of nothing else. How impossibly high the wall soared. These picks, so flimsy and inadequate. The slippery ice.

Mistake, her mind whispered.

Apaay clung to the bits of ice gouged into the wall, shaking. For so long she had wanted to prove that she could do more, *be* more, if only given the chance. The idea would not settle. It lived beneath her skin.

She thought of how relieved she'd been to leave Irnik behind in the courtyard and wanted to laugh at her foolishness. She had thought she could do this alone. She'd been wrong. Apaay wished for his help now, even knowing it was far too late for that. *I believe in you.* Those were the words she wished for.

Hauling up her deadweight another few feet, Apaay faltered as her thigh muscle seized in a white flare of pain. The foot pick skittered along the surface, and her stomach lurched as she dropped, agony searing through her shoulders as she shifted her weight to her upper body. Her boots scrabbled for purchase. A dent, a hairline crack to shove into. Slippery, slippery ice. Apaay had just managed to locate a hold when her other foot slipped from its anchor. She dropped even farther this time, the muscles in her back screaming.

Apaay couldn't move. The air cooling her bare head made her feel especially vulnerable. Sweat dripped from her body, and her only thought was how long she could cling to the cliff face before the picks gave out. Again, she pushed her boots against the wall. There was no hold. She blindly slammed the toe of her free leg into the surface and heard an unmistakable crack. She glanced down. A piece crumbled away, disappearing among the wolf pack.

One more, Apaay promised, driving one of the ice picks she gripped in her hand forward. She could not stop. She could not slow.

The pick made impact and shattered.

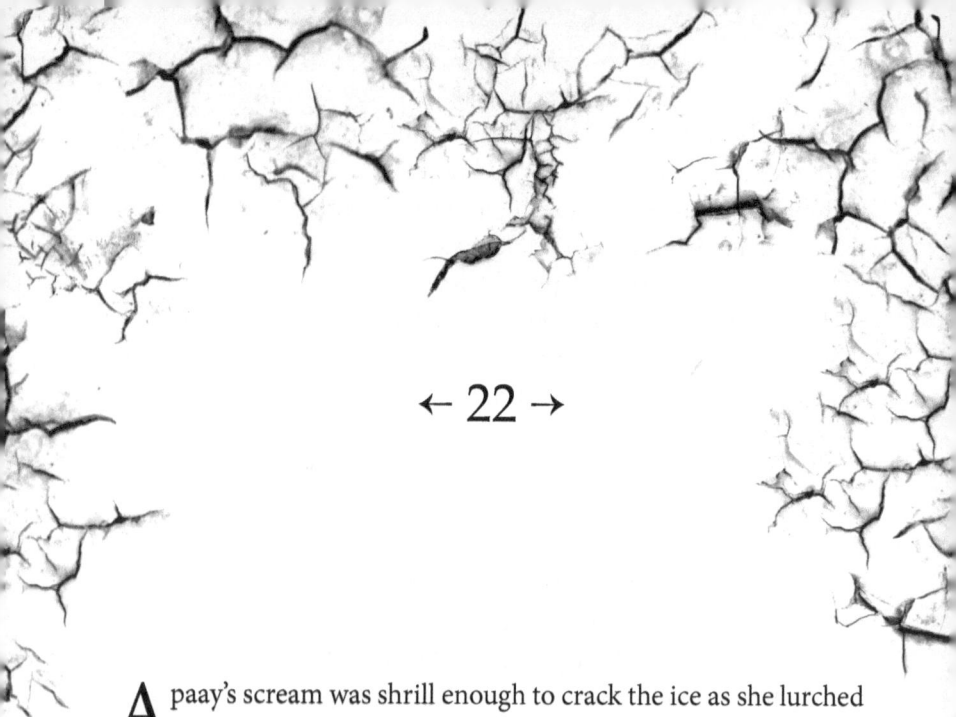

← 22 →

Apaay's scream was shrill enough to crack the ice as she lurched off balance, her other hand scrabbling for a hold, any hold, against the slick surface. She tried digging her fingers into a crack, but there were none. Her body bowed. Her abdominal muscles shredded with heat, wrist pained from the awkward angle at which she clung one-handed to the remaining ice pick. The space swelled around her. The sky loomed above. Only by tucking in her elbow could Apaay center herself and grab hold of the tool with both hands. Gasping for air, she pressed her body flat against the sheer ice, eyes squeezed shut. It was a long fall to the ground.

Her limbs trembled. Her gut churned. A single pick for her hands, and two for her feet. She would never reach the top.

Apaay rested her forehead against the wall. The cold seared. Below, the wolves writhed with frenzy, but she was strangely detached from it all. She was tired. She was so, so tired. She would kill herself to complete an impossible task. Save Eska, but now Chena and Ila, too. It was too much. She carried the weight of not one, not two, but four people on her back, and she could not hold on for much longer.

Her skin was all sweat. The pads of her fingers had blistered from being worn down to raw, peeled skin sticking to the inner hairs of her mittens. She did not know whether her feet picks were sturdy or if they were one impact away from shattering as well. Her body had reached its limit, and the only thing holding her upright was sheer force of will and a single question: What would tomorrow bring?

Salvation?

Or hell?

I love you. Apaay wished she had told Mama and Papa before slipping away like the thief she had chased after. What would they say if they saw her now, if they learned of the blood on her hands, the heart that was beginning to harden? If she told them she had tried to the best of her abilities but didn't think she could go on?

Apaay remembered Mama's fingers threading through her hair one night long ago, cheek pressed against the soft blanket after learning she would once again not be chosen to lead the summer hunt. Apaay had sobbed long and hard. Her heart felt as if it were breaking. She wanted so badly to show what she could do, and now she would not have that chance.

"I wish I didn't care," she'd said, the words broken and garbled. Her face stung, puffy to the touch. "It would be easier if I didn't, if I wasn't so weak." She'd tried, every year, without fail. They still didn't want her. She wasn't good enough.

"No, naaja." Mama clutched her hand, momentarily pulling Apaay from her sadness. "Don't ever think that. Don't ever stop caring." Voice pitched low, she whispered, "You love so fiercely. With your whole heart. That's where your strength comes from. Not from your skill in hunting. Not from tracking. Here." She pressed her palm against Apaay's breastbone. "Always remember that."

Apaay blinked sweat from her eyes as, somewhere in the maze, another wall moved positions with a harsh crunch. She imagined her thoughts as a drowsy wolf pup and ran her hand along its back, one long stroke to slow its deadly, anxious speed.

Think, Apaay.

She had not forgotten why she had come. She imagined Eska at her side, racing her to the top. Shoulder to shoulder, they would climb, hand over foot, and Apaay would get there first, and they would both pretend Eska had not let her win. Strong in body, strong in spirit.

By the time she had calmed, Apaay had a solution. She would simply have to use one of her foot picks as a hand pick. It was not ideal, but she could use one foot to brace herself while quickly plunging the remaining foot pick into the ice. If she didn't have two hand picks, she would have no way to root herself when reaching for the next hold.

Clutching the ice pick shoved in at chest level, she tried yanking one foot free but found it stuck. Taking a breath, she looked down.

The world rippled like a vast white sea, dots bursting in her vision. One of the wolves lunged, its claws scrabbling against the smooth wall, unable to grip or climb. Ice shot from its mouth in retaliation, but she was too far away and it fell short. Apaay's stomach heaved from the great height.

She tore her gaze away from the ground, the fatal drop reminding her of all she had to lose.

And Apaay decided she did not need her eyes. She needed only her hands.

Using her teeth to pull one of her mittens free, she reached down and began removing one of the ice picks attached to her boot by sense of touch. She fumbled for the knot and scowled at how tightly she had tied it. Apaay hadn't figured she'd need to *untie* it. After long minutes, the knot loosened and she extracted the wedge of ice, the strip of sealskin dropping away.

With the pick finally free, she reached up and slammed it into the wall above her head, body flush against the vertical surface.

It held.

With less stability, Apaay was forced to change the pattern of where and when she planted her holds: hands spread farther apart, feet shifted closer together, the single picked foot in the very center. Right hand, left hand, and then, using her upper body strength to remain steady, she braced her free foot against the wall and quickly shoved the foot with the pick higher, gouging it in. She had no hair. No mother. No home. And why was that? Because the Face Stealer had taken them from her.

The fury sent her up a step. Her picks dug in. Another hold. It hadn't been a choice then, and it wasn't a choice now. Apaay loved her people. She would climb this wall. For them. For herself. The contraction of her abdominal muscles pushed her higher, higher still, until she reached the top.

Apaay grabbed the lip of the wall, hauled herself over on watery arms, and collapsed onto her back, staring at the blank canvas of the sky, a raw-edged laugh slipping past her lips. By the skin of her teeth, or maybe the skin of her hands, she'd made it. And even if no one was here to witness the occasion, she felt proud of her accomplishment, an emotion she hadn't experienced in years. Her chest warmed at the feeling of self-love.

Once Apaay had calmed her nervous energy enough to stand, she examined her surroundings, her hand sliding into her pocket where the stone wolf resided, giving her strength when she needed it, that of her people. The maze extended for perhaps a quarter of a mile in each direction, the walls following its contours. Some extended halfway around the circle, while others blunted, leading to dead ends.

Since the wall was near ten feet thick, it was not difficult to traverse as Apaay peeked over the edge in search of the second mirror. She found it, unsurprisingly, in the very heart of the maze. After a quick descent, she reached the embellished frame, paw prints carved into its corners. With a deep breath, Apaay stepped through.

And fell, a sudden drop through the close, damp air. The force of impact as she hit the ground punched through her body—ankles, hips, knees. It was dark. She should have been used to it by now, but every time she stumbled into the shadows' thick wrappings, her pulse sped up, body curling in on itself, already seeking safety.

With a soft groan, Apaay rolled onto her back. At least the adrenaline had dulled the agony in her leg.

"Wh-who's there?"

It took some time to place the voice. Even longer to place the location. The long corridor, the stench of refuse and decay—the cells she'd discovered the very first time she'd traversed the labyrinth. The only difference now was the single torch flickering at the end of the hall. Someone must have visited recently.

After brushing herself off and checking to make sure there were no broken bones, Apaay knelt in front of the cell where the prisoner resided, saying, "It's me. Apaay." She removed her mittens and shoved them into her trouser pockets.

The man shifted in the back corner. The shadows cloaked him. "You came back." Hopeful. The emotion tugged at her. She wished he would come forward so she could see his face. Apaay wanted to look into this man's eyes, because that was how she came to know someone.

"I . . . yes." There was no point in telling him her return had been unintentional. He had a difficult life as it was.

There was a pause, his breathing—and hers—the only sounds. They understood each other in this way.

She shifted closer to the light, and he gasped. "Your head is shaved." Shock, and underneath, the edge of dismay.

As if she could forget. Apaay touched her scalp, the soft fuzz that would never be the same as her long dark locks. Her hood must have fallen away when she'd been airborne.

He shuffled a few inches closer. "How are you feeling?"

"What do you mean?"

"I mean your hair is gone. How have you been coping?"

Apaay didn't think she'd be more surprised if he physically knocked her over the head with a rock. No one had asked her this. Not Ila, and not, she added with a touch of folly, Irnik. But she had wanted them to. Something to show her they cared about her mental well-being. She couldn't help but resent them a little for their obliviousness.

Laughter strained, she slumped against the bars. "Not great." Not even close. "I'm thankful no one from my community is here to see me."

"What did you do, if you don't mind me asking?"

It was ridiculous how she immediately thought, *The right thing,* and more ridiculous that it had led to this tragedy. "I helped a friend and spoke the truth, which is apparently grounds for punishment."

"Yes," he murmured to himself. "I do know something about that."

Apaay wondered what he knew, but she did not want to scare him off. She kept her silence.

He said, after some time, "Did you find your sister's face?"

So he had remembered. Apaay assumed he had forgotten their previous conversation, as he did not remember much about his life before this. "No," she whispered. "I looked twice, and both times I came up empty. I'm beginning to wonder if it's even here." Because if it wasn't, then she had done all of this for nothing.

"The Face Stealer never keeps his prizes all in the same place. He spreads them out." She could barely make out his expression. "It's possible you were close to finding her face before, but then he went and changed the location."

"How do you know that?"

His blurry form sat up straighter. Almost a minute passed before he continued. "Because a long time ago I managed to escape this cell. I was searching for a face he had stolen from me." The next words ached. "I was never able to find it."

"You were caught?"

"Yes."

Something had happened to him then. His voice spoke of a violent past, a wound that had yet to heal and maybe never would. Whose face had he searched for? A family member, a lover, a friend? She wished she could see his expression and tell him he was not alone. They were reaching through the dark together.

Her question came low, tentative. "Did they punish you? When they discovered you had escaped?"

"I have suffered almost twenty years' worth of punishment," he replied heavily. "What the Face Stealer did to me then was not the worst of what I have endured."

An ill feeling squirmed in her stomach. The torture this man must have been subjected to made her falter.

Apaay wanted to see the face of the man she spoke to. It was essential. She didn't want to speak to him blind. She wanted to see all of him. "Won't you come into the light?"

He recoiled as if struck. "No. I can't. I—"

"Please. I promise not to hurt you."

She felt his stare, the intensity, even though she couldn't see it. "I don't want to frighten you."

"You won't frighten me." Yet her heart picked up speed.

"Are you certain?"

"Yes. You don't have to hide from me."

He moved without haste, someone who was suffering from pain or exhaustion or both. There was a scuffing sound, the hiss of cloth skimming along the ground. Apaay held herself immobile. She hardly dared to breathe lest she frighten him back into his corner. Rats scuttled nearby, the scratch of their nails loud in the enclosed space.

When he emerged from the streaking shadows, Apaay nearly let slip a gasp. Only a few feet separated them, save the iron bars of his cage.

Scars ravaged his face, as if some beast had torn it apart with nails and teeth and claws. The left side of his mouth drooped, and he had lost his left eye as well. The skin around the socket puckered, the scarring shiny and taut from the top of his brow bone to the flat plane of his cheek. His remaining eye, however, was perfectly clear. The shining pupil slid up and down her malnourished form before locking onto her face.

"Are you afraid of me?" he whispered.

"No." She was afraid of many things, but he was not one of them. She did not fear other people's pain.

"It's been a long time since I've seen another person," he murmured. "A long time since anyone has seen me."

Apaay grasped for what to say to this man, who was younger than she would have suspected. He couldn't be older than twenty-five.

Her words were simple and sincere. "I see you."

Wordlessly, he bowed his head. "I wish we could have had a proper introduction." His voice grated, stone on stone. "But since I can't remember my name, I'm not sure how to introduce myself."

As silly as it sounded, she wanted to give him a hug. It was completely endearing how polite he acted, considering they were both trapped in less than ideal circumstances. "Maybe—that is, if you don't mind—we can think of another name for you."

His nod was faint. "I would like that."

The naming process was not simple. It was not a piece of fluff plucked from the air. It was a deep, complicated occasion, one that grew roots strong enough to span generations and sustain the life of one's community.

Apaay did not know why or how this man had forgotten his name-soul, whether trauma had crushed the memory, or even if he was telling the truth. Either way, she would try to give him a new name. Or rather, *one* new name. Analak names held no regard for gender, and it was not uncommon for her people to have multiple names depending on their individual relationships with others.

Apaay wanted to give him that feeling of belonging. She wanted this name to embody him.

She took a long, hard look at the prisoner. A thinned face, hollowed out by hunger, cheekbones protruding. Lack of light had paled his grimy skin, and she wondered when he had last bathed. His head, she noticed with surprise, had been shorn at some point, though the strands had regrown to brush the tops of his ears. He, too, knew what it was like to feel untethered, lost.

Apaay tilted her head in thought. Who he was, who he had been, who he could be, what had led him here, what he had sustained.

"What about 'Masuk'?"

"Masuk." The name rolled along his tongue, as if he were testing its weight.

"There was a man from my village who passed on a few years ago. He went through a lot of hardship in life." Both his wife and daughter had died in childbirth. The man's father had begun to lose his memory and could not remember what his son looked like, or if he had one at all. "But he was kind to everyone. He was strong. I feel like his name reflects your strength: Masuk."

Survivor, in the language of her people.

His eyes flickered with what she believed to be gratitude. "Thank you."

Apaay glanced toward the end of the hall, where a single mirror had suddenly appeared, reflecting the glow of the torchlight. "I should go."

As she stood, he surged forward and clasped the bars with his bony fingers. "If you find a way out," he said, and the words, so full of hope, tugged her toward him, this young man who had known darkness for so long, "don't leave me."

If she found a way out. *If.* "How am I supposed to find you again? I don't know where this place is." But he might, if he had once managed to escape.

"Take one of the staircases to the sixth level. Just . . . don't leave me here in the dark."

She would never understand what he had endured. Someday, though, she hoped to learn of his story. "I won't," Apaay said. "I promise."

← →

After passing through another mirror, Apaay now moved cautiously down a corridor in another part of the fortress, the voices having returned at full force. Whispers and pleas and songs, women and children and men, leading her deeper into the bowels of the labyrinth, down winding staircases with sheer drops into a void.

Again, the guards were absent. They were not posted before the entryways. They were not conversing in the shadows or dozing against the walls. There was nothing and no one around, no footsteps save her own—a lonely padding of boots into the dark and the damp.

Irnik did not reappear. No doubt he was cursing her name in some hallway on the other side of the fortress, but a small part of her wished he would. Appear, that is. She had enjoyed his company.

The whispers rose in volume, a rich complexity, and they yanked her down a shorter set of stairs that led to a broad, airy hallway.

A door glowed at the end of it.

Apaay regarded the wooden door in wariness. Light streamed from beneath the bottom crack, and the corners were embellished with strange swirls. Thus far, she had only ever traveled through mirrors, but the voices shrieked and cawed and hissed, surging like breaking waves.

They demanded she go forward.

They demanded she set them free.

Jaw locked in resolve, she began to walk.

And walk.

And walk.

She must have walked near one hundred steps, yet the door grew no closer. The voices were thunder in her ears. She could not block them out.

Her footsteps slowed, then halted altogether. Harsh breaths punctured the silence. The distance to the door was no shorter, no longer. Nothing had changed.

Apaay ground her teeth together in frustration. Honestly, when had *anything* worked out the way she wanted it to? Riddles, tricks, and lies. Nothing was clear in the dark. Bowing her head, she was considering possible solutions when something shifted in her peripheral vision, and she stumbled back, a hard object digging into her lower spine. The door handle. Somehow by walking backward, she had managed to reach the door.

Blood pulsed at her temples. Something was out there.

Slowly, Apaay reached behind her. She couldn't see down the passageway beyond. *Out. Get out now.*

Pushing down the handle at her back, she slipped through the door and closed out the darkness.

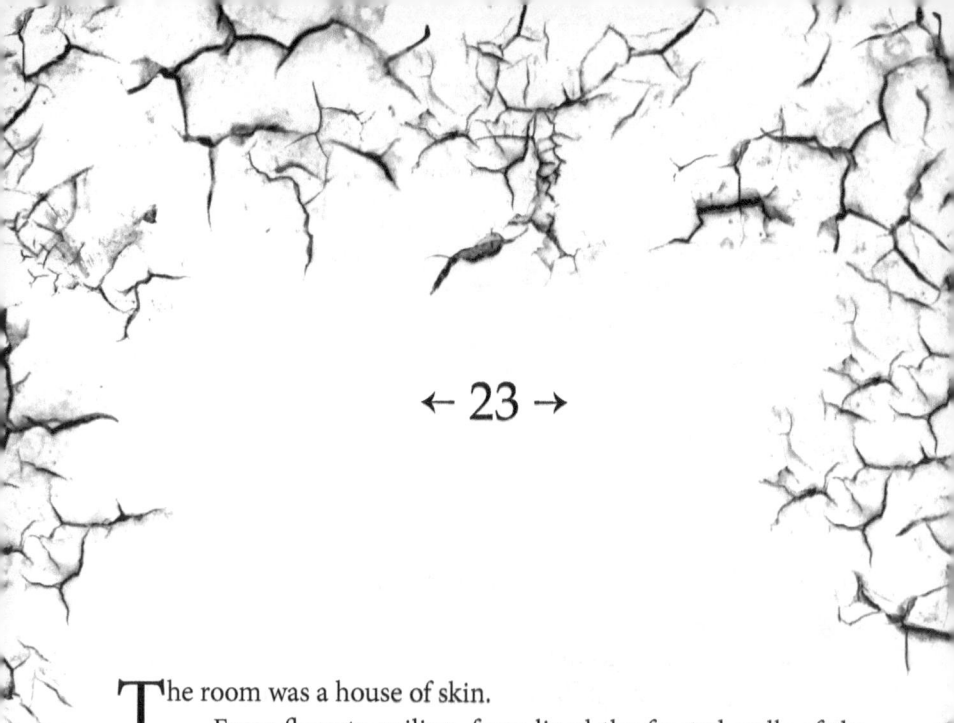

The room was a house of skin.

From floor to ceiling, faces lined the frosted walls of the long, narrow space, stretching into the dark, where they disappeared. Amber and bronze and brown, hints of red, hints of gold, light and dark, warm and cool. Occasionally, a paler complexion, or one of deepest brown. The faces sat silently on their shelves, all mulish mouths and slackened lips. Their eyes tracked her as she moved.

The hair along Apaay's body stood on end. The sight was so horrifying that it took a moment for her brain to process what, exactly, she was looking at. The screams had stopped, and it was soundless. She had never seen so many faces in one place before. There must have been thousands of them. Thousands of people who could no longer see, or taste, or speak. Years' and years' worth of stolen identities.

Apaay had grown up fearing the Face Stealer. He was as much a part of her culture as the spirits and gods, this demon who stalked the night. Dark, misunderstood. At times confusing and unreal. Upon her first encounter, Apaay had despised him, yes, but that had been different. She had looked at him through the eyes of a child, a monster come to darken her doorway and dreams.

But herein lay the evidence of his malevolence, a cache of stolen goods. It sickened her. What would cause someone, or something, to do this? What was the reason aside from instilling a legacy of fear?

She did not have time to dwell on questions, as she could not linger. Apaay scoured the bottom shelves first, searching anxiously. She sincerely hoped Eska wasn't displayed on one of the upper-level shelves, as she had no way to access them. Lost to the shadows, they had most likely gathered dust. Forgotten, those ones.

Many of the faces were streaked with dirt or mud or debris— evidence of a former life. They ranged from young to old and everything in between. No person was safe. No one left untouched.

When she stumbled across the newborns, her throat cinched tight. They had been laid gently on the shelves, as they were too small, too delicate, to be hung up. Some were but a few hours old.

She could hardly bear it.

It took perhaps an hour to sift through the bottom shelves, another forty minutes to scan the next shelf up. That girl's face was too round, that nose too narrow, no scar in sight. Her search grew more frantic as time went on.

And then she recognized a face she had seen quite recently. The one the Face Stealer had stolen from her village. The young boy Qavak. Were it not for the birthmark smudging his chin, she would not have recognized him. Such anguish twisted his features.

Reaching out, she ran a fingertip down his chapped cheek, then removed his face from the shelf and held its limp smoothness in her hands. He hadn't deserved this fate. Not at all.

"Dying for my company?" said a voice behind her. "Can't say that I blame you."

Apaay's pulse surged, and she whirled around, dropping her hand to her side. The Face Stealer stood a few feet away, leaning against one of the glittering shelves, a lazy smile curling his mouth. She hadn't heard him enter. His reddish-tan vest molded to his muscular form, highlighting the breadth of his shoulders, and instead of boots, he wore soft-soled slippers that hugged his ankles.

"I was—"

"Oh no," he said, that dark laugh twining around her. Leaning forward, he snatched the face from her grip and arranged it upright on the shelf. "We both know why you're here."

Even after he replaced Qavak's face, he remained close, angling his body toward her. "Can't resist me, can you?"

With a soft snarl, she shoved him away to give herself room to breathe. "Don't flatter yourself."

His irises flickered from molten gold to a playful blue green. "I do love a challenge."

"You're a monster," she spat.

"Monster." He tilted his head in consideration. "Can't say I haven't heard that one before."

"Demon."

"Really, how unoriginal can you be?"

The words swelled, they burned, they were white streaks of rage barreling up her throat, singeing her mouth, all the ways she wanted to rip into him. If she'd had her spear, she would not have hesitated to shove it through his chest. "Destroyer of dreams."

Mouth pursed, he studied her. He did not blink. "Now, that one . . . I have not heard that one before." His gaze skimmed over her bare head, the lack of hair.

"It's rude to stare," she said, fisting her hands so she would not give in to the temptation of lifting her hood.

"I was never one for manners."

He slipped away before she could draw breath. He moved like the wind: powerful, fluid, unseen. "Are you afraid?" He circled her as he'd done the very first day she'd noticed him sitting on his throne, uncaring, insolent.

The tip of his nose skimmed along her cheek, and she recoiled from the touch. "N-no."

His smile was all teeth. "Liar."

Apaay wanted to face him; she wanted to face him so badly. Giving this demon her back, leaving herself vulnerable—it went against every instinct. He could gut her. He could break her arms. He could do so many things, and no one would ever hear her scream.

The fear built, but Apaay squashed it as hard as she could, crushing it beneath her boot. *Don't let him see. Don't ever let him see how he affects you.*

She looked to the open doorway. There was no point in running. Not with the way he moved. Then again, Apaay had no interest in running until she completed her task.

Casually, she wandered past him to one of the shelves as he asked, "Did you find what you were looking for?"

Honestly.

With false sweetness, she said, "Why don't you spare me the games and tell me whether it's here."

"Ask nicely and maybe I'll consider it."

"Yes, because we all know how well that turned out last time." She had asked. And he had denied her.

His laughter stroked along her nape, and Apaay couldn't help how her pulse tripped. "Smart girl."

She scowled, though he couldn't see, and reached into her sleeve where she'd hidden the icicle from the maze, having not wanted to be completely defenseless. It had begun to melt from her body heat, but now that she pulled it free, it hardened from the air's chill.

"Smarter than I first assumed," he went on. "You managed to both escape from your cell—again—and find this room." Something close to admiration rang in the words, and maybe a hint of confusion as to how she had managed it.

"Did you think a few iron bars could stop me?"

"Yes, actually." His voice softened a touch. "I did."

"Your mistake."

"How did you do it? The only way out of the cells is with a key, and the only ones in possession of a key are the guards."

Shifting the weapon to her right hand, Apaay adjusted her grip. "As if I would ever tell you."

"Don't be shy. I can keep a secr— Ah."

Apaay's mouth went dry.

"The young guard who came to speak with me. Irnik, is it?" He chuckled in sly amusement, which only heightened the fire in her.

His arrogance was sickening. "Was it him? Did he give you the key? Poor fool."

When Apaay didn't respond, the Face Stealer sighed and stepped closer. Her bone-white knuckles ached from her hold on the weapon. She regretted killing that woman, but this was different. She had been a victim, like her. He was the true enemy here. The look on his face when she stabbed the ice through his chest . . .

He shifted behind her. She braced herself. "I didn't take any key from any guard. You underestimate me."

"Do I?"

She was taken back to the morning of her first kill. The sleeping woods. Wind racing across lush green grasses, like silver ribbon unspooling. Apprehension and the rush of adrenaline twining within her, that she was here, she would do this, and of what would follow if she made the kill, if she missed.

"Trust," Papa had said. "Trust in yourself."

With a slow exhalation, she'd released the arrow straining against the string of her bow.

And now Apaay stood on a different ledge, but with that same hope and wanting. Trust. Trust things would lead to where they needed to go, and that whatever happened was meant to be. When she had released that arrow, she had wanted to please Papa, but here, alone, there was only Apaay. It was past time, she decided, to trust in herself.

So Apaay took a breath. And struck.

She whirled. Her arm lashed out. The ice cut through the air, spearing toward his heart. Between one blink and the next, he vanished in a pocket of shadow.

Apaay lurched forward from the force of her momentum. She started to turn when something solid plowed into her back, and she slammed into the ground, the icicle snatched from her grip and tossed to the side, where it shattered. Large hands secured her arms against her chest, heaviness pressing down her legs. She jerked once and lay still, staring up at the Face Stealer with clenched teeth.

"If you wanted to kill me," he murmured, eyes strangely bright, "you should have aimed for my neck. Less coverage, you know?"

"Trust me," she growled, struggling in his grip. "Next time I won't miss."

He merely quirked an eyebrow, eyes narrowed above his straight nose. "That's assuming there will be a next time. Who's to say I won't kill you now?"

It was a monumental effort to keep her voice level. She felt his power prowling the room like a large cat. Felt it brush her skin. "You won't kill me."

"Really?" The edge of his mouth twitched, void of amusement. His features were lengthening: nose, mouth, chin. The skin lightened to a tawny hue. An elder stared back at her, wrinkles folded deep. "The way I see it, it would be no less than you deserve."

"You won't do it." Something sour curdled on the back of her tongue as she stared into the wide depths of the woman's pupils, but she would not give him the satisfaction of seeing her flinch a second time. Her body was screaming at her to run. "You want to know why?"

He tilted his head in curiosity, his hair falling forward. The strands appeared silky to the touch. "Enlighten me."

"Because you want to see what happens. You're wondering if I'll succeed or fail. You want to see if I have what it takes."

He made a vague sound in his throat. "Tell me, have you always been this bad at reading people?"

"Only people who have something to hide."

"And do I have something to hide?" He asked it as if this was a game they were playing.

"Yes." She just didn't know what yet.

To her surprise, he released her and rose to his feet, apparently tired of the verbal sparring. "If you're looking for your sister's face, you won't find it here." A provocative grin as he gestured toward the thousands of faces surrounding them, staring out emptily. "But feel free to waste your time searching."

The stone in her chest grew heavier. Masuk had been right. He did keep the faces in different locations. She wondered if the face Yuki looked for was there as well.

Swallowing down her disappointment, Apaay said, "Where is it, then?"

Another laugh. "As if I would tell you."

"You are a truly hideous creature," she ground out, pushing to her feet, though less gracefully than he had. "These people—" She lifted Qavak's face again. "They have lives. And you delight in ruining them."

A muscle fluttered in his jaw, so subtle she nearly missed it. "Yes, and I do such a very good job at it." He strode over and snatched the face from her grip. "Do you want to know how they beg? How they scream and pray someone will save them from this hell? *Do you?*"

The last words were spoken with the face of Qavak. "Take a look," he spat through the boy's small mouth, so at odds with the body of a powerful, fully grown man. "See what it is I can do."

Qavak's face disappeared, replaced with an aging woman, a boy with a hooked nose, a girl with washed-out irises, identity after stolen identity taking hold before reverting to his chiseled beauty as he said, "And you would be wise not to forget it."

Apaay swallowed hard and whispered, "How can you live with yourself?"

He shot her a cutting smile, and she wondered if it didn't hurt him a little to use it. "I don't."

Abruptly, the door to the room slammed shut. A harsh, sucking wind tugged at her clothes as the Face Stealer materialized behind her, a broad hand on her shoulder. "If you want to live," he murmured into her ear, "don't say a word."

Blood surged through her body. She looked to the door—shut. Was this a joke? Or was it possible someone was approaching, even though the fortress had been deserted?

Before she could respond, a blanket of opaqueness flowed from his hands, stretching into fabric and wrapping around her, where it flared and turned transparent. She felt its subtle weight. "To anyone else, you will look like my shadow." He stepped in front of her as the door swung open and Yuki paraded in.

Hands on hips, the young girl glared at the Face Stealer, not giving any indication she noticed another person hunched behind him. "What are you doing here? I thought I sent you on an errand."

"I finished early," the Face Stealer said, calm as could be. "See?" He tossed her a face that suddenly appeared in his hand. Apaay couldn't get a good look at it.

Lines marred the smoothness of her brow, her face drawn as she studied the face. "Fine." She tossed it back to him and began to pace the length of the room, at one point moving so close that Apaay was forced to hold her breath. "The mystery of the council gathering is solved, at least."

"And?"

Yuki stopped near enough that Apaay could reach out and touch the girl's delicately bared shoulder. "And they want to reinstate the alliance."

Beneath his vest, the muscles of the Face Stealer's back locked. "You can't be serious."

"Oh, I am."

"Why?"

She attempted to pat her hair into place but only succeeded in further tangling it. "The better question is, why not?"

"Ah, Yuki." He shifted his body, blocking the girl from Apaay's sight. "I know you enjoy your games, but don't try playing them with me."

It was difficult not to be impressed. The Face Stealer managed to sound both menacing and pleasant, as if he were discussing the weather while pointing a spear at her head.

The girl huffed, fabric rustling. Apaay guessed she had crossed her arms. "You never want to play with me anymore." She moved a few feet to the left, as if unable to stand still. "Apparently, there have been rumors about the Western Territory."

He made a noncommittal sound, though his back remained tense. "What kind of rumors? The Western Territory burned to the ground a long time ago. Or have you forgotten?"

Her mouth settled into a pout. "There's no need to be rude about it."

"What kind of rumors, Yuki?"

Worry darkened the girl's features. While it was not the first time Apaay had seen an emotion other than anger or torment, it unsettled her. The confusion made Yuki appear as she was: a child. "You were right before, about Nanuq. They say he's restless."

Apaay's eyebrows snapped together. There was that name again. *Nanuq.*

"Restless?" the Face Stealer asked. "Restless for what? He's already claimed half the free land."

"Jealous?"

"What does he want with the Western Territory?"

The Western Territory. Apaay sifted through the pieces of information she knew about the North's five territories. Wasn't the Western Territory where the wolf Unua had dwelled before they'd been conquered and wiped out in the war?

"From what I heard," Yuki said, "he has unfinished business to attend to."

The Face Stealer didn't respond, and Apaay had the sense he simply had no words. A rare occurrence. The information must hold some significance to him. "Are you going to rejoin the alliance?"

The girl shrugged and wandered in another circle around the room. She stopped at the face of a young man near Apaay's age. Her fingers brushed across his cheek, the gesture oddly yearning. "I haven't decided. I was thinking about it, though."

"Last time was a mistake. This time will be, too."

Her hand dropped, and she whirled on him, appearing small and frail and someone very much haunted by her past. "It was only a mistake because *you* interfered."

"I had no choice. Joining the alliance won't end well."

"You could join, too, you know."

"Not interested."

"I don't know why you're getting so upset over a piece of burnt rock in the ground. What's done is done."

"I know why you're doing this, Yuki." Rough emotion caught along the edges of his words. "The alliance is another chance for you, isn't it? Prove to your father your greatness, and maybe he'll love you?"

Yuki went immediately still, her shock plain. Whatever conversation Apaay witnessed, it was far more personal than the girl wanted it to be. For once, Yuki was caught in the demon's web, for she did not interrupt him as he went on.

"Tell me," he said. "Did he contact you following the war?"

"There wasn't time—"

"Answer the question."

"I *am*." Ice splintered as one of the shelves cracked in two, and a tumble of faces scattered throughout the room. One hit the toe of Apaay's boot. "He wanted death and destruction, so I gave it to him. But then you interfered, ruining everything. Now you're trying to interfere again. Stay out of it, Numiak."

A long-suffering sigh followed. "Believe it or not, I'm trying to *help* you."

Apaay seriously doubted that.

The girl waded through the faces, kicking them aside with a vengeance. "Let's not lie to each other. You only seek to further your own agenda."

"And you're so different?" Power pulsed around him, roiling like thick bands of smoke that draped over his shoulders and curled around his legs. "Take it from someone who's been there. It doesn't matter what you do. It won't make your father love you."

"Stop talking."

"People like us?" he said, voice hard. "We're not meant to be loved."

The words lingered in the air, as if unwilling to disappear for fear of being overlooked. Apaay had spent enough time in the Face Stealer's company to know he spoke in half-truths and lies, but she had never heard, never *felt*, this type of honesty from him before. Apaay wondered which version of the demon was true, or if they were both lies. She wondered if he had always been this way—a dark thief—or if he had once, perhaps, been human, too.

"I said stop talking," Yuki spat, pointed teeth bared and eyes glistening with moisture. "You're just jealous because the war took everything from you, while I still have a chance to salvage my life."

There was a terrible silence. Apaay glanced between them, the rush of blood crackling in her ears. Yuki and the Face Stealer glared at each other, and their shared pain was like sediment stirred up from a riverbed. What Yuki said must have been the truth of what the demon felt, because he said nothing, though he vibrated with tension. His power coalesced and dampened the light of the room.

Gradually, Yuki calmed and regained control over herself. Her smile was sleekly calculating. "Don't be bitter, Numiak." Apaay could smell the sea on the girl: burning salt and brine. "Besides," she said, "if Nanuq's restless, perhaps it would benefit me to pay him a visit, see if there's a way for us to come to an agreement, one where everyone wins."

"You mean you're not satisfied with all this?" He gestured to the hard, barren ice of the shelves and floor and walls, the utter lack of color and warmth.

With a snort, she flapped a hand, but couldn't hide its trembling. Apaay jerked back to avoid her touch. "You know this is only temporary."

The Face Stealer pressed a palm to his chest with a wounded sound. "Yuki, I'm hurt. I thought you enjoyed my company."

She loosed an exasperated sigh and whirled away, heading for the open door. "I don't have time for your dramatics. Send a message to Nanuq. Tell him I'm looking forward to getting *reacquainted*."

She slammed the door behind her with an evil little laugh.

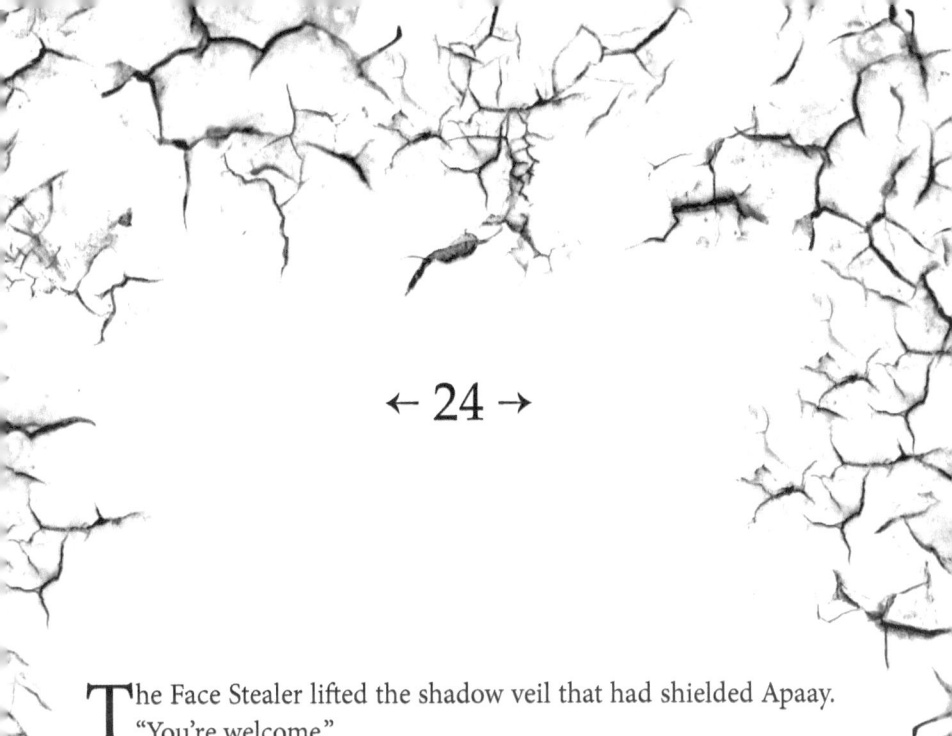

← 24 →

The Face Stealer lifted the shadow veil that had shielded Apaay. "You're welcome."

She moved as far away from him as she possibly could—all fifteen feet of it. "Funny. I don't believe I said thank you."

"Maybe not," he said as a wave of his power returned the faces to the now-repaired shelf, "but you will. All in due time."

"Doubtful." She would rather rip off her toenails.

The Face Stealer half turned away, though not before she noticed his jaw clench. Apaay did not know if the rare display of emotion stemmed from her response or his conversation with Yuki. She wanted to ask. The words pushed against her teeth. The history he and the young girl shared was deeply rooted, but something had poisoned the earth from which it grew. This talk of an alliance. Someone named Nanuq. Yuki's pain, and his—it was none of her business.

But she couldn't help herself. "Who is Nanuq?"

His voice changed, became rough like stone. It sounded as if he was fighting his anger, and failing. "Why do you want to know?" Slipping his hands into his pockets, he wandered the room, denying her his face, the darkening and lightening of his irises.

Apaay tracked his level stride, the line of his torso when he bent down to rearrange one of the faces that had slumped over on the shelf. She did not know why. She did not know where the urge came from. It was as if a cloth had been draped across her mind and she could not see to the other side. But she wanted to.

"He sounds important." And oddly familiar.

The Face Stealer did not immediately respond. Apaay tried to gauge his reaction, a difficult task with his back turned. Her resulting frustration startled her into taking a few steps back, the shelf digging into her lower spine. Since when had she ever cared about his reaction? The transition had been slight, from ignoring such clues to seeking them out.

The silence could take, but it could also give. So it was more of what he *didn't* say that told her so much. A space between words, allowing time to construct the smoothest of replies.

These words mattered, this subject mattered, and whether she saw the color of his eyes or not, the quiet spoke in subtle ways, proving how much he cared. Nanuq, whoever he was, must be someone from the Face Stealer's past. An enemy? It would explain the animosity.

With the face now upright, the Face Stealer shot a look over his shoulder and said, expression bored, "Depends on who you speak to."

Well, that told her exactly nothing. "Do *you* think he's important?"

A glimmer of surprise crossed his features before a slow grin spread, though not, she noticed, to his eyes. Those remained serious, contemplative. "You want to know what I think? I'm touched." Before she could answer, he shrugged. "In regard to the alliance, yes, he's important. But you had already gathered that, no doubt."

Again, this talk of an alliance. Except now it was no longer water or air—difficult to pin down. There was substance to it, as if discussion had given it solidity and life, enough to cast off the shadow of its past. Yuki was considering rejoining. A mistake, the Face Stealer had told her. Did he make that claim based on his own experiences, possibly as a former ally, or had he been separate, on the outside looking in?

"What is this alliance for?" Apaay asked.

"That," said the Face Stealer, "is a discussion for another time."

Once, she would have argued. Once, she would have fought and raged and demanded things of him.

Once.

Pressing the heels of her palms to her eyes, Apaay tried to sort through this new cache of information. She wondered what this man, Nanuq, could possibly want with the Western Territory, a stretch of land wiped clean. *Unfinished business.* She had no idea what that implied. Unfinished business from the war, an event that occurred nearly twenty years ago? Perhaps that was why this alliance was being reborn from the ashes—as a safety measure. Clearly, it held some significance.

"Are we done here?" he asked.

Not even close. If Eska's face wasn't here, there was little Apaay could do, but she was not leaving empty-handed.

Pulling the hood nearer to her face to ward off the chill he seemed to carry, she took a breath. Now was not the time for pride. Now was the time to open herself up to the risk of another shut door. He'd helped her before. Maybe he would help her again. "I want to know what happened to my friend Chena." And in case the Face Stealer decided to act oblivious, she added, "The girl they brought into the arena."

"This is what you've decided to waste my time with?"

"As if you had anything better to do," she answered with a scowl.

He crossed his arms over his chest and leaned against the icy wall. "I do have things to do. Very important things. Faces to steal. Lives to ruin." The shadows made him appear taller, broader, sharpening his angles. "You know, the usual."

Well. Good to know he hadn't lost his twisted sense of humor.

"What, no comeback?" he retorted at her lack of response. "It didn't stop you before."

Yes, but it was exactly that. *Before.* Before the arena. Before her head had been shaved. Before Chena had been captured. Before the truth of her imprisonment, the knowledge that she would most likely never escape from this place alive, set in.

"Tell me this one thing. Is she all right?"

"What are you willing to trade for this information?"

Suddenly wary, Apaay studied him for a possible motive. It sounded like another one of his tricks. "I don't have anything to trade you." She had nothing but the clothes on her back and her dreams.

"Oh, I wouldn't be so sure of that." He tapped a finger against the swell of his biceps. "I'm not looking for objects. More . . . favors."

She blinked. "A favor."

"Yes. In exchange for information about your friend."

"What type of favor?"

He said with a shrug, "Whatever I wish it to be."

Apaay shivered. The air was so cold here. "That doesn't seem like a fair trade."

He drawled, with a cunning look her way, "When did I ever say the trade would be a fair one?"

He hadn't, she supposed. It should not have surprised her. She didn't bother hiding her grimace, as he saw everything anyway. She would be indebted to the Face Stealer, this demon who gorged himself on the pain and suffering of others. But she had run out of options.

"What are the parameters?"

He pushed off the wall, stalked a few feet forward. The silver of his eyes winked as the ice did. And the stars. "It's simple. We exchange a blood oath to secure the deal. When the favor has been carried out, the oath is severed, and you are free to go."

The words chilled her. *Free to go.* She didn't like the implication. Until the favor was carried out, she would not be free of him.

"What is a blood oath?" She had never heard of one before. It didn't sound pleasant.

"A contract of a sort. You are binding your word to my blood. So long as I am alive, you are obligated to keep your word." The skin around his eyes crinkled slightly. "And don't get any ideas," he said, looking to the scattered remains of the icicle Apaay had failed to stab him with earlier. "I am very hard to kill."

Apaay chose not to react to that statement. Hard to kill, but not impossible. "What do I have to do?"

"So you accept?"

"I didn't say that." Not yet, anyway. "But if I agree to it, I want information, and your guarantee that you'll help Chena escape this place. I know a part of you despises Yuki as much as I do. I ask that you help my friend. She doesn't deserve to die here."

He looked at her as if she had grown a very large, very hideous second head. Hurriedly, Apaay touched her scalp. Still one head.

"You ask for your friend's freedom, but not your own?"

Apaay shrugged, unwilling to admit she was very low on hope these days. Chena had the best chance at life. Soon she would become a mother, and neither she nor her child deserved to grow up in isolation.

"I don't understand you," he said in bewilderment, one of the few times he had expressed something other than his usual stoicism or infuriating nonchalance.

She stepped back at the force of the statement, the bafflement he did not bother to hide. "Then that makes two of us." Because she *definitely* didn't understand him.

For one uncomfortable minute, neither spoke, each avoiding the other's gaze. Eventually, the demon said, "If I agree to help your friend, do you accept the conditions?"

"The conditions being I owe you a favor?"

He dipped his chin in assent. "Any favor I ask, at a time that is convenient to me. Should I call on you, the blood oath requires you to follow through."

Her gaze swept over the faces, all slack-jawed and void. It was easy to imagine they were alive and screaming at her to flee. "What happens if I refuse to comply under the blood oath?"

He laughed softly. "Impossible. The oath ensures it."

Bound by him. Bound *to* him.

These were dangerous dealings.

For once, she was not thinking of this decision in terms of pleasing others. She was not thinking of how this would prove herself to the community. This was her decision, and hers alone. She could do this. She had survived everything that had come before, and she could survive one more thing.

Pressing a hand to her forehead, she muttered, "I accept."

"What was that?" he crooned.

"I said I accept."

He looked as if he wanted to say something, but instead, the Face Stealer offered her his hand. A puckered scar folded the underside of his wrist into ridges of a long-healed injury. At her mistrustful glare, he said, "I need your hand."

She turned away from the scar. He could be hurt. He was not invincible.

Lifting her chin, Apaay placed her palm in his, surprised to find his skin warm and dry. Not that it would have made any difference, but she supposed she had expected to find it cold.

In his other hand, a whalebone knife gleamed. Apaay froze. It was the same blade he had used to sever her hair. Though he did not say anything, the memory was in his eyes. She remembered the pure green of his irises right before he had taken the knife to her scalp. Whatever the color had meant, it was long gone now.

He placed the edge against her open palm. "This might sting a little."

Apaay girded her stomach muscles for the bright flare of pain and upwelling of blood. A scarlet pool gathered in the well of her palm, the rust coating sinking into its creases, and she flinched, recalling different blood dribbling across an icy floor, limp silver hair. Hot saliva flooded her mouth. It did not matter how many times she pushed the thought aside. The memory always returned, more gruesome and vicious than before.

Next, the Face Stealer cut into his own palm. He, too, could bleed.

At her surprised expression, he muttered, "What were you expecting, smoke and shadow?"

Something like that.

Before she could protest, he grabbed her wrist and clasped their palms together, blood to blood.

Searing heat gathered at the point of contact and exploded up her arm. Apaay did not know if she screamed. Blood roared in her ears as white flashed through her vision. She wanted to snatch her hand away, pull it from the fire licking along her flesh, but could not. His touch pinned her, this heat that was both life and death.

Apaay shook her head in confusion. Sometimes she was looking at the demon. Other times she was looking at a girl—herself. His gaze, she realized, had become her own.

This was who the Face Stealer saw: a proud, clashing gaze; a stubborn chin; a mouth that refused to shut.

As quickly as the change occurred, she blinked and was again in her own body. Their hands dropped, and Apaay stumbled back. He must have done something to her. Taken possession of her in some way. She should never have agreed to this.

A lazy smile. "That wasn't so hard now, was it?"

"Bite me," she growled.

His dark, sensuous laugh teased along her spine. "Don't tempt me, wolfling."

The air sparked between them in the pale, glittering room, and Apaay could not pull her attention from the play of light splashing over his dark skin, the way the shadows drew near him, unable to resist.

This was a demon who had walked in darkness for a long time. He was still walking through it.

"Tell me what you know about Chena." After a pause: "Please."

"Now you're learning."

Her answering swear made him laugh.

"The girl was taken to a separate cell on the opposite side of the fortress. She was given food and water, and while she gained a few injuries from her capture, they aren't life-threatening. She's alive."

But for how long?

"What's Yuki going to do with her?"

He shrugged. "How should I know what goes on in that twisted little head of hers?"

"But you're her—" Truthfully, she didn't know what the Face Stealer was to the girl. Lover, slave, prisoner, friend?

"Friend," she settled on, because *chained dog* did not seem quite as forgiving.

"Yuki would be a fool to trust me with all her secrets, and she knows it. Honestly, I wouldn't be surprised if the girl spent the rest of her life in that cell, forgotten." Another halfhearted shrug. "She's nothing to Yuki."

"Then why doesn't she let Chena go?"

"Yuki likes collecting things. People, as a matter of fact. It's an unfortunate addiction."

Apaay studied him. She did not understand his motives. Sometimes it felt as if he worked for Yuki. Other times it seemed like he worked against her. It must be true, what the girl had said. He served his own agenda, whatever it was. "You didn't give away my presence earlier." For whatever reason, he had spared her. "Why?"

He stared at her for a long moment. Something in his face had changed too swiftly for her to recognize. Gone, like smoke on the wind. But she had seen it. It had been there.

"Honestly?" he said.

She waited.

"I truly haven't a clue."

It wasn't what she had expected. It was somehow a lie wrapped within a truth, or a truth wrapped within a lie. Not fully one or the other.

Apaay said, "I'm counting on you to uphold your end of the bargain."

His face shuttered, locked into the rigid mask she had grown used to. "You doubt me so easily? Maybe I should leave your friend in her cell to rot."

Apaay stepped back as if she'd been struck. The room subtly darkened. "After everything you've done, everything Yuki's done, can you really blame me?"

Emotion flickered and disappeared. Without the slightest bit of remorse, he whirled around and started toward the door.

"She's pregnant," Apaay whispered to his retreating back.

He stopped. For the first time, Apaay wished she could see his face, the play of emotions she was sure he would never let anyone see.

His voice was low, but she heard it all the same. "You're going to return to your cell now. I have things to do. Faces to steal." His expression was positively savage as he looked over his shoulder. "I'm sure you understand."

Reaching out in front of him, he touched a portion of the wall. Darkness knit itself into the shape of an archway that led to fired red shadows beyond. Before she could act, he shoved her through, back into her cell. "Check your pockets," he said, before the doorway closed, leaving behind the blank stone wall.

Ila appeared immediately beside her, gripping her hands, full of relief and concern. Questioning.

When Apaay slipped her hand into her pocket, her fingers met not hard stone, but something warm and sleek. Moving closer to the door, she brought the object into the light. It was a small, shadowy ball, its form soft and droopy. At her gentle prodding, the edges unfurled. A deep voice filled her ears.

Didn't think you'd miss it. A key carved of stone—clever. Even I wouldn't have thought of that.

Trembling, she crushed the shadow ball in her fist and chucked it across the cell to the sight of Ila's wide gaze.

She had failed Eska. Again.

It was a long, long night.

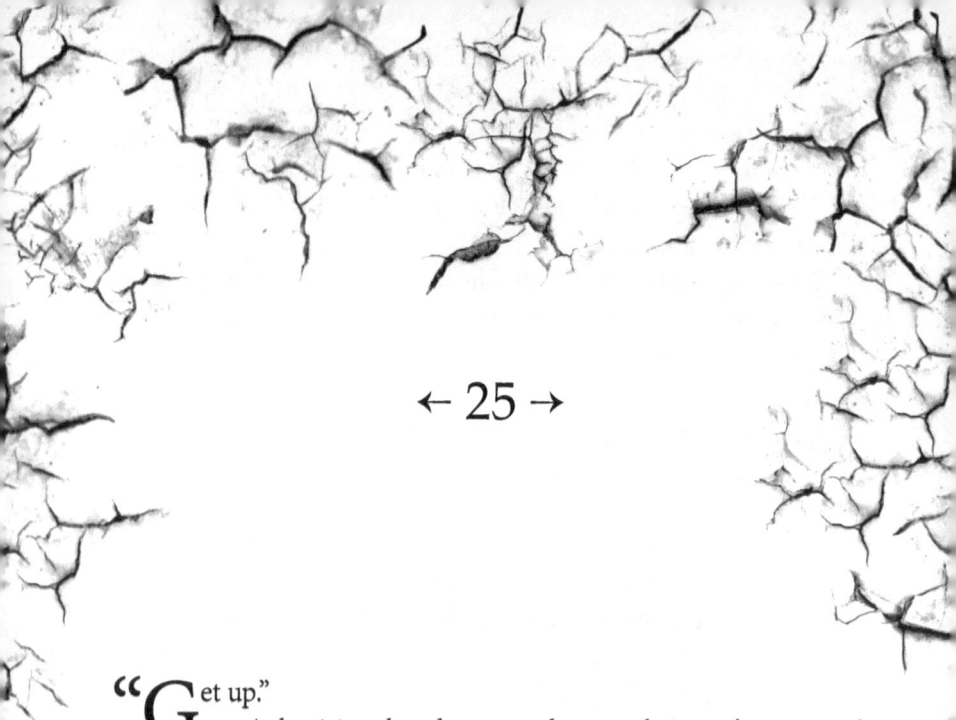

25

"**G**et up."
   A bruising hand wrapped around Apaay's arm and yanked her upright, tearing her from sleep. Her eyes met the hard expression of the guard. Ila sat to her right, wringing her hands in uncertainty.

"I said," the guard growled, hot breath wafting over her face, "Get. Up."

A chill rolled down her spine. Such sharp, sudden finality.

Yuki must have learned of her second escape attempt.

"All right," Apaay said, not wanting to worry Ila.

But after months in each other's company, Ila could recognize Apaay's emotions as readily as Apaay could recognize her friend's. The older girl grabbed the guard in a moment of fear, and the slap as he backhanded Ila across the cheek resonated in the close quarters.

Apaay thrashed in the guard's grip. "Don't touch her," she snarled.

"Then I suggest you move along. But first, give me your hands."

Her gut coiled from the rope scraping against her wrists, the slam of the cell door as he hauled her down the hallway. What reason would there be to bind her hands? She had no weapons, no means of injuring the guards without causing injury to herself.

But as the terror swelled and broke, she knew. This did not have anything to do with weapons. Apaay's hands were empty.

This was about taking away her power.

The central chamber had once again changed. On either side of the main walkway, the ice had melted into unrestful, gray-green liquid, which had swelled into waves that encompassed the stone path so Apaay stumbled through a delicate, light-infused tunnel.

The guard pushed Apaay to her knees at the base of the dais. Yuki and the Face Stealer surveyed her from their usual positions, the girl perched on the edge of her chair, the demon lounging with one leg outstretched. Apaay flinched as those piercing eyes swept across her face. Five days ago, they had clasped their bloody palms together, skin to skin. She began to wonder if it had been a dream.

"Leave us," Yuki snapped. The guard's footsteps soon dwindled.

Apaay was pulled into a depthless place. The light winked out. She gasped against the unbearable pressure crushing the air from her lungs, a brittle wheeze scraping her throat. Unable to support herself with her tied hands, she fell onto her side, lips tingling.

"Yuki," said the Face Stealer mildly. "Play nice."

The girl blinked, and Apaay was released from the girl's hold. Shudders consumed her body.

Surging to her feet, Yuki stomped down the stairs, cheeks stained a furious red. A tentacle of the freezing water wrapped around Apaay's neck, lifting her so her toes barely skimmed the stones.

"Where is she?" Yuki hissed.

With nothing to ground her, Apaay floundered. "Where is who?"

"The prisoner." Yuki leaned closer. They were nose to nose. Lines creased the corners of the girl's liquid eyes, an unsettling sight on a face so young. "Where is she?"

Finally, Apaay understood. The girl wasn't talking about her escape attempt. She was talking about Chena.

"I—" The tentacle tightened. Pressure built at her temples, throbbing hotly with the surge of blood. The Face Stealer must have taken Chena to a safe place. She was surprised by the wash of gratitude she felt toward him. "I don't—" She choked on a wheeze. Darkness. So much darkness. "I don't know what you're talking about."

"Liar!" Her voice deepened and boomed around the room, almost as if they were underwater. "Five days ago, the girl was here, but when the guard went to check her cell this morning, she was gone. I know you're friends. You were from the same sad, sorry community. You're the only one who would have reason to help her. How did you do it?"

Her attention flicked to the Face Stealer's relaxed form, and for half a second, their eyes met.

With a sneer, Yuki whirled on her heel, the tentacle drenching Apaay as it collapsed.

"How interesting. Cool, cunning Numiak, working behind my back." The jutting chin spoke of thinly veiled vulnerability. She didn't seem to notice that the netting had slipped from her shoulders and now trailed behind her, having caught on her heel. "I did not expect this of you."

His eyes creased with amusement. "You truly believe I had a hand in this? I'm rather disappointed."

"I know how you work."

He merely lifted one dark brow. The gesture spoke of whispers in the dark, smoke and shadow and all things unseen. "My dear Yuki," he said. "Why would I help the girl escape if I was the one who brought her here in the first place?"

It was a swift punch to the gut. Apaay gaped at him, but he was no longer looking at her. She was not of any importance.

It was silly to feel betrayed by this piece of information. But admittedly, she did feel betrayed. She had made a deal with him under the impression that he was at least partially on her side, and Apaay had nothing to blame but her own foolishness. With so many identities at his disposal, why would the Face Stealer need to be wholly one thing?

"Hm." The young girl tapped her chin in deliberation, though her eyes reflected doubt. "You do have a point." She walked through the water, perfectly round ice floes freezing beneath her feet so she would not plunge through.

"Helping the girl escape would only waste my time. And even if I did play a part in it, you would know if I left the fortress."

Slowly, Yuki nodded, every point the demon made helping to solidify the evidence that he had not helped Chena; it must have been Apaay, another mortal who did not belong here, who hadn't a chance to leave.

While the Face Stealer made himself scarce, the girl returned to the pathway and used a thin stream of water to tug on Apaay's hood until she scrambled to her feet. "Tell me where she is."

It was a blessing, Apaay supposed, that the Face Stealer had not informed her where he had taken Chena. Then she would not be able to divulge the information. "I don't know." Above everything else, it was the truth. "I was locked in my cell the entire time."

"This is your last chance, child."

"I'm telling you, I don't know!"

Yuki's thin, cracked lips pressed together, something terrifying and unhinged taking shape beneath the mask of her control. "Well, someone must be punished." A breathy laugh curled in the air, the sound skittering down Apaay's sweaty spine like claws as the water caressed her cheek. "And I think it should be you."

For once, Apaay did not have the strength for a comeback.

"It's amazing, actually, the number of coincidences there are in the world." The netting rasped along the ground as she circled Apaay, slowly. "Sometimes, things happen as if I had called on them myself. When Numiak was returning from his nightly activities the other day, he stumbled across something that might be of interest to you."

The Face Stealer emerged from the passage, an animal trailing in his wake.

"No." Apaay's knees went instantly weak, and she half collapsed onto the floor, arms still bound. Her small, shriveled heart disintegrated as the animal fought to break free, a high whine in his throat.

Nakaluq, whom she had believed to be dead.

"So he *does* belong to you," said the girl, voice near a croon. "Good. Very good."

In picking up Apaay's scent, Nakaluq strained against the leash. The Face Stealer shortened the rope, forcing the dog to sit at his feet. She wished she could touch him. Her wrists had been bound so tightly the tips of her fingers tingled from circulation cutoff.

"Apparently, the poor dog was wandering near the cairn searching for you. I admire loyalty, and he is quite the loyal pup." Her expression was almost pitying. "It's a shame he has to die."

← →

The force of her horror barreled into Apaay, pressure building as tears blurred her vision. "Don't do this," she whispered. "He's an animal. He doesn't know any better."

"Is that supposed to be my concern?"

Her mouth opened, then shut. "Haven't you ever loved someone who accepted you so completely, even your flaws?"

The girl's gaze was overly bright. She answered with a harsh, "No."

Apaay could not suck in air hard enough, fast enough. Nakaluq had been lost to her, but now he was here, having accomplished what he had been trained to do: find her, and bring her home.

This was all her fault. She had led him here. Sweet, loyal Nakaluq. Her friend.

Two years ago, a blizzard had overtaken Apaay and a small hunting party some ten miles from their village. Howling winds, a searing white world. They did not have time to seek shelter, and in a matter of minutes, she'd been buried. The packed earth bore down, too heavy for her to break free. If she tried to claw her way out, the little space she had for oxygen would collapse.

Curled around herself, Apaay tried to slow her breathing and conserve air. She did not know what had happened to the rest of the party, as they had been separated. Her heart beat like the wildest, most fearful drum.

Three hours later, her air had all but run out. Dazed and exhausted after attempting to dig herself free, Apaay had awaited death's quiet hands.

But then a stream of light pierced her fading vision, and the cold air slapped her awake. Nakaluq shoved his snout through the hole he'd managed to dig, crying, scrabbling at the snow encasing her with his nails. Trustworthy, driven by the need to serve. Loyal to the very end.

That night, with Nakaluq's aid, Apaay found the remainder of the hunting party, breathing, alive. But she would never forget how Nakaluq had searched for her first.

"It's really quite simple, child," Yuki was saying. "Tell me where your friend is, and I'll let your dog go."

"I don't know where she is. I don't know how she escaped or where she went or when. I'm telling you the truth." Apaay hardened her voice with conviction, her attention settling on Nakaluq every few seconds. He was trying to gnaw through the rope binding him.

Turning away, the girl said, "Fine." A brief nod at the Face Stealer. "Kill him."

"No. Don't!" Apaay shuffled forward on her knees, hands tied and utterly useless. She struggled against the bonds, the rope scraping her wrists raw so a warm trickle of blood coated her palms inside her mittens.

The Face Stealer clutched a knife in his hand, a piece of chiseled bone. Nakaluq's whines ricocheted off the walls, the vaulted ceiling. He strained against the leash, smelling Apaay's fear, the demon's intention.

Apaay pulled her arms apart as hard as she could, shoulder joints alight with agony. "You don't have to do this," she whispered to the dark, beautiful demon. If only he would look at her. *Look at me!* she wanted to scream.

The knifepoint skimmed across the dog's throat, beneath his chin. Nakaluq strained away from the weapon, eyes flashing white.

"Nakaluq," she said, the word already a broken thing. "Shh, shh, it's all right." Apaay could no longer move forward. The water had frozen around her knees, imprisoning her. "I'm here."

The sharp edge had broken skin, and a drop of blood hit the ice. Color cut into the pale scruff of his neck.

"Numiak will saw through your poor puppy's throat. What will it be, girl?"

Apaay ground her teeth together, fighting back the pain rupturing in her chest, the seams strained to bursting. It hurt to breathe. How had she gotten to this point? Three months ago, she'd been blissfully unaware of how pain ravaged the world. But the veil was lifted now. "I'm telling you, I don't *know* where she is or how she escaped. You have to believe me."

The girl thrust out her chin, the first sign of a tantrum. "This is how it will be. First, Numiak will cut off your dog's feet. He'll have nowhere to run."

"Wait—"

"Then he'll go for the eyes."

Her stomach churned, the taste of metal coating her tongue.

"Is that what you want for your dear pup?"

"Please, *please*." She sucked in a rasping breath. "I love him."

For some reason, this sent Yuki forward, her hands curled into fists at her sides. She was trembling. "You love him, and yet you left him to die out in the cold. You love him, and yet what are you doing to save him except begging like the pathetic girl you are?" Her rage was a massive shadow, cloaking everything it touched. "What would you know of love? You're nothing but a stupid child."

"I have been willing to die every day for the people I love," she said, face soaked with fluids and tears, "while you sit on your chair and build more walls."

"You have no idea what you're talking about."

"Whatever happened to make you so hateful, so angry at the world, I'm sorry, but this is not the answer."

"You know *nothing*," she hissed, stabbing an unsteady finger at Apaay. "I gave you chance after chance, you ungrateful *fool*. All I asked was that you find where the faces were hidden. A simple task." She scrubbed her hands over her face, her hair limp like a dead animal. The circlet still clung. "You couldn't do that one, small thing. And you—" Voice breaking, she collapsed onto her chair in shock at the spill of tears.

She was just a girl, swallowed up by a throne she would never grow into.

"If I can't be with the people I love," Yuki whispered, swiping at her damp cheeks in misery, "why should you?" She gestured for the Face Stealer to continue. "Finish it."

"No, no, wait. I'll do it. *I'll do it!*" Apaay screamed, the words drawn up from a place of such agonized terror she had never sounded more different. Deep, shuddering sobs fell from her half-frozen lips. "I'll do it. I'll kill him." She couldn't bear the sound of Nakaluq's pain. He was pure, and they were slowly destroying him.

Yuki raised a hand, calling for a halt.

Apaay didn't look to see if the Face Stealer had stopped his torture. She was hunched over her knees, trying to hold in her bleeding insides.

"That, child, is a most excellent idea. Guards, untie her bonds."

Apaay could barely concentrate on what was happening. The ice encasing her legs melted, and moments later, her bonds had been cut and Nakaluq was in front of her, burying his snout against her chest. Throwing her arms around him, she sobbed into his fur. The blood on her hands—his and hers—was warm and sticky. "I'm sorry," she whispered. "I'm sorry."

"I don't have all day. Or did you change your mind?"

She tightened her embrace. "I'll do it." She could do this one last thing. She could take away the confusion and the pain and send him among the stars. There, he would run free for all eternity.

Pulling back, Apaay gazed into his frost-blue eyes, a color like the sun glinting off the northern ice. She had failed him. She had failed so many people in so many ways, and it was not even the end. How many would die because of her inability to protect them?

Nakaluq bathed her face in warm, wet kisses, sensing something was wrong. He just didn't know what, and that he would be the one to pay.

The Face Stealer slipped the dagger into her hand and stood slightly behind her, probably to ensure she didn't do anything rash. The hilt was cold, even through her mittens.

Body curled protectively around him, Apaay placed one last kiss against the side of Nakaluq's snout. "We will meet again," she whispered through her tears, the words tender, the knifepoint pressed against his side where his heart beat in these last few moments. "And when we do, we will run and run." She could hardly push out the words. "And we will never stop."

The death was quick and clean, and Nakaluq experienced no pain as he left this life and passed into the next one. A clatter echoed in the chamber as the dagger slipped from her hand onto the ground.

Apaay collapsed onto his still form, body shaking with the deepest, blackest sobs. He was sleeping, that's all. He would wake soon, and they would tumble and wrestle together like old times. He would show her, as he had done over the years they'd shared, sleeping curled into each other, what it felt like to know you were alive and free.

"All right, child, get up." The girl's insufferable voice rang out. "Back to the cell."

"No, wait." She clutched Nakaluq's body close. "He needs to be buried." A dog was like family to the Analak and was always given a proper burial to ensure its spirit was laid to rest.

"Save your breath—"

"Let the girl bury her dog," the Face Stealer cut in.

Yuki bristled at the tone. Before she could speak, the demon went on. "I'll take her out to the garden. The earth has thawed somewhat. Then you won't have to worry about disposing of the body."

"*Fine.*" Whirling away, she stomped from the room. "Return the prisoner to her cell when it's done."

When she and the Face Stealer were alone, he grabbed the knife from where it had fallen, washed off the blood in the salt water bordering the walkway, and slipped it into the side of his boot. Apaay still hadn't moved.

Bending down, the Face Stealer tried to pick up Nakaluq, but she lunged toward him and spat, "Don't you dare touch him." She didn't feel entirely grounded. Something inside her had snapped when she'd shoved the blade into Nakaluq's chest, and there was no coming back from it. Not for a long time. Maybe not ever.

His eyes were gray. The color Apaay had decided meant he was thinking many things, but wasn't willing to reveal any of them.

Quietly, he stepped away and retreated down one of the passageways, forcing her to heave Nakaluq's dead weight from the ground and cradle him to her chest. Though clearly malnourished, he was still a large dog, and her arms shook from the strain. She trudged after the Face Stealer, trying not to think of the blood tracking on the floor, trailing back to the place where Nakaluq had died.

They emerged into a familiar garden, with the circle of benches and ice-encrusted trees. It had been, and still was, a crystallized extravagance. Above, the constellations dazzled, and she was greeted with another surprise: bands of green light flowing from horizon to horizon.

"This should do," the Face Stealer said, gesturing to a bare patch of dirt bordering the wall.

Apaay took a step forward before changing her mind. "Would it be all right if I buried him here?" She gestured to the base of an impressive pine. Nakaluq had loved sleeping beneath the trees in the summer. Since they did not grow this far north, there must have been some type of enchantment allowing for its survival.

A shovel appeared in his hand, which he leaned against the trunk. "Suit yourself."

Gently, Apaay laid Nakaluq on the ground. She brushed a hand over his ear, the inside soft. His body was already beginning to lose its warmth.

Normally, the deceased were buried at the same place they'd been born. Due to the permafrost, digging graves often proved difficult, so the Analak instead wrapped the deceased in caribou skins, laid them out on the tundra, and built cairns atop the bodies. By now, Nakaluq's spirit would have passed from the physical world to the spirit world. Perhaps he was now a band of light in the sky.

As Apaay began to dig, she said, "You knew this would happen, didn't you?"

The Face Stealer leaned against one of the trees, arms crossed over his chest. She felt, rather than saw, his exhaustion. "You'll have to be a bit more specific. Did I know your long-lost pet would wander into Yuki's territory looking for you? No, I did not. Did I know today would end with your dog dead by your hand? I didn't know that, either." For once, amusement did not lighten his voice. There was not the easy way in which he linked his thoughts together, always one step ahead, fatal in its smoothness. No, today his words were serious and severe, a thin layer of temper simmering underneath.

She sent him a wary glance before lifting the shovel and slamming it down. The top layer of soil had thawed into brown mush. "You knew there would be consequences, though." *Because of what you did to help Chena.* She didn't dare speak those words aloud, the evidence of his betrayal to Yuki. Not here.

Regardless, he understood what remained unspoken. "I had a hunch. Yuki enjoys her punishments."

"It was cruel." More than cruel. It was life-altering.

"She's had a difficult life. Abandonment as a child can really twist the mind. If you were starving, would you not gorge yourself on any food offered? What Yuki can't comprehend is that love can't be forced."

"Are you seriously defending her?"

"No, but whether it was cruel is unimportant. It was the price you were willing to pay."

Tightening her grip on the wooden handle, she slammed the shovel down again, satisfied with the resounding crack as it split the half-frozen underlayer. "I didn't know this would happen. I thought—"

"You thought what? That your friend would find freedom and there would be no consequences?"

She glanced around to see if anyone was near. "Yuki—"

"Is far away. She can't hear us."

Once again, Apaay wondered about the extent of the Face Stealer's power. Even standing fifteen feet away, its crackling energy buzzed, the low hum running like a current through her blood. It was familiar in a way she couldn't explain.

"Is it so bad," she asked, "to hope for something better?"

"Yes."

"Why?"

"You mean you haven't figured it out yet? Hope always leads to disappointment."

"Not always."

He tilted his head. "You're still here, aren't you? Your dog is dead. Your family is gone. You have yet to find your sister's face or kill me."

Apaay paused in her digging, muscles shaking from fatigue. She couldn't remember the last time she had felt physically strong. It used to be she could haul a two-hundred-pound seal back to camp single-handedly. Now she doubted she'd be able to carry a tenth of that weight.

Her mouth pulled downward. "You're right. About all of those things."

The demon watched her in unease, which in turn made *her* uneasy. "You're lucky Yuki didn't serve out a worse punishment."

"Trust me," said Apaay. "There is no worse punishment." Emotion rose within her like the swelling tide, ready to drag her down. She swallowed hard, but it did not prevent her voice from cracking. "I killed someone I loved today. I will never be able to erase that."

His brow furrowed, even as he searched her face. "It was a dog."

It had been months since she'd known what it felt like to feel full, both in her belly and soul. Months since she'd felt genuinely happy, and she wondered if she would ever be happy again. Now the wanting had scraped her hollow, and these words were cruel. How could the Face Stealer not see she had loved and lost? But maybe he didn't have a heart. Maybe all he had was a threadbare shred of puckered skin.

"His name was Nakaluq." Blood coursed hotly through her. He only had to open his mouth before the urge to stab him struck. "And he loved purely, far more purely than a human could, than a demon. What he gave me—it was given freely." Her look was stony. "But I wouldn't expect someone like you to understand."

That infuriating smile made a reappearance. "Because clearly you know so much about me."

"A demon who steals faces, ruins lives, sits on a throne next to a child who tortures others for entertainment and keeps his silence? I know everything there is to know, and all I had to do was pay attention."

"And yet I hid you from Yuki in the room of faces. I helped your friend escape. Does that still make me a monster?" A muscle ticked in his sharp, angled jaw. She had the sense her answer was important and would paint things in different colors than they had been.

"Do you think one or two good deeds excuses the grotesque pain you've caused so many?" Apaay looked down and continued her digging. The hole was nearly large enough and deep enough for Nakaluq's body. Her eyes burned. She didn't want to put him in the dark. She couldn't stand the thought of dirt sullying his pale fur. "I don't know why you did those things, but I know there was a motive. I just haven't figured it out yet."

"You seem certain of this. Who's to say my actions weren't simply altruistic?"

"Were they?"

He did not respond.

"That's what I thought," she muttered, adding more half-frozen soil onto the growing pile. Sweat beaded at her temples, wound down her cheeks and neck to soak into the fur of her hood. Her breath puffed hard. Dizzily, she shook her head. "Is Chena . . . did you return her to my village?"

"She is safe."

"You didn't answer the question."

He hummed in his throat. "You are more observant than I thought."

"I'm not surprised you underestimate me."

"Oh no, I stopped doing that a long time ago."

Apaay hid her surprise with a grunt as she stopped digging and knelt at Nakaluq's side, smoothing his fur one last time. Goodbyes were always hard, but this goodbye was forever.

"May you wander the land free of pain," she whispered, speaking the prayer to send his spirit into the spirit world. "May you drink from the clear mountain stream, and run through the green summer grasses, and dream beneath the stars." The last words she murmured close, away from the Face Stealer's prying ears, which were surely listening in. "May you reap the bounties of this beautiful earth." One last kiss to Nakaluq's temple, hot tears warming her chilled cheeks. "Until we meet again. Farewell, my friend."

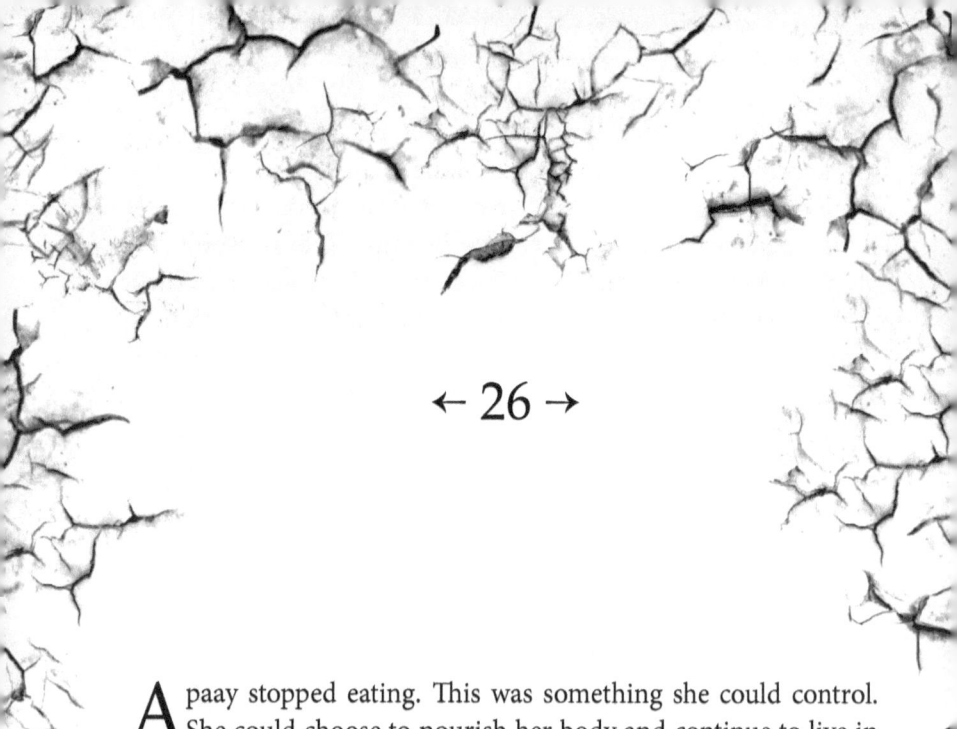

26

Apaay stopped eating. This was something she could control. She could choose to nourish her body and continue to live in squalor, or she could begin the process of choosing how she would die with what little dignity that remained. There was not much fat on her body. She was a bundle of skin, bones. It would not take long.

She separated the days like so: the days Irnik visited them, though Apaay no longer participated in the conversations, and the days he did not. The days they were fed, and the days Apaay went hungry. The days she and Ila spoke, and the days left to silence.

The hours Apaay was asleep.

The nights that were full of nightmares.

The days she dared to dream.

One such night, Apaay imagined she was back with her family in their ice house. It was dinner time. They roasted whale meat over the small fire warming their home, the fat popping and sizzling as it dropped into the flames. Eska tried snatching a piece of Apaay's meat, the greedy thing, Apaay laughing as she held it out of reach.

And now Papa was making shadow puppets on the walls, the ice saturated in warm golden light. A seal. A fox, sly and quick as it roamed. An owl soaring overhead.

Eska joined in, her slim, clever fingers curling and clamping into a wolverine, a hare. Mama, her dear little naajaluk, was laughing. Papa touched his wife's cheek, smiled.

And Apaay knew with certainty this was a dream, for Eska had eyes with which to see.

Ila tried forcing her to eat, pressing strips of raw seal meat against her stubborn mouth as she lay on her side, staring at nothing. *You need to eat,* Ila said, her gestures growing more urgent as the days, and then the weeks, crawled by. *Please, Apaay.*

She did not eat. She did not speak. The pain was locked away where no one could find it.

Tell me what happened, Ila would say. The girl grabbed her icy hands, held them close to her chest to warm them. *You're scaring me.*

Weakness ate at her body. Yet even after everything, some inbred instinct howled at her to fight back. The hunger pains grew almost unbearable. Eventually, they disappeared entirely.

In the evenings, she dreamed of standing in solitude near the pines bordering her village, unable to draw near. In the mornings, Ila would tell her how Irnik had brought extra food, seal and whale blubber to give her nourishment, strength. Always, Irnik would stand on the other side of the bars, watching her. His gaze was hot enough to burn.

And then, one day, something new. Ila pressed a hand to Apaay's pale, chilled cheek. *Irnik said Yuki will be gone next week. He says he wants to help us escape.*

But there would be no escape for Apaay. This she knew. The darkness called to her, and she would be a fool to deny it.

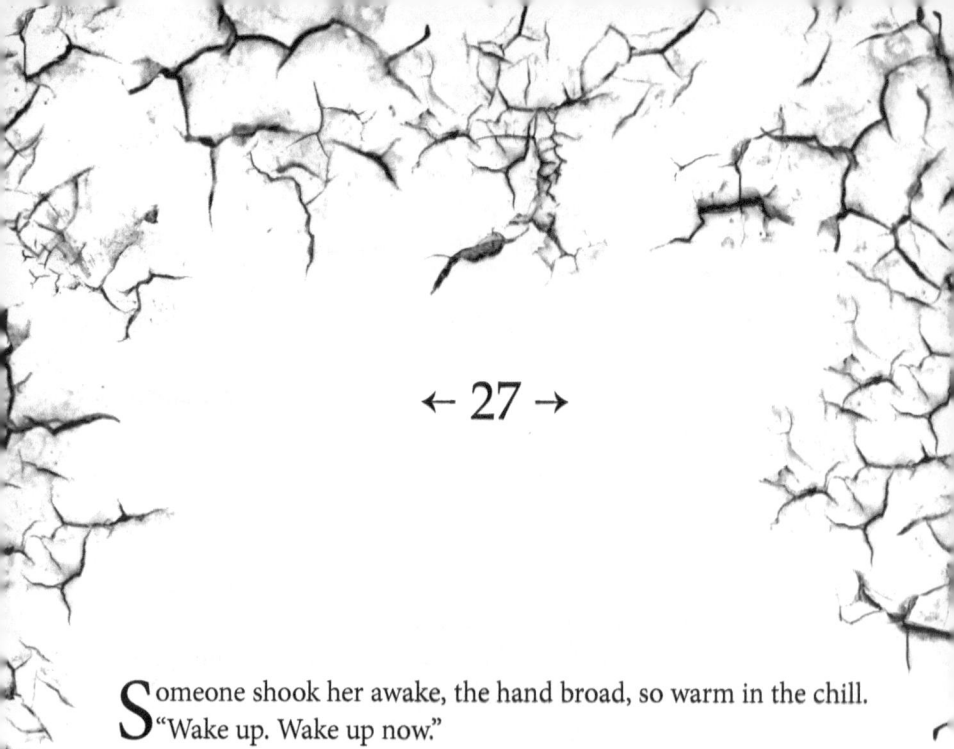

← 27 →

Someone shook her awake, the hand broad, so warm in the chill. "Wake up. Wake up now."

Apaay blinked groggily. Irnik crouched over her, his face tense, Ila hovering behind him. The cell door gaped.

"We need to hurry." Irnik hauled her up single-handedly, his gaze narrowing in worry. He should not be able to perform a task so easily. The bulk of layers concealed her malnourished frame, and if she were to remove her clothes, he would be able to see her protruding ribs, her shoulder blades like small bird wings. It should have worried her. It should have, but it didn't.

Without the support of Irnik's hand, Apaay sagged. Immediately, Ila wrapped an arm around her waist to keep her upright.

I don't know how this is going to work, Irnik said to Ila. *She can barely stand.*

I'm not leaving without her, the girl replied stubbornly.

His hands slapped together as he signed, his frustration evident. *What will you do, carry her? You're both half starved.*

She merely lifted her chin, daring him to argue. *If that's what it takes.*

They did not know. They did not understand. The guard who would help her, the girl who was prisoner. She was a shredded bit of cloth, worn out, tired. They spoke of escape, a free life, but what was the point? There was no point. It was yet another waste of time.

"I'm not going with you," Apaay croaked, pulling away.

"What?" Irnik's face slackened. "Yes, you are."

She nearly laughed. This man, who had probably never known life in a cage, should be so bold as to assume her thoughts, her ambitions, her last dying wish. "Don't you see? Yuki has won. The Face Stealer has won. They both have." She hadn't told Ila or Irnik about Nakaluq, what she had been forced to do. Every night, every day, she missed him. "If you're going to escape, at least get Ila out. She has something to live for."

Ila seemed to realize from Irnik's expression what Apaay suggested, and latched onto Apaay's arm.

Irnik watched her closely. "You do, too."

"No," she said, "I don't."

"What about your family? They're still alive."

Yes, and it made no difference considering she would never see them again.

"Is this about your sister's face?"

"What do you think?" In the beginning, that had been her aim—fulfill the promise she had made. But her words were little more than white fluff, melting at the first sign of heat.

"I think I know where it is," he said. "I think I know where it's hidden."

Pulling away from Ila's touch, she turned away so they would not see her pain. "I already found where the Face Stealer keeps his faces, and it wasn't there."

"There's more than one room. The main one, where he keeps most of the stolen identities, and a smaller room where he keeps only a select few."

For a second, her heart soared at the possibility, before it tumbled to the ground. How could he possibly know this? "You're lying."

Gripping her arm, he tugged her gently around. "I swear to you, I'm not."

His sincerity was true, from what she could see. But it still did not answer the most important question.

"If you knew all along where her face was, why are you suddenly telling me this now?" And why would Eska's face be placed in this room as opposed to the other? "I've been trapped here for *months*. You had all this time, and instead of helping, you watched Yuki and the Face Stealer torture me in silence. Why?"

They stood nose to nose. Their eyes matched—spitting, furious. Irnik, who was perhaps half a foot taller than her, did not look the least bit intimidating. She wanted answers. Now.

"You know how to hunt, right?"

Apaay hadn't even the energy to take offense. "Of course I know how to hunt." Sort of.

"Then you understand the importance of timing. Strike too soon, and you scare off your target. Hesitate, and you squander the opportunity." Ila appeared at Apaay's side, offering support. "That is why I haven't come to you until now. Change is coming to the North, and it's not safe to stay here any longer. This is the right moment. This is the time to act."

A flutter of hope in her chest. She squashed it before it had the chance to grow. "How do I know you're not lying? It's probably not even there."

"I have no reason to lie to you. I found the room during your last escape attempt, after you went through the mirror without me." The gleam in his eye caught the light. "The faces of three young women were in that room, one of which could be your sister. I don't know why it wouldn't still be there."

Apaay rubbed her forehead, ears open to the acoustics in the hall. This was usually around the time the guard checked on them. "Why are you helping us? We're nothing to you." It was nothing less than the truth, and yet the words tore something in her.

Irnik tilted his head in confusion. "That's not true. We're friends."

Friends.

The tightening in her chest eased. She was greedy for it. Human connection. Trust. "Really?"

"I want to see Yuki destroyed as much as you do." His gaze flitted from Ila back to Apaay and stayed there. "And no one deserves to die alone."

Ila hovered near the open door, having given up on reading their lips, as they spoke too quickly for her to follow. She awaited Apaay's decision. They both did.

"I don't know." How would she know this time would be different, that it would lead to success? It was truly exhausting to keep picking herself back up.

Apaay. Torchlight skimmed the proud angle of Ila's jaw. *Do you remember when you told me about the token you received from your first kill?*

Of course she remembered. Now that it was gone, she never wanted to forget.

You told me you wanted to prove to your father that you could make the kill, and you did. But do you want to know the reason why I think you made the kill?

Her throat bobbed. "Why?" she whispered, not sure she wanted to know the answer.

Her friend smiled, the warmth like a flood of light that Apaay couldn't help but draw near. *I think,* she signed, tapping a finger to her forehead, *it was because you believed in yourself. Deep down, you recognized the fire inside you. You wanted to prove to your father what you already knew: that you are worthy.*

Apaay was crying—deep, shuddering gasps. When had the tears come? She didn't know, but there they were. All over her face. All over her battered heart. A relief.

Ila tucked Apaay's face into her neck. Poor Irnik looked ready to bolt as she sobbed, all barriers down, a dam bursting open. Her head pounded, her throat swelled, but Ila shouldered both their weights, and shushed her, and poured love into the hole in her chest, and Apaay did not have to worry anymore, because here was someone who would carry her. How lucky she was, to have friends to pick her up when she had fallen.

"You don't need to go through this alone," Irnik said behind her. "You have us now."

Ila's embrace tightened in confirmation.

"And even if you didn't have us, you'd have yourself. And that's all you ever really need."

The words shot through her heart. *Truth.*

Voice muffled against Ila's neck, she said, "Are you *trying* to reduce me to a sobbing mess? Because it's working."

He laughed and touched her shoulder, drawing her back until their eyes met, his gaze softer than she had ever seen it. "Are you up for this? One last adventure?"

She snorted and wiped her face. Adventure. Right.

But she could do this. She had *been* doing this. She'd just gotten a little lost along the way.

With a nod to Irnik, she and Ila followed him down the corridor, her friend breathing heavily beside her, fear giving the sound a jagged edge. Apaay grabbed her hand and squeezed. Standing water slicked the stones, splashes resonating through the tunnel. The question was not *if* it attracted the attention of the guards, but *when.*

The stairwell was deserted, the steps worn smooth from use. One flight. Two flights. An echo of crashes and booms. Apaay recoiled from the third level, glad to leave the slow-moving river behind.

When they reached the fourth level, Irnik held up a hand, signaling for them to wait as he ducked around the corner. Apaay, who had yet to explore the fourth level but was too cautious to investigate, strained her ears for any sound save their breathing. The scuff of a boot. A murmur of conversation drifting down the halls, like wolves slipping through the whispering woods.

Ila was trembling. No, *she* was trembling. Ila was the one supporting her with strong arms.

Minutes passed. The silence, trapped in the labyrinth's stony grip, stretched.

Ten minutes later, Irnik still had not returned.

Apaay and Ila shared a look. *Do you think something happened to him?* Apaay placed her palm against her forearm and made a slicing motion for *injury.* She should have anticipated the possibility of separation. Irnik knew his way around the labyrinth. They did not.

I don't know. The older girl fiddled with her fingers. *Should we go after him?*

How? Neither knew where he had gone.

Apaay lifted a hand suddenly. There, coming up the stairs—footsteps.

It was not Irnik. His gait was near-silent, while these men were about as discreet as a whale giving birth. Apaay's hands shook so badly she could hardly make her signs literate. *Men. Stairs. Need to run. Don't know where. What to do?*

Ila peeked her head around the corner, and Apaay followed her example. The hall was vacant. Three doors lined one wall, with three on the other. If they climbed the stairs to the next level, their footsteps would ricochet in the enclosed space. They did not have long.

Apaay stepped as she would when hunting: toe, heel, featherlight. Reaching the first door, she pressed her ear against it. No sound. She yanked on the knob.

Locked.

The men had reached the landing, their raucous laughter skipping at the girls' heels.

Apaay tried the next door. She yanked on the handle and fell back from the force of it bursting open, then hurriedly shoved Ila through. Gently, she pulled the door closed, though not all the way. A sliver of an opening allowed them a view into the hall.

The men loitered near the stairwell in a tight circle, bulked in heavy, ice-encrusted furs, their faces hardened and chafed by harsh winds. One of the men must have made a joke, as the others clapped their mittens together in hilarity.

It became apparent the men weren't moving anytime soon. Holding hands, Apaay and Ila turned to appraise their hiding place. Two hundred pairs of eyes reflected back at them. Built vertically into the ground, stacked atop one another, leaning against the walls, the mirrors took up every available space. It appeared to be a storage area of some sort.

Reaching out, she tried passing her hand through one of the reflections but found it solid. A plain old mirror, then. The others were the same.

Ila came to stand next to her and stared at the girl in the mirror, little more than a stranger. She was, perhaps for the first time, looking into her own eyes.

In awe, Ila lifted a hand to her cheek. The girl in the mirror followed. She touched her lips, red like the berries that burst from the bracken in the spring. She touched her long, slightly upturned nose, marveled at her high forehead, the tapered chin. With every hesitant touch, Ila came to know herself.

Ila glanced from her reflection to Apaay, quizzical. Then she shook her head and went back to staring, her smile wondrous. They were nearly the same height.

Apaay smiled, too. *What?* She ran a palm over her fuzzy hair.

The color in her friend's cheeks deepened. *It's silly.*

Tell me.

I . . . Her hands fumbled for words, the ones that would best illustrate her feelings. *I never realized I was beautiful.*

The words both broke Apaay's heart and made it full. *You are beautiful. Of course you are beautiful.* But it had little to do with appearance. Ila's beauty came from strength, and courage, and the kindness of her heart. Apaay was so lucky to know her.

She turned to her friend. *Ila.*

In the mirror's reflection, Ila tilted her head in question.

After we leave this place, I want you to come home with me. She already considered Ila family, but she wanted to make it permanent. *I know my family will love you.*

A tear tracked down her friend's cheek, which she wiped away. *I would be honored.*

With her focus on the mirrors, Apaay did not hear the footsteps until they were outside the door, the hinges squealing as it opened. Three guards appeared in the mirrors' reflections, their shock plain.

The men recovered first. One bolted toward them, hand reaching for a weapon at his waist. An axe? Dagger? Apaay didn't wait around to find out.

Grabbing Ila's hand, she pulled her into the maze of mirrors. Running and running, faster, as fast as they could go. They fled to the pounding boots of war.

Apaay veered right, ramming her shoulder into a corner. Glass shattered. She changed direction, stumbling as she encountered seven different versions of herself, haltingly looking for the way through. The optical illusion showed her there were five or six different paths she could take, but that was a lie. She barged forward and slammed face-first into another mirror. Ila cried out as she reached a dead-end, then backtracked and stumbled into a reflection of herself. From the crashing and cursing and glass crunching underfoot, the guards were having an equally difficult time navigating their way through the maze.

Apaay stopped, rubbing the bruise already swelling on her upper arm. She had made too many mistakes already, and she could not afford to make any more.

The mirrors reflected every angle and then some, back to front to side. If they could escape this room, return to the hallway, find Irnik . . .

In the end, Ila led the way. There were too many turns and cutting corners for Apaay to determine their positioning, and Ila seemed to have an easier time spotting the right path, as she was not as exhausted or ravaged by hunger. She used her sense of touch to find the openings, trailing her fingers along the mirrors' edges.

But they were not untouchable. Apaay screamed as someone snatched her hood, yanking it so hard her spine snapped back. She whirled and flung out a hand, striking the man in his jaw. He went down as the remaining guards rounded the corner.

"Faster, Ila!" Never mind that Ila couldn't hear. It helped Apaay feel as if they *were* going faster. If she urged them faster, they would fly. If she wished for escape, they would break their way out, into freedom, into life.

The moment the mirrors fell away, Apaay put on a burst of speed, a cramp cutting deep in the side of her stomach. They had this one chance. Out the door, run, find a place to hide.

Thankfully, the door was unlocked. They stumbled into a snow-laden hallway, taking turns when they saw fit, which was, as far as Apaay could tell, whenever inspiration struck. Nothing mattered except distance. As much as possible, as soon as possible. They must leave those men behind. They must disappear.

A shadowed alcove provided them the necessary secrecy, and they huddled together in the cramped space, trying to make themselves as small as possible. Perhaps three minutes passed in silence, save their labored breaths. Moments later, the men flew past and disappeared into the distance.

They waited an indeterminable amount of time. Apaay had never sweated so much in her life. The hairs of her inner clothing layer clung to her skin in a slimy, gelatinous mass, and she seriously debated abandoning her parka to the alcove, except she would need it once they escaped. The tundra did not offer mercy. Without it, she would not survive.

Eventually, more footsteps. A single pair, the tread softening as it neared. Deliberate, as a hunter's would be.

Irnik emerged into their line of sight, gaze locked on Apaay, as if he had known their location all along. Ila gasped and lunged to her feet, throwing her arms around the guard. Apaay, however, stood much slower, gritting her teeth.

"Where were you?" she said, the words low. Sound carried far in these halls. In the shadows, it carried even farther.

Irnik eased back from Ila's embrace, his expression equally mistrustful. "Where was *I*? Where were *you*? I told you to wait in the stairwell. When I returned, you two were gone."

"Yes, because there were guards coming up the stairs and what were we supposed to do? Wait around for them to capture us?" Adrenaline was fire in her blood, setting her limbs alight.

"They saw us," she went on, her words falling faster and faster, no time, no time, *no time*. "They chased us through this strange mirror room, and one almost caught me, but I hit him and they went that way." She pointed. Her hand was shaking.

Ila scrunched up her face in concentration as she read their lips, trying to keep up with the speed of the discussion.

Irnik worked his jaw, biting back whatever it was he wanted to say. "Fine. This way."

"No." Grabbing his arm, she whipped him around. "You didn't answer the question. Where were you?" They shouldn't be here. They should be in the cell where it was safe, where no one could hurt her, where she could hurt no one. How long until their escape made its way back to Yuki and the Face Stealer?

"I *told* you," he ground out. "I went to see if the hallway was clear."

"For ten minutes?"

Blowing out a breath, Irnik pressed his fingers to his sweat-dampened temples. Strands of hair curled around his face, having pulled free from his braid. "You knew the risks when you decided to come with me. If you thought this would be easy—"

"I didn't say it would be easy, but you're not being honest with us."

"You can trust me. We're friends, remember?"

"Friends are supposed to be open with one another. Did you tell the other guards we escaped? Have you set us up?"

This last insult, above everything else, razed his features into something fierce. "No. No to all of those questions."

Apaay rubbed her burning eyes, torn between wanting to scream in frustration and weep in confusion. If this was a trap, they were already doomed. "Then *why*?"

Ila must have been able to catch a snippet of their argument, because she signed, *Apaay's right. You're not telling us something.* She jutted her chin out. *Where were you?*

With a low growl in his chest, he answered, *Doing what needed to be done. Now, are you coming or not? We don't have much time.*

Apaay scowled, but he was already walking away. Ila awaited her decision.

Secrets and darkness. They belonged to each other.

Apaay said, *Follow,* and they did.

They made quick work of the fortress, avoiding the areas stationed with guards, Ila trailing Irnik, Apaay bringing up the rear. Their luck did not last, though. Rounding a corner, they slammed into a dead end.

Ila glanced around. A single moonbeam floated through the tunnel and illuminated the opposite wall. *What are we doing here?*

Wait, he replied.

So they waited.

Apaay shifted in impatience, shooting Irnik a glare that told him exactly what she thought of this ridiculous plan. As the minutes crawled by, the thin, pale beam inched farther down the wall.

Nothing's happening, she said.

Look.

At first, she did not know what had changed. But then she spotted a key-shaped hole set within the stone, pulsing with light from within.

A thin white line split through the center of the wall. At the apex, two diagonal cracks appeared, spearing to the bottom of the wall, shaping the outline of a large triangular door.

Wordlessly, Ila and Apaay followed Irnik inside.

After discovering the first room of faces, Apaay had expected day: open space, a crystal chamber, the faces in tidy rows on shimmering shelves, displayed like gold or jewels, arranged to draw the eye.

This room was night: a damp cavern littered with oil lamps in each corner, the shadows sharp and severe, enclosing them. Only a few inches of space separated the top of Irnik's head from the ceiling.

Seconds after the door thudded shut, Apaay realized she hadn't heard any voices leading her here. None. But maybe that was because there were so few faces. Five, to be exact. They hung neatly on the back wall, lamplight highlighting the cheeks and brows, obscuring the hollows of the eyes, the nostrils, the indentation between the lips.

Apaay's pulse slowed, her body growing strangely heavy as she stepped farther into the room. They had time now. She could take as much time as she desired to look upon these faces and wonder who they were and why they were here. Deep down, she knew this was a false sense of security. Wondered if it was an effect of the Face Stealer's power moving in a shallow current throughout the room in his absence. They did not have time to waste. But it felt as if they did.

The first face was a young woman about Apaay's age. Classically oval, regal, with the most graceful eyebrows she had ever seen.

Apaay skimmed her fingertips across one cheek, the skin soft and oddly warm. Comforting, like a blanket of fox fur.

She moved to the next face, and froze.

Eska.

Sister.

Family.

Home.

Love. So much love she was gutted and had to lean a hand against the wall. Her body trembled. Apaay fought the desire to touch it, because what if it wasn't real?

The pain of missing her struck low in her belly. But it was the pain of seeing her, too. There were shades of Eska in these features, but not the full riot of color. This was the face of her sister, and yet not. The pupils had dulled. The mouth drooped, unable to smile. This was a shadow to Eska's sun.

"I'm coming for you," she whispered. "I promise."

Beside her, Ila signed, *Is this she?*

Apaay bit her lip, not wanting to look away. *Yes.*

Ila watched her, and Irnik. She felt their eyes. Waiting to see what she might do.

The last three faces were unfamiliar: a handsome man with scars roped around his cheeks; a woman with a wide, deep red mouth; and finally, another young man with winged brows and a cleft chin.

Irnik appeared at her side, a nervous energy about him. "We need to go."

Yes, they would go. Except—

Apaay faced him. "How did you know where this place was?"

The guard removed Eska's face from the wall, tucking it into folds as if it were a piece of fabric. He did this for the other faces as well, though she didn't know what purpose they served, or whose faces they had been, or if these people were still alive.

"It's complicated."

"Yes," she drawled, eyeing him. "You said that." Apaay held out her hand, suddenly wary. "I'll take Eska's face." He was keeping something from her. She didn't know what. She only knew the feel of lies upon the tongue, and his was a most burdensome weight.

He hesitated, and Apaay tensed, prepared to fight for it if necessary. She knew something had been amiss when he'd disappeared earlier. She wondered where he had gone. If his secret would be their death. "The face, Irnik." Her eyes were hard.

Wordlessly, he handed it over, and she slipped it into her pocket. It would be safe there, because now that she had it, she would never let it go.

"Come," he said. "If the guards saw you and Ila, then we need to hurry."

"Oh," a voice crooned at the door, "I'd say you're about all out of time."

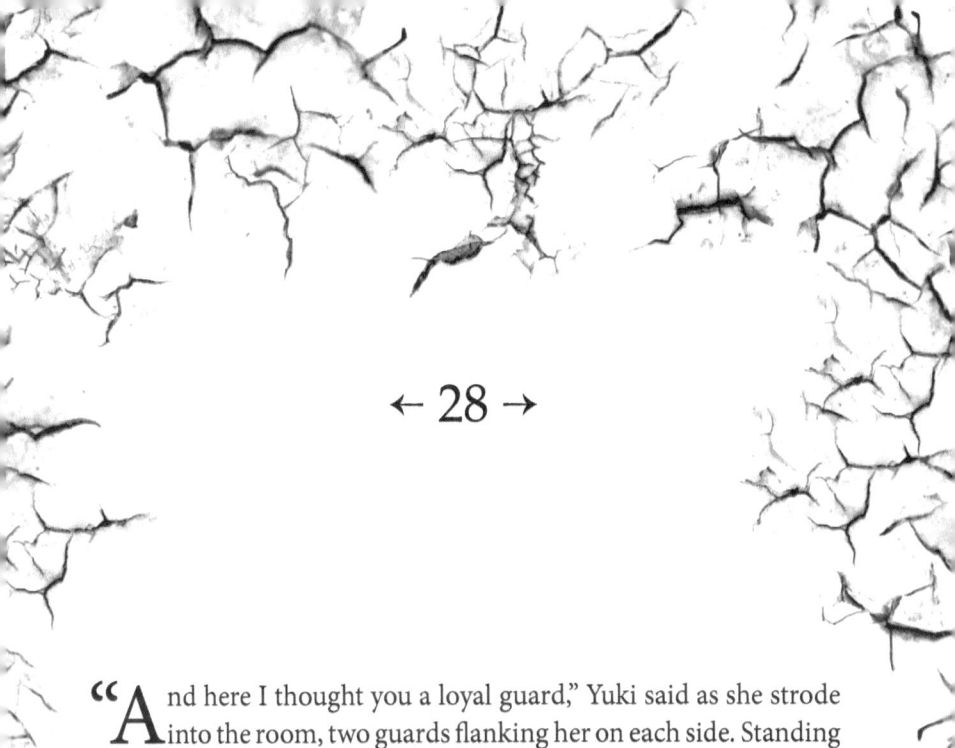

"**A**nd here I thought you a loyal guard," Yuki said as she strode into the room, two guards flanking her on each side. Standing beneath the squat ceiling, the girl appeared much taller than usual. "It just goes to show. You can't trust a pretty face. My mistake."

Apaay tucked Ila close, uncomfortably aware of their cramped position in the corner. Waves of heat beat against her trousers from the oil lamp near her feet.

As Irnik stepped toward Yuki, the girl clucked her tongue, something deadly uncoiling behind her eyes. "Ah-ah. No farther, traitor." One of the guards pointed a spear at Irnik's heart. If he decided to strike, it would not miss.

Irnik's smile was cold, fleeting, gone. "Let's play nice, Yuki. This is a simple misunderstanding, nothing more."

Her pupils seemed to suck in all the light, leaving none for them to see. "What is there to misunderstand?" Hands clasped loosely behind her, she strode around the room, even being so bold as to turn her back on them. "You have committed treason by freeing two prisoners without my knowledge. On the contrary, I understand everything quite clearly. I thank you, though, for leading me to this room. I've been looking for it for a long time."

"You mean your demon pet didn't tell you where it was?" Apaay spat.

"No." Her sleek, slender shoes hissed against the ground. She did not appear the least bit concerned. "Numiak is quite secretive when he wants to be."

The girl's attention settled on the wall where the faces had hung moments ago. Almost imperceptibly, her lips thinned. "We can do this the easy way or the hard way. Your choice." Pressing her palms together, Yuki turned and smiled. "Return the faces you found to me, and I might reconsider killing you."

Irnik shifted his weight to the balls of his feet, braced for battle. His back swelled with breath and strength. "We both know that's an empty promise." Across the way, the guards spread out, two heading for Irnik, the other two for Ila and Apaay.

Yuki's gaze didn't waver from Irnik, and Apaay had the sense she knew where every player in this maddening game stood, even those who were not present. After all, she had set the board. "You know nothing of the sort."

"Tell me why you need them, and maybe I'll consider the offer."

Laughing lowly, she studied him through her eyelashes. "You are playing a dangerous game."

Beneath his clothes, the muscles of his back locked, shoulders to waist. Apaay had the strangest urge to press a hand against his spine, to remind him he was not alone in this. He had Apaay and Ila to fight for him. With him.

But the moment passed.

Irnik said, "And I'm afraid you will find yourself on the losing side."

The temperature in the room plummeted. Frost crystallized around Apaay's nostrils, and her nose burned with each inhalation. The flames shriveled and wavered from the sudden cold, a hideous shriek clawing through the cramped room as a thin layer of ice raced along the stone walls and down to the floor, the sound burrowing into her ears.

"Kill them," Yuki snarled, "and bring the faces to me."

Apaay did not have time to decide the next step, whether to flee or fight, as the guards were moving, and Irnik was whirling, his hand flashing toward her as he said, "Catch," and tossed her one of the daggers hidden up his sleeve. Apaay fumbled to catch the weapon before it hit the ground, some inbred instinct roaring at her to *get away*. The blood, the pain, the greed—this was not her world. She had been thrust into it, shoved into the sea without knowing how to swim. There was the creaking ice. There was Yuki, a slender pillar of rigidity, whose word was law. There were the stocky, broad-shouldered guards, violence flaring in their eyes as Apaay yanked Ila behind her and crouched in a fighter's stance. The need to defend was a caged animal prowling inside her.

Two of the guards broke off and lunged for Irnik, who wielded an axe that seemed to have appeared out of nowhere. Light glinted off the curved ivory blade, and then he was a blur of motion, a streak of untouchable darkness that drew Apaay's gaze as his powerful shoulders lifted, the axe held high, and swung down, down, shearing through cloth and flesh and bone. A splintering, the strangulation of a choked off scream. The guard crumpled as Irnik drew a second guard into his space with invisible threads.

The other two came for her.

The men's spears had a longer reach, but Apaay did what she could dodging strikes, attempting to slip under their guard and stab them in the gut. She did not think of her damp palm sliding along the hilt, or of the searing heat in her chest. Her mind was a storm, telling her to go here, step there, quickly, quickly now.

And she tried. The men pushed her back and struck with fatal blows, and still she did not yield, feeling Ila's quaking form at her back. She would overtake them, Apaay thought woozily. All was not lost. This was one more obstacle, nothing more.

Yet it wasn't enough. Her bones were brittle twigs. She moved in starts and bursts of flagging energy, so different from the girl she had once been, the one who had bulled through wind and ice, the one who had promised her family not to worry, because she would return. And something broke further in Apaay, the force shattering her very core, because that girl . . . who was that girl? Tears sprang to her eyes. That girl was little more than a memory now. She had died along with Nakaluq.

At the realization, she faltered. One of the guards rammed her into the ground with a kick to her stomach. Too exhausted, too slow. Her skull cracked against stone.

White exploded behind her eyes, then receded in a red haze. Someone was calling her name, the word electric with fear—*Apaay, Apaay, Apaay*—louder, ascending into a harsh near-scream. Apaay rolled away seconds before a spear buried itself where her head had been moments before.

She swiped wildly at the guard's leg, cutting into the muscle of his thigh, then scrambled away before he could counter the attack, nearly ramming headfirst into the wall as her boot slid across the ice that had crept along the ground.

Turn turn turn she needed to turn around if she wasn't fast enough—

A hand on her shoulder. Someone jerked her back. Ila—Ila was grabbing the weapon from her hand and shoving Apaay behind her, standing tall, a shield.

With a howl, Ila launched herself at the guard while Apaay slumped in the corner, trying to catch her breath. Acute throbbing spread across the base of her skull. Apaay massaged the ache and grimaced at her weakened state. Her legs had liquefied, trembling so hard she locked her knees to remain upright. Without the wall for support, she would have slid to the floor.

Fighting ensued. She couldn't bear to watch, and yet she was unable to look away. The violence sucked her into its force, Irnik on one side, dragging two men down with knees to their chests, Ila on the other, no strategy or skill, nothing but a burning desire to end this. She attacked with the same ferociousness Apaay had witnessed following her hypothermic ordeal, as if some beast slumbered beneath her skin.

A hard lump swelled in Apaay's throat. She remembered sitting with Ila in their cell, alone save the drip of water. *No one will remember me,* Ila had whispered, the confession a pinch of air.

This place, these people, had stolen the life Ila could have had. They had decided who she was and what she deserved. They had deemed her inferior, had stunted self-exploration, denying her the chance to know her true self. *You are nothing*, they said. *You are less.* But they were wrong.

For there was the resilience, the quiet steel. Here, amid battle, she burned bright. One day, when there were no longer walls to contain her, Ila would rise to greatness. With so much fire within her, how could she not?

"You incompetent fools!" Yuki shrieked, the sound bloodying Apaay's ears. Two guards lay dead, but the remaining two fought with everything they had.

Perhaps it was fearlessness, the uncaring way in which Ila slashed at the enemy, all passion and no control, but it confused the guard long enough for Irnik to jump into the fray and slit his throat. In the space of a single breath, he had felled a fully grown man.

Yuki hissed, hands lunging for unprotected Ila as the door flew open. Deep in the bowels of the hall, a horde of guards approached.

It happened too quickly for Apaay react. A dark tunnel appeared as if having winked into existence, and Irnik rammed his shoulder into Yuki's side so she fell through the space with a bloodcurdling screech, vanishing as the wall knit together over the tunnel's entrance. Despite the girl's absence, the guards didn't falter, determined to see these escaped prisoners to a bloody end.

"I'll hold them off," Irnik said, eyeing their opponents. Damp tendrils clung to his scalp, sweat flicking onto her cheek as he whipped his head around. "You and Ila run. Find someplace to hide."

Apaay cut him a level look. "You don't need to do this."

"I'll come find you when it's safe."

"But—"

"Go."

This was wrong. It was wrong for him to stay. It was wrong for them to flee. They should stay together, fight together. Like family.

Yet the guards poured into the room like a breaking wave, and Apaay hurriedly signed what Irnik had said to Ila. The older girl nodded, her expression strained. It was difficult to breathe in the confined space, even more difficult to see. Two of the oil lamps had extinguished, the walls sinking inward.

Irnik drove the guards back, cutting a narrow pathway to the door. Ila broke free of the mass first, and Apaay had nearly reached the doorway when arms banded around her chest and neck, depriving her of air. She twisted in the man's grip, wrapping one leg around his calf so he lost his balance, arms wheeling. Then he turned and ran.

A bit shaken, Apaay moved into the hall before patting her pockets, checking for Eska's face.

It was gone.

"No." She wheezed the word. Like dead, brittle leaves.

She patted her trousers again, shoved her hands into her pockets and grasped for something that was no longer present. Once, twice she whirled around, searching the ground for a small puddle of loose skin.

The guard was halfway down the corridor.

The sight of his dwindling form brought her deadened limbs to life. Torchlight smeared into streaks of red-gold heat, lighting her path through the darkness. Not again. Never again.

"Apaay!"

At Irnik's booming voice, she stuttered, glanced over her shoulder. The man's footsteps faded.

Ila thrashed as a guard yanked her down the opposite hall. Her feet scrabbled for traction, her back arched to pry herself from the man's touch, a hoarse cry muffled behind the palm smashed against her lips. She managed a blow to the man's knee before he slammed her against the wall, her body slumping forward.

Apaay took one step toward her friend before she stopped. Eska—

"Help her!" Irnik, swamped by three men, couldn't reach her. He sliced through one guard's belly, but a second plowed into his side. Through the doorway, she glimpsed the room littered with bodies. A gurgling sound traveled the length of the tunnel, the wet slap of skin on skin. Hot saliva pooled in her mouth.

Her focus cut from Ila—hissing and clawing at the wall, fingers digging into stone in one last stand of defiance—to the deserted hallway. Ila's gaze burned, a desperate plea. Apaay could hardly speak the words. "He took Eska's face!"

Irnik grunted and threw one man against the wall, plowing a fist into his jaw. "What?"

A fissure ruptured in her chest, the two halves of her heart straining toward different people, both important women in her life.

A dry wind shrieked through the passage.

The guard howled and snatched his hand away, fingers streaked red. Ila had bitten through the man's fleshy palm. Blood dribbled down her chin, and the man backhanded her across the face, the crack sending Apaay forward two steps before she again paused. Her gasps came harder as the weight of this choice bore down. Time—she needed more time.

Another glance down the now-deserted corridor. Almost a full minute had passed. Night had swallowed the man's shape, and the clash of weapons had diminished, and still she stood, pinned by uncertainty, her pulse fluttering in her throat like delicate moth's wings. That man would take Eska's face to Yuki. After all she had done, the horrors she had endured. Apaay would never see it again.

Irnik snatched a fallen weapon from the ground. He sliced, blocked, and twisted in effortless grace. "What are you waiting for?" he bellowed. "Help her!"

Ila vanished around the corner.

Apaay should step forward. Had their positions been switched, Ila would not have hesitated, and yet Ila did not have a sister waiting for someone to save her from eternal darkness.

She had to choose, and someone would suffer. She wished things were different. She wished this power had not come to her, to decide who was more, who was less, because it was easy. It was easy to place her wants and needs before Ila's, before Irnik's. Here, starved for any sort of choice, it was easy to be selfish.

She had come here for one reason only: to bring her sister home.

Irnik glanced over, and their eyes met.

Apaay stumbled back. "I'm sorry," she whispered.

Then she bolted after the guard, Irnik's voice chasing her into the dim. The man had a few minutes' head start, but he was not untouched. A trail of splotches guided her easily through the maze of halls. This must have been the guard she'd wounded earlier.

The labyrinth rang with her footfalls. Apaay slowed when she reached a fork, then veered right to pursue the blood trail, streaks thick and uneven as if the man had stumbled and dragged his leg behind him before climbing to his unsteady feet. The stains, an oily sheen in the low light, morphed into splotchy smears. The man was bleeding out. His blood, dampening the stones like water upon the ground, would lead her to victory.

The faint scuffs of his stumbling gait reached her ears. Apaay skimmed a hand along the curved, ice-encrusted wall, using it for support when the last of her strength began to flag. It would not be long now, but she gritted her teeth, pushed through the searing heat gnawing at her abdomen, the slow seizing of her calves.

When she next rounded a corner, he was there. Thief, coward, a man all but gone. But she stumbled at a glint of light, the stationary object he fled toward at the opposite end of the hall.

A mirror.

Moonlight pierced its plain silver frame. A white, glassy fear crept along her nerves like frost upon the ground.

If he reached the mirror first, the game would end. Yuki would win. Nothing would change. Apaay would find herself back in that choked damp hole, chained. Someone with neither family nor a home.

Everywhere, she burned. Taut, aching thighs. Shoulders and back, chest and throat. It seemed impossible that she should have the energy to run faster, farther, but she hadn't a choice except to push and push, until she may as well have been flying.

At the sound of her giving chase, the guard quickened his stride, his limp more pronounced, trousers soaked black. The space between them dwindled: ten yards, five yards, three. He wavered. Reached for the rippling surface.

Apaay rammed him from behind, arms banding around his chest. They plunged through the mirror together, freezing air cutting on either side as they clawed at each other in free fall. Apaay managed to ram her elbow into the man's nose before the floor rose from out of the dark. She slammed atop him in a crumpled heap, limbs barking from the impact. A muffled groan slipped out.

For long moments, she couldn't move. Her head pounded. Her teeth rattled. And yet time was a swiftly moving river, draining into the sea. She must rise.

Gingerly, Apaay rolled her wrists and ankles. Nothing broken or sprained. The guard was still, one of his ankles bent at an unnatural angle, chest rising and falling shallowly. He had lost a lot of blood.

Moving slowly, she crawled to the man's side, her focus locked on his face for any twitch or sign that he would wake. She fumbled through his pockets and shoved Eska's face into her trousers before the man's fist shot out.

Pain exploded through her cheek. Apaay ducked her head as her eyes watered, her ears ringing from the force of his blow.

He tackled her, and they rolled, Apaay adjusting her center to prevent him from pinning her, like when she and Eska would wrestle to let off steam. But this was not a game. The man was all brawn, in his prime. He brimmed with life, while she guttered out. He could break her so easily.

Large hands swallowed her shoulders as he dropped his weight onto her legs. Apaay dug her heels into the ground. She tried to buck him off with her hips, her breath like splintering glass. She clawed at his clothes, her head shoved against the hard ground by one of his massive palms, and Apaay felt the scream building, barreling upward, because she was not strong enough, she was not limber enough, she was a jumble of nerves and deflated spirits, and she couldn't *reach*—

A surge of energy poured into her limbs. Apaay twisted her body with bared teeth. Eska was counting on her. *Pop, pop, pop*— joints cracked along her spine as she gained leverage. She flung out an arm and cuffed the man on the side of his head, then plowed her fist into the pulped flesh of his thigh wound.

He flinched away with a guttural bellow. Apaay scrambled to her feet, tripping in her haste to get away, and felt him clasp his fingers around her right ankle. She threw her weight into her left leg, thigh muscle burning with the strain, unwilling to give in, unwilling to give even the smallest inch. There must be a mirror nearby, one that would take her from this room, this man.

Lowering her center of gravity, she poured all her remaining strength, every tattered scrap, into jerking her right leg forward. Her left knee groaned at the weight it bore.

And the man simply let go.

She flew into darkness, tucking in her arms to prevent further injury at the impact. Five steps, and the guard was there, his hands hard, lifting her emaciated body up and slamming her into the ground.

Apaay's chest seized, lungs collapsing into hard knots. Her choked gasps drowned out a nearby splintering.

He grabbed her arm and dragged her across the slick surface. Apaay flailed, managing to twist her body and kick his bloody flesh, and the guard released her, now on his knees. Red drenched her boots and hands. His blood, not hers.

Apaay swayed on her feet, unable to place her full weight on her left ankle. Before she could reconsider, she sent a powerful blow to his temple. The man twitched and lay still.

Apaay swiped at her damp hairline, her hand trembling so hard she accidentally poked herself in the eye. The darkness cloaked everything, pressing in.

No, that wasn't true. There was light. A faint bluish glow emanated from beneath her feet, extending in every direction. No beginning and no end, the sight like dread, like death.

Ice.

← →

Slowly, Apaay sank to the ground, as her legs could no longer hold her weight. Water churned beneath the frozen surface. She was her grandmother as a young girl, struggling against the current as water dragged her down. It was no longer a memory she could shove into a dusty corner. It was not the past. It was now.

Apaay hung her head, eyes squeezed shut. Sweat prickled her brow. She was not outside on the frozen sea. She was still in the fortress. This wasn't real. She had left home, remember? She'd left the coast, and the frozen nightmare, far behind.

It didn't matter, though. Convincing her mind of the illusion did nothing to quell the roiling sickness, because she had already *seen* the ice, had already processed the image, and now the shaking ripped through her body with enough force to level her. She wished there was a way to slap sense into her past self. *Listen,* she would say, but it was too late now. Those memories swelled, gorging themselves on her fear.

First, a plan: to get off this ice. Then she would figure out what to do next.

Two hard raps against the surface deemed it solid. No discoloration to indicate weaker areas, as far as she could tell. At this point, she cared about little else.

Apaay wandered across the vast expanse, her soles whispering against the eerie blue surface. No sun, no moon or stars to guide her. Even in their absence, she usually had an idea of north or south, east or west. Not here. Not in the in-between.

Every ten steps she halted, listening for the slightest shift or creak.

She was even afraid to breathe too loudly.

Winter was a time of both loss and joy for the Analak. Loss of daylight brought a frozen sea—an end to isolation as they used dogsleds to cross the open water and trade with their brother and sister communities. They were a diverse people connected through common interests and ways of life. Food, song, language, dance—in such ways, they were linked. Different, yet the same.

While Apaay had only ever visited villages in the coastal regions, more Analak lay inland, scattered throughout the Central and Southern Territories. They did not subsist on seal or whale, animals birthed from frigid waters. Rather, they lived off those of the earth.

If the weather was willing, Apaay probably would have visited Laya, one of her good friends from a neighboring community.

Instead, she was walking a land that was not her land, across ice that was not the ice she knew. This ice lied. It was not the same color. It did not have the same smell. And another thing. She had the uneasy feeling she was not moving any distance at all. The landscape, the bare, flat plain, never changed.

A sharp crack sounded.

Apaay stopped cold.

A loud, grating sound filled the room. It was her breath, she realized, harsh as it puffed past her lips. She stood there for long minutes, hands pressed against her trembling legs, her grandmother's trauma embedded deeply in her. The silence that followed was not the reprieve of a long-winded sigh or hard bout of crying, but rather a truth you turned your back on, even as you felt it scrape along your spine, a single, curved claw.

She eased forward a step.

Another crack.

Apaay flinched. The space was so great it masked the direction the sound had come from. Anywhere. Everywhere.

She looked down, squinting to better see in the dark. Smooth, unblemished ice.

Sweat coated her skin, a thick layer of damp, her clothing itchy and constrictive. She needed to sit down and catch her breath, but she didn't have time. If she could spot the crack and the direction it had come from, she would know which area to avoid.

Apaay had begun to turn when she saw it: a line snaking from out of the darkness, moving with impossible speed.

She ran.

Faster and faster and faster, tearing through the endless gloom. Her boots pounded the surface like her heart, like two powerful beating drums, while the shriek of solid ice beginning to split apart roared from behind. She was back on the ice, a young girl who had believed herself invincible, when she was nothing more than skin and bones, easily broken, easily fooled.

A glance over her shoulder. Her injured ankle rolled, and she faltered, barely catching herself before going down. Apaay lost precious seconds regaining her footing.

Last spring, when the ice had begun to thaw, a man from a neighboring community had drowned at sea. Three days passed before anyone had found his kayak, floating upside down in open water. No one ever found his body.

She did not want that fate.

The sound of fracturing ice chased her through the room. Apaay searched for a way out, but she didn't know what she was supposed to look for. A stretch of beach? A large stone she could clamber up before the ground gave way?

It didn't matter, in the end. The cracks snaked into view, spreading out in thin, threadlike fragments, breaking the smooth surface into a thousand facets.

Apaay dropped to her stomach, arms and legs splayed out to increase her surface area over the ice. Air condensed where her mouth touched the surface, spreading and receding with her wheezing.

As the ice shifted beneath her, water began to seep through the cracks. The shock of cold speared through her.

Apaay squinted at the area a few feet ahead, where the cracks hadn't infiltrated. If she could drag herself forward, the ice might be solid enough to support her weight.

Arms spread, palms flat against the ice, she pressed down slightly and inched forward, legs dragging behind her. The frozen surface crunched and shifted from the movement, but held.

She did not dare move faster than the slowest crawl.

Unfair—a darkly fleeting thought. It came alive, how utterly *unfair* it all was. Sometimes she'd ponder it, unfold those corners of her mind and look down the long line of hardships she'd faced over the months, like gouges in the pristine earth. And she would ask herself why. Why *she* was the one to suffer. Why there was suffering at all. The world was nothing more than a picked-at scab, blood welling from the touch of dark thoughts.

Everywhere, Apaay ached. She had no outlet for the pain save her eyes, which itched and burned and from which tears now flowed. A part of her wished to return to her cell, where it was safe, predictable. She had to hold on, just a while longer. Just until she escaped this room, and found Ila and Irnik, and they tore free of the labyrinth's icy hold. Then she could find a place to rest, and break.

Her hand pressed down. And down.

Right through the ice.

Thin veins buckled, and a massive crevasse ripped open the ground, the impact shuddering through her chest. Water gushed over her hand.

The slab she rested on abruptly broke off, and Apaay screamed. Without the stability of the larger mass, the ice floe started to bob, forcing Apaay to press herself harder against its surface, her fingertips digging into the edges. But she wasn't centered. Gradually, the slab tilted backward from the uneven weight distribution. The slippery surface sent her sliding toward the edge. Her hands scrabbled uselessly, so desperate to cling, but then the ice floe flipped, and black water closed over her head.

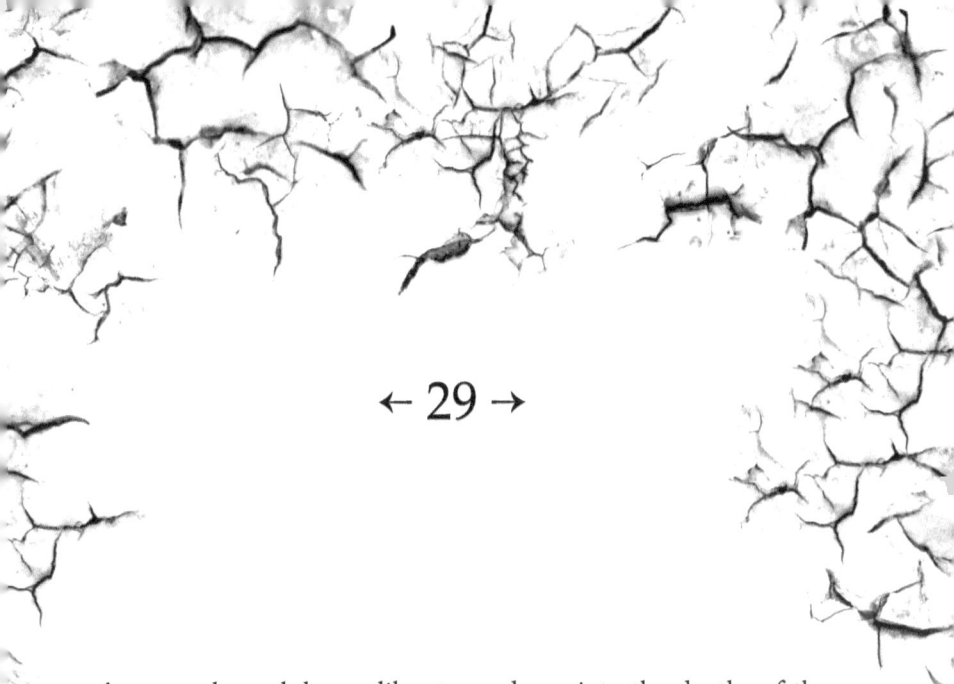

← 29 →

Apaay plunged, heavy like stone, down into the depths of the sea. The water was ferocious and demanding, so hungry after being starved for so long. The cold seared her skin and salt scoured her eyes, rapidly leaching her of strength. She had stared at death often enough to recognize its face, and this time it would not let her go. Apaay felt how tightly it squeezed, how desperately it clung. She had not the will to resist.

So she sank. And death's jaws welcomed her in.

It was strange. For so long, she had feared the ice, the darkness lurking beneath. She did not know what awaited her below, in that swallowing abyss. She only knew it was separate from everyone she loved, and she did not want to go. She did not want to leave this world unfinished. There were plans to be made and celebrations to be had, and a future bright and burning.

Her chest cinched tighter with the need to breathe. Yuki had wanted this, her demise. This hell had hardened Apaay, had all but destroyed what was good, but in her shattered state, it had also unearthed something buried long ago, stashed away out of fear, shame.

She had found Eska's face. Her dear sister, nearly lost.

More importantly, she had found herself.

She was not Ila or Chena or Mama or Papa or Masuk or Eska or Silla.

She was Apaay.

She was enough.

Her body came alive, legs propelling her upward, toward that ring of glowing white light piercing through the void. She shed her mittens and clawed at the ice with unbridled ferocity as panic broke over her. Kicking furiously, Apaay slammed her shoulder against the slab of ice. It barely moved.

Again, she rammed the frozen ceiling, her movements weighted. The fracture where the ice had broken was an illuminating white scar, and Apaay pressed against the crack as her chest seized and blood pulsed behind her stinging eyes. If she could push it upward with enough force, the slab would flip, allowing her to break the water's surface, into air and wind and light.

Her fingers skimmed the top. She kicked and shoved upward, palms flat. The ice was heavy, her arms so weak.

Then her clothes dragged her down.

Apaay plummeted through the water. Her ears popped from the pressure, the light thinning, squeezed by the water's dark fist. Bubbles burst around her head in white froth, a shock of sound as she dropped. She was going the wrong way. She needed to go *up*, but she was too heavy, and the sopping fur weighed upon her shoulders and legs and back, as if determined to take her with it.

She tackled her parka first, the heaviest of her clothes. The sodden coat clung, trapping her right arm against her stomach. Apaay flailed, kicking furiously, ensnared by the cold water that wanted her to breathe, but she clamped down on the need to inhale. This was death. She knew it in her cold-riddled bones. She had taken her last breath of air, and soon water would take its place, filling her eyes and nose and mouth.

Down she sank, the water like a thousand stabbing shards of bone. Still, she tore at her parka, imagining her fingers as claws, shredding, slicing, gouging their sharp points into the bindings, ripping it to pieces. It would not take her. Not today, not ever. She could do this; she could shed this weighted skin.

Her lungs withered, air steadily leaking out.

Her movements grew more lethargic, the sopping fur cutting into her neck. She needed to breathe. She needed—

The parka slipped free.

Her thoughts were a haze as lack of oxygen set in. Dimly, Apaay turned her attention to her boots, fingers numb and fumbling, and managed to shuck one off before her twitching muscles stopped responding.

Small bubbles drifted above and were lost.

Apaay hit bottom. Silt plumed in the water, a murky cloud fanning around her head. The pressure built, too great to resist. She gasped for air. Her thoughts cut off from the water's shredding force.

The salt burned.

She drifted, limbs nudging against the soft ground, eyes half open, seeing nothing. Her mind unraveled. The cold whispered, so gently in her ear, to rest for a moment, and she wanted to scream at the voice to go away, for it was not welcome here, it was not welcome anywhere.

Apaay rammed into something hard. She was almost gone, a half-drowned ghost of a girl, but she held on to consciousness long enough to reach out, her fingers brushing a solid frame surrounding a warmer, viscous substance. With the help of the underwater current, she pushed through.

The blast of water knocked her forward, throwing her from the submerged room into one of the passages. She rode the wave until it petered out and she sank into a sprawling heap.

Apaay heaved, her gruesome retching filling the corridor. Salt water poured from her mouth and splattered onto the stones, a bitter, sour stench. Her body shuddered through the heaves.

Eventually, the vomiting tapered off. Slumped onto the floor, Apaay sucked in deep lungfuls of air, her limbs twitching from shock. At first, she thought herself dead, but surely death would not be this painful. Her bruised, battered body throbbed, but oh, the air tasted so pure she would have happily lay there drinking nothing else for the rest of her life.

Surprisingly, her parka and boot had come to rest near her head. Even more surprising, they were completely dry. Everything was dry. Even her hair. It was yet one more thing she did not understand about the labyrinth.

Wincing at the ache in her hip, Apaay used the wall to help herself stand. She pulled on her clothes and was relieved to find Eska's face still in her pocket. A moment later, footsteps sounded, and two people rounded the corner.

Ila and Irnik stuttered to a halt, gasping, and Apaay drank them in—their bedraggled forms and widened eyes, their presence and distress. They were alive, they were whole, they were *here*.

But a separateness lay between them now. The shadow of what Apaay had done. She felt its solidity, like a wall built stone by stone.

Ila and Irnik were together.

Apaay was apart.

I'm sorry, she signed to Ila, every piece of her heart infused in those words. They sounded inadequate. She was not surprised. Ila had needed her, and Apaay had turned her back.

The older girl watched her warily, half shielded behind the guard. There was a hardness to her expression Apaay had never seen before.

Irnik glanced between them, no doubt able to feel the tension. "We'll have time for apologies later," he said. "Did you get your sister's face?"

She glanced at Ila, but the girl had turned away. "Yes."

"Then let's go."

"We'll never get out of here alive," Apaay managed as they flew down the corridor, torches extinguishing as they passed. Darker and darker, and then the light was gone.

"Have a little faith, why don't you." Even after felling nearly two dozen men, he hardly sounded out of breath.

Stone gave way to ice, then transformed back to stone as they pushed through the thick, gray light. The hallways curved, circling the central hall, the labyrinth's very core. Water stained the stones black. Apaay slipped and would have gone down if Ila hadn't caught her.

The girl dropped Apaay's arm and pulled ahead.

Irnik checked over his shoulder for guards. "When we reach the ground floor, we'll take a left. We'll use the outside garden to escape." They raced around a corner. "The walls are enchanted, but leave that to me."

Moments later, they reached the stairwell. The footsteps of what sounded like a hundred guards thundered, pulsing through the soles of her boots, and a sickening fear took root, because this, out of every form of torture she'd been subject to, was real. This was the end.

Irnik had already descended the first flight of stairs, Ila behind him, when Apaay stuttered to a halt. She remembered then, a promise made in the darkness and the cold.

Masuk.

"Wait!" But Irnik didn't wait. He probably couldn't distinguish her voice among the rumbling, which grew louder by the minute. "There's someone I promised to help. I can't leave him!" Masuk had mentioned his cell was located on the sixth level. They were heading in the wrong direction.

Near the bottom of the second landing, Ila turned. By now, Irnik had reached the first level and was halfway to freedom.

Go with Irnik, Apaay signed, hoping Ila could read the gestures in the grainy light. *I'll catch up.*

The older girl hesitated, hands curling into fists. Then she squared her shoulders and nodded.

They went down.

And Apaay went up.

The guards had yet to reach the stairwell when she topped the fifth-floor landing. Apaay fully intended to race up another flight of stairs, except there were none. This was as high as she could go.

Stepping free of the stairwell, Apaay looked around the deserted area. A walkway ringed the domed ceiling of the cavernous room, with a railing protecting her from the sudden drop. She was almost certain Masuk had mentioned the sixth level, but he had probably meant the fifth one. There weren't any passageways this high, merely doors. So many doors. Fifty, at least. Shut, locked, hiding their treasures, or prisoners, within.

She no longer cared about keeping silent as she sped around the length of the floor. Irnik and Ila would have reached the ground floor by now, and if Irnik hadn't realized Apaay had vanished, he would eventually. She hadn't meant to ruin his well-laid plans or put their lives at greater risk, but they had not seen Masuk and his deplorable living conditions. If she did not free him, no one would. He was trapped in the dark, but soon she would lead him into the light.

Apaay tried the handle on every door she passed.

Locked.

Locked again.

As loudly as she dared, Apaay whispered, "Masuk? It's Apaay. Tell me where you are."

A few doors contained iron bars set in the top of a small square window, but she was not tall enough to peer through the slats. Some doors had round handles. Others had long handles, or square handles, or handles located on the right side instead of the left. She could not open a single one.

Around the hall she flew.

Once to check the locks.

Twice to call for Masuk.

A third time to check the locks again.

When she reached the stairwell a fourth time, Apaay slowed. If she continued to run, her legs would collapse, and then what good would she be? The stairwell was alive with noise. A man bellowed in pain. Irnik? Had Yuki reached them? If only she had more *time*.

Apaay slumped against the old worn stones. Masuk had said the sixth level, right? She had not imagined it. He was not here.

Unless . . . *had* it been her imagination? Maybe he'd said fifth and she only *thought* he said sixth. Or maybe he'd said the fourth level. But that was where she had just come from, and she didn't want to risk running into the guards.

Groaning, Apaay tilted the back of her head against the wall.

So many doors.

Her mistake came in a moment of clarity. Apaay, recalling every horrible trial she had endured, realized she had approached this all wrong. In the labyrinth, *mirrors* were gateways, not doors.

Masuk was not chained behind a door. He was chained behind a mirror.

To see things clearly, she must look in the spaces between. If she were wanting to hide a prisoner in plain sight, where would she look?

Above, she decided. No one ever looked up.

Apaay circled the floor twice, head tilted back. After a few minutes of fruitless searching, she changed tactics yet again. She should not be looking for the source, but a by-product of the source. Where there were mirrors, there were reflections.

Moonlight slanted through the gloom in pale streaks. The railing gleamed, vertical slats carved in the shape of breaking waves, froth stemming from its rounded top. She ran her hand along the edge, making sure to keep out of sight should anyone look up. The noise of battle spread and softened, as if moving to a different location in the fortress. Unfortunately, there was no reflected light she could see.

On the third time around, Apaay analyzed the railing more closely. It stretched in a continuous length around the walkway save for one small space perhaps two feet wide, as if a chunk had broken off. If she stood in the gap, her toes would align with the very edge of the floor. Then, a drop into space.

Brow pinched in confusion, she ran her hand along the railing until it dropped into nothing. Ice, then air. There didn't seem to be any reason for the gap, and yet—

Peeking over the edge, Apaay checked for guards. The way was clear.

She stood on the edge, toeing the sudden drop. The thought of taking a step forward crossed her mind, like a spark of light on metal. She couldn't deny its presence. She did not know how such a small thing could carry such weight, but maybe it wasn't so small. Maybe something's size had nothing to do with how much weight it carried.

With one hand clutching the ice, Apaay stretched out her right foot.

The space in front of her was no longer empty.

A spiral staircase of glittering crystal materialized in a ripple of air, winding to the top of the domed ceiling, where a circle of reflective glass winked at its apex, awaiting her.

Sixth floor, indeed.

There was little time to second-guess herself. Apaay climbed the staircase quickly, and when she reached the mirror hanging a few feet above her head, she stuck up her arms, grasped for a ledge, and pulled herself up and through.

That familiar damp odor greeted Apaay as she hurried to the farthest cell and fell to her knees, shivering beneath her sweat-soaked furs. "Masuk, it's me." In the distance, a high-pitched scream pierced the gloom.

Near the corner, the darkness whispered and took shape. "Apaay?"

The knots in her back unwound in relief. "I'm getting you out. Can you walk?" She had never seen him stand.

"Yes, but my legs are weak." He shuffled forward, and torchlight bathed his ravaged face, his scars shiny with perspiration.

"I'll help you. But we're leaving. Right now."

He nodded. Waiting. Expectant.

And Apaay's heart sank with the realization that she did not have a key.

"No," she whispered. The chilled iron seared her forehead. How could she have forgotten something as important as a key? Stupid. So, so stupid. She'd been so focused on escape—escape the cell, escape the guards, escape the labyrinth—that it had slipped her mind.

"Masuk," she whispered, unable to say it.

But he already knew. His expression fell, withdrew, and for the first time since meeting him, she realized he had smiled, however briefly, at knowing he would step beyond these bars. Such a lovely smile, now gone.

"It's all right," he managed.

But it wasn't. It was the opposite of all right. It was a sentence to the bleakest of lives. She had opened the door, given him a small glimpse of hope, and slammed it in his face.

Apaay slumped forward, unable to hold herself up. Why hadn't she thought of the key?

"I'll fix this. I told you I wouldn't leave you, and I won't." She must find Irnik and Ila. Assuming they had reached the garden safely, Apaay would need to sneak to the first level and ask Irnik for one of his keys. Not that it would fit this lock, but she had to try, she *had* to—

A shadow darkened the line of the hall, blotting out Masuk's stricken expression. Apaay froze, staring into his terrified eyes as he stared into hers.

Someone was at the door.

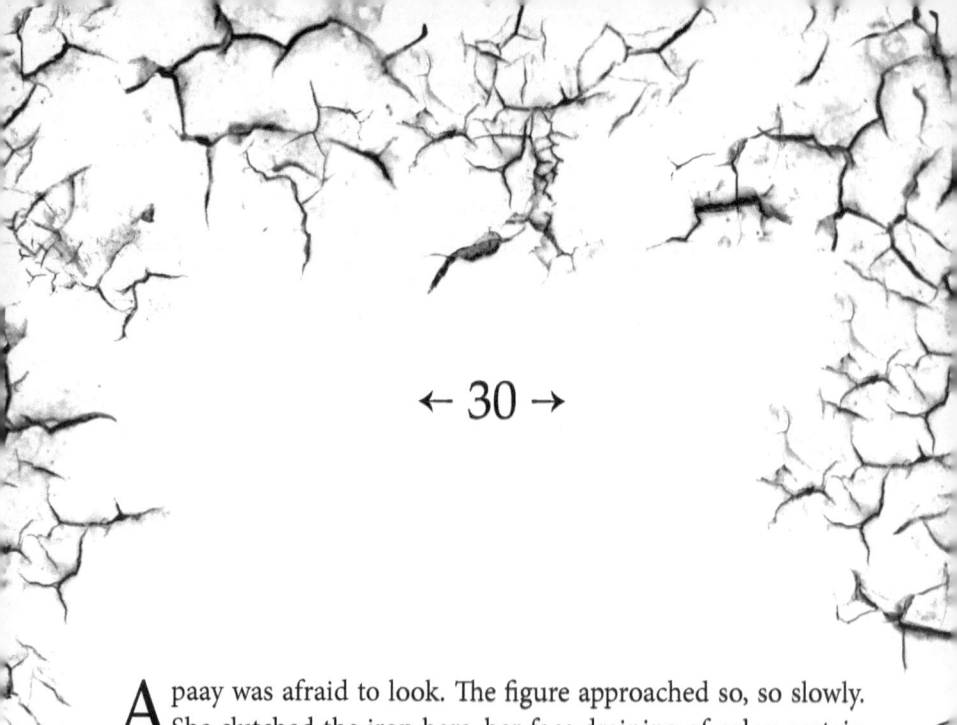

Apaay was afraid to look. The figure approached so, so slowly. She clutched the iron bars, her face draining of color, certain that any moment a spear would punch through her back. Masuk had scuttled to the corner of his cell, using the shadows to conceal himself. Apaay did not have that luxury.

The figure stopped behind her and grabbed her arm, pulling her up.

"How," Irnik said, his eyes flinty, "did you find this place?"

Her body sagged. Not Yuki. Not the guards. Just one guard—this one.

Behind him, Ila stared at her, face bloodless and, Apaay hoped, relieved. Maybe this wasn't a blessing as she had originally thought. Irnik looked as if he wanted nothing more than to throw her off the nearest cliff.

"I—" The excuse lodged in her throat.

He gripped her shoulders, gave her a little shake. A vein throbbed in his temple. "Speak."

With a growl, Ila stepped between them, shoving him away. Surprised, Irnik released her, silently watching as the girls checked each other for injury. Ila winced as Apaay pressed against the girl's shoulder joint.

Pulled muscle, Ila said. *I'm fine. Irnik knew a shortcut and we lost the guards.*

Guilt swelled against her ribs. Ila was speaking to her again, even if she did not deserve it. *I'm sorry. For what I did to you.* She reached out as if to touch Ila's cheek, then let her hand fall. *I understand if you don't want to be my friend anymore—*

Stop. A small, watery smile. Her love was plain. *It is done.*

Yanking Ila forward, Apaay wrapped her arms around her friend, breathing her in. *Good,* she thought, because nothing else needed to be said. *Good.*

"I apologize for shaking you," Irnik told her, hands in his pockets. His attention slid to the cell and the prisoner within before darting away.

"You knew he was here?"

Irnik released a frustrated sound, his fingers tunneling through his hair. The flicker in his expression was not one thing, but rather many: irritation, guilt, possibly even affection. "Yes, I did. Now tell me how you knew about these cells."

Apaay answered because she *chose* to, not because he ordered her to. "I found it when I was sent into the labyrinth the first time. There was a mirror I walked through." Then, she had thought it would lead her to Eska's face. That was before learning of the labyrinth's unpredictability. "I promised Masuk if I found a way out of here, I would help him escape."

The light cast pockets of darkness across Irnik's face. She had never seen his expression more closed. It was very unlike him. "Masuk?"

Apaay crossed her arms, refusing to let his suspicion deter her. "He couldn't remember his name, so I gave him one."

Ila, who had been reading Apaay's lips, signed, *Survivor.*

Yes, Apaay signed back. Ila, at least, understood the sentiment.

"Do you have the key to his cell?" she asked.

He clacked his teeth together. "No, and we're wasting time. We were almost at the garden, and now we've wasted even *more* time. If you hadn't run off, we could have escaped by now. You risked all our lives for a prisoner. Do you realize what could have happened?"

"No one asked you to come back for me. I told Ila to go ahead and I would catch up."

He snorted. "And you thought she would have left you?"

Of course not. That's why she'd said it.

Lifting her chin, Apaay said once again, in an unwavering voice, "I'm not leaving without Masuk." She didn't flinch at his fury. It was all hot air anyway. Besides, she had made a promise to the prisoner. If she could not keep her word, then she could not keep anything.

Irnik made a sound between a curse and a growl, shooting Apaay a furious glare. "Fine," he muttered. Stepping around her, he pulled a key from his pocket and inserted it into the lock. A heavy *thunk* crashed in the dark. The door swung open.

"I knew you were lying" was all Apaay said before brushing past him to crouch before Masuk, who huddled against the back wall. The stench of urine and excrement was so strong she was forced to breathe through her mouth.

Apaay smiled and held out her hand, an offering. "Everything's going to be all right." She would be damned if she forced him into deciding. This was his choice alone to make.

He jerked his chin at Irnik, expression wary. "Who's that?"

"He's a—friend." An angry, confusing, frustrating friend, but still a friend. "He's going to help us escape, but we need to hurry."

After a moment of torment, he grasped her hand. His was large, and cold, and dead in a way only suffering in silence and darkness could do to someone, but he stood and allowed her to lead him from the cell for the first time in nearly twenty years.

Masuk had a terrible limp. Five steps down the hall, his legs buckled, dragging Apaay down with him. Irnik threw one of the man's arms over his shoulder, using his strength to half carry Masuk down the passage while Apaay and Ila trailed behind.

When they reached the mirror set into the floor, Irnik went through first, followed by Ila, then Masuk, and finally Apaay. Apparently, Irnik hadn't the patience to help the prisoner down the stairs, instead leaving that job to Apaay and Ila, which was to say, mostly Ila, since Apaay could barely stand. With no railing to protect them from the long drop below, it took close to ten minutes to descend the staircase.

"About time," Irnik said when they reached the bottom.

"Well, maybe we could have gone faster with a little *help*," Apaay snapped, curling her hands into fists so she would not be tempted to slam them into his face.

"It was your choice to bring him, not mine." He set off toward the stairwell before she could answer.

Masuk murmured, "He seems like a lovely fellow."

Sure. If you considered broody, foul-tempered guards lovely.

They traveled in single file, Masuk and Apaay bringing up the rear at a hobble. Eventually, they reached the stairwell, now abandoned. Down one flight, past the fourth level, to the third. When they reached the landing, Irnik lifted a hand. They stopped, huddling together against one of the walls. Apaay stiffened from the splash of dark water a few feet to her left.

Footsteps, coming closer.

The guards blew past the stairwell entrance one level above. As soon as the footsteps died, they continued their descent.

By the time they reached the first level, Apaay was panting as hard as Irnik. Her throat burned with thirst. She had made it this far, but truthfully, she didn't know how much farther she could go.

Masuk, too, was fading. The distance between Apaay and Masuk and Irnik and Ila lengthened like a piece of fabric stretched to sheer. He slipped on the slickened stones, and Apaay braced to catch him. Exposure tinged his toes a faint blue.

"Here." Apaay knelt to remove her outer boots, peeling them away from her thinner, soft-soled slippers, which unfortunately weren't waterproof. "Put these on."

He swayed, staring at her shoes with a small frown. "But your feet—"

"I'll be fine. You're in danger of getting frostbite. They might be small, but they're better than nothing." She helped him slip on the fur-lined boots, his hand braced on her shoulder. They were the cleanest thing about him. "Better?"

He nodded gratefully. "Much."

They caught up with the others a few minutes later in the central chamber, the five mirrors appearing more ominous than they had, reminding Apaay of all that had occurred. Such terrible, terrible things.

She gritted her teeth against the stabbing sensation in her abdomen. "Almost there," she heaved to Masuk.

Irnik and Ila had reached the opposite entryway. Apaay didn't remember where she had entered the labyrinth or how, but the exit must be close. The air sparked with urgency, need driving them onward, and Apaay, even in her weakened state, was sure she had never run this fast in her life. So many things had been taken from her, but what awaited her beyond these walls—warmth, family, air as wild as it was free—would welcome her home. She would hunt with Papa. Cook with Mama. Share jokes with Eska.

But the dream shattered.

Apaay screamed as a tendril of ice water wrapped around her ankle and jerked her backward, dragging her along the ground, back to the sea and the girl who stood atop it, among everything that was hers. Apaay scrabbled for a hold, but her mittens did not have any traction. One hard jerk, and her head cracked against the stone.

"Leaving so soon?" Yuki cooed with a feral smile, her hair in wild disarray. Lifting a delicate hand, she gestured as if to wave hello, and the liquid rope moved with the motion, hefting Apaay up until she dangled above the thrashing waves.

"It's rude not to say goodbye, you know." One snap, and Apaay plunged into the sea.

The frigid water closed over her head, greedily sucking her down. Darkness became her world. Ice squeezed her lungs and locked her muscles into stiff boards. It was exactly like the first time, exactly like the last time, and the rush of panic would never change.

She floundered. Pumped her arms and kicked her legs and strained toward the light, so hazy behind the churning gray water. Apaay fumbled to shed the heavy parka, and she swore if she survived this day, she would make Yuki pay.

Something hard knocked against her. A hand latched onto her arm and propelled her upward. Apaay broke the surface and gasped, blinking water from her eyes to see who had saved her, how she had managed to cheat death.

Masuk.

Yuki was too busy giving orders to pay attention to Apaay and Masuk as they swam to the walkway and heaved themselves up on shaky arms, flopping onto their backs. Either Yuki didn't notice Masuk had jumped in after Apaay, or she didn't care. Probably the latter. Masuk was not a threat. This man had faded away for years, and he was almost gone.

Apaay clenched her teeth together to stop their chattering, her breath frail and white. Every part of her curled away from the chill spreading through her body, searching for warmth. Yuki, ever the fan of slow acts of torture, did not order the guards to finish them off, and Apaay, in her fatigued state, was not surprised. With no fire to warm her, she would surely die.

Lifting a hand, Yuki gestured for the guards, all fifty of them, to close in. Irnik concealed Ila as much as he could with his body, a difficult task without a wall against their backs. They were fully surrounded.

"I knew there was something suspicious about you," Yuki murmured to Irnik as the guards parted to let her through. A light sheen of sweat glimmered at her temples, her body vibrating with volatile energy that sizzled in the air.

She stopped a mere foot away. "You called me Yuki."

He matched her smile, teeth for teeth. "Is that not your name?"

"Yes," she replied, as if they were sharing a joke like old friends. "It is."

Apaay and Masuk hobbled to their feet, bodies jerking with shudders, water dripping onto the ground. Apaay leaned on him, and he on her. The waves grew more violent, lashing at their legs.

In the months that Apaay had been trapped here, she'd learned a few things about Yuki. The girl rarely showed fury. The angrier she became, the sweeter she spoke. This killing calm masked a rage that had simmered for years, and there was no stopping it now.

Yuki knew something. And from the look she and the guard shared, Irnik knew something, too.

"If we're going to stand here staring at each other all day," Irnik said, "the least you could do is pay me a compliment. It's rude, you know."

"I don't believe I was finished speaking," she said, swatting aside a greasy lock of hair.

Lips curved, he gave her a small bow. "My apologies. I believe you mentioned how I called you by your name?"

"Yes." Those ink-black eyes, like two round pearls, gleamed. "And this is the interesting thing." She laughed, a manic sound that sang against the ice and revealed just how far Yuki had truly fallen. "Only one person has ever called me Yuki, and it certainly wasn't Irnik. No, Irnik was too stupid to do anything but grovel. He never questioned me." Clasping her hands in front of her, she said, "If there's one thing I despise, it's a liar."

"Interesting, considering lying is what you do best."

Between that clash of wills, no one existed but them. This fortress did not exist, or the guards, or the ice throne, or Apaay and Ila and Masuk, three prisoners having almost escaped to freedom.

The silence stretched.

"Maybe you can fool them," Yuki said, "but you certainly can't fool me." She flashed that sickly sweet smile. "Isn't that right, Numiak?"

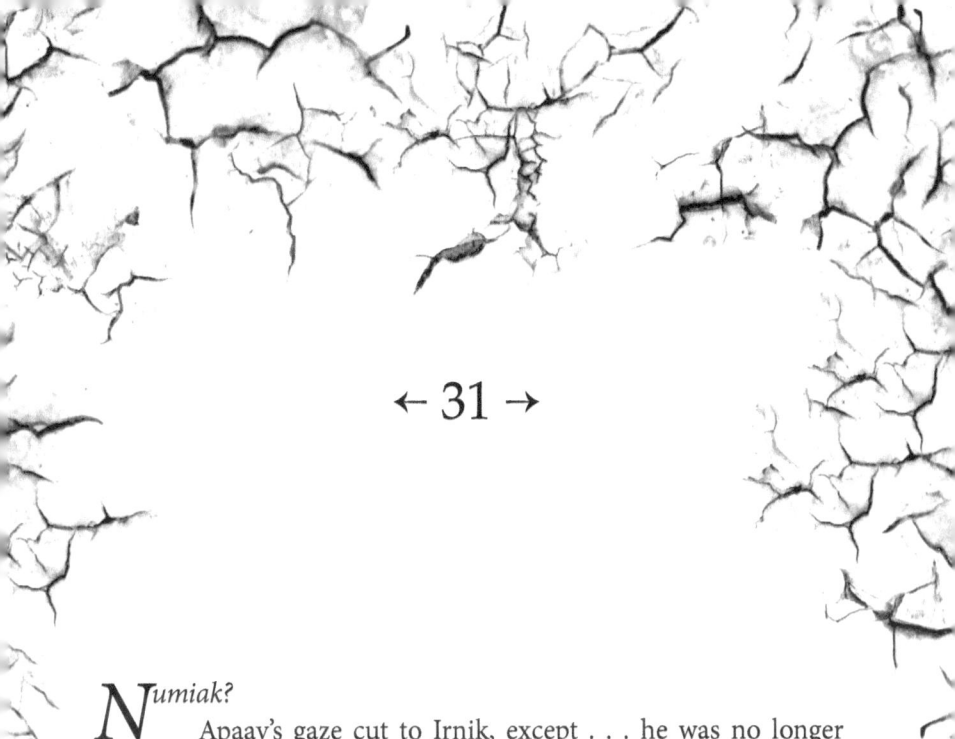

← 31 →

Numiak?

Apaay's gaze cut to Irnik, except . . . he was no longer Irnik. The face of the guard, the one who'd helped them escape, had melted into chiseled dark features, straight black brows, eyes of every sort of color, a beauty found only in dreams.

The Face Stealer.

She couldn't move. The ground had been ripped from her, the world flipped upside down. This could not possibly be real. He was a flame, brightly flickering, easily extinguished. But his form did not waver. It was solid, and cast a shadow upon the ground.

The words throbbed in her chest, like a bruise. How? And why?

"How long has this charade been going on?" Yuki demanded, taking a step closer. The guards awaited their orders. "Weeks? Months?"

Years, thought Apaay.

All this time the demon had worn another man's face, slipped into his skin, manipulated his body. He had become someone else. Someone who did not exist. Someone, Apaay realized with a sinking heart, whom she had believed to be her friend.

But he was not her friend. He was the source of her pain, and she had unknowingly revealed to him her weaknesses. She had been blind. All this time and she had never known.

Ila, equally appalled, clapped her hands over her mouth.

Yuki looked lost. Her small mouth trembled. She, too, must have trusted this man, confided in him.

"Answer me!" A funnel of water shot skyward, looming over them.

The Face Stealer didn't answer. Beside her, Masuk's face had taken on a slack quality. Apaay wrapped an arm around his waist when he swayed.

"How dare you," Yuki hissed, stepping within his personal space. The wave plummeted back into the sea. "You thought you could outwit me? You thought you could save these wretched mortals without my knowledge?" Her laughter grated, and it went on, far too long to be natural. Apaay cringed at the soul-sucking sound. "Sweet Numiak. You forget who I am."

The Face Stealer answered with a sleek, even smile. "On the contrary, Yuki, it's *you* who have forgotten who *I* am."

"And who are you, might I ask? A coward who hides behind the faces he steals?"

The smile fell. "Your enemy."

The violence in that statement sent Yuki back a step. Delicately, the young girl cleared her throat and half turned toward Masuk. "Who's this?"

"You mean you don't recognize him? The deplorable conditions he's endured? The half-dead look about him?" The demon had not moved, had not dared to. Fifty spears were pointed at his chest, and he was the only thing standing between Ila and their sharp points. "Surely you recognize one of your own prisoners."

Beside her, Masuk stiffened. Apaay's legs trembled from supporting his weight.

"Hm." Yuki sent one last glance to the starved man before dismissing him, apparently deciding he was indeed her prisoner and had been locked away for so long she had forgotten he existed.

"Now you're uncertain," he murmured.

The girl, who had begun to pace, faltered. "No," she said furiously. "You confuse uncertainty with my lack of caring. Why should I care about a half-dead man?" She resumed her pacing and stopped at the edge of the walkway, staring down at the gray-green lather foaming on the water's surface. The guards tracked the movement, awaiting her command.

"Tell me this." Turning, she crossed her arms. They were like twigs or icicles or something equally breakable. "How long have you been working against me? From the very beginning?"

His answer was vague and exactly what Apaay would expect of him. "Long enough."

"I thought we were on the same side."

"The mistake is yours," he murmured, irises a cool green, "in believing a prisoner could ever be on the same side as the one holding the key to the cell."

"But you weren't a prisoner. We were equals. It was like you said: I have something of yours, and you have something of mine. Soon the alliance will be reinstated. If we joined forces with Nanuq . . ."

A muscle fluttered in his jaw at that name—Nanuq. "Not interested."

She bit off a curse. "You weren't at the council meeting. You don't know what his vision is. It might align with what you want."

"What I want," he said, lethally soft, "is impossible, because it no longer exists. Or have you forgotten?"

Her eyes widened a fraction before she leaned forward and hissed, "*Don't* throw the past in *my* face. I offer you a chance to move forward, to start again."

His gaze offered little warmth. "Like I said. Not interested."

An animalistic snarl ripped from her throat. "Then perhaps you'll be interested in *this*." Water exploded upward, twisting in the air before surging toward him, and he pushed Ila aside seconds before the force slammed into his chest, sending his body cracking into the stone wall. The deluge of water kept him pinned.

"You forget, Numiak, who's in charge here." Teeth bared, she sent a second tunnel of water to join the first. Its roar filled the chamber, twining with Yuki's delighted peals. Ila cowered from the sight. "But don't worry. I'll remind you."

It was as if the darkness merged with him, because one minute he was there, and the next he had vanished, having somehow enfolded himself into the shadows to reappear in an alcove across the room.

"That's not very nice," he said, wiping the coils of sopping hair from his face. "Honestly, Yuki. Where are your manners? We have guests."

"I'll show you nice." She launched herself forward.

A blink, and he was gone. The darkness was his shield, molding to his form so he was neither material nor immaterial, living nor nonliving, using the lack of light to shift between locations. The shadows were, for him, an in-between place. He was night, and night was him, and there had never been another.

In her half-delirious state, it was difficult for Apaay to keep track of his movements. He seemed to pull the shadows from the corners in which they dwelled like scraps of fabric, weaving their threads into ropes, which curled around Yuki as she pummeled him with a mountain of churning liquid.

He jerked the tethers forward, swung them around with Yuki attached to their ends. He released her, and she flew. Straight toward the icicles protruding from the domed ceiling.

Apaay, fully prepared for the sight of her impaled body, braced for the spattering of blood and flesh. But the ice melted and refroze against the dome's contour, allowing Yuki to slide down its curved surface, until a wave deposited her safely on solid ground.

There was a dazed look in her eye, like the splitting of a half-healed wound. Apaay knew that look. She was *wearing* that look. As if the young girl had never thought this person, whom she had trusted, would intentionally try to harm her.

The Face Stealer laughed. *Laughed.* "Come now, Yuki. Aren't you having fun? I know how much you love your games."

Games, yes, Apaay thought. *But not these.*

Yuki only enjoyed the games she won.

But this was not about winning or losing. It was more. It was about people, it was about relationships, it was about power, it was about privilege. It was about everything *but* the games.

Something had taken root in the girl, and it had festered and molded and tainted her in some irreversible way. Her expression was vicious. But there was something else. A fragility, a frailness. The way this girl braced herself against the blows spoke so loudly it was impossible to overlook. A thin, hard shell that had cracked, like a bird's egg.

This was a girl who had loved a life, and cherished it, and lost it.

They clashed again, shadow against water. The Face Stealer glided around the room, held aloft by strips of night. Darkness parted darkness, a curved black blade. He struck, then slipped aside. Winked out of existence, reappearing only seconds later. Yuki chased him, her attacks sloppy with frustration and palpable rage, her shape a streak of silver gleaming beneath the low light. A wave of water trailed behind, frothing and spitting foam.

No matter her intentions, he eluded her. Did Yuki not know? She could not touch night. She could not touch smoke. Tendrils slipped around his arms, breathing as he did, alive. Without them, he was a man, but curled into the shadows, he descended into myth.

The darkness crooned.

Demon.

The Face Stealer drifted across the roiling water on a dark cloud, swallowed by a small pocket when she came too close, bursting into being behind her, too fleeting to capture. The oil lamps doused as he passed, until Apaay was forced to squint to make out their forms. She remembered the room of faces, how he'd shielded her with his power. An all-concealing cloak. It had *become* her.

Yuki bared her teeth in frustration, shaping the water into what appeared to be a large polar bear that chased him throughout the room. Then she dove beneath the waves.

Apaay and Ila shared a glance, one of stricken alarm, at the realization that Yuki was far more dangerous out of sight.

The ground trembled. Something enormous was coming to life beneath the surf.

A colossal stalagmite punctured through the water right beneath the demon. Apaay gasped as it shot skyward, as it touched the soles of his boots before he vanished. When he reappeared, the ice came for him again, and then a third time, as if Yuki knew where and when he would materialize before he did so.

"Poor Numiak, always running." She let loose a laugh and skipped across the icy protrusions.

His expression was unreadable. He wasn't able to avoid both the bear and the stalagmites. Yuki managed to corner him on the opposite end of the chamber, a massive rumbling filling the space as one of the columns cracked at its base and swung around, its curved peak reshaping into a sharp point. An enormous icicle barreled toward the Face Stealer's heart.

That demonic smile made a reappearance. A promise—of terrible, terrible things.

Apaay almost felt bad for the girl.

As soon as the weapon brushed his chest, he became mist. But Apaay understood, as the Face Stealer reappeared in some far corner near one of the arrow-shaped archways, that Yuki had anticipated this, his disappearance. Already, she was turning. Already, a long line of water snaked in the opposite direction from where the demon now hovered. Her teeth were bared and tears coated her cheeks, an expression of pure loathing, fueled with the fire to hurt him, too.

It happened too quickly for Apaay to comprehend.

The water struck.

Ila screamed.

High above, the stalactites rattled, a dusting of crumbling ice. Chunks rained down. Apaay stumbled forward five, seven, twelve steps across the slippery stone as she cried, *"No!"*

Lurching into one of the distracted guards, she knocked him aside, reaching for Ila as the older girl went airborne and crumpled against the wall. When the guard snagged her arm, she hissed and spat, clawing at his face, at any patch of skin. Behind her, a muted groan.

"Ila," she managed through chattering teeth. Her trembling dissolved into violent jerks, her body failing to produce enough heat to warm her organs. She slid to the floor, no longer able to feel her fingers or face or toes.

As a small wave deposited Yuki onto the pathway, the guards parted to let her pass.

Night bloomed like a dark flower in the vaulted chamber.

Apaay bowed her head as a dry wind howled and scraped along the icy walls. When she lifted her head, he was there. The darkness gravitated toward him, blotting out the moon. A darkly beating heart.

Shadows settling along his shoulders and back, he strode forward, much of the dim easing into watery gray light.

Yuki's nostrils flared. "One more step," she said, the words agonized, "and she dies."

The image was brutal and clear. Ila, held aloft by a liquid hand, toes skimming the ground. Ice slivers crowded against her throat, sinking into that delicate skin.

"This," said the Face Stealer, gesturing between Yuki and himself, "is between you and me." The guards shifted in his presence, and his voice was lethal in its softness. "No one else."

"That stopped being the case when you tried helping these prisoners escape. Try again."

Without breaking eye contact, he stepped forward.

The shards pushed in deeper, and Ila gasped. Yuki's mouth pinched. "I mean it."

"Let the girl go. She's nothing to you."

"Don't tell me what to do."

"I'm not telling you anything. It was more of a . . ." Another step forward, palms raised. "Suggestion."

He continued his slow approach.

Emotion flared in Yuki's gaze. Apaay had seen glimpses of her vulnerability, but eventually the walls always rose, higher and stronger than before. Now the girl was stripped, every part of her locked and wooden, sharp edges worn down. The look in her eyes was like raw, pink skin. She had been pushed too hard, too far.

"I always believed we worked well together because of our differences," Yuki murmured. She chuckled even as her face crumpled. A swift, merciless undoing. "But we're the same, you and I."

"Oh?" Casual. He was nearly within arm's reach. "How so?"

She said, with a look of utter defeat, "We're both alone."

The Face Stealer faltered, and Apaay didn't know whether it was intentional, but the slip allowed Yuki an opening. A band of water encircled him. It spiraled around and around, tightened, then held.

She yanked him beneath the sea.

As soon as the water swallowed them, its surface smoothed to a glassy calm. Apaay didn't know what to feel. A part of her wanted the Face Stealer to drown, because when she thought back to every hideous, gut-wrenching occurrence, the moment she had stepped upon this cut path, everything began and ended with him. He had stolen Eska's face. He had brought Chena here. He had caused Nakaluq's death. He had kept his silence.

But if he died, she would never escape this place alive.

Apaay shifted her focus away from the water, relieved to find Ila relatively unharmed save a few scratches on her neck. A ring of guards surrounded her, but their attention lay elsewhere. If the Face Stealer survived his attempted drowning, they would need to flee, and quickly.

Apaay dragged herself to the water's edge, waiting for a sign or splash. Waiting for him to breathe.

A few bubbles disturbed the surface.

Apaay leaned forward.

A burst of water. A splintering of sound.

Yuki sat atop the cresting wave, smoky tendrils wrapped around her throat. She flailed, and cursed, and wished death upon the Face Stealer, death upon his family, as the demon arose from the water's deep, his expression wild and unleashed.

"You don't remember?" he said, voice chilling. Bumps rippled up Apaay's arms for an entirely different reason than freezing cold. "You killed them. You and that bastard Nanuq." The tendrils tightened further. The guards, upon realizing what was happening, charged forward, their shouts ringing against ice and stone.

With a final jerk, the girl slumped forward. He flung her body against the wall, where it cracked and lay still, the delicate ice circlet no more than crushed shards.

The blow had snapped her neck.

It was far too late by the time the guards reached her. With Yuki's death, the lashing waves settled.

But the Face Stealer wasn't done. His eyes blazed, a hard, oxidized black. A wave of crushing night swamped the guards, and it was the last thing they would ever know. It filled their eyes and noses and mouths, squeezed their organs, burned them to ash. A reminder, always, of who he was and what he could do.

He appeared at her side a moment later. The dampness lifted from her clothing, as well as Masuk's. Ila bolted down the walkway and threw her arms around Apaay, who gripped her friend's shoulders and arms before inspecting the wounds at her neck. The shallow cuts were already beginning to scab over.

You're fine, Apaay said, needing to say it, if only to reassure herself. Ila was unhurt. They were almost free.

Voice low, the Face Stealer said, "Let's go."

Apaay tensed at his nearness. His eyes still held that dangerous glint. She'd always known he was powerful, but witnessing that power was another matter entirely. It lingered in the air, electric. He had killed fifty men without a blink.

She stepped away from him, feeling faint. "Who's to say you won't take us to some equally terrible place?" It was not an unlikely possibility. There was not one thing she could trust with him.

"Either you come with me of your own accord, or I drag you from this room. Your choice."

"That's not a choice. That's a threat."

His power snapped against her skin in frustration. "Then how about this. Do you want to live, or do you want to die? Is that choice enough for you?"

That wasn't fair. He'd backed her into a corner, backed them all into a corner. Ila and Masuk were depending on her, too. The prisoner could barely stand as it was. She couldn't carry him and herself.

"Fine," she said through clenched teeth. "Lead the way."

Wordless with unrest, they followed. Soon, they had reached the garden. The stars were delicate pinpricks, as if a cloth with holes poked through had been cast over the sky.

Apaay had wondered how they would scale the wall encircling the glittering trees, but she should not have worried. With admirable efficiency, the Face Stealer manipulated the shadow to encompass their group of four, lifted them over the ice, and deposited them on the other side.

For the first time in months, she walked the land as a prisoner freed, and yet Apaay had neither the energy nor the time to appreciate it. They hurried across the barren, rock-strewn land, she and Masuk leaning heavily against each other. The night was still, and the only peaceful thing.

"You're going too fast!" Apaay called, stumbling through the snow. Since she no longer wore her sealskin boots, the thin slippers were already beginning to dampen.

He didn't bother turning around. She had difficulty distinguishing him from the surrounding night. "You're going too slow. Hurry up."

"But—" She frowned at Ila, who also appeared confused by their breakneck pace. "Isn't Yuki dead?"

"No. The blow will only last for a few minutes at most."

"But you snapped her neck."

"Yes, but she can only be killed by a certain poison, and unfortunately, I have none in my possession. She heals quickly."

They picked up the pace.

With the Face Stealer among them, Apaay did not experience the same disorientation she had upon first reaching the in-between. In less than ten minutes, they reached the wolf-shaped cairn. The Face Stealer placed a palm against the stone, then held out his other hand.

"Take it." He was gazing at Apaay. "Everyone else, grab onto her."

Apaay stared at his hand, not making any move to touch it. A relatively harmless gesture, coming from someone who was anything but.

"While we're still alive," he said, voice hardening with urgency.

"You'll excuse me if I hesitate," she snapped. "I still don't know whether to trust you."

"Only a fool would trust me. But where I'm taking you will certainly be better than your life here."

She suddenly remembered Eska's face in her pocket. "Are you returning me to my village?"

"No. It's not safe."

"My sister—"

"Can wait."

"But—"

"Do you want to die?" His pupils were blown wide. "Because you will if we do not leave right now."

Apaay may not have trusted him, but she heard the truth in those words. And maybe a tremor of fear.

Dropping her gaze, she placed her hand in his, the touch reminiscent of the deal they had made—the blood oath. With her free hand, she clutched Ila's fingers while Masuk looped their arms together.

It felt like the coldest she had ever been and the warmest she had ever been. Her world squeezed into the smallest point of being, then exploded into light. Mountains guarded their front and rear, trees dotted sporadically throughout the white landscape. There was no hint of the sea.

Before the Face Stealer could shift away, she tightened her grip on his hand. "I need to return to my village. My family needs me."

"There's no time." His gaze swept from her legs to her face. "You need sleep, food, and recovery. You're nearly dead on your feet."

"No." She pressed closer, lifting her chin so she could look at him fully. "We go now."

Tendrils pulsed around his form. They seemed to appear when he experienced rage or frustration or some other strong emotion. "We'll go when I say it's safe."

It was never more clear to her that Irnik was not, and never had been, real. Irnik was a face he had stolen, a role he had played. This man was a demon. She could never forget that. "Then I'll return there myself."

Apaay took two steps away from the cairn before he yanked her back by the hood, cold air slicing along her exposed scalp. "If you step past the cairn, Yuki will be able to track us. It offers a protective barrier. No one can find us here."

"If she finds you, then it will be nothing less than you deserve," Apaay spat, knocking his hand aside. "Either take me to my village, or I walk."

"You're not thinking this through."

The simmering heat in her gut helped beat back some of the exhaustion. "I'll do whatever it takes to return to my family. You can't keep me here."

They stared at each other for an immeasurable moment. The demon, and the girl. Surrounded by snow. Free.

But it didn't feel free to Apaay.

Turning to Ila and Masuk, he said, "Go to the lake and wait for me. If anyone approaches, tell them who you are. They know to expect you."

"What lake? There's nothing here." It was the first time Masuk had spoken to the demon.

Something hardened in the Face Stealer's expression, but he pointed west. "Keep walking straight. You'll know it when you see it."

Ila signed, *I want to go with Apaay.*

No, the Face Stealer said, and Apaay vaguely recalled her hypothermic ordeal. Upon returning her to the cell, Ila had fought him like a mother wolf protecting her young. And the Face Stealer had signed to her.

Apaay should have put the pieces together then—how unusual it was that both Irnik and the Face Stealer had known how to sign.

It's not safe, he continued. *One ridiculous girl is all I can handle at a time.*

Apaay huffed out a half laugh. Ila, after shooting him a mistrustful glare, lunged forward and caught her in a tight embrace.

Reluctantly, Apaay drew away. *I'll see you again.*

The Face Stealer gripped her hand. *We'll be back.* He touched the cairn, and they were thrown once more into darkness.

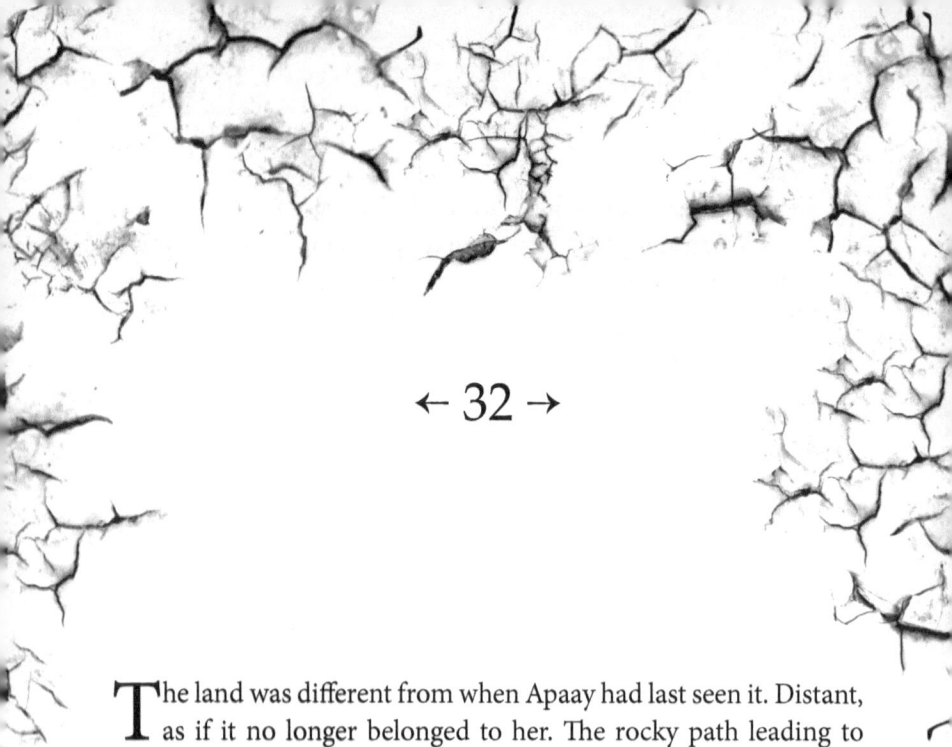

← 32 →

The land was different from when Apaay had last seen it. Distant, as if it no longer belonged to her. The rocky path leading to the sea appeared aimless. The pristine snow less lustrous. Even the brine carried upon the wind had dulled.

Since they had arrived at a cairn located a half mile from her community, it did not take long to reach it. Her legs trembled with weakness, but she hurried forward through the soft, new-fallen snow. Her heart swelled and lifted as if with song. She couldn't wait to surprise her family. They must celebrate somehow. Dancing, perhaps, to the beat of oiled drums.

Apaay ascended the steep hill that overlooked the ice houses, breath puffing hard. A smile began to spread across her face as she topped the rise and looked down, thinking yes, she had made it, she was here—

The ground was blackened ash.

The Face Stealer came to stand beside her, impossibly quiet. Apaay didn't understand what she was looking at. The snow was . . . No, there was no snow. She was looking at the bare earth, the snow having melted away. There were no homes. There were no dogs, or skins drying, or children running about. There was absolute stillness. The stillness of death's quiet hands at work.

Was this a dream?

Apaay stumbled forward in confusion. Something was not right. That was all she knew. *This is not right.*

She was not close enough to distinguish the shapes strewn across the scorched ground. They could have been anything: clothes, stores of frozen meat, overturned sleds. The forest encircling the village was bare, burned trees protruding from the austere earth. Everything else looked to be rubble.

"Apaay."

The Face Stealer's voice, soft and smooth like glacial ice. It was the first time he had ever spoken her name. Until this moment, she hadn't even realized he *knew* her name, as she had only recently learned of his Irnik charade. But—yes. Apaay was her name.

Her feet, having turned numb from the damp slippers, carried her down the hill. The pressure in her chest squeezed the closer she came to the wreckage of what had once been the place where she had sewn her first pair of boots, built her first kayak, shared her first kiss, butchered her first seal. These scattered remains were no longer her community. They were the ashes of her home, the ashes of her people.

She kept looking though, scanning the area for life. A flash of color, a cry of pain, a dog's high whine.

No one was here. She was alone.

"Naajaluk?" She was seven years old. It was night. The woods were thick and dark and deep, her voice shrill in the mist, until a figure emerged from out of the dark, beautiful and bold and strong—Mama, who would find her, always.

"Naattaluk?" She was ten years old. It was day. Her cheeks hurt from smiling as she lifted the warm, limp body of a snow hare she had snared, and Papa swept her into his strong arms with a booming laugh, swinging her so high it felt like flying.

"Naajatikaaq?" She was twelve years old. It was dawn. Her skin was chilled beneath the furs, and Eska pulled her close so there was no space between, sister to sister, two hearts beating as one.

Stumbling down the path that had enclosed the ice houses, Apaay blinked away tears as she approached the area in the back.

There was an abandoned boot, its twin half buried in the earth farther on. A small, sooty doll. The splintered remains of a child's sled.

When she reached the space where her home had proudly stood, she stopped, unable to move. Apaay no longer knew whether she was breathing.

In the circular space, the dirt slightly discolored, snow having melted away, lay three body-sized lumps. Charred scraps of cloth remained, a few tatters of fur like wisps in the wind, the rest blackened. Her throat thickened with emotion, a stone she could not dislodge, and she gagged. The stench of singed flesh was strong.

Mama and Papa and Eska. Her beloved family.

Gone.

"No. No no no no no no no." Apaay collapsed, as she could no longer stand. Her body wouldn't let her.

Curling over herself, she rocked back and forth as the wind picked up speed and snow began to fall, so soft compared to the hardness of this feeling. *No,* she thought. *No.* It was the only word that made sense. She grabbed hold of it, this anchor, this heavy weight of denial that prevented her from floating away. If she kept moving, kept rocking back and forth, this could not be real. It could never be real. This was an illusion, a nightmare made flesh, and Apaay knew if she stopped, if she let the silence fully blanket her, then the truth would destroy her. It was already destroying her.

"Why?" she whispered to nothing and no one.

"That's how Yuki works," the Face Stealer said behind her. She jerked at the intrusion, having thought herself alone. "You destroy something of hers, and she destroys something of yours." The sound of his breathing encompassed her. "I told you, back at the labyrinth, what would happen if you crossed her. You didn't listen to me. Luckily, Yuki is someone who very much acts on her emotions. It wasn't difficult to guess her intentions. She hates nothing more than having to witness the love of a family when she has none."

The words struck her like scalding water. "You knew this would happen? You *knew*?" Her breathing came faster and faster, and it still felt as if she were drowning. How could she have ever believed him to be a friend?

"I knew." His words held a different quality, something she could not put her finger on. "But you should not believe everything you see."

Apaay clutched her chest, feeling as if her heart were shredding into pieces. It seemed so long ago, that day she and Nakaluq waited on the ice. She remembered how still the land had been, like the space between exhalations. Even then, she had not been fast enough. She had not been strong enough. And now they were gone.

"Leave me," she growled, forehead touching the scorched earth. The dirt was cold. "I don't care about Yuki or you or whatever conflict you've pulled me into." Gritting her teeth, she squeezed her eyes shut, stinging water pushing at the seams. "Go back to the labyrinth, demon. Leave me to grieve in peace."

"I'm not leaving without you," he murmured. "And if I must carry you back, then I will."

She felt neither exhaustion, nor cold, nor fear.

The wind sounded like weeping.

When he touched her arm, Apaay jerked free and pushed to her feet. "Don't touch me. Don't you understand? You did this." The shudders quaked into her soul, and she stared into his onyx eyes and wished he had drowned back in the labyrinth. "You took Eska from me. My parents—"

"I was not the one who tried to kill your family," he grated, hand slicing through the air, eyes wild and burning, burning, burning. *Demon.* "I did not burn your village to the ground."

"But you did. None of this would have happened if you hadn't come here in the first place. Why? Why did you do it?" She could hardly choke out the words, so thick were they with hate and betrayal at having trusted someone who had badly deceived her. "Everything you touch you destroy."

His face was somber. "If you would just listen—"

She stumbled back. The wind gusted, lifting away the layer of ash. "Stay away from me."

"Apaay!"

Whirling around, Apaay tore through the burned remains of her home and cut a path through the forest, disappearing into the trees. She listened for footfalls behind her, but the Face Stealer did not follow. The wind grew more violent by the minute, thwacking against the branches as she pushed through the thickening flurry, sobbing so hard she stumbled blindly onward.

How had her life come to this?

The worst part was Apaay did not understand. Not her memories, not her thoughts, not her dreams. They were bits of broken glass, scattered, unable to depict a picture clearly. Some piece of her felt as if these seemingly unrelated incidents—Eska's face, the labyrinth, befriending Ila, the blood oath, even the Face Stealer posing as Irnik—had in some way been inevitable. But she did not understand why or how or for what purpose. She did not understand why the path ended at her ruination.

Apaay gagged, tasting ashes on her tongue. A wayward root caught around one of her slippers, and she nearly crashed into the ground.

Her legs would not move fast enough. Snow dragged at them, and a sense of dread welled up, crashed down. The trees were gray smears bashed by a cold white wind. Soon she left the woods behind, memory leading her to the place where it had all begun.

The sea.

Snow led to a tumble of stones, and then the ice. Her slippers pounded against the glassy sheet, unwavering and without fear, because she was not afraid of drowning, she was not afraid of death's watery grave, not anymore.

She was afraid of being alone.

Breathing hard, Apaay eventually halted at the place that was both a beginning and an end. The breathing hole lay a few yards away, a layer of water having frozen over it.

She didn't know what to do.

Reaching into her pocket, Apaay pulled out Eska's face, holding it tightly so the wind would not snatch it from her. It was lighter than she had expected, limp like a piece of cloth. She looked upon its loveliness, ran a finger across the tiny white scar at her sister's temple—consequence of Apaay thinking it would be a good idea to steal Papa's tools and practice spear-fighting.

Gently, she tucked the face back into her pocket.

The wind screamed, driving Apaay to her knees. Catching herself with one hand, she tried curling into a huddle to shield herself from the howling gusts that scored and scraped and clawed, the cold stabbing her skin, and they may as well have shredded open her heart. The pain was so great she could not hold it inside.

"Why?" she growled, snow piling up, caging her in. She slammed her fist into the ice.

In the distance, something popped sharply. This time, she did not flinch.

Louder, voice hoarse. "Why?"

Slam.

A furious, choked-off wail. "Why?"

Slam.

Weeping, a stream of tears. "Why?" *Slam.* "Why?" And now screaming, bared teeth, the wrecked expression of a wounded animal, a wounded heart. "Why, why, why—"

Slam.

Slam.

Slam.

The snap and crack of ice hurtled toward her. Apaay collapsed onto her side, shuddering, as fluids leaked from her eyes and nose and froze against her skin. Below, the frozen plane fragmented, as it had done decades ago for her grandmother, before Mama had been born, before she'd been even a thought in her grandmother's young mind. The rush of water roared through the cracks.

All . . . all was not lost. Apaay clung to that flame, so small yet so bright. She cupped it in her palms, mittens curved around the sliver of warmth, wanting to keep it safe from harm. *Hold on,* she urged it. *Hold on.*

It felt like this sometimes during the long night. She was convinced someone had wrapped her world in black cloth that would never again be lifted. She would fall asleep to darkness, and wake to darkness, and walk through life in this dark eternity. But then there would come a day, an awakening, of a gray-touched horizon: the first hint of sun.

With so much uncertainty, Apaay clung to the things she knew. She was alive—beating heart, warm breath. She had escaped the labyrinth, even after she had accepted death. Wished for it, even. But it didn't matter. She had fled the labyrinth to return home, except there was no home to return to. Her community was in ruin, her family bits of bone. Yuki had broken her slowly and thoroughly, and then, as if that had not been enough, had ground her into dust. The girl had taken everything.

The ice buckled, shoved apart from the water's brute force. She barely felt the cold seeping through.

Curling into a tighter ball, Apaay sucked in deep gasps of air and fumbled for her pocket, that bit of solid rock Ila had shaped into a wolf. At its smooth texture, her frantic pulse eased, slow, slower, to a more manageable pace.

No, that was wrong. Yuki hadn't taken everything. It would be easy to succumb to an even darker place, but she forgot how bright the stars could shine, if only she let in the light. Who was she? Apaay. She was Apaay and she was her people, which could not be stripped from her as easily as her hair had been shorn. Speaking Analak, *being* Analak, was in the manner of all things. How they danced, and ate, and hunted, and walked, and raised children, and smiled, and slept.

And she was not alone. She had Ila. Chena, with her unborn child. Even Masuk, who understood what it meant to be forgotten. These people in her life, made beautiful by their trials and hardships, were the only ones left.

She must return to them.

Except Apaay didn't know how to locate the cairn where they'd separated, not without the Face Stealer's help. And as desperate as she was to find her friends, she would not, could not, call upon him for aid. They were not friends, as he had told her when he still wore Irnik's face. When she'd believed him to be true.

Apaay bit her lip hard as the emptiness yawned inside her, a stark reminder of all that she had lost. As she sank deeper into the water, she recalled the snowy peaks that had surrounded them, how their massive bodies seemed to scrape against the sky. The Atakana divided the Central and Western Territories, and snaked down into the Southern Territory as well. The cairn, and wherever the Face Stealer had sent her friends, must be somewhere within that range.

Regardless of her current situation, Apaay would not give in. She would find a way to return to them, free of any sort of master. If she could survive the labyrinth and Yuki's mind games, if she could emerge from that frozen hell with breath in her body, she could find her friends. It would be a long road, and a hard one, but she had walked longer, harsher paths. She had spent time in solitude and had survived. She had clawed through blood and pain and despair with only a shred of hope to lead her. And maybe she was weakened and broken now, but she would be strong again. Someday. One day.

It was decided, then. Apaay would find Ila, Chena, and Masuk, and they would form their own family. They would find a place untouched by darkness and begin again, as her people had done for centuries. It would not be like this. It would not be one bleeding heart after another, a trail of devastation, but rather something pure. A beginning without end.

Cautiously, she uncurled her body from the depression in the ice. After sliding on her stomach until she reached a solid area, Apaay climbed to her feet and turned around.

There, on the slope of the rocky shore, stood the Face Stealer.

They stared at each other across the frozen sea, a shroud pulsing around his form, diminishing the longer she looked at it. The storm did not seem to bother him, and Apaay wondered if he was even cold, or if he felt nothing at all.

Within the span of two breaths, he had materialized in front of her. Before Apaay could speak, he said quietly, "Your family is alive."

She opened her mouth. Closed it. Licked her trembling lips. "You're lying."

His eyes glittered in the half light. "I tried to tell you, back at your village. You wouldn't listen to me." The shadows wreathing his neck uncoiled, soiling the pale fur of his parka.

She couldn't remember what he had said, truthfully. She only remembered they had not been the words she so desperately needed to hear.

The demon's attention flitted to the ice, though it did not seem as if he were avoiding her gaze. "Yuki has eyes and ears everywhere. I didn't want her knowing that her plan had failed. I was not able to save everyone. There wasn't enough time. But your family is well. They are safe."

People had died. *Her* people. But her family . . .

"I saw the bodies." Scorched fur, cracked bone. Her stomach roiled.

"You didn't look closely enough. They were caribou, not human."

Apaay sucked in a breath, held it. Indeed, the fur she saw had been caribou. But her family's clothes were sewn of caribou as well.

"I have lied to you about many things," said the Face Stealer, voice pitched to carry over the howling storm. "But I would not lie to you about this."

Apaay wanted so badly to believe him, believe *in* him. But she remembered Nakaluq, that whalebone knife heavy in her hand. She remembered Ila cowering from the polar bear Unua, unable to fight, unable to see. She remembered the crystallized chamber filled with stolen faces, Chena burdened by chains. After everything he had done to those she loved, how could she possibly trust that his intentions were true? How could she ever forgive?

She could not.

"I don't believe you."

His eyes snapped to her face, twin fathoms without end. Those eyes had seen a thousand lifetimes and would see a thousand more. There, churning against the turmoil and the rage, lay a sorrow so sharp it seemed to cut into his insides, the wounds bleeding out unseen. A human, unreachable pain.

Chin lifted, Apaay stepped back, waiting to see if he would stop her. But he only watched as she turned and plunged through the battering wind, back toward her village, forging a fresh path through the snow. Apaay could not trust the demon's word, but she could trust Eska, and where they had come from, and the land from which they had been born.

So she went to the tree. That lone conifer that had miraculously escaped the fire's wrath, the one that reminded Apaay of peace. And when she reached into the space near its frosted roots and rested her hand upon a square of silken rabbit fur, Apaay, who did not think she had any tears left to shed, curled against the tree and quietly wept, body limp with relief.

The Face Stealer had been telling the truth.

Like sediment upon a riverbed, the realization settled. She had assumed him to lie, as was his nature, yet he had done her this kindness when it had mattered most. Who was the Face Stealer, this demon of mist and night? She didn't know. She just didn't know.

Apaay slipped the scrap of fur into her pocket next to Eska's face and the carving of the wolf. Somehow, he had convinced her family to leave their home behind. And somewhere in the Atakana, they awaited her.

The air around Apaay seemed to thicken, causing the hair along her arms to rise as the sensation of an unwelcome presence materialized nearby. Otherworldly. Tugging at her edges in a way she didn't understand.

Apaay eased back, her pulse a dull thud in her ears, and spotted the Face Stealer's form through the flurry. Even from this distance, she sensed his hesitation.

What did he want with her?

A sudden gust plowed into her back, and the Face Stealer vanished, his shadows swallowed by the squall's intensity. Apaay braced herself against its force, teeth gritted. She would need to find shelter soon, a place to decompress, to deliberate these next vital steps that would lead her to family, friends. But she didn't want him following her. She wanted to forget this demon. She never wanted to look upon his face again.

Snow spewed from the sky in heavy sheets, and the veil did not lift. The blizzard's wail pitched to a high keening, a raw-edged scream that slipped through her blood and bones and *became* her—a force, a storm. The path was clear. Now was her chance.

Take it. Take it and run.

She fell into the white and disappeared.

ACKNOWLEDGMENTS

We've come to another road at last, but whereas the previous one was ending, this one is just beginning. That's the great thing about working on a series. More books to write! It was the greatest pleasure writing Apaay's story, and I can't wait for the many years to come as this series unfolds. However, there are many people who need to be thanked.

My thanks first goes to my editor, Heather, who saw the heart of the story and seriously made it shine brighter and more beautifully than it ever had before. Thank you so much for sharing my vision of Apaay's journey.

Again, to Jennifer, who believed.

To Beth, the best critique partner and author friend anyone could ask for. Thank you so much for always taking the time to read my work and give me advice.

To Faryn, who gave me the cover of my dreams!

An extra thank you to Neil, who provided feedback concerning the mythology and culture of the Inuit of Nunavut, Canada.

To my parents, who stand by me no matter what I decide to do with my life, which happens to be many things! Knowing that I always have a place to call home grounds me when things are drifting and uncertain. To Leah and Cameron, who cheer me on from the sidelines. Thank you for your love and guidance, the times of peace and the times of war. Sibling relationships should never be boring.

Lastly, to my readers. These stories are always for you.

Alexandria Warwick is the international bestselling author of the Four Winds series and the North series. A classically trained violinist, she spends much of her time performing in orchestras. She lives in Florida.